Slaughter of the Innocents

Tristan Grandillon's voice remained as even as the ice on a frozen lake. "I'm here to speak with you about Gerald Cummings and the slaughter of all those innocent people last December."

"I don't know what you're talking about," he said tensely. Could this be another test of his silence?

Grandillon said nothing as he stepped next to Blake and hooked his hand beneath the driver's door of the car. No words were needed to convey his message as the muscles of his arm bulged and the wheels of the car rose from the pavement. With the strain showing only slightly in his face, Grandillon slowly lowered the car before standing and dusting his hands. "Now do I have your attention?"

Other Leisure Books by Steve Vance:

The Abyss
The Asgard Run
The Hyde Effect

SHAPES

STEVE S VANCE

LEISURE BOOKS NEW YORK CITY

A LEISURE BOOK ®

September 1991

Published by

Dorchester Publishing Co., Inc.
276 Fifth Avenue
New York, NY 10001

Printed in the United States of America

SHAPES

PART ONE:
The Players

CHAPTER ONE

They were young, happy, and wonderfully in love with each other and with their lives. When Monday morning, June 19, dawned clear and bright on I-70, a few miles east of Goodland, Kansas, their car had just broken down and they had the grand sum of only forty-three dollars. But Harrison Joseph "Harry" Mitchellson, twenty-one, and Marsha Dale Cooper, twenty, seemed surprisingly carefree about the whole matter. They were convinced that the world was basically good and as they embarked on their exploration of it, they would muddle through somehow.

Between them, Harry and Marsha had already killed nine people.

"It looks dead to me, baby," Marsha said as she peered under the hood of the seventeen-year-old car. Extremely attractive, with long blond hair and sparkling blue eyes, her one hundred and twenty pounds drew the attention of almost every man she encountered, and, once attracted, the poor lugs had no chance of resisting her well-scrubbed, cheerleader looks. "Should we just shoot it to put it out of its misery?"

Harry laughed, though he *had* shot holes in more than one automobile. "No need to waste the ammunition, sugar. This pathetic piece of metal is long gone." Six one and about a hundred seventy pounds, he had neatly kept black hair and a beard and the disarming grin of a traveling salesman. "Tell you what, let's push it off the highway into that thicket over there. It slopes pretty steep here, so you get in and steer."

It took less than five minutes, since the grading was quite sharp and Harry, despite his wiry appearance, was really very strong. With the stolen and now abandoned vehicle hidden from casual notice, the two young people walked back to the shoulder of the road and surveyed the sparse amount of traffic.

Marsha looked east into the dazzling morning sun and then back to the west. "Why don't we hitch back to that town we just passed, um, Goodland? I'll bet we could pick up another car inside an hour."

Harry nibbled reflectively at his lower lip. "I don't think so, babe. Nobody knows that we've come this far east, and even if we don't off anybody when we pick up the wheels, some good citizen's liable to get a look at us and give the description to the FBI. Instead, what do you say we look for some lonesome male traveler and ride with him to Missouri or Indiana before we do him? That way, we can dump the body and have the car for maybe three or four days before anybody misses him. We could be in Maine by then."

"You think of everything, don't you?" The girl yawned daintily. It had been a long night, and now she was tired and hungry. "I hope that the Good Samaritan comes by soon. I'm bushed."

Harry draped an arm about her shoulders and they began to walk. "Losing your stamina so soon? Shoot, I remember a time not so long ago when you could steal a car in Biloxi, drive all night to Tucson, and run a scam on the mayor and the school board before noon the next day."

The pair walked and reminisced, laughing often, for nearly a half hour before a likely candidate slowed down in response to their raised thumbs.

The car was a real beauty: a 1957, black-and-white, Chevrolet convertible in apparently pristine condition. Its finish sparkled like ice in the gradually spreading sunlight, and even though the air was still slightly chilled, the middle-aged-looking driver was cruising along with the top down. Well-padded with a bare pink scalp, ringed by rather long brown hair, the man's fat, friendly smile seemed made to order for Harry and Marsha.

"You kids look in need of a little assistance," he observed after stopping a few yards past them.

The two trotted eagerly toward the waiting car. "You bet," Harry replied in an equally friendly tone. He opened the passenger door, allowed Marsha to step into the backseat, and then joined her. "We've been walking all night. You're a godsend."

The man turned to look at them, still smiling, but with a slightly quizzical gleam in his eyes. "Really? You must have come right through Goodland, then."

Marsha took Harry's little finger in her hand and quickly bent it back almost to the breaking point.

Harry gasped. "Yeah, uh, sure we did, but, well, we don't have much money, and we figured that it would be better to stick to the highway than to spend the night in a park."

The driver nodded and laughed. "Good thinking. My name's Poduano, Dominic Poduano." He extended his hand to Harry. "Call me Dom."

Mitchellson shook hands with him warmly. "I'm Harry Mitchellson, and this is my fiancée, Marsha Cooper." Harry gave their real names easily, because, in spite of a series of robberies, rapes, and murders that spanned the entire western half of the country, neither had ever been arrested. They were young, in love, murderous, and careful.

"Pleased to meet you, Harry, Miss Cooper," Dom stated.

"Marsha, please."

"Sure. Where are you kids headed?"

"Oh, east," Marsha answered. "I've got some relatives in Maine, and Harry and I are going to stay with them until we can get jobs." She squeezed Harry's arm tightly. "Then we're going to be married."

"No kidding? Congratulations! I'm heading for New York, myself. Indigo Lake. Ever heard of it?"

"Sure, I have. It's gorgeous."

Dom beamed even more brightly, which Harry would have thought impossible. "I'll be glad to take you as far as there. Your company will be well worth it. In fact, as a kind of pre-wedding gift, I'd like to pay for your meals and motel bills. How's that sound to you?"

Harry and Marsha, both of whom were already assessing methods for killing this loquacious and friendly man, were quite surprised by this offer. "That would be great, Dom, really," Harry said. "It's really nice of you to do something like that for a couple of strangers."

"Ah, young love, it's the best there is." Dom turned toward the steering wheel and eased the car onto the highway. "I was young once, too, a *long* time ago."

"I'll be glad to help out with the driving, then."

Without looking back, Dom waved his hand. "Thanks, anyway, but that's one of my many eccentricities. I know it's silly, but nobody works the pedals of this little girl but yours truly."

"Right, I understand." To himself, Harry added, *At least, nobody else drives it until I razor your guts all over the virgin forest floor somewhere between here and Indigo Lake.*

"I hope you two don't mind riding with the top down," Dom called over the wind that was already whistling through their ears. "There's nothing in all the hospitals in the world as good for you as fresh, clean air!"

"Love it, Dom!" Harry yelled back.

After a couple of miles had passed, Marsha leaned close to Harry's ear and whispered, "Are we going to do this guy right now, babe?"

Harry shook his head. "Let's see how hospitable he really is. Hell, if he's really going to supply us with food and a bed all the way to New York, there's no reason to zap him until a few miles this side of Indigo Lake. No fuss, no fuzz."

"Good," she said, patting his thigh. "I'm tired and I'm going to take a little nap." She rested her head on his shoulder.

"Don't worry about a thing, sugar. It's smooth sailing now."

More than a thousand miles away in San Francisco, Monday dawned bright and promising. Blake Corbett awoke in his hotel room to a day ladened with fear, a legacy he inherited from a night in a government facility six months before. Tonight the moon would be full again as it had been that night.

A novelist, Corbett specialized in the horror genre, the old-fashioned kind which dealt with the classical villains: vampires, ghosts, prehistoric remnants, and zombies. And werewolves. He had never actually believed in the supernatural, but as a fan and writer of horror, he had immersed himself in it for more than twenty years. If most of those years had been confined to the lower financial echelons of the literary world, existing from book advance to book advance, it still had been a glorious life for him. He'd been one of the very few people who had been allowed to devote himself to a career that he really loved.

Then last December 14th had arrived and brought with it his opportunity to test the reality of a supernatural world he'd never taken too seriously.

A particularly savage serial murderer, Gerald Cummings, had been hunting people throughout the country during the previous year, and Corbett and three friends—college student, Meg Talley, newspaperman, Douglas Morgan, and self-proclaimed genius, Nick Grundel—were convinced that this killer was not just another disenchanted or sexually perverted loner acting out his sickest fantasies, but a real, living embodiment of paranormal evil. They'd even stated as much on national television. Cummings always killed on the nights of a full moon.

Finally, the authorities had captured the madman and confined him for observation at the Institute of Natural Sciences and Research, a government-run compound in an isolated area of the Diablo Mountain range, not too far south of San Francisco. Blake, Meg, Douglas, and Nick, as well as more than two hundred members of the international press corps, had been invited to visit the Institute that night in December so that they could witness for themselves that Cummings was no supernatural fiend. A maniac, yes, and one of the most awful people ever to walk the earth, but still a man and not a werewolf.

That night had been the worst of thirty-six-year-old Blake Corbett's life. The official government version was that a genetically engineered virus had escaped from one of the labs and had infected the unsuspecting assembly of doctors, patients, scientists, and reporters. More than a hundred had died that evening. No one was allowed to leave federal custody for more than a month, until it was conclusively proven that they were not carriers of this new, terrible virus. At least that was the government story. After all, how could they admit they were holding a family of werewolves?

Finally released from the smothering protection of the government in April, Blake, Meg, and Doug had been among the lucky ones. But young Nick Grundel had not been so lucky. Emotionally, of course, they had all been changed by that one god-awful night, and Blake's response was to retreat totally from public life.

But his literary agent, Rodney Witty, was not particularly interested in Blake's personal feelings. Blake's name was hot, following all the publicity he'd garnered last year and Witty had been determined not to allow Blake's bruised sensibilities to kill his professional momentum. The agent's prodding had managed to get Blake out of his dingy, little apartment in Los Angeles and back into circulation. Blake knew that Witty hoped that the same tactics that had bullied Blake into appearing at this horror convention in San Francisco would maneuver him to get behind the typewriter again soon.

As much as it surprised him, Blake had to admit that the convention had been good for him. Meeting people again hadn't been the ordeal he had anticipated. After all, what did he have to fear from them in the *daylight*? And he had actually drawn strength from the attention of the fans of his numerous horror and science-fiction novels. Even the standard public reading—this one from his 1985 novel, *The Whispers of Darkness*—which he had never enjoyed doing in his sixteen years of convention appearances, had gone comparatively smoothly.

But the convention had taken place over the weekend of June 17–18, making this Monday the 19th, and Blake knew what would take place at the Institute at midnight tonight. It was a long drive from San Francisco to his fortress-like apartment in LA, about three hundred fifty miles, and he planned to finish that last mile before the stroke of twelve.

Hurriedly, Blake dressed and checked out of the hotel at eight, bade a brief good-bye to the convention's organizer, and walked from the lobby through the glassed-in elevated walkway which led to the parking lot, where his aging, loyal little import awaited him.

As he pushed his dark-rimmed glasses up on his nose, he looked through the glass at the already heavy flow of morning business traffic, and reflected again on his agent's insistence that Blake attend this convention. What he had experienced at the Institute had been about the worst thing he could imagine, and his overall concept of life was irreversibly altered by it. But turning into a mushroom in his dark, hot apartment was no answer either. Maybe he couldn't tell the world the truth about that night due to the conditions of his release from government custody, but that didn't mean that he had to isolate himself from that same world when his only real moments of concern and fear popped up every month or so.

Running his hand through his short, dark brown hair, Blake took a deep breath of the gasoline-scented air coming from the parking garage. It smelled sweet to him. In spite of what would happen tonight, he felt free.

His car was parked on the fourth level, and with no valet service, he had a long walk before he finally reached it. Fishing for his keys and parking stub, he thought about dropping his suitcase into the trunk along with the "survival bag" that he carried with him whenever he left his apartment. But he decided that he would feel a lot more comfortable and secure if his tools were resting beside him on the front seat. The survival bag contained dried wolfsbane, a cross, a pistol, and six silver bullets.

At five-seven, there was a quiet strength to Blake's blocky form. Despite what tonight might hold for the bookwormish-looking author, he seemed relaxed, unconcerned, as he bent to unlock the car door.

"Mr. Corbett?" said a smooth voice directly behind him.

He literally jumped and whipped around, thrusting the survival bag before him as if its icons would protect him even through its leather exterior.

"What do you want?" he demanded sharply.

"I'm sorry to have startled you," the man said.

"My God, you almost gave me a heart attack—" Abruptly, Blake's jangled nerves relaxed when he recognized the tall, sun-bronzed man. "What can I do for you, uh, Grandillon, isn't it?" He'd noticed the blond-haired conventioneer with the "I'M TRISTAN GRANDILLON" name tag during the weekend. It was difficult to overlook a man who had so many young women flocking around him. But it wasn't until that instant, in that dark and cold parking lot, that Blake realized just who he was—the government. Blake was certain that Grandillon had shadowed him all through the convention to insure that Blake didn't break the agreements and violate the documents he'd signed to secure his freedom from custody at the Institute.

The man nodded. "Tristan Grandillon," he said, pronouncing the last name "Gron-*di*-yun." "I'm flattered that you remember me, since we were never introduced."

Blake sighed and placed his suitcase and bag on the hood of the car. He felt certain that he wouldn't be breaking camp any time soon. "We weren't officially introduced, Mr. Grandillon, but we certainly saw a lot of one another over the past two days, didn't we?"

"That's right," he admitted. "Your appearance was the reason I attended the convention."

Blake leaned against the door and folded his arms. His half-smile contained no humor. "Let's not waste each other's time, Grandillon. Just tell me if I reacted like an obedient trained animal or if I failed the test and you're here to return me to the strangling bosom of the United States government. I didn't tell anyone what really happened that night at the Institute."

Grandillon raised an eyebrow. This, apparently, was the extent of the man's surprise register. "Mr. Corbett, I assure you, I do not work for the government."

"Yeah, right, you're just my biggest fan."

"No. Actually, though I've read some of your work, I wouldn't call myself a fan." That voice remained as even as the ice on a frozen lake. "I'm here to speak with you about Gerald Cummings and the slaughter that took place at the Institute last December."

A ghost slipped its hand through Blake's flesh and ribs to clutch his heart in its dead fist. "I don't know what you're talking about, man," he said tensely. Could this be another test of his silence?

"On the contrary, Mr. Corbett. You're the only person who does understand what I mean. And I've got quite a bit of information to impart to you. Perhaps you would be interested in talking with me further if we were—"

"Cut it out, Grandillon! Drop the act!" Blake's voice spilled over with fear and anger. "Your secret's safe! I'm not going to write the greatest book of my entire career! I know you people will be watching me for the rest of my life, but you don't have to be so damned obvious about it!" He grabbed his bags and again jammed the key into the doorlock.

Grandillon said nothing as he stepped next to Blake and stooped to hook his hand beneath the driver's door of the sub-compact car. No words were needed to convey his message when the muscles of his long, brown arm suddenly bulged like cords of flesh-colored rope and the wheels of the car rose slowly some eighteen inches off the pavement.

Corbett stared disbelievingly as he stumbled several feet away from the car. The keys were left dangling in the lock.

"Oh, my God," he whispered.

With the strain showing only slightly in his face, Grandillon slowly lowered the car to all four tires before standing and dusting his hands. "Now, do I have your attention?"

Blake nodded mutely.

"Good. I don't care to engage in such ostentatious displays, but our time is limited, and I wanted to prove to you that I'm not a government agent assigned to monitor your activities. Are you convinced?"

"Yes," Blake replied quietly. "Who are you and what do you want with me?" His hands were slowly and deliberately working toward the latch on his survival bag. He doubted that the cross or wolfsbane would have any effect, but the bullets, though made of soft silver, would still carry a lot of impact.

"Actually, my name *is* Tristan Philibert Grandillon, though I've employed many aliases throughout the years." His eyes flickered to the catch of the bag. "I'm being scrupulously truthful with you, Mr. Corbett, and I hope you'll return the favor. Please leave the bag closed."

Blake's fingers stopped just above the catch.

"I assure you, I have neither reason nor desire to hurt you, but to protect myself I will do whatever you force me to."

He can lift a car with one hand, Blake reminded himself. *My arm would be like spun sugar to him.* "All right, Grandillon. You've told me your name, so what do you want?"

It was Grandillon's turn to lean nonchalantly against the side of the car. "I represent a group—a very exclusive group—of men and women who are quite interested in the Cummings affair. We schedule national gatherings every five years, and our next one is set for the week of July the Fourth, just a few weeks from today. We'd appreciate it if you would address our meeting concerning what occurred at the Institute during your period of detainment there."

"I can't talk about that," Corbett said swiftly. "They told me what would happen if I ever hinted . . . My friends, Doug Morgan and Meg Talley, already have disappeared in just the two months since our release, so I know that the government wouldn't hesitate to reel me in, too."

"Perhaps your friends have just gone into hiding."

"No, they would have notified me somehow."

Grandillon shrugged. "Who knows? Maybe your telephone calls and mail are being monitored. But that doesn't matter. Our gathering is being held at Indigo Lake, New York. It's a well-known summer resort, so no suspicions would be aroused if you decided to spend some time there to recuperate from your recent ordeal."

Corbett *did* want to talk to someone about it, to spill some of the cumulative horror from his soul, and he was also desperate to find out what that incredible display of brute strength meant in the midst of this insanity. But he just couldn't shed his fear of having his very thoughts overheard by the limitless ears of the FBI, CIA, or whatever department there was in charge of his case. "No."

"Well, it's your decision, of course. My associates and I won't harass you in any fashion. In fact, if you'd like, we will agree to break off all contact right here. Permanently."

That, too, upset Blake, as everything seemed to do these days. "Without explaining how you did that?" he asked, gesturing to the car.

Grandillon's almost too-handsome face broke into a smile to reveal perfect rows of even, white teeth. "Yes. But I will give you a couple of clues and an assurance. The assurance is that my group's meeting will take place on a private island at the lake, and our security systems will allow us to be certain that no unauthorized persons will be permitted on the island or within effective listening distance."

"The clues?"

The grin grew even wider. "One: what I did with this small automobile was a minor talent inherent in the members of my association. Two: the affliction from which Gerald Cummings suffered was merely the first stage of a profound physical evolution."

Blake's mind staggered with sudden understanding. He *had* witnessed that kind of power before! Cummings, in the heat of his murderous transformation, had been able to rip bodies apart, batter down steel doors, and lift a police car off his own chest.

"Christ, do you mean *you're*—"

Grandillon laughed and raised his hands, as if showing that no tufts of fur grew on his palms. "Whatever else you discover is up to you, isn't it?" He took a small business card from his coat pocket and handed it to Corbett. "Our address. My advice would be to memorize it and destroy the card somewhere between here and LA. If you decide to attend, the important week is July second through the eighth, but any time before that is fine, too, if you'd like to stay for a real vacation. Some members are already gathering there.

"As I said, we won't attempt to contact you any further. Your insider's knowledge would be most helpful to us, but we won't demand your cooperation. We aren't the government."

"Do I have to answer you right now?" Blake realized that there was no way that he could refuse to attend, even if he was unable to vocalize his intention to do so, yet.

"Of course not. Your attendance or absence will be your answer. Good-bye, Mr. Corbett." He turned and began to walk into the black depths of the parking lot.

"Wait!" Blake called. "What if I'm being monitored right now?"

"You aren't," Grandillon responded without turning to face him. "We know that you are closely followed very little of the time."

"How can you know something like that?"

"Because *we* have been following you since you were released from the Institute."

Then the tall man disappeared into the darkness along with the echoes of his voice to leave Corbett alone with an entirely new set of hopes and fears.

The woman stood very quietly in the shadows cast by the empty security kiosk until long after Tristan Grandillon had strolled out of her sight and Blake Corbett had cranked his small car and driven out of the garage. Her eyes seemed to glow whitely in the darkness, shining with the excitement and disbelief that filled them.

Kelly Brynn Davis didn't believe in heaven or hell, God or Satan, an afterlife, psychic phenomena, Yetis, flying saucers, the Loch Ness Monster, spontaneous human combustion, or anything else that couldn't be caught, catalogued, dissected, or otherwise scientifically defined or explained.

She especially didn't believe in werewolves.

Due to this deep-seated disbelief and distrust in life itself, Kelly had spent sixteen of her thirty-nine years as an avid reporter for *Proof!*. Like its older sister magazine, *Skeptical Inquirer*, *Proof!* examined thousands of reports of totally unproven paranormal phenomena and events from mind reading to hollow earth theories in the light of rational, scientific thought. But unlike the *Inquirer*, which was a scholarly and evenhanded enterprise, *Proof!* existed solely to discredit these reports even if it had to produce its own "evidence" of mistakes or chicanery. If the reporters were unable to uncover the truth of a claim, they were encouraged to falsify their own proof.

Kelly Davis had enthusiastically done that on several occasions and had come to the horror convention to write yet another report on Blake Corbett and his ludicrous contention that werewolves actually existed. Corbett had found himself a bloodied target of her pen before, though, and had successfully avoided her throughout the weekend. Her last-ditch plan had been to ambush him in the parking lot; instead, she had overheard one extraordinary conversation and witnessed a performance of strength that had taken her breath.

It's only a small car, her inner voice pointed out.

So the hell what? she answered herself. *It's still got to weigh over a goddamned ton! Could you do it? Do you know anyone who could?*

All that Kelly knew for sure was that werewolves didn't exist and that something very weird was being planned for a place called Indigo Lake, New York, during the week of July the Fourth.

She also knew that she would be there to watch it.

CHAPTER TWO

That Monday the eastern seaboard was blanketed in a long gray belt of clouds that slowly and steadily dumped inch after inch of rain. Temperatures were normal to high, however, and this combination of heat and moisture created a steam bath throughout most of the states east of the Mississippi.

The boxcar was no cooler or more comfortable than any other place beneath the shroud of dampness. It had hauled a load of heavy machine parts in the recent past, and one crate had broken open to bleed thick, pungent black oil over much of the wooden floor. The warm wind had blown rain through the half-open door for most of the afternoon, and the humidity seemed to have sunk into the dark stains and forced the dried oil back to the surface with all of its odoriferous power. The boxcar reeked of it. The four people inside would have been hard-pressed to argue that they were better off inside the slowly rocking car than they would have been outside in the rain.

"It's days like this . . ." began one of the men. Jimmie Ray Condon was seventy-two, as wizened and gray as Grandfather Farmer in a Rockwell painting, and his respiration was heavily compromised by emphysema, so that he usually had to pause for breaths several times during the course of a sentence. ". . . days like this that make me realize how . . . bad I wasted my life." He looked at the walls, which seemed to be sweating oil.

The man who sat next to him, sharing the side of the boxcar nearest the open door and the flow of air that it provided, was about fifty, if appearances could be trusted. He, too, was quite thin, but there was no gray to be found amid the glossy blackness of his too-long hair and unkempt beard. He had a hatchet-faced profile and eyes that seemed to mock himself as well as the listener when he spoke. For now, he was going by the name of Neil Thomas Merrick.

"Kind of late for regrets, isn't it, Jimmie Ray?" he asked with a grin. "Besides, if the Devil appeared out of thin air right now and offered to make you eighteen again by snapping his fingers *if* you'd swear to live your life again as a CPA, you'd kick his tail so far up his ass that the pointy end would come out his mouth."

Condon laughed brokenly. "Yeah, I guess . . . I guess you're right," he said. "I had my chance . . . anyhow. Back in . . . the forties, right after I got back . . . back from Japan, out of the Army. I was . . . I was a real suit-and-tie monkey, making good scratch, with a little wife . . . an' I gave it all up for this." With one veined and spotted hand, he felt along the folds of his voluminous cast-off coat and produced a small bottle of liquor. Sipping slowly seemed to settle the ragged breathing and allowed him to ease back into the story at the point at which the gasping had interrupted him. "Believe it or not, I was in insurance . . . I was good, too, damned good—"

"Shut up." These words, as a monosyllabic grunt, instantly silenced both men. Their eyes leaped toward the opposite end of the boxcar where in the deepest shadows the massive man who had spoken sat, immersed in the blackness like something that could live only in the absence of light.

Then the man, a giant at six-feet-five and almost three hundred pounds of swollen muscle and bulging gut, moved. He was as black as the darkness that surrounded him, and as he stood, he grunted.

Condon grinned a shaky, nervous grin. "Something up, Banky?" he asked in a whisper.

Jeff Larman Banky reached his feet and sighed with the effort and pain of standing. His right knee was still a raw knot of agony from two days ago, when he had fallen from a flatcar and come within six inches of having his head sliced from his shoulders.

"Yeah, sumthin's up," he said, like thunder, "and if either one of you sonsabitches wakes up the kid, I'll rip out his eyeballs."

"The kid" was the fourth person riding in the stinking boxcar. He was, indeed, much younger than any of his companions at seventeen, though he looked even younger than that. Asleep in some ancient excelsior in the back of the car, his five-foot-ten and one-hundred-fifty-five-pound frame could have belonged to a high-school freshman, for the lack of marks and weathering it displayed. None of the three men had ever seen the boy before. He'd been in the car when they'd hopped it during the morning down in Roanoke and hadn't said spit to them since. But they had little doubt that this was his first experience on the bum, despite the quick and hooded looks he had given them.

Jimmie Ray knew what lay immediately in store for this particular blue-jeaned runaway. "Aw, come on, Banky, don't climb him. He's just . . . just a baby."

"And prob'ly clean, too," Banky said as he limped

toward the sleeping boy. Banky would much rather have had a woman, but the boy would have to do.

"You could at least wake him up and ask him if he wants some first," Neil Merrick pointed out softly.

"And you could shut your hole or get it shoved fulla sumthin' you don't want, too," responded Banky.

Condon put his hand on Merrick's arm and shook his head. He didn't run with Banky, but he'd seen the huge man on various lines over the past fifteen years, so he knew that those threats carried real menace. Banky was a monster who could easily beat the piss out of all three of them and toss them through the open side door.

Merrick simply shrugged and leaned back against the sweating wall.

Banky's walk was a short and agonizing one, and only his powerful lustful cravings blocked out the sharp, tearing sensations that radiated like spokes from his knee as he stooped next to the kid. There were some things that not even pain could cool.

"Shit," sighed Jimmie Ray to himself.

Somehow, Banky got his considerable bulk to the floor next to the boy without awakening him. Figuring that this was going to be rough no matter what tactic he took, he slapped his meaty hand over the boy's mouth and went for his belt with his other hand.

What happened next was so swift and unexpected that both Condon and Merrick felt as if the shadows had flown out of the corners to enwrap their heads and distort their vision. The kid, who had slept through the ponderous approach, came instantly awake at Banky's heavy touch, and did not lag in his reaction to the situation.

The boy's arm whipped from his side into Banky's, catching him at the elbow and blasting the large hand clear of his own face. With perfect coordination and speed, his leg shot up to smash against the side of the big man's head with enough power to knock him backwards onto his huge butt. The kid rolled away and came to his haunches like a gymnast.

Most other hobos would have retired from the conflict at that instant, deciding that a little loving was nothing to fight for. But Banky wasn't like ninety-nine percent of the other destitute men who rode the rails. He'd made his approach to this skinny little white rabbit, and resistance, even resistance that knocked his senses askew and set his right knee afire, only served to fan his rage and desire.

"You little bastard!" he rumbled. "I'm gonna ream you like a fence post!" He shifted his great weight into a forward surge.

The kid moved like lightning. He faded to his own left and out of Banky's flailing, half-standing grasp and then snapped a kick into what he knew to be the man's injured knee.

Banky's right leg gave way and his body thumped to the floor of the car before he began to scream. The cries were ear-shattering and as terrifying as anything Condon and Merrick could remember having heard. Banky seemed to wrap all of his weight around the blazing joint, and he rolled to his back clutching it, his mouth wide in agony. The kid stepped safely out of the way to watch, rather than pressing his advantage.

Again, Banky's tremendous well of fury overflowed. Rolling onto his left knee, he continued to wail as he lunged for the kid in an awkward, three-legged stance. The boy glided easily away, like a dancer, before abruptly reversing his flight to charge directly into the off-balanced attacker.

Banky was on his way to the floor and unable to stop himself with his bad knee when the kid darted between his flung-out arms and smashed his own knee with every ounce of his weight into the big man's jaw. He, too, erupted with a cry of pain, but Banky's head snapped back like a tether ball before he slumped to his side. His skull thudded onto the wooden floor and blood gushed from a half a dozen new gaps where his teeth had been.

Incredibly, Banky once more tried to reach out and clutch the quicksilver wraith who evaded him. This time, the boy landed four tight, flashing punches to Banky's face in the span of a heartbeat. When Banky fell this time, it definitely was over.

"Damn, damn, damn!" the boy hissed as he limped quickly about the rear half of the boxcar.

"Son of a bitch," whispered Jimmie Ray in awe.

"You can say that again," Neil added.

The kid's knee apparently was only bruised, because he swiftly began putting his full weight on it and stopped grunting curses to himself. Returning to the unconscious Banky, enraged, he started kicking his leg into that long and fleshy midsection.

"Hey, kid . . . kid, don't kill him!" Condon pleaded. "He's out, you've . . . busted him up good. That's enough!"

The boy stopped punishing Banky's body and stared at Condon and Merrick for an instant before turning back to the man and swiftly going through his pockets. They all proved to be empty of anything that interested him, and he stood for a moment above his conquered enemy as if carefully regaining control of his anger. Then he walked toward the two men.

"I got no money, kid," Jimmie Ray said edgily. "Nothing . . . nothing you'd want."

"Me, neither," Neil stated.

The boy looked surprised by their reactions. "I'm not a thief," he told them with apparent sincerity.

The men understood the kid's reasoning: Banky had attacked him and lost, therefore anything that he possessed was fair compensation for the boy's trouble. Both men breathed sighs of relief.

"Where's this train heading?" The kid's reddish-brown hair was swiftly plastered to his scalp by the blowing rain as he stared out the door.

"All the way, up to Van Buren, Maine," Condon, the old veteran, replied. "End of the line. Where you headed, son?"

The kid didn't turn away from the door. "Nowhere. I'm just waiting."

"For what?" Merrick asked.

"Liberation," was the quiet answer. "April second and liberation day."

Merrick glanced to Condon and made the universal finger-rotation sign for scrambled brains.

"You know, son . . . if I was you, I wouldn't ride this . . . iron all the way to Maine," Condon wheezed.

The kid finally turned away from the door and sat leaning against the wall next to it. "Why?" His voice was calm, cold.

Condon took another swig from the bottle, which was getting dangerously close to empty, and then measured his response. "You got sweet moves, boy, sweet as sugar. Do any boxing?"

"Some," the kid admitted.

"Street bopping, too, I'll bet."

"Who hasn't?"

"I never saw any . . . anybody take old Banky down so clean . . . or so fast . . . but he's going to come to sooner or later."

"Maybe," Merrick muttered.

"And he's going to be royally pissed . . . believe me. Now, I know that you can . . . take him in a stand-up, but he's . . . real strong, real strong, and mean as sin." Long pause for breath. "You're tough, but he'll get you. He'll castrate you."

"I'm not afraid of that tub of shit," the boy said.

"You'd better be. He's crazy. You seen it. Hurt like he was, he kept coming, didn't he?"

"Yep. Maybe I should take precautions, then. Break his other knee and his elbows, too. I think I could sleep pretty safe then."

Merrick laughed. "Damned straight."

"No, don't hurt him anymore." Condon's fine-lined, parchmentlike face suddenly looked even older in the faint light that penetrated the layer of clouds outside. "I know what Banky did . . . was really bad, rotten, but you gotta under . . . understand him. He's been through a lot. Some bad stuff's come down . . . on him. Lost his wife and kids back twenty years . . . ago. A fire. A lot more stuff."

"Things are tough all over, man."

"Some folks don't make it tough on theirselves. Some folks it just happens to."

The kid sighed and closed his eyes. He, too, seemed a little older now and very tired. "Okay, okay. What are we close to?"

Merrick took a quick look at the undistinguished countryside that was flowing by them. "What'd you say, Jimmie Ray? Indigo Lake? Around there?"

The old man nodded. "Just this side, ten minutes. A big, slow curve maybe a mile up ahead." He knew the lines, all right.

"This is a nice place, I guess?" The kid asked this with a slight grin.

"Real nice, a resort. Good place for a runaway to hide out . . . lot of different accents there, so nobody would notice . . . a Georgia boy too much."

The kid's eyes locked on Condon's, and there was the slightest telltale hint of surprise in them.

Jimmie Ray chuckled. "I been around, son. What'dya say?"

The kid thought for a moment and then stood. "Why not?"

"Good. Better get ready to hop it . . . that turn's coming up right soon."

The train did slow considerably on the uphill grade, but as the kid poised in the open door, Condon could tell that he'd never done this before. He didn't look scared, but he was taking a long time to consider his moves.

"Better take it soon, son . . . before we top the hill and straighten out at the curve," Condon said casually.

"Yeah, sure," he answered, still staring at the rocky soil that was sliding by a few feet below him.

"Don't rush him. We've got time," Merrick told Jimmie Ray.

Condon found himself a bit startled by this new guy's unexpected knowledge of the terrain, but he said nothing.

About a half-minute later, the boy flashed a look to them, sucked in his breath, and disappeared over the edge. He landed on both feet, took a half roll, and skidded a short distance in the wet grass just beyond the raw stone and mud base of the slightly elevated track. Nothing seemed to be broken, and, all in all, it was not half bad for his initial venture.

"*Aloha oi*, Ketchel!" shouted Condon with a wave.

The kid raised one hand in response as he came to his knees.

"He'll be okay," Jimmie Ray whispered. "He's a piece of work, that one . . . a real hitter."

Neil Merrick stepped to the open door with a smile. "I guess that's my cue to say so long, too, old man."

Condon coughed raggedly. "Here, man?"

"Yes. I always wanted to see this place. I hear it's the Tahoe of the Northeast."

"Right. Well, you take care of yourself, Neil. Watch out . . . watch out for the low spots in the road." He extended his hand.

Merrick shook it firmly. "I'll catch up to you down the line, out in Shakytown, man. Watch your ass until then."

Jimmie Ray Condon knew that his lungs were too far gone for him ever to see California again, but he kept the grin right up until the time that one of his best friends in the past five years stepped out of his boxcar for the last time.

They walked in the rain for four miles without saying a word. The kid had nothing to say, and Neil didn't want to upset him.

They were still far from Indigo Lake, walking slowly along an empty two-lane blacktop, when the clouds finally squeezed out their last drops of water and then cracked their gray shell releasing the rays of the early-evening sun. Neil glanced skyward and nodded.

"Thank God for small favors, huh?" he said.

"Yeah," the boy mumbled. He had the wispy beginnings of a beard on his chin and jawline.

"My name's Merrick, Neil Merrick."

"Good for you."

He was a real hard case, all right, but Merrick still liked the kid and had the notion that he wasn't as tough as he tried to project. "Don't tell me, I'll bet they call you Red, am I right?" The boy's hair was more brown than red, but it was something to promote the conversation.

"Nope, they sure don't," answered the kid.

"Oh." They walked a few yards more. "What do they call you, then?"

Finally the boy grinned a little. "That old man on the train called me 'Ketchel.'"

"So he did, so he did." Merrick wiped the remnants of the rain from his eyebrows. "Do you know why?"

"The only Ketchel I've ever heard of was Stanley Ketchel, a great middleweight champion about eighty years ago. Maybe the greatest ever."

"Maybe. But before he was a pro champ, he was a legend on the rails."

"Really?"

Merrick nodded. "Like a lot of guys at the turn of the century, he got around the country by hopping freights, and he proved right away that he could fight like a son of a gun. Nobody on any of the lines could stand up to him, and all that a fellow had to do to become king of the hobo jungles was to walk in and say, 'I'm Ketchel.'

"Plenty of other people got to know about him when he went pro. Kicked the guts out of the best middleweights in the world, and put Jack Johnson on his ass, but to the 'bos he remained a mythic figure, like a god with knuckles. He was so famous that even today, eighty-five years in October since he was shot in the back of the head by a sniveling coward of a ranchhand, they still talk about him in whispers, like most people talk about war heroes."

"You sound like you've done plenty of research on the subject," the boy observed.

"I have, son. Let's just say that I'm working on a book."

"Uh-huh."

"Yes, my masterpiece. As long as there're railroads, there'll be hoboes, and as long as there are hoboes, Stanley Ketchel will never really die. Now, whenever a 'bo sees some guy who can really play a tune with his fists, they compare him to Ketchel, big or small, black or white. But you really look the part. Ketchel was five-nine. You?"

The kid stared ahead at the nothingness that lay before them. "About that, I guess. Maybe an inch taller."

"One fifty-five?"

"I haven't weighed myself in a few days."

"What weight did you box in?"

The boy grinned. "'Fifty-six."

Merrick laughed shortly. "Maybe you *are* Ketchel, come back for a few hours to give me the chapter that will top off my book."

"Sorry. My name's Wyler, Chris Wyler."

"Pleased to meet you, Chris." Without awaiting a reply, Neil pointed down the flat road to a distant outline of buildings. "There's our destination. Indigo Lake. The town itself is nothing special, but up around the lake is gorgeous, believe me, with a great vacation complex right on its shore."

"You've been here before?"

"Yep, a time or two."

"Maybe you know some place where we can flop for the night without having to worry about the spiritual brothers of Man Mountain Banky," Chris said.

"I just might at that. But I don't really think you have to worry about defending yourself and your 'virtue.' You sure plowed through Banky in record time, and he was a pro football player back in the seventies, before you were born."

"That must have been where he got his bad knees."

They were on the outskirts of Indigo Lake, in a town, where the corner bar seemed to be the center of activity.

"Hungry?" Chris asked as he stopped before the smoked-glass front window of O'Hanlon's Bar and Grill.

"You know it, man," replied Merrick, "but I don't have any money, and I know of a place where we could get—"

The kid shook his head. "I'm sick of beans and week-old pumpernickel. I want steak and potatoes, with beer to wash it down. You game?"

"Hell, that sounds great, but we'd have to sweep a lot of floors for just one meal."

"If we're lucky, we won't have to raise a broom. Come on." He walked into the bar, and, with a what-the-hell shrug, Neil followed.

There was no cover charge and therefore no employee at the door of the crowded bar, but one of the three bartenders picked up on the pair as soon as they stepped into the hazy, yellowish light of the big front room. Chris walked directly toward this man, a big, beefy individual with more hair showing over his shirt collar than on his head.

"Evening," Chris said as he rested his elbows on the counter.

The response was less cordial. "Show me some ID or take a walk, little man."

"Hey, sure, I'm legal," Chris told him as he dug a black wallet out of his jeans. Producing a laminated driver's license with his picture, he handed it to the big man.

The bartender squinted at the card suspiciously. "*You're* twenty-one?"

"Right. Twenty-one and two months."

"When were you born?"

"The second of April, 1974." Actually, Chris Wyler had come into the world on that date in 1978.

The bartender realized that he had met his legal obligations and painted on a friendly smile. "Sounds good. What can I give you gentlemen?" he asked, returning the fake license.

"A mutually beneficial business proposition," Chris answered.

The pleasant look immediately evaporated and was replaced with exasperation. "Listen, kid, I got an automatic dishwasher and a gal who sweeps up seven nights a week for a room in the back, so if you're hungry I suggest you try the Salvation Army."

Merrick laid a hand on Chris's shoulder as if to guide him out of the bar.

"Hear me out, man," the boy said coolly. "Every bar's got a bigshot loudmouth who rides the other customers like he was a bronco buster, right? And you don't toss him yourself because he supplies you with a regular flow of cash. Point him out to me, and I'll clean his clock, send him home early, and give you a couple of nights of peace without worrying about your reputation being damaged with the rest of the clientele. What do you say?"

"And for this service I pay you—"

"A meal for the two of us."

"So who pays for all of my broken furniture?"

Chris grinned, feeling that he had the man hooked. "I'll make sure that the loudmouth swings first, so you can take the damages out of his bar bill."

"Unless *he* beats *you*. I know you haven't got a penny on you."

"In that case, I go to the workhouse for thirty days and you get my salary. Okay?"

The bartender actually chuckled at that. "Listen, boy, I see by your license that you're from Athens, Georgia, which means that this is probably your first time in the big city, isn't it?"

Chris said nothing, even though four or five Indigo Lakes could have fit in the city limits of Athens, Georgia.

"You're probably tough shit down there, but the bad guys up here will use you like toilet paper, get me?"

Chris's face remained impassive as he stared the man down and said, "We won't know that until we try it, will we?"

The bartender spat another laugh. "Okay, hot dog, see that jerk over there, the one with the punk haircut and the five mouth-breathing puppy dogs ready to lick his butt when he tells them?"

Chris found the man easily enough. He looked about thirty, six-one or two, maybe two hundred pounds; his clothing was sadomasochistic chic, and his eye makeup was less than subtle. "I see him."

"That's Maurice Willets. He has to prove how much of a man he is at least once a week by picking a fight and beating some poor sucker bloody. You take him and the whole menu is yours."

"Thanks, mister." Chris started to move away from the bar.

Merrick caught his arm. "Chris," he whispered,

"you don't have to do this. I can get us a better dinner than anything this place could offer."

Wyler simply winked and strode across the room to where Willets stood, regaling his idolizing audience with tales of his latest exploits.

". . . so I told him that I don't take any talk like that off of *anybody*, especially not a slant-eyed gook," the man was saying as Chris approached. "For some reason, he got offended by that, so we had to do a little dance. He's going to be in the hospital for another month or so, and wired up for longer than that."

"Right, man, yeah," laughed one hanger-on.

"That'll show 'em to come over here and take an American's job away from him," another added.

"I don't like to be the enforcer all the time, but, hell, some things you just can't let go, you know?" Willets stated solemnly.

"Like being Asian in KKK County, U.S.A.," Chris observed as he passed the group on the way to a table directly behind them.

"What'd you say, assbite?" Willets demanded loudly.

Chris stopped walking and faced the man. *This is going to be easier than I thought*, he told himself. "Nothing much, just that we should all try to be more tolerant of one another. If I lived in Japan, I wouldn't want them to hate me because my eyes are round."

Willets laughed breezily at that, and his followers took their cue from him.

"Lookit this, Maurie, we've got a *philosopher* here," one guy said. "A bleeding heart pablum puker! He must be the last flower child."

"He's going to be a bleeding flower child unless he ups and flounces out of my sight." Willets used his middle finger as a pointer and jabbed Chris's chest firmly. "Get me, Southern shit?"

Chris smiled. Perfect. "I don't believe in fighting,

mister, but I'm afraid I'll have to ask you not to touch me again."

Sizing up the markedly younger and smaller boy, Willets hissed, "See how you like this touch!" before swinging a high, hard right hand at Wyler's head.

Neil was ten feet away, ready to stop the massacre if the taller punker began to connect solidly, but he stood paralyzed, mouth slightly agape, at what happened in the next half minute. Against Banky, Chris had looked remarkable, but he had been facing a partially incapacitated foe, who had retained little of the quickness of his professional football days. Willets, on the other hand, was younger, in obviously good shape, fast, and somewhat experienced in the martial arts.

But Chris was a demon. With combinations almost too fast for the eye to register, he wreaked havoc on the body and face of Maurice Willets. Every move and punch that the taller man attempted was blocked or slipped and then countered with blazing fists, feet, and knees. When he tried to use his feet on the kid's most obvious targets—groin, knees, and face—he failed to make any significant contact. When he desperately closed in on the boy to use the strength of his corded arms in a grappling match, Chris faded out of his reach and landed a pair of thumping shots to the gut that dropped Willets to his knees, retching.

It was all over in an astonishing amount of time and without the shattering of a single beer mug. Maybe this kid *was* Stanley Ketchel reborn. Neil had witnessed things more fantastic than reincarnation.

"All right, that's enough!" the head bartender growled, though he wasn't looking particularly displeased. "You two break it up or I'll call the cops!" He knew that Willets was finished, and there was no reason to let the kid mutilate him.

Willets's entourage gathered around him, stunned,

and with clumsy, solicitous hands tried to pull him up. Maurice came shakily to his feet, and, with his friends' help, he stumbled out of the bar. Chris watched them go without comment and then sat at an empty table.

"How's this, Neil?" he asked. "Close enough to the kitchen?"

"Yes, sir!" Merrick answered happily as he hurried to sit across the table from the boy. "This looks just about perfect to me."

It was the best meal either had eaten in a long time. The waitresses—no friends of crude Willets—couldn't do enough for Merrick and the boy, and even the other diners and bar patrons made a few congratulatory stops at the table. Maurice Willets and company had not been very well liked at O'Hanlon's Bar and Grill.

"Well, you're Ketchel's size but you use Dempsey's methods for keeping food in your belly," Merrick said as he slowly savored his coffee and apple pie with French vanilla ice cream, the best dessert offered by the establishment. "When he was a kid, before he made a name for himself in the ring, he traveled the rails, too, and when he hit town, he'd either scrounge out yard work for a meal or head for the nearest saloon and beat up the local bully for beer and sandwiches."

"Looks like I'm not original in anything much, doesn't it?" Chris asked wryly.

This boy is not a hood, Merrick noted, *he's had education, a background of some privilege. He's not an animal, even if he fights like one.* "Jack was only fifteen when he did it, and, of course, *you're* twenty-one."

Wyler grinned and knocked back the last of his beer.

Darkness fell as they ate, and they found themselves faced with the question of where to spend the night. Chris was ready to ask the head bartender/

owner if there was a back room they could use when Merrick reached a decision and stopped him.

"Sit back down, Chris. I've got it covered."

The kid's eyebrows rose in mute question.

"We're going to have the finest beds this town has to offer."

"There must be some really charitable hotel owners around this place."

"You got us the meal. Let me worry about this."

Chris watched a skimpily dressed waitress as she cleared the next table. "It's in your hands, man."

Neil hadn't been lying, Chris decided as he and the man walked wearily up the long drive toward the gates of the Indigo Lake Resort. The place looked great. It encompassed this entire half of the crystalline lake, with widely spaced vacation homes that were larger and more impressive in appearance than anything the town had to offer. A number of small docks buttressed the smooth waters that glistened like strings of pearls in the moonlight, and in the center of the lake, was a large island connected to the shore by an artificial wedge of paved land that cut through the surface of the water with knifelike precision.

It looked like the type of place that would cost a month's salary for an overnight stay, and Chris wondered just what in the hell he and Neil were doing marching up to the security station located at the center of the gates.

A uniformed guard laid aside a copy of a best-selling horror novel, as he stood to greet them. "Good evening, gentlemen," he said with genuine warmth.

"How are you, Chester?" Merrick responded with easy familiarity, though the guard had shown no sign of recognition. "My young friend and I would like to check in for the night."

Right, and I get the feeling that it's going to take more than kicking the giblets out of some overripe punkoid to buy a bed at this place, Chris thought.

With startling civility, the guard said, "Certainly, sir. Your name, please?"

"Neil Thomas Merrick," Neil replied.

The man's smile became even broader and more sincere. "Mr. Merrick, so very good to see you again, sir! You're somewhat early this year."

"See you again," Chris replayed within his mind. This guy hadn't acted like he'd ever seen Neil in his life before tonight. The boy noticed that even as he enthusiastically welcomed Merrick, the guard was deftly punching away at a computer keyboard.

"And your friend is?"

"Christopher Wyler," Merrick answered. "He's not a member of our association, but I wish to provide him with our hospitality for the evening and perhaps longer."

"Of course, sir." The guard consulted the readout screen, nodded to himself, and touched a button which buzzed open a standard-sized doorway in the kiosk just to the left of his cubicle. "I'm sorry to be so bound by regulations, but I'll have to ask you to step inside for a moment to recite your canon, if you don't mind."

"Surely." Neil clapped the boy's shoulder firmly. "Wait here, Chris, this won't take a minute, and in just a few after that you'll be nestled in the softest bed on this side of the Atlantic."

"If it's a board between two cinder blocks, it'll beat the last place I slept," Chris said.

Chuckling, Merrick stepped into the tiny alcove in the guard station. The door instantly slipped shut behind him. Naturally, Chris had no way of knowing what was occurring within the enclosure, but he was able to hear faintly Neil's voice slowly and carefully speaking several lines of dialogue, like an uninspired student reciting poetry before the class. The guard was watching his computer screen with an increasingly pleased expression covering his face. After perhaps forty-five seconds, he said, "Very good, sir," into a microphone and flipped yet another switch on the control panel.

The door zipped open, and Merrick stepped out.

"The patterns match to within degrees, sir," the guard told him. "Again, may I say how glad I am to welcome you to this year's meeting."

"Thank you, Chester."

Do I have to recite "The Charge of the Light Brigade"? Chris wondered.

"You and your young friend will be staying on the island, I take it?"

"Yes."

"Then allow me to summon a car for you."

This guy must be a millionaire, Chris thought as a long, dark Rolls Royce appeared at the gates from somewhere within the resort and he and Neil seated themselves in the rear of it. These "associates" of his must be in the Fortune 500. But what in the hell was Merrick doing riding a boxcar along with an eighty-year-old asthmatic and a horny giant with bad legs?

The car quietly motored through the shoreline collection of resort houses and across the land bridge to the island. In the dark, Chris could tell little about his surroundings, but when he saw the huge, four-story mansion, lit by lights in maybe half a hundred windows and the outside by dazzling floodlamps, he knew that very few people other than the extremely rich ever saw this place close up.

Man, you've fallen into the real stuff this time, Chris thought.

The silent chauffeur stopped before the mansion's vast front porch, and the two passengers climbed out of the car and walked up the elaborate staircase. They were met halfway by one of the most heart-stoppingly gorgeous people Chris had ever seen.

"Neil?" the gorgeous woman asked from a couple of

steps above them. "Neil Merrick?"

Neil smiled hugely but with still a touch of uncertainty. "Yes, and you're—"

"It's me, Gabrielle!" she cried happily.

"Gabby!" Merrick launched himself up the two steps, engulfed the red-haired woman in a tremendous bear hug, and then swung and squeezed her all the way up the staircase to the porch. The way they hugged and laughed and kissed left no doubt that they knew one another *very* well, even though neither had recognized the other at first.

Feeling like a nonswimmer in deep water, Chris followed the pair up the stairs.

"Oh, you devil!" Gabrielle said in a delightfully accusing tone when Merrick placed her again on her feet. "You promised last time that we would stay in touch, and what do I get? Not one word in five whole years! Thank you very much!"

"The best intentions, my dear." Neil laughed.

"What on earth have you done to yourself?" she asked. "At the last meeting, you were—"

Neil coughed abruptly and used his eyebrows to indicate Chris's presence.

Gabrielle turned her glowing face toward the boy. "And who is this simply beautiful young creature?"

Chris was thoroughly captivated by the woman's awesome looks. Her red and glistening lips, pink-and-white complexion, and flashing green eyes all seemed to have been achieved without the aid of cosmetics, and the breathtaking body in the tight, white gown was far beyond any exercise fitness expert's ability to produce. In the young man's mind, there were two kinds of feminine sexuality: the dark and brooding fire that is addictive to a man as surely as any illegal drug and the boldly joyous sunburst that can overwhelm a guy and leave him wasted and as empty as a deflated balloon. Gabrielle surely was the latter.

"Forgive my manners," Merrick said. "Gabrielle,

this is Mr. Christopher Wyler, my boon companion and perhaps the greatest natural martial artist in the Western hemisphere. Chris, allow me to present Miss Gabrielle Francoise Secretain, certainly the most beautiful and delightful young gentlewoman it has been my great good fortune to have become acquainted with in all of my global wanderings."

"How do you do, Miss—" Chris's attempted greeting was smothered in his lungs by Gabrielle's sudden and entirely unexpected kiss. Her delicious lips seemed ready to gulp him down like an appetizer, and when his own lips parted purely in reflex, her tiny, hot tongue darted between them with an energy that was like a flame in his chest.

As abruptly as she had clasped him to that marvelous bosom, Gabrielle turned away to clutch Neil's arm again. "Come in, you two! Everyone will be so ecstatic to see you! Pepe is already here, and so are Colin and Barbara!"

"Really? It seems that we'll have a grand turnout for this session," Merrick observed. "Come along, Chris."

Chris stood for a moment alone on the porch and tried to summon up the strength to follow the pair. Jeez, what a reception! He hadn't had a clue that Neil was involved with people like this. A million questions bombarded his numb brain, but one rang clearer than all the rest.

He wondered if Gabrielle Francoise Secretain had a weakness for seventeen-year-old runaways with less than perfect police records but who had really kind and pure personalities?

CHAPTER THREE

The fat guy had incredible stamina.

Harry Mitchellson was surprised at the way Dom Poduano was able to sit behind the wheel of the '57 Chevy for fourteen out of the seventeen hours that they had been on the road together without so much as a complaint about *deadenus gluteus*. He'd taken a one-hour break for each of the three meals they'd eaten that day and, true to his word, Poduano had cheerfully paid for Harry and Marsha's portion of each check. But other than those necessary breaks, he'd remained cemented in place, skillfully guiding the beautiful vehicle toward the northeast. Even when Harry and Marsha called for pit stops, Dom had waited for them in his idling pride and joy.

Well, he is a traveling salesman, Harry told himself, *and I suppose that means he had to build up a tolerance for long stretches of driving. Probably setting himself up for massive prostate trouble in five or ten years.*

At dusk, Dom had the decency to put up the top,

but his stream of friendly, wide-ranging conversation continued unabated as the darkness became complete. Marsha was asleep on Harry's shoulder again, and he was convinced that Poduano was going to drive straight through to New York when the man suddenly seemed to realize that that was the full moon beaming so brightly up in the sky and not the sun. He glanced at the dash clock.

"Good grief, it's almost eleven o'clock!" Dom said, surprised. "Why didn't one of you kids say something?"

"I never like to disturb a man while he's doing good work," Harry replied.

Poduano laughed. "Sure, but, shoot, man, I could have talked and driven all night long. Wouldn't be the first time." A large green-and-silver highway sign flashed by on their right side. "Did that say Marshall?"

"Uh-huh. Next exit a mile and a half," Harry said. "Would that be a good place to stop?"

"Fine place," answered Podano. "Plenty of motels just off the interstate, good rates, gas. Yes, sir, if you kids agree, I believe that's where we'll pitch our tents for tonight."

"I think I can speak for Marsha when I say, the sooner the better."

Marshall, Illinois, was not a metropolis, by any stretch, but as Poduano had claimed, it offered a large selection of overnight accommodations. They chose a Benny's Lodge that looked clean and boasted a prominent vacancy sign.

After parking in the lot before the main office, Poduano turned quietly for all his bulk, and whispered to Harry, "Before the girl wakes up, would you two prefer separate rooms or do you want to share one?"

Mitchellson smiled at the man's remarkable sense of propriety. "One," he said softly. "We *are* going to get married, Dom, and we don't want to take advantage of your generosity."

Poduano waved a hand. "Don't give it a thought, son. Just your company makes up for all of this to an old gabhorse like me. I'll sign in so you don't have to disturb the little lady for a few more minutes."

Harry gently roused Marsha while Poduano was inside the office. "C'mon, babe. We're at the motel."

Marsha blinked slowly and rubbed her nose. In the bright, electric-blue moonlight, she looked like a blond angel. "We gonna kill 'im now?" she asked sleepily.

"Not tonight. He's a real sugar daddy, and we're going to let him bend our ears all the way to New York before we take a chance like that, okay?"

"'Kay." Marsha began to straighten various bits of clothing; she'd slept through much of the day, and Harry could tell that he probably would be in for a rough night. "Am I going to have to let the old walrus have a free one in exchange for the hotel room?"

"You know, I really don't believe so. I think that the bastard honestly just wants our company." The wonder of such a situation was easy to read in Mitchellson's normally well-disguised voice.

Poduano returned with the keys a few minutes later. "We're going to be next-door neighbors," he said jovially. "Two-oh-two and 204. Right up there. Cable TV, if you kids want to watch anything tonight, but I have to ask one favor of you."

Uh-oh, here it comes, thought Marsha. She was ready to do what she would have to.

"I'd like to be on the road again by eight in the morning, so if you'll be ready for breakfast by seven, I'd appreciate it."

Harry and Marsha, the loving murderers, held one another's hands and nodded in innocent agreement.

* * *

The curtains were parted in the otherwise dark room, and the moonlight streamed in like liquid platinum. It fell across the thick carpet and onto the bed where the two young people lay. On the bedside table, Harry's digital watch read, "11:58."

Marsha couldn't sleep now. Her hand drifted from her side to the chair on which her skirt lay neatly spread out. The wide white leather belt slipped easily from its loops into her fingers.

"Harry," she whispered gently, "you awake?"

"Hmm?"

"Wake up, Harry. I want to do it. Now." The moon was full and very powerful tonight. "I gotta do it, Harry."

"Right now?" he asked wearily.

"Yes."

He raised his head from the pillow and the looped belt went over it and cinched tightly about his neck in one practiced motion. He gasped, taken by surprise, but already his body was responding the way every man's body responds to strangulation. His hands searched hungrily for her naked breasts.

"This now," she hissed commandingly, "and then the big thing, the real thing."

He couldn't have spoken if he'd tried.

True to his word, ebullient Dom Poduano was up early the next morning. By six-fifty-five, he was knocking none too gently on the door next to his room to rouse the two kids so that they could get up, clean up, dress up, and show up for breakfast before the eight o'clock departure time.

Dom liked the pair, even if they weren't married. The guy was a good talker and the girl was one heck of a looker, and he knew that they would provide good company all the way home.

"You old folks circulating in there, yet?" he called.

"Getting late. You never stand still in this life, you know. It's either go forward or slide back." He knocked again.

Amid various coughs, grunts, and snorts, a pair of feet approached the door, and an instant later it swung open to frame a tousled-headed Harry in his underwear, looking like death warmed over. "Dom?" he asked fuzzily. Dark rings under his eyes made him resemble a raccoon. "What the hell time is it?"

"Seven in the A.M.," Poduano answered. *I know you're young, boy, but you've got to take time out for rest occasionally*, he noted mentally. "We need to be on the road in an hour. Are you and your little lady going to make it?"

Harry scratched his hairy chest. "I don't know, man. We appreciate the ride and all, but, damn, it's really early, you know?"

Before Dom could reply, Marsha stepped into the doorway at Harry's side. She looked fabulous. Already washed, brushed, and dressed, she seemed to radiate youth and good health. And attractiveness. It seemed as if she had used the night to recharge and nourish herself, while Harry had dissipated.

"Don't worry, Dom," she said brightly, "you run down to the restaurant, and I promise I'll have this sleepyhead as presentable as he gets in ten minutes."

"Roger and over and out," Poduano responded with a big grin. He made a miniature salute as he turned on his heel and headed for the stairs.

That Marsha, she sure was something.

CHAPTER FOUR

Chris Wyler was, to put it mildly, shocked by the way
in which Neil Merrick had been accepted by the
members of the association on Caprice Island, though
he masked it well beneath his road face. Chris had
taken Merrick for another 'bo, nothing more, and to
discover that the guy was wealthy—wouldn't he have
to be to belong to *this* group?—was quite a shock. The
bed he had slept in on that first night really was the
best he'd ever had.

At first, his stay was terrific. As Neil's good friend,
Chris was waited on by eager-to-please servants, fed
the finest foods he'd ever tasted, and fawned over by
the thirty or so incredibly attractive and healthy
women and men of the association. After nearly a
month on the road, it was a nice change of pace, all
right.

But it had soured quickly enough. To an independent and self-contained person like Chris, the role of

houseguest rode heavily, and even the fact that no one ever asked questions about his home, destination, or age only lessened his unease for a few days. He may have been given almost anything that he desired, including a couple of nights with one of the beautiful and eager maids, but he was still treated like a retarded child—or maybe a pet animal.

The members of the association had some mysterious secret that they were unwilling to share with Chris. Conversations ended in mid-word when he came into the room, and body language took on an entirely new aspect as intense messages were passed supposedly behind his back. Chris didn't care about not being a part of the "in" crowd; he didn't want to know their glorious or dirty little secrets. What did bother him was the fact that they were making all of these changes in their routine due to his presence.

Even good food, a soft bed, and a little maid named Audrey could keep him on the island for only three days.

On Thursday, June 22, Chris found Neil after the typical sumptuous breakfast and thanked him for his hospitality while explaining that it was time to move on.

Merrick seemed honestly shocked and a bit upset. "You're leaving so soon? But I had certain plans for you, Christopher, plans that will change your life far beyond anything you can imagine."

When I left home, "certain plans" had been made for me, Ace, Chris thought. "Thanks, anyway, Neil, but I'm not really the junior executive type. When the mood hits, I have to jump that iron and ride. You've got to know the feeling."

They were alone in the vast, lavishly over-furnished den. Merrick was ensconced behind reams of *The New York Times*, and Chris stood next to him. As Neil folded the business section of the paper and laid it aside, Chris was once again amazed at the transformation that seemed to have come over Neil in only three days. He was clean-shaven and his hair had been trimmed, but his body seemed to have undergone definite physical changes. When they had first met, Neil had to be an inch or so shorter than Chris and perhaps a slightly starved one hundred and forty pounds. Now, however, he seemed to be at least six feet and closing in on a fit one-seventy. The guy was a human chameleon.

Or maybe Chris's late-night sessions with Audrey were inciting his imagination in more than the most obvious ways.

"Chris, let's not continue to blow smoke at each other," Neil said. "I've been touring the country by rail for the last five years, and that's plenty of time for me to be able to recognize a youngster who doesn't know the first thing about hopping—and debarking —freights. Oh, you can take care of yourself, all right, no doubt about that, and you must have worked that punch-for-pasta gimmick a number of times. But Monday's ride was your first gig as a hobo, correct?"

Feeling he owed Neil the truth, Chris nodded. "I've mostly been hitchhiking. I'm a fast learner, though."

"I don't doubt that, either. As for age . . . hmm . . . sixteen?"

"Seventeen."

"Since April second, I take it. And your 'liberation day' will be *next* April second, when you turn eighteen."

"That's right. Legal adult. No runaway charges, no school ties, just one punch-drunk hobo named Wyler against the rest of the world. So you can see why I don't want to stay in one place too long."

Neil stood and clapped the boy's shoulder. Maybe he was wearing lifts in his shoes these days, Chris thought. "Son, I can't think of a better plan than for you to stay in one place—right here—for the next nine months. You'll have security, privacy, companionship, and the chance to map out your future without having to defend yourself against the Jeff Bankys of the world every time you close your eyes."

"I don't want to take advantage of you and your friends, Neil. I'd feel like a flea attached to the best dog in town if I hung around here for another year."

"And living in boxcars would be better?"

"I'll get a job, pick up some money fighting. There are plenty of unsanctioned matches where they don't check your age and ID too close as well as the occasional battle royal—"

"'Battle royal'?" Merrick interrupted. "Do you mean those barbarous spectacles where eight or ten teenaged boys are blindfolded and put into a ring, and the last one left standing wins the 'prize'?"

"I picked up a hundred bucks that way in Missouri three weeks ago," the boy answered. He extended his right hand. "It was terrific to meet you, Neil, and to find out that you've got a lot going for you. Maybe we'll wind up in the same car again someday."

Merrick glanced at the hand but didn't touch it. He seemed to be trying to reach some difficult conclusion, and when he spoke again, it was with an almost explosive energy. "Two weeks more."

"What?"

"Stay here, in the resort for two more weeks, and then I can explain the offer that I'm willing to make to you. Agreed?"

Damn, how did I get to be the fair-haired boy? Chris asked himself. *Maybe he is an eccentric millionaire with a yen for an heir, and who am I to refuse a windfall fortune?*

"Chris?"

"Listen," he sighed, "I don't know who or what you think I am, but I'm no Boy Scout. I've got a police record, and I'm not on the road because I want to become steeped in the primitive essence of our country. What I'm trying to say is—"

"You're not up for adoption, Chris." Merrick laughed. "No sudden wealth, but something far greater than that. I'm not going to ask anything of you, so you can relax on that account, and what I'll be in a position to offer you over the week of the Fourth will free you from all of your problems—money, health, age—for the remainder of your life."

It sounded like a dream, the golden opportunity that existed only in ephemeral daydreams, and Chris Wyler couldn't bring himself to accept it. He'd been through a lot in his seventeen years, much of it unpleasant, so he found that he could no longer take the words of others at face value. His defense mechanism was always active, his innate polygraph alert to statements that sounded too pat and too good.

"I don't think so, man," he finally said. "I appreciate the thought, but I'll have to pass."

Merrick responded with an exasperated grin. "You don't make it easy, do you, bub? All right, let's try this. You'll need a stake to get on your way again, so I want to hire you for the next two weeks."

The kid's eyes remained hooded, if not hostile. "As what?"

"The . . . uh . . . the director of the athletic department. It's a real job, no training required, all you'll have to do is dispense basketballs and badminton equipment and make sure the place is locked up after eleven each night. The salary is a rent-free room and five hundred dollars per week."

"Five hundred?" Chris responded incredulously.

"In cash. It's the going rate. You can ask the girl who has the job now."

"The girl I'm going to knock into the unemployment line, you mean."

Merrick gave a brief nod to indicate that he had strode, eyes open, into the jaws of this not-too-well-hidden snare, but that was his only concession. "We're in luck there, too. The current director has just tendered her resignation."

"Bullshit," Chris said.

Neil shrugged. "How can I argue with incisive reasoning such as that? All right, son, walk out on this opportunity if you must, but you should know at least what it is you're giving up."

"So tell me."

The man shook his head. "Not yet. That's not how it's done. You won't have to put up much to collect on this, just a little faith, and to show that all you have to do is hang around. Here or at the athletic building. Walking out now wouldn't prove your independence so much as your stupidity."

What's there to lose? Chris wondered. *I can't read anything into this guy, no motives, and I know I ain't that cute. For two weeks, why not?*

"When do I report to work?" he asked, knowing that he would miss a lot of the perks offered by the mansion but unable to face twelve or fourteen days more of playing house pet.

Merrick smiled with satisfaction. "I knew you were a smart cookie."

"I'm also as broke as all ten of the commandments."

Five minutes later, alone in his room, Neil Merrick picked up his telephone and said simply, "Brundage." Within moments, the second party was on the line.

"Leslie? This is Merrick," he said officiously. "Please have your things together and be ready to move into the house within the hour." He smiled slightly as the expected reaction burst from the receiver. "Yes, this Fourth. Don't thank me. You've worked hard for the opportunity, and I wish you the best of luck.

"No, don't worry about that, either. The position has already been filled."

For a man with an itch to get to New York, Dom Poduano certainly seemed to be taking his time.

He was still driving twelve to fourteen hours a day without showing any signs of fatigue or saddle sores, but he hadn't chosen the most direct route. From Marshall, Illinois, on Monday night, they had proceeded almost due east, rather than northeast, so that tonight, Thursday, the twenty-second, they had wound up in Towson, Maryland.

Marsha was fed up with all of the traveling and eager to kill the fat man and be on their way to Maine. Harry was barely able to contain her impulsive energy by pointing out that they were getting further from the scenes of their latest crimes by the day and promising that if Poduano didn't pull a sharp turn to the north on Friday they would seriously consider taking care of the problem in a decisive fashion.

So when they checked into a Little Genie motel that night, both of the young people were edging toward their limits of endurance. Though they were literally riding in the best situation that they could have prayed for, it seemed that something had to give. Certainly Harry was looking for some form of relief, however temporary it might prove to be.

Blake Corbett was asleep in his apartment in Los Angeles. His rest was deep, dreamless, and wonderful; he was allowed very few nights like this these days.

When the telephone rang next to his bed, he awoke with a start and cursed his nervousness. The next full moon was still most of a month away, but that didn't seem to matter to his ever-present anxiety. Without bothering to turn on the light or to find his glasses, he fumbled the receiver to his ear.

"Hello?" he muttered. Just a month short of one year before, another phone call had begun this apparently unending nightmare for him.

"Corbett?" demanded a clipped, no-nonsense voice. "That you?"

Blake coughed. "Yes. Who—"

"It's me, Douglas Morgan."

Blake's eyes grew wide in the darkness. "Doug? Man, it's great to hear from you! Where are you? I thought that the government had—"

"There's no time for old home week, Corbett," Morgan interrupted. The former columnist for the *Los Angeles Chronicle* had gone through that December night with Blake, Meg Talley, and Nick Grundel, so he knew all of the secrets that Corbett was being forced to keep by the government. "This line may be tapped. How's your financial situation?"

Blake was confused and unsettled by that. "Uh, pretty good. My notoriety from last year has done wonders for my book sales, and there's a chunk of money from a movie deal I've just signed. Why?"

"I want you to get all of the ready cash together that you can. Go to every automatic teller in the city if you have to. Then be ready to take it on the lam, maybe for months or even years, until we can get the country to listen to the truth. Or you can tell me to go to hell right now, and we'll never bother you again. Will you help us?"

"Who?"

"Meg, me, and Nick. This is too big for the government to quash, and unless we act now, Nick will spend the rest of his life in isolation."

Oh, my God, Nick Grundel, Blake thought. *My associate. My friend. And now one of them.*

Could he actually help that young man regain his freedom?

"Corbett?"

He drew in a breath. "Okay. Yes. Where do you want me and when?"

Morgan told him and then hung up without so much as a good-bye. For a long time, Blake Corbett sat in the darkness and replayed the horror of the past six months through his mind.

It was starting again.

CHAPTER FIVE

It would have surprised anyone who had known Blake Corbett throughout his adult life, but he had five thousand dollars in cash secreted in his apartment. In a real way, he owed his affluence to the mad killer, Gerald Cummings.

Financial irresponsibility and alimony payments had ensured that Blake would spend much of his career poised on the brink of bankruptcy. But if his notoriety the year before from publicly pursuing "the Mangler" and labeling the once-a-month mass killer as a werewolf had done anything positive in his life, it had been to give his book sales a healthy boost and to place two more of his properties with film producers. As a result, Corbett had more money than he'd ever had, and the certainty that mere money could never mean as much to him as it had when the world had been a saner, more understandable place.

So why did he have five grand in a shoe box on an overhead shelf in his bedroom closet? For much the same reason as was apparent in Douglas Morgan's call: in case he needed to make a quick trip out of town. And maybe out of the country.

It was after 1 A.M. when Blake took the five thousand and quietly left his apartment. The adjoining parking lot seemed to be empty of observers, at least to his eyes, but he knew that the security man at the gate could easily be in the employ of his friendly neighborhood government watchdogs and eager to telephone his superiors about this odd, unscheduled, late-night jaunt. Once, not so long ago, Blake would have considered such thinking paranoid, but now it was only reasonable.

He had to have his car, though, and he certainly couldn't smuggle it out under his coat.

Blake had fifteen thousand dollars more in the bank, but he knew that he wasn't going to get very much of that out at this hour. There were perhaps a dozen of the automatic banking machines throughout the city, but they all were wired into a central computer. So when he withdrew the pre-set limit at the first one—one thousand dollars—and he was refused at the second—"LIMIT ONE THOUSAND DOLLARS PER EVERY TWENTY-FOUR-HOUR PERIOD"— he took the hint and bypassed the other ten outlets. You didn't have to hit A.B. Corbett with a brick.

Six thousand bucks was not a bad grubstake to start off this escapade, but he still wished that he knew just how long that stake would have to last.

Just before 2 A.M., he left for the rendezvous.

A thirty-year veteran reporter Douglas Morgan had well-honed instincts, and all of these refined senses told him that this whole deal was a setup. An inside informant privy to the innermost secrets of a deeply buried government agency designed solely to protect the most important discovery since the development of the atomic bomb decides to blow the whistle by contacting a widely read, and discredited, columnist for the *Los Angeles Chronicle*? Yeah, sure.

But he still couldn't afford to dismiss the calls.

Morgan knew from the first telephone call to his home on a night in May—less than a month following his own release from the Institute—that this was no joke. The mysterious caller recited details of an ordeal that Doug personally had lived through, details that only another firsthand observer of the December massacre could have known, details that were too much beyond the average human experience for even a horror fiction writer to concoct. The caller claimed to be dedicated to spreading the truth about Gerald Cummings and lycanthropy, and to this end he had revealed to Morgan the method in which Nick Grundel could be rescued from his enforced detainment at the Institute. After the call, Doug and Meg Talley immediately went underground, using Doug's newspaper contacts to keep them hidden from the authorities.

Which was why forty-eight-year-old Douglas Morgan was sitting in a parked car on a back country road at three in the morning.

"This thing stinks like a hog on a hot day," he said to the other occupant in the car.

Margret Patricia "Meg" Talley zipped up her tight leather jacket and responded with a quizzical look. "What do you mean, Doug?"

The dour-faced man touched the light button on his wristwatch and compulsively checked the time. "Just that this whole deal seems a lot more like a scam to catch you and me than to help Nick escape custody."

Meg cinched the straps at the tops of her boots a little tighter. "Who'd want to trap us? For gosh sakes, Doug, we were living in the open, in our own homes, until two months ago. If somebody wanted to trap us, why didn't they just roll the paddy wagons up to our doors then?"

"I said it smelled. I didn't say I knew why," he answered. "It just seems strange to me that anyone inside the government would be so interested in exposing the truth about lycanthropy that he would risk his career—hell, his freedom—just to keep us up to date with the classified details of the whole investigation. And now to tip us off where and when Nick's being transferred—"

"I suppose it proves that our mysterious 'he' is as committed to revealing the truth to the world as we are and that he realizes that we'll need irrefutable evidence in order to prove it. Nick's infected now. They won't be able to deny our story when they see what happens to him under the influence of the full moon." Meg glanced through the window at the clear, starry sky above, thankful that there was no moon.

"Yeah. You're right, I guess. I *hope.*" Morgan checked his watch again. "But it still doesn't feel right."

"Do you want to call it off, then? Try to help Nickie some other way?"

"No. If they get him out of the state, we'll never be able to track him down. The van should be along in about ten minutes, so you'd better get out of sight."

Meg opened her door and stood, peering into the dark and forbidding forest that pressed in closely on either side of the empty road. It was on a California dirt trail that she had first encountered a monster called Gerald Cummings. "Okay, boss, but if he doesn't show in half an hour, you'd better not leave me out here alone."

Though he was a longtime resident of Los Angeles, Douglas Morgan had no experience as a film actor or any inclination toward acquiring any. But he did have contacts in the business who got him, even while in hiding with Meg from the government bloodhounds, several fairly intricate pieces of special-effects equipment. He thought that he also had the knowledge necessary to utilize them successfully.

The car sat on a hill overlooking a long stretch of the deserted road, which gave Morgan an unobstructed view of any vehicles approaching from the west. From that direction at about three-fifteen, Morgan saw the first pair of headlights come bouncing along so he took it on faith that it was their target and set off the carefully distributed special effects.

First he activated the fuse to a small flash grenade and tossed it into the road. It worked beautifully, almost too much so. Morgan was staring directly at the rolling device when it burst in an eruption of searing white light that screamed into his darkness-swollen pupils. He roared with pain and curses as he clutched his eyes.

"Doug! Doug, are you all right?" Meg called from the concealment of the forest to the left of him.

He fought to regain his control. "I'm okay! Don't come out!" He blinked rapidly, seeing only a painful sheet of white radiance before his face. There was no time for this now. "I can handle it!"

He had been holding a cigarette lighter, which he dropped in the sudden pain of the flare, and as he frantically worked to clear his eyes, he also scrambled about on his hands and knees to find it. Luckily, he had tossed the grenade about fifteen yards down the road, saving himself from real retinal damage, and within seconds he could at least see the road. Snatching up the lighter, he fired a pre-prepared fuse and dropped it into the napalm-like jelly that he and Meg had mopped over the road.

This material flared up almost as swiftly as had the grenade, though not as brightly. In a breath, the road was filled with a dangerous-looking orange fire. The jelly had been shored with a second semi-liquid substance that inhibited the fire as thoroughly as the jelly promoted it, thus assuring that the forest wouldn't go up in a similar blaze, but an uninformed observer had no way of knowing this.

Morgan stood in the road between the fire and the rapidly approaching headlights and estimated the time of arrival of what he hoped was the government van. Thirty seconds at most.

"Right," he grunted to himself. The most elaborate part of the effects had to be enacted next.

It hadn't been absolutely necessary to use it, but the next illusion would add authenticity to their plan—if it worked as his film technician contact had promised. It was a life-sized dummy with a simple motor that caused the arms and legs to work in a feeble, injured fashion. Dragging the prop near the leaping flames, he positioned it face down, switched on the motor, and lit the flammable clothing that covered it. Then he stepped back and appraised the illusion.

Damn, it *did* look good. Just like some hapless driver who had been thrown from his car after wrecking it and had caught fire when doused with the flaming gasoline. The scrabbling limbs added a morbid, but definitely effective, touch to the picture.

"One more player to position," he whispered.

While he wasn't an actor, he knew that he had the talent required to play this particular role. Finding a place close to the fire, but not too close, he lay in the road on his stomach and did his best to look dead.

The van careened up the hill and skidded to a stop seconds later. It was so close to Morgan that it kicked gravel into his face.

"Good God, that man's still alive!" shouted a shocked voice from within the vehicle. "Get the extinguisher!"

It's working! Morgan thought.

"Lennox! Hold it!" snapped a second man's voice.

"He's on *fire*!" the first man responded frantically. "We can't let him burn!"

"I said wait! Our orders are to remain in the

transport vehicle until we reach Montello."

Damn! Morgan felt more the victim than the perpetrator, pinned like a bug between the fire to his left and the headlights of the idling van. His hand, pressed beneath his body, trembled with a fearful eagerness.

"We can't get around the wreck, anyway, so I'm—"

"You're going to follow orders, Lennox!"

"Then let *me* go put it out, you assholes!" shouted a new voice. That was Nick! "I'm not under any damned orders!"

"Shut up, Grundel," replied the driver, apparently the officer in charge. "You know we have the right to place verbal restraint devices on you if you—"

"Screw the orders!" Lennox shouted. "I'm going to put that fire out!"

"Lennox—oh, all right! Toland, give him a hand. Get the fire out and push the car off the road."

Thank God, Morgan thought. *Now for the fun part.*

He kept his eyes tightly shut and tried not to breathe noticeably, but he could hear the two men leaving the van and running toward the fire. He hadn't counted on their having extinguishers, and he realized that if they doused the mechanical dummy and discovered what it was before they approached closely enough for him to implement the next step of the plan, he would be up the creek.

"Is he still alive?" asked one man.

"He's moving, but, hey, there's somebody else down! Over here! I think he's dead!"

"You check him while I take care of this one!"

Morgan could barely restrain himself from shaking his fist in triumph.

Footsteps rushed to Morgan's side, and the would-be rescuer dropped to his knees. Morgan waited, fighting to remain "dead," until just the right moment, when the man grabbed his shoulder and rolled him to his back to check for injuries.

"Blink and I'll blow your head off!" Morgan whispered as he shoved the .38 beneath the man's chin.

The government agent's eyes grew wide, and he made a strangling noise but said nothing.

"Lean over me, like you're trying to help." When the uniformed man responded and stooped to within range, Morgan swiftly popped open the standard issue holster and appropriated the man's sidearm. "Now, call your partner over, and do *not* try to warn him or somebody's going to get hurt."

"Okay, sure," the man answered. Louder, he called, "Hey, Matty, come here!"

Matty Lennox was enthusiastically spraying down the prop fire and beginning to have serious doubts about the struggling man whose life he supposedly was saving when he heard his partner's shout. "What is it?"

"Just come here, will you?"

Lennox shut off the extinguisher and trotted across the road with it tucked beneath his arm. "There's something screwy about this, Frank. That's not really a man—" His voice was lopped off by the sight of two handguns flickering in the firelight, both in the hands of the man on the ground.

"Not a word!" Morgan hissed. Lennox began to raise his hands by reflex. "Get your damned hands down!" The man complied quickly. "Now, put the extinguisher on the ground and lay your gun beside it. Don't try to tip off the guy in the van or I'll be forced to do something I honestly don't want to."

The agent did as he was ordered. "I don't know what the hell you think you're doing, mister, but we're federal operatives, and this stunt will guarantee you a long stay in a cold climate," he stated tightly.

"Shut up. Come over here and help me to my feet. The two of you are going to walk me to the door of the van, and I'll have a gun in each of your backs." So far, everything was going better than a congenital pessimist like Doug Morgan could have believed. Too good?

The men were trained and trusted government employees, but neither of them was anxious to chance death or paralysis. They obeyed the hijacker's demands without hesitation, even though Morgan wouldn't have shot them. Of course, they didn't know that.

The large van had a sliding door on the side much like a school bus or a delivery truck. With Morgan playing the injured victim between the husky agents, the trio limped to the open door and stopped. The next step in the drama came when Doug took his hands from behind his escorts and rested them on their shoulders, with the handguns pressed against their necks.

"What the hell?" shouted the driver. He went for his own sidearm immediately.

"Hold it!" Morgan snapped. "I'll kill them, man!" The driver froze. "Take it out and toss it onto the ground! Slowly!" *God, I hope the damned thing doesn't go off and blow a hole in my ankle.*

It didn't. But while Morgan and his prisoners watched the heavy weapon fall, the driver's hand surrepticiously drifted toward the dash.

Morgan noticed just in time. "Do you *want* me to kill somebody, you jackass?" he demanded. "Touch that radio and I start shooting!"

"No, no, don't shoot!" the driver replied nervously.

"Will you just do what he says?" screamed Lennox. "This guy's not kidding, and it's *my* neck!"

From within the dark van, a familiar voice called, "What's going on? Are we making a side trip to Cuba or something?"

Morgan grinned. "Just a short stop to make your next connection, Grundel."

"Morgan?" came the surprised response. "Is that you, man?"

You didn't have to impart that little bit of information to these guys, Nick, he thought. *But, what the hell?*

"The very same. Ready for a change of scenery?"

"You'd better damned bet I am! They've got me locked up back here!"

Doug waved the gun in his left hand toward the driver. "Get him out here."

The man shook his head swiftly. "I can't do that. Not this man—"

"Do it!" Morgan commanded sharply.

"You don't understand! We *can't* release *him*!"

This isn't right! Morgan sighed silently. *They never resist a man with a gun in the films! I might have to shoot one of these guys to prove I'm serious. But can I?*

Apparently, his indecision appeared to be more like dangerous determination to Frank Toland, the first agent Morgan had taken prisoner, because he said, "Don't shoot! I'll do it!" He leaped into the van.

"Toland! You know what this man is!" the driver shouted.

"He's somebody who hasn't developed an affinity for the trappings of masochism!" Nick Grundel responded loudly. "Get these cuffs off me, Morgan!"

Doug motioned with the gun again. "You heard the man."

Toland quickly disappeared into the windowless darkness of the van, while the driver seethed impotently, and within seconds Toland reappeared with a short, black-haired man dressed in a white hospital uniform and matching tennis shoes. The second man was grinning broadly.

"Nick?" Morgan asked in surprise. The voice had been right, but the face didn't seem to match.

"Hot damn, Morgan, I never believed you'd care enough about me to take on the whole damned government!" The young man laughed as he danced down the steps to join Doug and Lennox in the road. "This is great! Let's get the hell out of here!"

"Nick?" Morgan repeated, still puzzled. "What's happened?"

In sudden realization, Grundel slapped his clean-shaven face. "It's the beard, man, you've never seen me without it!"

That was true. During the months that Morgan and Grundel had pursued their supposed "werewolf" with Blake and Meg, the twenty-four-year-old, self-proclaimed genius had sported a full beard and mustache and Doug had never glimpsed the face underneath it.

Nick's expression turned slightly alarmed. "It's *me*! I'm Nick Grundel, you dim-witted yellow journalist!"

Morgan nodded. "That's you, all right. Pick up that gun."

Chortling, Nick snatched the driver's weapon from the road and gazed a little maniacally at the three government agents, who now were on the receiving end of the pistol. "Wow, if I were a vindictive and somewhat homicidally inclined sort rather than a peace-loving marshmallow, I could really get some back right now, couldn't I?"

The three men flinched visibly.

"There's no time for this foolishness, Nick," Morgan said brusquely. "Get to the car."

"What car?"

"Mine, over there, beyond the fire."

Grundel took a last look at the men who had been involved in his illegal captivity for the last half year and raised the gun threateningly. "I guess it's good-bye then, gentlemen," he said viciously, and aimed the gun at Toland.

"Oh, God, oh, Christ, I let you go, Grundel!" the agent cried.

Nick said, "Bang!", before turning and sprinting

into the ditch on the right side of the road in order to dodge the still-formidable jelly fire. "Let's move our asses, Morgan!" he called over his shoulder.

"I've got things to do here first, kid." At his terse reply, the trio of agents again stiffened expectantly. "All of you get into the rear of the van," he ordered.

The men reluctantly moved into the back of the vehicle, which had held their prisoner who they were transporting from the Institute to yet another secrecy-laden government facility. Morgan climbed into the van and, while pointing one handgun at the three, began scanning the dash. Finding the built-in radio, he smiled and sent a bullet crashing through it.

The noise was tremendous within the van and the sharp curses from the captives added to it.

Morgan watched as the sophisticated communications set disintegrated into an arcing mass of expensive junk, and he knew that there was no reason to waste a second bullet on it. "You can charge that to my account," he remarked. "Now, I'm going to ask you fellows to stay inside the van until my passenger and I are well away from here."

"We'll get you, you crazy bastard!" the driver promised.

"Shut up, stupid!" whispered Lennox.

With a brief salute with the gun in his right hand, Douglas backed out of the van. Before he returned to his own car, however, he took thirty seconds to shoot out all four tires on the idling vehicle. Then he ran as athletically as the youthful Nick around the fire and leaped behind the wheel of his waiting automobile.

As the three embarrassed and frightened men cursed him from within the van, Douglas Morgan roared away from the site into the enveloping night. Alone.

When Nick Grundel ran by the bright barrier of the special-effects fire, he felt better than at any time since that night in December when he'd learned the terrible truth about Gerald Cummings. Sure, the overpowering, smothering, and undeniable reality of what he himself had become boiled in the back of his mind like a vast black cloud, but for right now, he was free again. Whoever would have figured that taciturn and yet acid-tongued Doug Morgan would have gone out on a limb like this for him?

He charged to the rear side of the car toward the passenger door and ran right into a dark form that had been invisible in the night. The form fell in one direction with a high-pitched squeal as Grundel tumbled in another with an equally startled cry.

"I got a gun here, you idiot!" Grundel shouted. "I'll put a bullet in you!" As if in demonstration, Morgan's gun roared once back at the van.

"Nick, no! It's me! Don't shoot!" the form whispered desperately.

Grundel squinted, attempting to identify the slender, leather-clad figure. "Who are you?" The gun remained trained in that direction.

The figure quickly reached up to remove the black motorcycle helmet and allow a mass of long, auburn hair to fall from beneath it. "It's Meg, Meg Talley!"

He stared at her for an instant, and an emotion that his own abrasive personality had denied that he possessed threatened to overwhelm him. This was like Christmas! Nick took a step forward and lifted Meg, who, at five-six, was an inch taller than he, completely off the ground.

Meg couldn't have been more startled by Nick's reaction than if he'd shot her. "Nick! Hey, I'm glad to see you, too, but we don't have the time—" Her words were cut off by his mouth finding hers.

They kissed for several seconds, until Morgan began shooting out the tires of the van.

"Nick, we've *got* to go!" she finally managed to say.

Grundel placed the young woman on her feet and

whipped open the car door. "You, first!"

"No, not in the car! Come with me!" She took his hand and dragged the confused man with her into the woods.

As ever, Nick's dry and entirely inappropriate wit returned. "This is a great idea, Talley, but shouldn't we wait until we've made our escape?"

"Will you be quiet? This *is* our escape!"

"On foot?"

"Of course not! Now, hurry!"

"But what about Morgan?"

"He's our blocker! He's going to draw off any pursuit while we go in the opposite direction." They burst from the dark woods onto an ancient dirt trail that had been totally invisible from the highway, only fifty feet away. Parked in the middle of this trail was a light-weight motorcycle which, though small, was capable of carrying two people. Meg instantly took a long dark coat and a second helmet from the rear of the vehicle and tossed them to Nick. "Put these on!"

He caught the coat but missed the helmet. "Do you know how to drive a bike?"

"Of course! Hurry!"

He wasn't convinced. "I'm driving."

"The hell you are—" The noise of Morgan's car firing up cut her off and injected new urgency into the moment. "We have to leave while the car's motor covers the sound of ours! Let's go!"

Nick managed to slip the helmet over his head, but he failed with the coat before Meg literally pulled him onto the back of the motorcycle and kicked it into remarkably silent vibrancy. They sped off along the overgrown and rutted trail with the headlight boring a white cone into the darkness ahead of them and Nick's coat flapping like a kite's tail behind.

When they were at least a half mile away, Grundel, who was having an unequivocally wonderful time holding onto Meg's waist, leaned close to her ear and shouted, "Just where are we going, anyway?"

"Across the river, outside of Merced!" Meg called back without looking away from the treacherously narrow road. "We're going to meet Blake and then join up with Doug and get out of the state before daybreak!"

"Corbett's in on this, too?"

She nodded.

"Man, I'm even more beloved than I realized!"

Morgan laid down some rubber in getting away from the bright fire, but once he was a quarter of a mile or so away, he eased up on the gas and glanced back. He could still see the fire, of course, but there was no sign of pursuit. He knew that the agents couldn't have changed all four tires so soon, but he also knew that it was not uncommon for government agencies to dispatch two vehicles on every undercover mission, with either the first running as a decoy or the second as a transfer vehicle in case of mechanical failure.

He pulled to the side of the road and waited for almost two minutes. When he saw the band of fire that blockaded the highway explode in sudden fury near its center, he waited no longer and quickly got back into his car. That had to be a government honcho blowing through the flames like a kamikaze. No civilian driver would have endangered his own car that way.

The pursuing vehicle, another van, moved like a bat out of hell. Morgan's car was large enough to have carried Meg's cycle in its trunk, and was a well-cared-for and very fast model which Doug handled with an aggressive proficiency. Still, the trailing van began to close the distance between them with remarkable speed, and Morgan was forced to floorboard his car along the dark and winding hill roads. He wanted to draw off any pursuit from Meg and Nick, but that didn't mean that he wanted to get caught.

The chase began toward the direction of San Francisco. Morgan hoped that this would give the government hounds the idea that he and the escapee were trying to make the airport there, so that any radioed alarms would be focused in that direction and away from the two young people on the motorcycle.

Like a Southern moonshine runner and his revenuer birddogs, the vehicles rocketed along the roads and highways at speeds that sometimes surpassed one hundred miles per hour. Doug didn't hear any gunshots behind him, but he was certain that the thugs wouldn't hesitate to squeeze a few rounds into his gas tank if it looked as if he and Grundel, represented by Counterfeit Charley, an inflatable bogus passenger in the seat next to him, were slipping away from them. In the planning stages, he had felt certain that he could lose any pursuit among the hills, but as he charged farther and farther from the Merced meeting point, he realized that he would need at least fifty miles to shake these guys. Fifty miles that he didn't have if he were to leave with Meg and the others by daybreak. And he certainly wasn't going to turn back toward Merced with these guys still on his tail.

It was a good try, Morgan, he told himself, *and if you'd been Mario Andretti, it might have worked to perfection. But. . . .*

There was only one way left to him to insure the success of the most important part of the mission. Holding the speeding car on the writhing ribbon of road with one hand, he picked up the receiver of his car phone with the other and began punching a number that he had memorized only two days before.

CHAPTER SIX

Blake Corbett sat in his darkened car and waited.

It was nearly four A.M., the sun would rise in less than an hour, and he was parked on an empty suburban street next to a public telephone, waiting. Was he crazy?

Not entirely. Morgan's call had made it clear that he and Meg were going to spring Nick from the Institute's custody somehow, and they needed Corbett and his cash in order to escape the state and reveal the details of the Cummings affair to the world. He couldn't turn his back on these people who had become like members of his own family.

So, there he was, alone, wired with excitement, totally unaware that this particular location was deserted simply because it wasn't a very safe place to be after dark and before sunup. In fact, his first inkling of danger came when four kids tried to pry off the hubcap of his left front tire, apparently without noticing that the driver was reclining behind the wheel.

"Hey!" he yelled out the open window. "What are you doing? Get away from there!"

The kids, three punk-type boys in their mid-teens and a girl of perhaps twenty with strangely glistening eyes, jumped as a startled unit and hissed like angry cats.

"Shit!" whispered one. "You said the piece of junk was abandoned!"

A second kid grunted, "So what?" and stood, revealing himself as a tough-featured light-heavyweight in spite of his relative youth. He held a tire iron in one oversized hand.

Oh, great, and me with six thousand dollars in cash in my pocket! Corbett thought. Of course, that wasn't all that he carried in that pocket.

The large kid took a couple of steps to the window and leaned over, a mean smile adding even more menace to his made-up face. "Why don't you step out of the car, sir, so we can explain a few things to you?"

Blake slipped his unlicensed handgun from his coat and laid it across his upper left arm. "First, let me introduce my friend to you."

The response was beautiful. "Holy Jesus!" the kid exclaimed.

"Deke, what's wrong, baby?" asked the girl. Then she and the two other boys saw the weapon. The effect was just as rewarding in them.

Corbett kept his voice to an authoritative whisper, "Now, you and your monkey buddies get the hell off this street before you blow this operation and I have to slap every one of you behind bars!"

"Yeah, uh, I mean, yes, sir!" Deke answered. He whistled piercingly and the entire group scattered from the street like papers in the wind.

It was a small moment but a satisfying one.

All was quiet for five minutes more, then the night air was agitated by the engine noises of a small motorcycle. Actually, though it was loud enough in the dying darkness, it also was comparatively subdued when matched against the average motorcycle, and Corbett paid no attention to it until it stopped next to his open window and the driver asked, "What are our chances of hitching a ride west, mister?"

"Meg?" he responded in surprise.

She laughed in relief as she removed the helmet. "We made it, Nick!"

Her rider, a strange mixture of top coat and white pajamas, slipped his helmet off, too, and revealed a grinning face that was at once eerily familiar and just different enough to be uncomfortingly off-center.

"My God, it's Nick Grundel!" Blake stated as he opened his door. "They got you out of there!"

"They did that, Mr. Poe," Nick answered, extending his hand.

They shook enthusiastically. "But the beard, man. I've never seen you bald-faced before."

"Prison issue," Nick answered, rubbing his chin. "Just like these sharp threads."

Meg zipped open a saddlebag on the motorcycle. "Don't worry about that. We planned for all contingencies." She pulled out a pair of jeans and a wrinkled pullover.

"Despite it all, you look terrific, Nick," Corbett told him. Inadvertently, he glanced at the brightening sky, even though he knew that the moon wouldn't be full for about three more weeks.

Grundel noticed. "Don't worry, man. It's only what, the twenty-second?"

"The twenty-third, Friday morning," Meg supplied.

"And the next full moon's not until July seventeenth," he continued. He stripped off the white hospital blouse and slipped on the blue pullover. "As you can guess, I'm pretty conscientious about keeping up with the phases of the moon." Taking the pants, he ducked into the backseat of Blake's car.

Corbett took a deep breath. "It's true, then, what we

surmised? You were infected by Cummings?"

"They didn't hold on to me at the Institute because of my charming personality," Nick answered as he struggled within the blackness of the car.

The chill seemed to sweep through Meg, too. "And you've . . . changed?"

Nick didn't seem at all upset with the direction of the conversation. "Yessir. Six times: First in January, last time on Sunday night, and next on July—"

"July seventeenth, we know, we know." Meg sighed. "We've been pretty concerned about that, too. If you'd rather not talk about it, we'll understand, Nick."

"No problems on this end."

"What's it like? Really?" Blake had written about such things hundreds of times, but never from the standpoint of a true believer. Now he had an actual representative to question, and nothing other than the moment held any interest for him.

"Want to check your hunches against the jackpot, right, A.B.?" Nick actually laughed a little. "Let me tell you, son, you've never dreamed—"

"Nick, not right now!" Meg interrupted. "Have you finished? Blake and I need to get out of here before someone notices us."

"In that outfit, every heterosexual male in the state has noticed you already, Margret. But climb aboard. I've never been known for my modesty, anyway."

The young woman rolled the motorcycle toward the rear of the car. "Can we get this in your trunk, Blake?"

Yeah, just as soon as I move out the yacht and emergency hang glider, Corbett thought. "I'm afraid not, Meg, at least not without throwing out the spare tire and the luggage I brought along, and then we'd have to tie down the trunk lid."

"I just thought that we might be able to use it later," she told him a bit sadly.

"If I'd known that you were bringing it, I could have

rented a trailer or something. What about Doug's car?"

She shook her head. "He's going to leave it behind, at the airport in Fresno, to try to throw the investigators off our trail."

Corbett shrugged. "I'm sorry."

"Oh, well, I didn't have you for very long, little girl, but you did your job well." She glanced at an alley next to the telephone booth. "I'll leave it over there for some lucky kid to find in the morning."

"Let me," Blake said quickly. As he rolled the motorcycle over the curb and sidewalk, he mentally added, *I wouldn't take odds on it being here until morning, even if that's only a few minutes away.*

Within a minute, all three were in the car, waiting once more. "When should Doug make it here?" Blake asked.

Meg checked her watch. "I would have thought he'd have shown up by now. He must be having more trouble than he'd expected with the pursuit."

"Take it from me, Morgan drives too wild to have to worry about being caught by anything slower than a Lear jet," Grundel stated. "He'll be here."

"I hope so," Meg whispered.

Four minutes later, when the telephone rang with sudden shrillness, the waiting trio were startled, but only to the point that they chuckled in embarrassment. None of them was expecting a call.

"Who would be calling a public telephone at this time of morning?" Meg wondered idly. "Or at any time, for that matter?"

"Dopers," Nick replied, as if from experience. "Somebody trying to complete a drug deal, either to buy or sell. In case you hadn't noticed, this isn't the most appealing section of town."

"Tell me about it," Blake muttered with a slight smile that neither of the others understood.

"I just hope that whoever it's for doesn't show up to answer it," Meg added.

The phone continued to ring.

Blake's mind was like that of a detective, continually touching, probing, outlining, searching for a new tangential direction for an answer. *What if*, he thought, *that call is for us? Who would it be*?

"Meg," he said in slow realization, "have you and Doug been here before?"

"Of course," she answered. "Two days ago. We knew that the authorities wouldn't expect us to join up in Merced, since none of us have any contacts here—"

"I mean right *here*, on this corner?"

"Sure. We scouted it for the meeting. Why?"

"Because Doug may have taken down the number of that telephone and that—"

"That may be Doug calling!" She leaped out of the car to grab the receiver from the hook, and the men hurriedly followed her. "Hello? Who's calling? Doug?"

"Meg? Is that you?" Morgan's voice asked tensely. The sounds of his car could be heard distinctly in the background.

"Yes, yes! Where are you?"

"Somewhere between Oakland and Stockton! I haven't been able to shake the bastards, yet!"

"It's almost sunrise, Doug! Swing back to the south so that we can link up and leave together—"

"No, Meg! They'll catch the three of you, too! That's why I've called. I want you to leave! Now!"

"What? Without you? We can't do that, Doug!"

"You have to! That's what it's all about! You've got Corbett and his contacts, and, more important, you've got Grundel. Set it up so that the next time he changes you can present it in front of the whole goddamned country! Show them! Prove it!"

"We'll wait for you in Fresno!"

"You can't take that chance! Head east!"

"Doug, we can't just *leave* you!"

"Let me speak to him!" Corbett demanded.

"Blake wants to—" Meg started to explain.

But Doug cut her off. "No time for that! After I've lost these jerks, I'll go underground and maybe we can connect later, somewhere, but for now so long! And don't let me down!"

"Doug, Doug!" Meg screamed.

Nick pulled the receiver from her hand and shouted into it, "Listen to me, you stupid macho meathead! You're not impressing anybody with this self-sacrificing routine . . . Morgan? Morgan!" He slammed the receiver onto its hook. "The big idiot hung up!"

Meg seemed close to tears. "He told us to go on without him, to make sure that the entire country watches the next time Nick changes, to convince them . . . What can we do now, Blake?"

Corbett, only hours into the plan and realizing that his next decision would either divorce him from all involvement or make him a fugitive from his own government, hesitated. If he stepped back now, the truth would eventually become known, wouldn't it? After all, there must be eighty or ninety of *them*— doctors, scientists, reporters, all of the unfortunates who had witnessed Cummings's transformation and then had been infected by the insane monster—still in custody at the Institute and Nick was free. But did he even want to be in the same state the next time that terrible madness overcame Nick?

He looked at them, and they stared back. They were just kids, really, kids whose eyes held no answers and instead seemed to leech away any thoughts that might be forming within his own mind. He hadn't asked to be placed in this situation. But he hadn't refused it, either.

"We don't seem to have much choice, do we?" he said. "I suppose we head east." They quickly returned to the car with him.

"You know," Nick remarked as they passed through Merced into the first leg of their long journey, "freedom of information was mostly a rumor inside the Institute. I wasn't even sure that our buddy, Cummings, was dead until Meg confirmed it."

"Dead and buried," Blake replied. "Or dissected and bottled."

"I wasn't sure that he *could* die. But even more surprising, she says that our very own myopic scrivener did the honors of killing the bastard."

"I had a hand in it," Blake said simply.

Nick paused, as if still unconvinced. "I'll make a deal with you. If you explain to me how you were able to knock off an immortal and invulnerable creature from Nightmare City, I'll tell you how I managed to grow myself a brand-new left hand after they chopped off my old one."

After he hung up on the furious Nick, Morgan drove for twenty minutes and thirty miles more. He cut back to the northeast and was actually closing in on Sacramento in a brilliant dawn when he seemed to have finally made good his escape. The van had dropped out of sight, and he shifted to the west to avoid the approaching city.

Now what? He was officially a fugitive. He had taken a weapon to force government employees to turn over a federal prisoner to him. He had partially destroyed a federal vehicle, and he had fled from other federal agents, who were attempting to arrest him. None of these factors boded well for his continued freedom unless he managed to go underground and elude the countless numbers of deputized eyes that would be searching for him every minute of every day and night.

To remain a fugitive, a shadowed figure, not able even to contact his wife and children beyond the last letter that he had left by his wife's side as she slept on that morning he had left her. . . .

But it wouldn't be for very long. He had faith in Blake Corbett. In about three weeks, Nick would go through that incredible transformation for a seventh time, and somehow Corbett would make it a *public* activity without endangering any lives. That would display the reality of Nick's condition in such a way that there would be no possibility of effective government denial. After that, all of Morgan's own "crimes" would be washed away by the literal flood of scientific knowledge to be gleaned from this discovery, perhaps the most important in the history of the human race.

All that Doug Morgan had to do, then, was remain free until July 17.

What happened next was a combination of a number of things: the earliness of the hour; the effect of the dazzling sunrise; and Morgan's own preoccupation with his immediate future. The bus came to nearly a complete stop at the corner stop sign, and the driver glanced to the east as he slowly pulled across the highway into the westbound lane. Though he saw a dark blotch amid the brilliance of the new sun, the driver was unable to gauge its speed accurately.

The average car traveling at forty miles per hour needs the length of half a football field to negotiate an emergency stop. Morgan was topping eighty-five miles per hour when he saw the bus.

It was sort of ironic to Morgan that he had whipped through winding mountain roads at higher speeds without once losing control only to encounter this sudden roadblock on a long and level straightaway. Reflexively, he hit both the brakes and the horn, realizing that neither would do the least bit of good, and, as expected, the car spun into a slide. Doug was such an experienced driver that he was able to regain steering control and straighten the car without locking the brakes, but by then there was hardly any room left to maneuver.

There was no other traffic in sight, but the huge bus was effectively blocking both lanes. The sides of the road were free of obstruction, but unfortunately the highway was bordered by a pair of wide and deep ditches. Still, if Doug hit the bus he was dead, along with a few of the passengers. He wrenched the wheel to his right.

Morgan was not an habitual seat-belt user, but on this occasion he had locked it about himself before undertaking the high-speed escape, and this saved his life. The ditch acted as a launching ramp when he hit it, and the speeding car became completely airborne long enough to flip through an entire three-hundred-sixty-degree roll, before it crashed onto its wheels. Doug was a little too stunned to appreciate fully the effect, however.

Once the car was on its wheels, the wild ride continued. Skidding in the dirt and short grass of the roadside, it turned sideways and caught like football cleats in artificial turf; the rolling car was in contact with the ground much of the time, unlike the first rotation, and Doug was jolted by every impact of metal and earth.

When the thundering chaos eventually spiraled into silence, the car was on its roof and Morgan felt as if he were being cut in half by the seat belt which was dangling him upside down. *Thank God for oversized and overpriced American automobiles*, he thought.

He was too numbed by shock to feel pain from any injuries he might have sustained in the accident, but his mind wasn't so addled as to have forgotten about the possibility of fire. Working with clumsy hands in this inverted world, he somehow unfastened the belt, dropped to the roof of the car without killing himself, disentangled his legs from the steering wheel, and crawled through the completely shattered window in the driver's door. He was beginning to hurt now, though his brain was yet too bruised to separate and isolate the various pains.

Crawling at least fifty feet away from the upturned vehicle, Morgan scanned the empty surroundings for any signs of help. No dice. The bus hadn't even stopped to see if he had survived the accident.

I have to get out of here, he thought. *Somebody will come by sooner or later and the police will be notified.*

Ignoring the pinkish film of blood that was dripping into his eye from a cut above his brow and a constricting sensation about his chest, Morgan pushed himself to his knees and then worked his feet beneath him. He took a step.

"Oh, God!" he screamed, staggering in agony. His right ankle had been shattered in the crash. "Damn, oh damn!" He clutched at the trunk of a nearby tree and used it to lower himself to the ground. "Goddamn it, not now! Not now!"

He had intended to take a couple of minutes to marshal his strength and then somehow make his way into the forest and out of sight of possible traffic. Beyond this, he had no plan at all and little hope. But he wasn't allowed even this small respite. The government van appeared in the distance and roared toward his overturned car.

They came out of the van like an invading army. There were six of them, all with drawn guns and expressions as solicitous as IRS investigators. *Well, we took 'em for quite a ride, didn't we, old boy*? Morgan thought with some satisfaction.

"Good morning, gentlemen," he said with admirable aplomb. "What can I do for you?"

CHAPTER SEVEN

The room was hermetically sealed.

Fifteen by twelve feet, it was very nearly a hollow cube. Without furnishings and every flat surface the same dull shade of battleship gray, it induced dimensional distortions and eventually hallucinations in anyone unfortunate enough to be enclosed within its featureless confines. Entry and exit were possible only through a single large panel controlled from the outside, as were the admittance of food and the evacuation of waste material. The air circulated through vents which were so well concealed as to be invisible.

In fact, the only immediately evident break in the monotonous environment inside those walls were the camera lenses built into the metal fabric. Dozens of camera lenses.

At present, the only inhabitant of the room was a naked child of approximately six years old. He sat huddled in the center of the chamber and shivered with the cold which enveloped him.

"Good morning, Eugenia."

Dr. Eugenia Daugherty looked away from the screen and its images of the trembling child to acknowledge the arrival of Dr. Isador Redmond into the observation chamber. "Hello, Isador."

Redmond, a tallish, thin man with graying blond hair and heavy spectacles that tended to magnify his small blue eyes, removed his light summer coat and laid it on the rear of one of the many chairs in the room. "You're at it early this morning, aren't you? It's hardly seven."

Eugenia turned back to the screen. "I was waiting to hear the results of the transfer of Grundel to the Nevada facility, and I thought I'd check the progress of our prize pupil until word came in." At forty-four, Eugenia was seven years younger than her associate at the Institute, though with her nondescript brown hair and rather hard face, it was difficult to make any age distinction between the pair.

Redmond walked to her side and peered at the screen. "So, how's he doing?"

"See for yourself."

"A little boy this time, eh? What's his mass?"

"Twenty point two-seven-five kilograms."

Redmond nodded. "Sounds about right for the size. Any signs of excretia?"

"None. It's recycling solids, liquids, everything, and still seems relatively healthy after eighteen days of abstinence."

"'It,' Eugenia?"

The woman smiled without warmth. "I hardly think that we can agree on a standard sexual pronoun, Isador. It's displaying male genitalia now, but you know that it's capable of mimicking females and neuters with ease."

"True, true. I'm just old-fashioned, I guess. I see the

genitalia and I make the call. What's the temperature in there?"

"I've lowered it to twenty degrees farenheit."

"Maximizing the expenditure of energy?"

Eugenia's smile grew wider. "We know that it cannibalizes its own tissues for energy, so I'm diverting a large portion of that energy into providing heat. This will hasten the expenditure and allow us to see sooner just how far it can reduce itself before necrosis sets in."

"It's my guess that dementia beats necrosis to end the self-digestion." Redmond straightened. "Well, five'll get you ten he grows a thick coat of fur in the next ten minutes."

Before Eugenia could reply, the intercompartmental communications device on the wall next to the double-chambered door buzzed briefly. Dr. Daugherty rolled her chair a short distance to her desk and touched a button on a panel located there. "Yes?"

"Dr. Daugherty?" a young man's voice responded over the intercom. "I have a verbal report on the transfer of Nicolas Grundel, per your written request."

Eugenia's eyes brightened. "Of course. Come in." She opened the door from the same panel.

The man who entered was no more than twenty-two, short and wiry, with flighty red hair and one of the best scientific minds in the country. Naturally, brilliance was such a common commodity at the Institute that this young man would remain low in the pecking order—so low as to be employed as a messenger—for months to come. He seemed eager, not so much to deliver his report as to witness the project in the lab.

"Yes, LaPiere?" Eugenia said.

Peter LaPiere was on the bottom of the totem pole,

but his free-spirited personality would not be hammered into any subservient tin mold. "Got the report on Grundel," he said in an offhand manner as he walked swiftly by the two doctors and peered into the screen which was focused on the captive in the next room. "He's really getting small, isn't he? Pretty soon he'll take a big bite and there won't be anything left but a hole with a mouth."

"Never mind that, LaPiere. Tell us about Grundel," Eugenia demanded.

LaPiere continued to stare at the subject. "Uh, yeah, just like you guessed, Morgan intercepted the van and tried to spring the guy."

"Tried to?" Redmond repeated.

"Well, he did, but they caught him." Inspiration struck the young scientist. "Say, have you thought about obtaining a sample of this little fellow's brain tissue and subjecting it to intense—"

"LaPiere, you're here to report!" snapped the woman.

He did glance at the two of them with that, if only for an instant. "Okay. Morgan cut off the transfer van in the hills, near Newman, by using some Hollywood pyrotechniques to make it look like he had a car wreck. He liberated Grundel and took off like hell."

"Was anyone hurt?" Redmond interrupted in spite of Eugenia's exasperation.

"No. It came off smoothly," LaPiere answered. "Anyway, Morgan lit out and the backup van followed, just as ordered. They shot up almost to Stockton and then cut back toward Brentwood, when Morgan started to pull away. They'd lost visual contact with him when he went out of control and flipped maybe ten or fifteen times."

"Morgan crashed?"

"Right. On a straightaway with no traffic around." He looked to Redmond. "Have you people compared cellular makeup when this thing is one form, instar, and completely metamorphosed—"

"LaPiere! You will complete your report or I shall make certain that you receive an unsatisfactory rating for this semester!" Eugenia said threateningly. "What happened in the wreck?"

"All right, Morgan smashed his ankle, and the security boys arrested him, but he's fine otherwise."

"Grundel?"

"Either he got away or he was never in the car. They found an inflatable doll in the wreckage, so that's probably what they took to be Grundel during the chase."

An odd expression came to Eugenia's eyes, and it seemed to be as much triumph as surprise.

Between glances at the captive, LaPiere continued, "My guess is that Grundel was never in Morgan's car. The guys in the first van couldn't see if he got into it or not, so I figure that he faded into the woods around Newman while Morgan took the security guys on a wild-goose chase. And Grundel slipped right through the cracks."

"Has the forest been searched?"

"As we speak. No luck, yet. Probably somebody else picked him up. Both Margret Talley and that writer, uh, Blake Corbett, are missing. The girl's parents claim they haven't seen her in a couple of weeks, and Corbett was in his apartment last night, but he ain't no more."

"Very good, LaPiere," Eugenia said slowly. "Thank you."

"Sure, any time." The young man grinned. "Say, do you mind if I hang around for a while? This kid is fascinating."

Redmond seemed ready to agree to this, but he was cut off by Daugherty. "You have your duties to attend to, LaPiere. That's all."

LaPiere sighed. "Thanks, anyway. I'd like to review the tapes on this case after he finally checks out."

"You know the procedure," stated Eugenia. And that was that.

After LaPiere had gone, the two doctors looked again at their subject in the sealed metal room. It no longer had any visible genitalia, or hair, or fingers or toes; its skin had become tight, slick, and poreless, like stretched plastic, an excellent insulation against the cold. Better than fur.

The creature seemed to possess some ability that they hadn't yet observed, something like ESP, as well, because it stared directly at the lens, climbed wearily to its feet, and tottered directly to the camera. "Please," it whispered in an almost angelic voice, "let me go home now. Please."

Daugherty and Redmond stared at one another. "Do you think it's entered mental senescence?" she asked. "It seems to have reverted to infantilism mentally as well as physically."

"Perhaps he's reached the point where he's forced to ingest his brain tissue for sustenance," Redmond answered. "I believe that this particular case has almost reached its conclusion."

"Let's try one more angle before the opportunity's lost," Eugenia said, her smile both beatific and horrible.

On the screen, the creature begged, "Please! I'm hungry and cold and I want to go home!"

But Eugenia answered, "Let's find out if it can develop gills."

PART TWO:
The Stakes

CHAPTER EIGHT

Marsha had had enough, and Harry knew that when she reached this point there was no use fighting her. Somebody would have to die to get him back in her good graces.

"I mean it, Harry," she said as the two young lovers prepared for their sixth day of traveling with Dom Poduano. She looked gorgeous in the white shorts and red-and-white sailor top that Poduano had purchased for her on Friday when he'd decided to spend the day shopping. "I'm fed up with spending fourteen hours a day in the back seat of that damned car."

"But, babe, he *is* paying all of the bills, keeping food on our plates and a bed for us to sleep in," Harry pointed out.

"We could do all of that if we had the money that he carries in that fat wallet and the car."

"I know, but if we do him, that'll bring the heat down on us just when we don't need it."

Marsha put her hands on her hips and gave him that

no-nonsense look. "Harrison Joseph Mitchellson, if that flabby Italian doesn't turn north when we leave this morning and *you* don't do something about it, I suppose I'll have to take care of the matter myself."

Oh God, Harry thought. It was a tactic as ancient as the relationship between men and women, and it was still every bit as effective as the first time it had been employed. How could he turn the tide of thousands of years of human history?

"Don't worry, sugar, I'll take care of everything." He sighed.

Since Towson, Maryland, was about as far east as one could go without hitting the Atlantic Ocean, Harry and Marsha had expected Dom to swing north or maybe northeast. As soon as they hit the highway, though, Poduano jovially announced their destination for the day. "Either of you ever been to Kentucky?"

"Kentucky?" Marsha repeated incredulously.

"Beautiful state, terrific people," Dom said. "Everything you've heard about the place is true. I think that we can make Owensboro by midnight if we cut back on our mealtimes."

Marsha's lips went very pale, and she slipped her hand across Harry's leg to sink her small, sharp nails into the big muscle that ran along his inner thigh.

"Yes, yes!" he whispered tersely. "As soon as we're in the clear!"

The opportunity came forty minutes later. They were headed southwest, well away from any urban areas, and apparently the only car for miles in any direction. The landscape was marshy and flat, with a heavy growth of brush beginning just a few yards from the highway. A nice place to hide a corpse.

Harry leaned forward and rested one hand on Poduano's shoulder. "Dom, how about pulling over up here for a minute?" he called over the whistling wind. Naturally, the top was down.

Poduano glanced back at them. "Something wrong?"

Harry maintained his friendly smile. "Not really, but I'd like to talk to you about something."

Poduano shook his head slightly. "Couldn't it wait until lunchtime, Harry? Owensboro's a fair piece away, but I believe that we can make it if we keep cruising."

Harry had a certain charm that allowed him to smile and walk away with the bank accounts of compliant elderly women or to convince a normally savvy new car salesman that he really *would* return the latest model following a trial spin without a company representative along for the ride. But he knew, too, when the time for a warm grin and a facile phrase was past, and he was prepared for this, as well.

Marsha was in no mood for gentle persuasion. Harry pulled the .44 from his coat pocket and touched its cold barrel to Poduano's neck.

"Pull over, Dom," he ordered.

The big man turned at the sensation of the gun metal, and his eyes dilated with shock. "Harry," he said slowly, his tone a combination of pleading and disappointment, "we're *friends*!"

"Then do as I say, 'friend.'"

Marsha giggled quietly to herself.

Poduano carefully eased the car to the side of the road and switched off the engine at Harry's direction. He sat very stiffly and stared straight ahead as he awaited the next demand. "You're not going to hurt me, are you, Harry?" he asked. "I'll give you my money and my credit cards without any trouble."

"And your car?"

Dom hesitated until Harry prodded him with the gun again. "Okay, yes, yes! Take it, take it all! Just don't shoot me, Harry, all right? Haven't I treated you good? Free food—"

"Fine as wine, Dom," Harry interrupted. He looked to the side of the road and at the swampy ground with the heavy, obscuring thickets. "Let's go for a walk."

The terror was injected into Poduano's voice almost tactilely, like jets of ice water. "You don't have to hurt me, Harry! Really! You can leave me here. There aren't any other cars around! Or you could—yeah, you could tie me up to a tree or something, and by the time I got away, you could be miles and miles away from here! I wouldn't even tell the cops your real names—"

"Want to get blood all over your upholstry, old boy?" asked Harry coldly. "Let's go."

Poduano began to cry, a strangely unsettling sight in a man so mature and large, but he followed Harry's instructions. Harry kept the gun trained on Dom as he exited the car, and Marsha momentarily considered accompanying them. She wasn't eager to miss out on the fun, but a long glance at the soft earth away from the highway caused her to decide to go easy on her new white shoes.

As he marched Poduano into the nearest thicket, Harry's thoughts were more on the anticipatory joy of driving that glorious car than on the imminent murder.

Marsha got behind the wheel first, however. As she waited for Harry to finish Dom off, she checked her makeup in the rear-view mirror, and played with the wheel for a couple of minutes to get the feel of it. It was okay, she supposed, as far as cars went, but it wasn't that different from a Toyota or a Volvo, except a lot bigger. She didn't understand what Harry saw in it that was so damned fascinating. Of course, he was a man, and all men were idiots when you come right down to it.

A single shot rang out in the quiet morning air.

"Atta boy, baby," Marsha said happily. Old

Sureshot! One did the trick. "That's the way to do him!" A flush of excitement welled within her, the same hot combination of joy and the delicious fear of discovery that accompanied every killing, plus sexual arousal, as well. Bouncing the heels of her hands on the steering wheel with rhythmic urgency as she waited for the triumphal appearance of her smiling champion, she hummed a familiar TV theme song.

Minutes passed, as did a couple of cars, which made Marsha uneasy. She didn't like the idea that someone might establish her presence at the site of a dead body which would be found sooner or later. But Harry remained back there, behind those heavy bushes, having his fun with the late Dominic Poduano.

"Just get the wallet and the money belt and let's go, *Harry*," she whispered with a touch of anger. "We don't have time for all of your favorite perversions now."

She waited ten minutes before calling to him. No answer. Actually, there were no sounds of any kind to indicate that *anyone* was doing *anything*. Marsha had a sudden vision of her boyfriend firing a bullet into Poduano's head, that shell completely penetrating the skull to kill the fat man, and then the same bullet ricocheting from a tree trunk and smashing into Harry's startled features. It was a frightening thought.

"Harry! Are you okay, baby?" she shouted as she stood on the front seat of the car. "Harry, answer me, goddamn it!"

The only replies were the distant sounds of traffic.

"Oh, damn." She sighed. Sliding across the front seat, she opened the passenger door and gingerly tested the soft earth with her fresh white tennis shoe. Okay, maybe something *did* go wrong back there and maybe he needed her help, in spite of the mush that she would have to slog through. With the fortifying breath of a true martyr, Marsha walked toward the thicket.

Marsha was worried for Harry's safety, because, in her own way, she did love him. But more frightening to her was the thought of being alone again, without a man to fulfill her needs and to take care of these distasteful activities that she chose to delegate to them. Marsha was quite self-reliant and capable of making her own way through the world; in fact, she might have been the epitome of real feminism in many ways, but she *chose* to play the role she did in relationships. Harry Mitchellson had proven to be the most nearly perfect lesser half she'd ever encountered.

Though she had been calling loudly and petulantly from the car, Marsha approached the thicket cautiously. Her pistol was smaller and more easily hidden than Harry's ostentatious .44, but in her experienced hands it was just as deadly. Silently, she slipped through the brush, as beautiful as a dream and as dangerous as a viper. She parted the bushes.

Harry was on the ground—at least, what was left of him. His face and most of his head was gone, and what remained above his neck was nothing more than a cupful of brown-and-red pulp that steamed visibly in the thin morning air. Poduano was kneeling over Harry's supine body like a penitent.

Marsha's honed instincts deserted her. "You bastard!" she screamed.

Poduano's face snapped toward her, and a second shock, even more powerful than the first, exploded on Marsha's senses. Dripping bits of Harry's brain were dangling from the man's grinning mouth and there was a single neat bullet hole in the center of his forehead.

Old Sureshot Harry never missed.

Screaming mindlessly, Marsha fired without realizing that she was pulling the trigger. A second bullet hole appeared as if by magic in Poduano's head, and he flipped backward to land with a squishy sound in the moist ground. Marsha ran to Harry's body, even though it was painfully obvious that he was beyond any help.

"Oh, God, oh, baby, what has he done to you?" she whispered as she stooped next to the awful ruin of his head. She was actually *crying*. "What—why didn't it stop him when you shot? Christ! I don't understand—"

Poduano sat up.

Marsha shrieked so piercingly that she did severe damage to her vocal cords, though her numbed brain wouldn't allow her to take notice of the pain. Her gun held four more shells, and she sent all of them slamming into his face and neck from close range. But he didn't go down.

Chunks of bleeding flesh were torn from Poduano, but his only concession to the shots was small, breathy grunts not from pain but from the effect of the bullets' impact. He pushed himself to stand while Marsha hysterically squeezed the trigger again and again on empty chambers. Only when the monster reached for her did she scramble, searching for Harry's huge cannon. When the icy hand touched her elbow, she broke and ran.

Marsha Cooper had seldom encountered a situation that she couldn't deal with in one way or another, but the only thought that seared through her mind as she ran, screaming, toward the car was escape. Not to investigate or to understand or to turn the events to her benefit, but to escape from this fragment of unreality which couldn't be accepted or endured. Despite his ponderous weight and the bullets in him, Poduano was fleet-footed.

Marsha could hear him just behind her, laughing.

The thicket parted with vicious little bites at her face and arms, and the car suddenly sprang before her eyes. It looked like heaven.

The top was down, naturally, so the young woman didn't bother to open the door; instead she vaulted over it into the front seat. Her muddy shoes slid across the upholstery like skis on snow, and she bounced into the floor while violently colliding with the dash. For a moment, she sat there, limply, as her consciousness swam through dark and dangerous waters.

"Ah, there you are," said a voice from above her. Poduano stared down with an obscene smile splitting a face that was mutilated by gunshot wounds. He licked his lips and walked around the front of the car. "That's fine. Just wait right there."

"Oh God! Oh God!" Marsha screamed, instinctively reaching behind her head to catch and twist the key in the ignition.

The car had a straight-shift transmission, and it had been left in first gear. Because Marsha was not depressing the clutch as she turned the key, the auto didn't crank, but it did lurch forward like a startled colt to slam into a surprised Dominic Poduano. He went down with a short cry.

Marsha sat on the floor for a full five minutes without opening her eyes. She'd never been this terrified in her life, not even when her stepfather had tried to rape her seven years before and she'd been forced to kill him with a steak knife. That had been almost unendurable, but it had been understandable; her stepdad had been a man who had died like he was supposed to. But Poduano . . . She'd *shot* him, time and time again, and he'd kept coming after her. She hugged her bare knees to her chest and shivered desperately in a suddenly awry and unfathomable world.

Slowly, Marsha's inner strength reasserted itself. "Okay, kid," she whispered to herself, "you don't know what the hell he was, but you *killed* him. He's dead! Number four. Right now, you have to get out of here." She climbed back into the muddy seat with almost arthritic deliberateness.

The highway was still empty. But someone would

come along eventually and see a frightened, pretty blonde sitting in a forty-year-old car with a dead man beneath its front wheels. In that event, if Marsha couldn't charm or bluff her way out of the circumstances, she would be left with some very sticky questions to answer. She cranked the car.

Another consideration arose at that instant. She needed money, and Poduano had plenty—thousands, it seemed—in his wallet and in a gigantic money belt. The thought of touching that gross and now decaying body made Marsha's skin crawl, but she was nothing if not pragmatic. Killing the engine, she stepped out of the car and walked carefully around to the front of it.

He was there, all right, just behind the left front wheel, which had bounced across his chest and crushed it. He lay face up with his eyes open and a surprised expression filling them. He wasn't breathing, as Marsha ascertained before getting too close to him, and though his head and neck were splotched with red, there was no fresh blood pumping from the wounds. All in all, he looked pretty disgusting.

"Damn it," she whispered as she stooped to the pavement and reached beneath the car toward the dead man's coat pocket, where he kept his wallet. She was exposed to any potential westbound traffic in that position, but that danger receded into insignificance when compared to being forced to touch this *thing*. She wasn't even going to try to drag the corpse out of sight for nothing on God's green earth could make her return to the thicket where Harry was laid open like tomorrow night's dinner at the beefeaters' convention.

Her fingers closed about the wallet. It felt fat and full of warm juices, the kind of feeling that excited Marsha more than the touch of any lover. As she drew the money from the coat, her silent stream of curses died beneath a slow, beaming smile. She kissed the wallet.

"Yeah, baby," she said, "it's just you and me now."

Poduano grabbed her wrist.

Marsha screamed incoherently, irrationally. She had shot this creature in the goddamned head and then run over him with a car, and he was *dead*! Dead people didn't wake up and grab your arm! She screamed with the entire force of her soul, and in some distantly isolated portion of her mind she wondered why her lungs weren't turned inside out.

Poduano worked himself out from beneath the car while maintaining his grip on Marsha's wildly thrashing arm.

She fought him with a strength and ability that belied her cheerleader appearance and had surprised more than one man, but it made no more impact on Poduano than had the bullets. While the dead man sat up, she gouged out one of his eyes with her free hand, almost ripped off an ear, and tried desperately to sink her nails into his carotid arteries, but the results were no more effective than simple love taps.

Poduano looked at Marsha with what was left of his face, smiled again, and began to pull her trapped hand toward his mouth.

"No, please!" she shrieked. "Jesus, what do you want? Take the money, please, just don't hurt me!" She didn't realize that she was paraphrasing Poduano's own words of minutes before. "Oh, God, please!"

Dom parted his lips to reveal the bloody ruin behind them, where one of Marsha's bullets had penetrated his cheek and taken out most of his teeth. His tongue was swollen and bright-red, in stark contrast to Marsha's fingers, which were already darkening to blue from the vise-like pressure at her wrist.

"What do you want?" she cried again. "Christ, *please*!"

He began to lick her hand. She very nearly fainted when the cold lump of flesh darted across her palm and between her fingers, and all she could offer in resistance was a faint, animalistic whine. Her former facile self-control evaporated, leaving behind the ugly possibility that she really had lost her reason.

Poduano's sick ritual lasted for a few minutes, during which he liberally coated Marsha's hand in a viscous mixture of blood and saliva. Then, as the young woman's mind began to shut down, he released her. Her shock was so intense that she even forgot to run away.

Sucking the taste of her from his lips, Poduano staggered to his feet and threw back his head. He stared fixedly through his remaining eye at the thin, paintbrush ridges of clouds that hung directly above them. Marsha was so deeply entranced by him that her terror actually receded. Something was happening here, something marvelous, something more vital than Harry's death and more important even than her own life.

Dom began to glow. Not like the sun or a star. It wasn't an explosion of light. Marsha's clear and guileless face caught and reflected the flowers of colored light that bloomed and died all about Dominic Poduano's exposed flesh like brief flickers of lightning. The light played about his body in random patterns, little currents of electricity that shone with all the shades of the rainbow, and Poduano began to sing with the ecstacy of it. His song contained no more words than had Marsha's screams, but there was a melody that warmed the cool air as it escaped his damaged lips.

Thank you, Jesus, Marsha thought, *for showing this to me*.

In the midst of this kaleidoscopic display of light and sound, Dom started to disintegrate. First the long brown hair that fringed his pink skull simply dropped away in clumps and strands, as if it were being cut from within his head. It dropped to his shoulders and was caught by a breeze and disappeared along the highway. His brows and lashes followed suit, so that he stood before her completely bald and still gazing into the blue distance above.

The dislodged eye which hung by a sinewy thread of flesh on his cheek suddenly dropped and landed with a wet plop onto the pavement by his foot. His remaining teeth spilled out of his mouth, but the song continued.

Slowly, Marsha returned from wherever the nearly religious impact of the moment had sent her, and she thought, *This is like that movie, where the guy falls to pieces, The Fly.*

As if in harmony with her observation, Poduano's mangled ear, flashed with a brilliant red burst and dropped in pieces from his head. Then his very skin began to flake away. Strips and sheets of it were ejected from his body as if the dancing light were performing a medical debridement fractions of an inch beneath the dermal surface. These bits were snatched by the wind and carried away.

I have to get out of here, Marsha thought frantically, in the grasp of her returning fear. She tried to stand but she was almost paralyzed by what she was witnessing. So she began to crawl away, with one eye peering over her shoulder at the metamorphosis.

Poduano's mutation gathered speed. With the flowing waves of radiance which cloaked his body gaining in brilliance and frequency, he began to shrink so quickly that Marsha thought the ground had given way and he was disappearing into the swamp below the highway. Within the space of a couple of Marsha's breaths, he was half a foot shorter and almost half the weight of the man who had stood before her only an instant earlier.

Once more, Marsha was overtaken by the immensity of what she was witnessing. She stopped crawling and leaned numbly against the gleaming rear fender of the car.

Poduano's hair returned like the growth of a plant played fast-forward on videotape. It appeared in luxurious fullness all over the clear scalp and shot upward to fall in fine waves over his head and down to his narrowed shoulders. It was bright, shining, healthy . . . and blonde.

Beautiful, Marsha thought.

His eyes, partially hidden by the new hair, were affected next. The empty socket began to boil with blood and tissue while the undamaged eye filmed over with a thick membrane the color of an unripened lemon. This must have caused tremendous pain, or so it seemed to Marsha, but when her gaze strayed to Poduano's mouth she saw his wide smile flashing small and perfect white teeth. The song turned into laughter.

"Marsha," he said quietly, but it wasn't Dom's voice anymore. The membranes clouding his eyes were sky blue. "Ah, there you are!"

"N–no, no," she whimpered, pressing against the car.

Poduano took a step forward, and the shoe fell from his remarkably smaller foot. He looked like a child wearing adult clothing, he looked like—

"*Me*!" Marsha cried. "Oh, Jesus Christ, you're *me*!"

"You recognize yourself," Poduano said happily. "You'd be shocked to learn how many people never catch on, even though they're looking into a mirror." The creature continued to walk toward the rear of the car.

Some of Marsha's fear boiled into rage. "No, you can't be me! You—this is crazy! It's impossible! Stop it! Stop it, you stupid monster!" In a complete reversal of her efforts to escape, she launched herself at this incredible *doppelganger* as if it were *she* who had undergone the transformation from Marsha Cooper to a wild beast.

The thing which had been Dominic Poduano was still wily and fast, though. Rather than meeting Marsha's assault directly, it sidestepped, tripped her, and then leaped onto her back with a mad, joyous cry as she slammed into the street. It rained blows on her with clenched fists, even as it laughed with boundless glee. But the weight and pounding hands on her back were hardly noticed by Marsha amid the flood of agony that had washed over her in the collision with the rough paving. Her nose was broken, her arms scraped raw like fresh hamburger, and her mouth was flooded with the coppery taste of her own blood. When Marsha was in pain, her reactions immediately focused on revenge.

The creature astride her was still flailing away, though with comparatively little force. The terrifying strength that it had possessed as Poduano seemed to have vanished with Poduano's weight which it had used to clone itself from Marsha. Its power was no more than her own now, and it seemed to lack her fighting instincts. She knew that she could take advantage of this new vulnerability.

Twisting like a snake, Marsha rolled free and clipped its jaw with her muddy foot. The monster dropped limply onto its back with an exhalation of breath that sounded like a faint sob.

Marsha came to her feet, bleeding, ragged, and, for the moment, lost in the sexual rush that was inspired by the pain and rage erupting within her. "All right, bastard, you've got it!" she hissed, leaping onto the monster's chest.

It was the most insane and erotic sensation that she could have imagined, sitting on top of her own twin, feeling her own body through the baggy men's clothing, watching her own face turn red and then darken toward purple while her hands squeezed the life from her own throat. It was weird, but it also was incredibly rewarding.

Marsha felt so damned powerful that she actually believed that she could squeeze until this freak's head popped off like a champagne cork. When the thing's tongue protruded like some swollen limb, she spat on it; and when the membranes in its nose burst in a pair of scarlet sheets, Marsha realized that in killing herself she might literally be destroying a part of her soul that was concerned only with suicide. She laughed aloud.

But when the multicolored lights began to play across this second Marsha's face, everything changed.

"Holy Jesus!" the real woman shouted, releasing her hold and falling away from the slim body. "No, not again!" The thing was already beginning to transform, however, and before Marsha could scramble to her feet, she saw the monster spit out a pair of bloody teeth and then replace these canines with long, gleaming fangs. Out of all of the madness that she had endured in the last few minutes, this little impossibility came nearest to shattering her mind.

Her cry was barely past her lips when the monster with her body was atop Marsha and those terrible fangs were sliding into the flesh of her neck like razors slicing paper.

The Poduano/Marsha/vampire creature didn't kill the young woman, at least, not with that first bite. It remained over her throat for a time, drinking Marsha's hot blood and the strength that it contained, and then it left her lying like some deflated infant's bottle while it returned to the car. Marsha tried to stand and run, but she was so weak that the best she could manage was a half turn to one side and a bleating whisper for help from all of those countless cars which still refused to pass the scene of this assault.

After retrieving the keys and opening the car's spacious trunk, the creature returned to her.

"No, no more, please!" Marsha begged. Real tears, real terror. She used all of her energy to raise her hand.

"Got to go now, baby," the monster replied in her voice. The fangs were gone once more, replaced with regular teeth. "Places to see, things to do, all before the big reunion at Indigo Lake. Up!" It bent and, with great effort, lifted Marsha in its arms. Then it walked with short and laborious steps to the waiting trunk.

"Ohhh, please," Marsha said in little more than a sigh, "not in there, not in the dark, please. . . ."

The monster gasped a bit. "Take it from me, kiddo, very soon you'll be much more comfortable back here than you would be trying to sit in the front." It balanced her for an instant on the edge of the trunk and then rolled her roughly into the interior. She landed with a thump and a soft moan of pain. "Now, why don't you try to get some rest?" it asked before slamming the trunk lid.

Moments later, the car cranked and drove swiftly west.

Marsha lay alone in the blackness, without Harry or her gun or anything to protect her from the dark. It was a worse hell than any lake of fire. She prayed to any deity that might hear her for deliverance from the unbroken night, and, for just a second, she thought that her prayers had been answered. Her staring eye hungrily drank in the rainbow-hued lightning flashes which were dancing inside the trunk.

Then she realized that the lights were originating from her own itching face, arms, body, and legs, and she screamed as she'd never screamed before.

Breakfast at Caprice Island in the center of Indigo Lake was just like any other meal at the exclusive resort, which meant that it consisted of a number of elaborately prepared courses served with continental aplomb by a complete and well-trained kitchen staff. The quiet eloquence of an internationally renowned string quartet drifted through the still atmosphere of the dining area, and the conversation at the long table was erudite and muted.

Of the thirty-three individuals expected to attend this quinquennial United States reunion, eleven were already on the island, and were gathered for breakfast.

Among them was Neil Merrick. With a deft series of motions with both hands, he caught the attention of a young serving maid and placed his order for the morning meal. Practically the mansion's entire staff consisted of certified deaf mutes, who were unable to lip read. They were extremely well paid for meeting these qualifications.

"May I say that you're looking particularly dazzling this morning, Gabrielle?" Merrick observed while the maid relayed his order to the kitchen.

Gabrielle Secretain flashed a smile. "You not only may say so, I believe I'll have to insist upon it," she replied.

Neil chuckled. "My pleasure." He sipped his wine. "Plans for today?"

She sighed, though with delicious luxury. "The usual, I suppose. Swimming, tennis, perhaps some horseback riding in the early evening. Join me?"

For all of his nearly unimaginable advantages in health, independence, finances, and experience, Neil felt the dark hand of depression threatening to wrap itself about his heart on this beautiful summer morning. The reunions were intended to be joyous affairs during which members of the human race's most exclusive club could exchange tales of the last five years and make plans for a future that stretched far beyond the average person's vision, and usually they were. But at this gathering, the last before the advent of another century, the members of the association were faced with a number of potentially serious matters.

"Neil?" Gabrielle prompted delicately.

His expression warmed when he looked at her. "Forgive me, my dear. I don't believe I can join you today. There are a few things that I must attend to, I'm afraid."

"Such as?" It was clear that to Gabrielle life held very few matters which couldn't be either ignored or avoided by taking a private jet to some more agreeable surroundings.

"Well, first there's Rosalie." It was spoken quietly but with unavoidable import. Rosalie Moorcroft was a member of the association whom they might never see again, not an easily accepted eventuality for these individuals.

It affected Gabrielle, too. "Has there been any new information?"

"None that I'm aware of."

"Then, we don't know that she's dead."

"That's correct, and I ardently hope that she's alive and in a position to regain her freedom. But the reality is that we've heard nothing from her since last December, when she went underground to investigate the Cummings affair."

A serving maid arrived with Gabrielle's first course, and the woman casually averted her face from the girl's line of sight. The staff signed sworn statements that none of their number could read lips, but human beings had been known to lie from time to time; thus it never hurt to take reasonable precautions.

"I thought this writer, Corbett, was scheduled to brief us on what he knows of her fate," Gabrielle stated.

"He's been invited to tell us what occurred at the Institute during the so-called 'mutated virus epidemic,' but we have no way of knowing if he even met Rosalie and, if he did, that he knows now which person she was and what happened to her." Neil laughed grimly. "We aren't even certain that he'll accept our invitation to speak to us."

"That should be of no concern."

"You're right, of course. If he proves to be stubborn, I'm sure Tristan can deliver him in a week or so."

Gabrielle paused in her graceful attack upon her eggs Benedict. "And worry over this will monopolize your schedule for today? Believe me, the *only* way to release yourself from unpleasant thoughts is to drive them out of your system with sun, exercise, and glorious abandon."

It is all so simple for you, isn't it, my beautiful hedonist? Merrick asked silently. Aloud, he continued, "In addition, I have a couple of preliminary committee meetings to attend. I'm sure you've received notification of them."

Gabrielle dismissed these purely secular dealings with a flutter of her hand. "That's *business*, and I refuse to allow my reunion to be compromised by *business*. Besides, preliminary meetings are nothing other than warm-ups. I haven't attended one in seventy-five years."

I know, Merrick thought. "I feel that I should sit in on them."

"What will they focus on?"

Neil saw his first course arriving and allowed it to be spread in place before he answered. "The one at eleven this morning will address the problem of our dwindling numbers. You realize, of course, that with the almost certain absence of Rosalie and the presumed death of Michael in '93's Chicago crash, our grand total is now down to only thirty-three members." Michael Kurland's untimely death in a major airline crash two years before had been a terrible blow to the association, many of whom had survived similar accidents in the past. But they all understood that the incident, occuring right after the jet's takeoff, hadn't allowed Kurland the time to prepare for the impact and subsequent conflagration. He had been very young, both in age and experience.

Gabrielle allowed herself a rare serious expression. "Thirty-three. That is well below the recommended fifty, isn't it?"

"Alarmingly."

"But we'll be inducting new members on the Fourth."

"Yes, three," Merrick conceded. "Audrey, Leslie, and Charles. The most we've inducted at one time in half a century. But that will still bring our total to only thirty-six—thirty-seven if our hopes for Rosalie are answered—and the 1990 committee limited initiates for this session to only two."

Gabrielle had seldom seen Neil or any associate this glum during a reunion, and she didn't appreciate the pall that it threatened to cast over her own enjoyment of the summer. "I have the feeling that you intend to propose a change at the preliminary meeting today."

"One of two, actually," he replied. "Either we change the initiate restrictions and allow every associate attending this reunion to introduce an apprentice which would double our number at the next reunion—"

Gabrielle's face registered genuine shock, but she said nothing.

"Or we shorten the indoctrination period from five years to a reasonable three months or half a year. We all know that effective mastery of the talent can be achieved in that time."

Gabrielle *did* respond to this, and her attitude was that of a believer who had just heard blasphemy directed at holy writ. "Neil, think of what you're saying! You know that the five-year period is used not only to perfect the initiate's self-control, but to examine thoroughly his psyche and determine if he will be stable enough to become a full associate."

Merrick nodded. "Certainly, but I also know that the psychological evaluations can be accelerated at the same rate as the physical indoctrination. Gabby, we have to wake up and smell the coffee! This is vital to our own interests—"

"Please, Neil!" she interrupted emotionally. "I don't like to talk about things like this." There was nothing coy or self-deprecating in the admission. What Gabrielle found uncomfortable to consider, she chose to ignore, as did most of the members of the association. "Besides, this isn't the time to introduce major policy changes like those. That's part of the agenda for the next reunion, the millennium."

"We can't wait another five years!" Neil stated with a little more emphasis than he had intended; a few of the others at the table glanced in his direction. "What happened in December quite probably bollixed up everything."

"Cummings, you mean? Do you think he was—"

"One of us. Yes. That 'mutant virus' tale was just a little too pat and coincidental for my taste, and there's no doubt, is there, that a person in rudimentary transformation stage could have killed a hundred, a hundred and fifty victims trapped within a sealed building. The government now *knows* that we're real. The blanket of disbelief which was our greatest defense is gone. And very soon they'll come for us."

"Neil, you're frightening me."

"Good. Almost certainly they've discovered the truth about Rosalie. If she's alive, they haven't released her as they did Corbett and so many others. Once they've thoroughly investigated and probably dissected her, they'll understand all of our mysteries, and I have no illusions about whether they'll regard us as threats to the rest of humanity. They'll be hunting us with more diligence and far more effectiveness than the Inquisition ever did."

Gabrielle winced. That period of history held especially painful memories for her.

"I'm sorry to be so cruelly blunt, but we've all closed our eyes and turned away from these things for too long," he continued. "When they come for us, I, for one, feel that we should respond with more than thirty-six members. We have to face problems like this one and the trouble that Dom is causing."

"Dom?" she repeated, eager to steer the conversation away from this depressing subject. "What about him?"

Merrick's expression told Gabrielle that this news wouldn't be any better. "He's the subject of the second preliminary meeting this afternoon," he answered. "He seems to have gone into mental degeneration."

The woman caught her breath. "Have there been any reports?"

"Only in the media. Two highly incriminating ones in the past week. You heard about the truck driver who was killed in Illinois on Monday, didn't you?"

She shook her head.

"It happened the same night Chris and I arrived at the island." Neil sighed. "Well, he was attacked by a nude young woman, according to the only witness, and his throat was torn out by human teeth."

Gabrielle rolled her eyes. "Another of those damaged minds who believe in vampires, but that's no evidence that Dom was involved with—"

"The head was gnawed off, Gabby. Completely. And they still haven't found it. You know how fond he is of brain matter."

This shook her certainty, and it showed in her expression. But she attempted to recover quickly. "All right, if it were Dominic, all that proves is that he's been careless, not necessarily that he's entered into a degenerative state. Are we to condemn him for *carelessness*?" For all the members, mental degeneration held the same terror that cancer or AIDS wielded over their uninitiated brothers and sisters.

"I would agree if it weren't for the report from Maryland on Thursday night." When Gabrielle's face remained clear of recognition, Merrick felt a certain amount of disgust at her intentional ignorance welling within him. "Surely, you've heard of the massacre?"

"Um, well, no," she said with embarrassment. "I've been busy. . . ."

Merrick adored this enchanting woman seated to his left, and normally he found her self-imposed isolation from what the uninitiated termed "the real world" delightful, but even the most endearing traits could sometimes become irritating. Rather than mentioning it, however, he simply explained, "Thursday night, in a little town north of Baltimore, a group of devil worshippers were planning to celebrate a grave desecration ritual of some type—"

"Oh, Neil, that proves it! Dom doesn't believe in Satan and all of that demonology mummery."

"Please, Gabby," Merrick said, with remarkable gentleness. "The Satanists aren't at issue here, but the man who carried off all thirteen of their still-bleeding heads is. This person slaughtered the cultists within a couple of minutes and with the savagery of a wild beast."

"Did anyone see Dom commit the murders?"

"No, no one still living. The caretaker of a small church did witness a young man march away with a sack over his shoulder, however."

Gabrielle pointed her fork at Neil as if ready to use it as a weapon. "Then it could have been any of the associates, you or me or—"

"Who among us is that addicted to brain matter, Gabrielle? And who would take such chances to get so much of it?" These cold, simple questions brought the conversation to a total stop.

Gabrielle was very close to Dominic Poduano. They were practically contemporaries. Dom was only thirty-seven years older than she, and if something as terrible as mental degeneration could claim him, how safe was she? After a long silence, she spoke with an uncharacteristically subdued voice, "What do you think the committee will recommend?"

"Perhaps nothing. We're still expecting him sometime next week, and if he attends, in all likelihood, he'll be subjected to a covert investigation by everyone on the island. That should tell us a lot. But if he doesn't arrive, I suppose an official team will be selected before the end of the reunion to track him down."

"And if he is beginning to lose his faculties?"

Merrick shrugged. "Confinement. Termination, eventually."

Gabrielle closed her eyes tightly. It had happened before, but only occasionally. Sometimes the point arrived when nothing else could be done about the situation. But it wasn't anything that was spoken of in polite company or thought about too frequently.

Neil saw the struggle threatening to envelop the usually bright, spirited woman at his side, and it hurt him. He took her hand in both of his. "You see how it is, don't you? We—we're not certain that it's he who is behind these things, but if it is, he's at least become very disorganized, killing more than a dozen people in one place and even speaking to a witness whom he left alive. At worst, he's entering dementia, and we simply can't afford his exposing our existence to the world. You understand, don't you?"

She nodded numbly. In their extended lifetimes, the only constant was the physical mind, and when that began to slip away, when the strictest self-control could no longer guarantee mental integrity, perhaps then death lost its awfulness. "I understand. But he's still so young."

Neil recognized the heart of her fear. She was only thirty-some years younger. "This doesn't mean that everyone will deteriorate at so youthful an age," he told her. Merrick was less than a century younger than Gabrielle himself. "You may attend the committee meeting, if you wish, to make sure that Dom's interests are competently represented."

She shook her head. "Let's drop it, shall we? There's nothing we can do about the future, so why belabor the point?" She glanced down at her half-finished first course as if her appetite had suddenly deserted her, and then she looked about the room. Tapping her wine glass with her stainless steel knife, she attracted the attention of the other ten people at the table and the young man who was standing at the doorway to the dining area, supervising the staff. "Please excuse me," she said with the familiar lilting tone that denied that anything could be wrong with her world. "Has everyone been served?"

They all had.

"Then I'd like to ask your indulgence for a few minutes while the room is cleared." The responses to the request were only smiles. Who would refuse Gabrielle Secretain?

Taking his cue, Charles Gladden, a stocky, thirty-year-old initiate, who was so close to full membership that he dreamed of its ultimate freedom every night, took a small repeating flashbulb device from his coat pocket and held it at shoulder level. A touch of a button caused a brief and very bright burst of white light almost as powerful as a camera flash, and three of the four hearing-impaired serving maids immediately turned to face him. A swift signing motion with his hands sent the girls hurrying from the room. The fourth had her back to Gladden and failed to see either the initial flash or its reflection from the richly polished wooden furnishings in the room. A name tag identified her as Shannon, and she continued to prepare an associate's second course from a wheeled tray beside the table.

It would have been a simple matter for the man being served to alert the maid to the situation, but that was not his responsibility. He watched with merely casual interest as did the others while Gladden, the hearing head of the household staff, circled the table and approached the young woman from behind. He grabbed her roughly and painfully by the upper arm and spun her around to see his swiftly moving and clearly angry hands.

The associates' eyes, which had witnessed cruelties beyond the average man's ability to conceive, were hooded by lazy lids as Gladden sharply scolded the girl, slapped her startled face, and sent her fleeing from the room in tears. He then followed her to the doors, locked them, and turned to face the gathering.

"To whom may I be of service?" he asked respectfully.

Gabrielle raised an eyebrow that the hypersensitive Gladden recognized and responded to with a quick step to her side.

"It is my great pleasure to lend whatever assistance that I may, *Mademoiselle* Secretain," he said. The other diners went back to their meal and conversation.

Gabrielle turned the keen-edged knife between her fingers so that it caught the light and sent it bouncing freely throughout the large room like shattered silver spars. "Please remove your coat and roll up your left sleeve to the elbow, Charles," she ordered.

The man neither hesitated nor flinched. "Of course, *mademoiselle*." His formal morning coat was off and across his right arm in an instant; his white shirtsleeve was neatly rolled back on the other. The exposed arm was well-muscled but quite pale. The employees at Caprice Island were not hired to tan on its beautiful shores. "Please proceed at your leisure, *mademoiselle*."

With practiced efficiency, Gabrielle took Gladden's

hand in her own, drew the offered wrist close to her face, and, with her mouth positioned greedily above it, used the knife to pierce his flesh. As Gladden sucked in a hissing breath for which he would be profoundly embarrassed later, blood fountained into Gabrielle's lips. The woman fastened her mouth over the source and drank with soft moans of pleasure.

Neil Merrick smiled and raised his wine glass with a whispered, "Skoal."

CHAPTER NINE

It was not a situation that their previous experiences had prepared them for, and neither Meg nor Blake responded to it in completely admirable fashion. Who could have foreseen someday driving cross-country, dodging police, and keeping one eye on a living, entirely corporeal werewolf?

"Wondering what I'll look like, right?" Nick said from the backseat without opening his eyes. Meg and Blake had believed he was asleep. "I don't know, either, since I haven't seen any pictures of myself during it, but it's a good bet that I'll make a close cousin to old Gerald Cummings. One of a more modest height, of course."

"You're letting your delusions of importance get the better of you again, Nickie," Meg stated firmly. "Not everyone in the world has your name impressed on their prefrontal lobes in indelible ink, you know."

Nick struggled into a sitting position. It was three days since his escape from government custody, and his black beard was already beginning to fill in his roundish face, making him look scruffier than ever. "Don't give me the things-are-hunky-dory-and-you've-not-changed-an-iota-in-our-estimation routine, folks. When three people are in one car and one of those people is a genuine lycanthrope, it's pretty easy to guess what's on the minds of the other two." He yawned. "Besides, Corbett must be sneaking peeks at me. His driving has improved noticeably."

Blake was behind the wheel, as he had been for much of the time since Friday morning, and he looked none too rested and dapper himself. "Nick, to us you're a werewolf for maybe six hours every four weeks or so, and that means that for the other six hundred and sixty-six you're the same sweet-souled saint we met last year."

"Six-six-six," Meg said thoughtfully. "You know, I believe it fits the circumstances." She took a long swallow of her iced tea.

"Okay, okay," Nick said. "From now on I'll know that the two of you consider me a raving maniac only during my monthly disorders."

Meg almost strangled on her drink. Her laughter was an explosive result of her humor, exhaustion, and tension. She was as committed to the stated mission as either of the men and even Morgan, though they'd heard nothing from him since early Friday's telephone call. But she was separating herself from much closer family ties than they. Blake was divorced without children and saw his parents no more than twice a year, anyway, and the twenty-four-year-old Nick had no closer relatives than a first cousin he hadn't seen since the '80s.

But nineteen-year-old Meg still lived at home, when she wasn't at college, the same home in which she'd grown up as an only child with a powerful fascination for horror films, literature, and television. It was this unabated fascination that had interrupted her college career when Gerald Cummings entered into the West Coast mass-killer sweepstakes the year before. Convinced by the evidence connected with the murders that Cummings was a living werewolf, Meg had begun her own investigation. In fact, one night as she drove along a lonely, country road, looking for Cummings, he had attacked her car, turning it over, trapping her inside.

Later in the hospital, Blake, Nick and Doug had paid her a visit. Blake and Doug had teamed up to investigate the murders and Nick had quit his job as a grocery clerk and in his usual fashion had gone off to investigate on his own. But the man had decided that since Meg was the only living witness to have seen Cummings they would interview her. From that time, the four had worked together to find out the truth, and their suspicions were horribly confirmed at the Institute last December.

Meg had been released from the government's custody along with Blake and Morgan in April. When she had decided to join the two men in freeing Nick and getting the truth to the world, she hadn't told her family why she was disappearing or what she was planning to do, and now she missed them more than she'd ever imagined possible.

She continued to laugh as Blake and Nick responded with quizzical stares. "Don't you see?" she finally managed to ask. "Nick . . . he—he has 'the monthlies'! Nick Grundel!"

Blake caught her meaning and joined her amused reaction at the incongruity of it, but Nick was not so delighted.

They left the city limits of Valentine, Nebraska, and headed northeast. They still had no set destination in mind, though they felt a little less conspicuous than during the first hours of their flight. Even before they had left California, Grundel had persuaded Corbett to lay out one hundred seventy-five dollars to pay an old acquaintance for quick painting Blake's little red compact green and replacing its license plates with a realistic-looking Wisconsin set.

Leaving Valentine, the three passed a private residence which contained an ostentatious satellite receiving dish in its front yard. And Blake was struck by an idea.

"Say, have either of you heard of Captain Midnight?" he asked.

He had momentarily forgotten that both of his passengers were self-confessed horror/science fiction/fantasy film freaks, who had spent much of their spare time during the previous year's search for Cummings engaged in marathon trivia contests.

Meg was first to respond to the question. "Let's see, 'Captain Midnight' began on radio around 1940, moved to television in late '53 or '54 and ran for nearly two years, before being syndicated as 'Jet Jackson, Flying Commando.'" She glanced back at Nick with an obvious, if unspoken, challenge.

He smiled confidently. "The name change came about because the original TV show was sponsored by Ovaltine, which retained the rights to the character, so that throughout the syndication run the 'Captain Midnight' name was crudely dubbed over. He was played by Richard Webb, and his sidekick was portrayed by Sid Melton, who was known as . . ." He returned the challenge to Meg.

She had to think about that one for a moment, but it came to her with a sudden brightening of her expression. "Ichabod Mudd!"

Nick inclined his head in respect.

"So, who played the scientist Tut?" she demanded.

He, too, had to consider that one. "Uh, Soule, Soule . . . uh, Olan Soule. Right?"

"Whoa, hold on!" Blake said with a grin. "I mean the *other* Captain Midnight, the fellow in Florida who disrupted the HBO satellite transmission back in the mid-eighties to protest the scrambling of the signal. I think he was a dish dealer, and that's how he signed himself when he slipped his printed message into the HBO broadcast."

"I seem to remember a little about it," answered Meg, "but I was only ten or eleven."

"Same here," Nick stated. "So what?"

Blake sighed, suddenly feeling very old. "So I think that's our answer. Captain Midnight used his satellite receiving dish as a transmitter. He made the switch over with a surprisingly small amount of difficulty and equipment. Scared the military establishment spitless that a civilian could monkey around with a high-tech process that way."

"And?" Meg said leadingly.

"And that's what we're going to do."

Nick snorted derisively. "Oh, sure, we're going national with 'The Nicolas Grundel Freaks R Us Show.' 'See good old Nick do his best imitation of a mythological shape-shifter,' while Grandma and all of the little angels have the opportunity to make trenchant comments concerning the lack of moral fiber of any pathetic jerk who would allow himself to be infected—"

"Nick, please," Meg said. "I'm sure Blake didn't mean anything like that."

"That's exactly what Blake meant," Corbett told them.

Meg looked shocked.

So did Nick, though his shock modulated to sly understanding in an instant. "When you said you wanted to show the world, you really meant it, didn't you?"

"That's right. I'm sorry for whatever emotional distress this will cause you, but this is hard ball. We're all federal fugitives, and if we're going to make this entire effort worth our trouble, we're going to have to go with our most powerful hitter. That's you, Nick."

"And what do you suppose we'll use for equipment?" he asked.

"There must be twenty million satellite dishes in this country. We'll rig one on the sixteenth of next month, prepare to tap into some major cable station, turn on the juice at a few minutes before midnight to explain the purpose of the affair, and then focus the camera on you and let you convince a planet of the reality and seriousness of our cause."

"From a suitably solid cage, of course. Believe me, we'll need one hell of a strong one. The one at the Institute barely held up against me, and there were even rumors in the underground of some escapes during the seizures." Nick closed his eyes. "I don't want to kill anybody."

"We'll find some effective restraints," Corbett assured him. "Ten or fifteen million sets will carry the transformation live, and with videotape, every news program in the world will broadcast it before the week's out. They'll track and catch us, probably by the next morning, but by that time the story will be out."

"Yeah," Grundel said slowly. "I believe it'll work, A.B."

"Well, I don't!" Meg responded with abrupt passion. "We're doing all of this to prove that the government is sitting on the biggest story in history, not to exploit you as some—some sideshow exhibit, Nick! If you go through with something like that, you'll be labeled for life."

Acerbic, plain-spoken Nick Grundel, who had never had a kind word for anyone, smiled warmly at the young woman. "I am what I am, hon. If we're going to convince anybody of this crazy reality, we'll have to show 'em the bug-eyed monster, and I'm the only one we got. It's not something I'm proud of, but apparently there's not a damned thing I can do to change the circumstances."

Meg turned her face away from both men and stared

out at the flat landscape, which was broken by the occasional house and satellite dish.

"That's what we'll do, then?" Blake asked.

The old Nick shifted into place like the falling visor of a war helmet. "Sure thing, just as soon as you can come up with the technological genius who can convert a receiver to a transmitter using nothing other than bed springs and chewing gum. Or can *you* pull that trick off yourself, Skipper?"

Blake pounded the heel of his hand on the steering wheel and whispered, "Damn!" His enthusiasm had outrun his resources again. Surely, with diligent application they could ferret out some backyard Edison capable of performing the deed, but he doubted that such a discovery would come before the next full moon or before the money ran out. Or before the federal Sherlocks caught up to them.

Then, with every bit as much spontaneity and impact as the broadcasting dish idea had hit him, the second portion of the answer popped into his mind. In their three days of traveling together, the exigency of their circumstances had pushed this sensational bit of information completely out of the forefront of his mind. He hadn't told either of his companions about Tristan Grandillon. So he did.

Caprice Island was strictly off limits, even to the guests at the lakeside resort, but Kelly Davis was certain that that was where the heart of the mystery lay—if there were any mystery at all. Yet, she couldn't deny it any longer. After what she had seen in that San Francisco parking lot between Blake Corbett and that Grandillon character, added to the misty rumors circulating throughout the resort, Kelly instinctively knew and believed in the impossible.

Kelly Davis, a dogmatic reporter, who had on more than one occasion falsified evidence to "prove" that some claimant faked his presentation of the so-called

supernatural—that same Kelly Davis had accepted
the reality of lycanthropy in the real, modern world.
Gerald Cummings had been a legitimate physical
monster who had killed maybe a hundred people at
the Institute and this Grandillon, lifter of automobiles, was another. In fact, she was convinced that
Indigo Lake held a thriving community of the hairy
bastards.

Using her reporter's skills, Kelly had established
contact with the most reliable and free-spoken grape-
vine in the area: the children. From them, she learned
many things, such as the fact that *no one* was allowed
across the sea road and onto the island, that the
incredibly wealthy people who did visit that walled,
hallowed spot seemed to congregate most thickly at
regular intervals of five years, and that this summer
marked one of those gatherings. After a little more
discreet inquiry, Kelly finally was rewarded with a
name that might prove helpful to her, even though it
was only a first name.

Chris Somebody was little more than a child himself, a teenager who quite recently had been placed in
charge of the resort's gymnasium and recreation hall,
at the abrupt departure of the young woman who
formerly had held that position. Chris was new
around Indigo Lake, a quiet, withdrawn sort, who,
nevertheless, seemed like an okay guy to the kids.
Rumor had it that he was a runaway from down South
who was very handy with his fists. Now he was Kelly's
target.

Tough guy or not, Kelly had no doubt that she could
get what she needed out of him. She was an old hand
at this game herself.

And talking to someone who had actually been on
the other side of that wall out there seemed to her to
be infinitely preferable to visiting the place herself.
For some reason which seemed to originate from
deeply within her darkened soul, Kelly Davis was

becoming more terrified of that strange retreat as the hours passed.

Chris Wyler had intended to watch that night's movie. He really liked *Mad World* and had never seen the restored version, so he made a quick security check of the rec room and gymnasium and explained to the few people still there where he would be if they needed him for anything. Everything appeared to be copacetic.

Until he reached the front door.

Maxwell Buhl was coming in. Buhl, called "Bonzo" by the kids, was almost a living caricature of the ex-Marine that he was. Six-three, one-ninety-five, with a face like a half-finished rock sculpture, he also was every bit the bully that Maurice Willets, late of barroom notoriety, was.

Chris had known him for four days and already hated Buhl's guts.

Buhl wanted to fight. He had won some sort of service championship while in the Marines, and Chris's performance against Willets had already become widespread. Naturally, Buhl now felt that he had to prove himself against this teenager who was nearly half a foot shorter and forty pounds lighter than he. It would be gentlemanly, of course, with training gloves and headgear, but the light in the man's cold eyes left no doubt as to the seriousness of the fight.

Chris wasn't the least afraid of Buhl, but he wasn't stupid, either. He tried to beg off, as nowhere in his job description did it say that it was his duty to spank the guests, but his very employment gave the imperious Buhl the leverage he needed. He *ordered* Chris to box.

Chris fought defensively at the beginning of the encounter, picking off, slipping and blocking Buhl's punches. The ease with which the boy accomplished this caused the ex-Marine to swell with embarrassment before the small group of people who had assembled to watch them. This embarrassment swiftly translated to rage. The wrestling mats on which they stood nullified most of their footwork, and this meant that Buhl was not faced with a darting and dancing opponent, yet he still was unable to hit cleanly a smaller opponent who was standing only a couple of feet in front of him.

Unlike Buhl, Chris felt no need to humiliate whomever he fought, and he would have been satisfied to confine his own counterpunches to harmless slaps aimed at the man's stomach and sides.

Buhl couldn't leave it at that, however, and his breathing grew heavy as he stepped up the pace in order to land a solid, hurting blow on Chris. Chris hardly seemed to notice the effort as he parried the blows like a mind reader, sometimes using his unexpectedly long reach to stop Buhl's punches before they'd even completely begun. Despite his impassive face, there was a definite glint in his eyes now, too. Chris Wyler liked to fight, and he did it very well.

Since boxing wasn't working for him, Buhl fell back into his martial-arts training. Missing a right cross as he'd missed a dozen before it, he slammed his elbow back into the boy's face with a solid sound that could be heard by all watching the fight. Chris grunted and took a step back, more surprised by the unexpected illegal blow than from pain.

Buhl then swung his knee upward at Chris's testicles.

But Chris knew the game, now, and he was ready. He moved his hips just enough to allow the knee to ride up the outside of his right leg and responded with a real left hook to Buhl's liver and, as quick as a heartbeat, landed another to the man's chin. The first blow froze Buhl's reactions in a rush of pain that penetrated every inch of his body, and the second knocked him on his ass. Chris almost kicked his teeth in.

Chris stared at the glazed expression that coated Buhl's face like a layer of translucent plastic for a long moment. His own right cheek was already beginning to swell and discolor from the impact of the elbow, but he still felt good. He would have felt even better had he pitched about three more shots into that slack and entirely vulnerable face, though he pushed down the beast inside him which demanded retaliation.

The young man walked away from the goggle-eyed ex-Marine sitting on the mats without a word, pulling off the gloves as he went. There went the job, he knew, but he still had over four hundred bucks left of his first paycheck, which was enough to get him to the next stop on the roller-coaster ride of his life.

It probably would have been pragmatic for Chris to pack up his meager possessions and fade away into the night, but he figured that he owed Neil Merrick the privilege of firing him to his face. So he took a shower, instead.

He felt good, just as he usually felt after a fight. He wasn't the smartest guy in the world, but, goddamn it, he could fight. When you do something better than just about anyone else and you enjoy it, there are few sensations as gratifying as performing that special activity to your own standard of excellence. You don't even have to win all of them.

After toweling down, he pulled on his jeans and shirt and set off barefooted for his room.

CHAPTER TEN

Marsha's world now was four-and-a-half feet wide by three feet long by thirty inches deep. It contained hard metal implements, one large rubber tire, a can that reeked of gasoline—she felt that half of the air available to her consisted of gasoline fumes—and her clothing, which had been dragged from her body in stages.

Her world was almost totally dark.

The monster drove like one, taking curves at incredible speed, slamming the brakes like a ditch digger trying to force his shovel through hard earth, and accelerating as if intent upon breaking the car's gravitational ties to the earth. Within her limited world, she suffered from these maneuvers. Without bone or muscle to resist and to protect her, she was thrown about the interior of her little prison like a kite torn in every direction by powerful winds.

Her body yielded to these stresses and flowed, as fresh dough flows through the strong fingers of the baker, into whatever portion of her world that the laws of physics dictated. Once there, the body took the shape imposed upon it by the infinitely more static metal walls and flooring. At times, she was pinned in one spot with her nostrils and mouth down, trapped between the boundaries of her prison and her own fluid flesh.

For days that dragged on with the slowness of a stream of water eroding a stone, the monster kept her in this state. It would come at irregular intervals to open up the trunk and flood her black hell with light that seared her flesh with agonizing intensity even as it assured her that she hadn't yet lost her sense of sight. Then the creature would lean over, revelling in Marsha's helplessness, and take another portion of her ebbing soul away in its awful mouth.

At these times, while Marsha dangled from its hands like a sausage skin filled instead with thick mucus, often her barely defined and functional lungs were able to inhale something close to a breath. Then she would concentrate all of her terror, rage, and profound loss into a single scream that would rip through the air with the painful energy of a bolt of lightning.

June 27th dawned bright and clear at Indigo Lake, but for Tristan Grandillon, the day brought more than just nice weather.

Grandillon was the association's equivalent of the U.S. Marines. Though he possessed wealth and influence as formidable as any other member of the exclusive group, he was not content to relax and expect life to provide him with an uninterrupted flow of entertaining, sterile sensations. Tristan craved action, even danger, and due to his very basic advantages he was far more capable of dealing with such circumstances than any uninitiated human being

could be. He had volunteered to approach Blake
Corbett at the San Francisco convention and entice
him to attend the reunion, and now he was tackling
the problem of Dominic Poduano with his characteristic flair.

That beautiful morning brought with it what
Grandillon considered to be an important development in the Poduano affair. Tristan stared at the
readout on his computer screen:

"Location—Doland, South Dakota.

"Item—Doland City Police Department Report.
Felony, multiple homicides. Time of report, 5:03 A.M.
(local). Time of commission of crime (estimated),
3:00 A.M. (local). Details: upon suffering mechanical
failure of automobile (1994 Pontiac LeMans, stock
#84009, four-door, silver and gray, license #DOX-
KID), victims hailed passing vehicle (description incomplete, two-door sedan, black and white, possibly
Chevrolet, possibly vintage, possibly convertible).
Motorist (male, six feet, 300 pounds, Caucasian,
balding, description possibly unreliable. See secondary entry) agreed to render assistance, at which time
motorist achieved apparent physical metamorphosis.
(Sex unknown, height and weight unknown, apparently non-human anthropoidal, description highly incomplete and of questionable veracity and accuracy.)
Attacked occupants of first vehicle, killing three of the
four. Identifications tentative. Rexford Arthur
Dunham (17, Caucasian, Doland, South Dakota),
Beatrice Victoria Chalmers (17, Caucasian, Doland,
South Dakota), William Spencer Sobach (18, Caucasian, Clark, South Dakota), with one survivor, Erika
Nancy Robinson (17, Caucasian, Doland, South Dakota).

"Investigation—On-going, no pertinent information available, updates to be provided as situation
warrants.

"Comments—Information provided by single surviving witness must be considered in light of distraught condition of witness, especially with regard to the supposed physical 'metamorphosis' of alleged attacker. Hysteria and possible drug abuse must be factored into conclusion. Extreme mutilation of homicide victims suggests multiple attackers of psychologically disfunctional states and/or attack by wild animals. Investigators are advised to utilize the widest parameters throughout the investigation while maintaining a rational approach.

"End report."

That, Grandillon felt certain, was what Dominic Poduano was up to now.

The computer screen swiftly displayed three other accounts of "unusual" criminal activities. The association's tentacles reached into the computerized files of police departments all over the country but as intriguing as these reports were, none of them fit Poduano's MO nearly as well as did this first entry. With the printout of the account as ammunition, Grandillon used a privilege accorded to each member of the association. He called for an emergency meeting.

It was not the most popular of early-morning activities among the associates, but it was well attended.

The presentation was straightforward and persuasive. Within five minutes, everyone agreed that this report did detail the activities of either a present or potential member of the association, who was in all probability Dominic Poduano, and that it was in the best interests of the association to locate and isolate this person. The member who applied for this detail came as no surprise to the others.

"How will you find him?" Neil Merrick asked. "It's difficult enough to recognize one another under the best of circumstances, and if Dom suspects that he's being sought, there will be no way of telling who he is."

Grandillon smiled, already planning his tactics. "Believe me, my friends, I understand the seriousness of this matter, with its possible ramifications for all our futures, but part of the reason I've accepted the assignment is the attraction of the challenge.

"I know Dom well, very well. He won't miss the reunion, and he chooses to travel by car. Since this is the final week before the opening—the Fourth is exactly one week from today—and this last incident took place in South Dakota, we can be fairly certain that he'll be heading east or southeast, in order to reach the lake in time. I'll take three or four of our security people and begin the search outside of Doland, working our way east."

Though Merrick had known Poduano for far longer than Grandillon, he had had no close dealings with the man for quite some time and had seen him away from the reunions only once in the last thirty years. Tristan, on the other hand, made it his business to know all that he could about the personalities, idiosyncrasies, and tendencies of every official member of the association, thus becoming as expert as possible on this ever-changeable group. Under other circumstances, he would have made an excellent FBI agent.

"It still seems like an impossible task to me, even if he is traveling this way," Neil observed. "As I said, you won't know *who* he'll be, and your only hope will be to witness another of his signature murders."

Grandillon nodded, but with self-satisfaction rather than agreement. "But I will know what he'll be driving."

Merrick looked confused.

Grandillon explained, "Four years ago, Dom came into possession of a mint condition 1957 Chevrolet convertible. Since that time, it's been his pride and joy. He takes meticulous care of it and never travels in any other vehicle if he can help it. It shouldn't be too difficult to spot a black-and-white, thirty-eight-year-old car, and once that's done, we'll decide what measures need to be taken with *Signor* Poduano."

As much as she resisted *business*, Gabrielle Secretain was in attendance at the early-morning meeting, too. "What do you mean, 'measures'?" she asked. "You're only going to talk to him, aren't you? There's no reason to do anything drastic."

Grandillon was a little more than half the beautiful woman's age, and he, too, had been born in France. These factors, added to his natural, political demeanor, dictated Tristan's elaborately cordial response. "*Mademoiselle*, you have my greatest assurances that every possible care will be taken with *Signor* Poduano. I'm confident that I shall be able to convince him to accompany me to the lake for further investigation without resorting to unpleasant tactics."

"But you said you'd take along security people," she responded accusingly. "Why should you need those— those thugs if you aren't going to . . . Tristan, he hasn't done anything *that* terrible!"

Grandillon could only shrug. Clearing his throat, he added, "I have had dealings with the rare unfortunate who suffers from cerebral degeneration, Gabrielle, and if that is Poduano's affliction, I will have to take appropriate measures to protect the integrity of the association."

"Oh, God," she whispered.

"Shall I take the necessary steps?" Grandillon asked. "Every moment we delay takes him further from the scene of the last attacks."

A brief round of discussion followed, and it fell to Neil to act as spokesman. "Do what you must in order to ascertain the identity of the individual, Tristan. The security force is at your disposal, and we trust that you will be discreet."

"You may count on it," he assured them. His smile belonged to a hunter on the scent of fresh game.

The twenty-four members of the Indigo Lake Security Team were, technically, also members of the association. Vania Crawford knew this, of course, just as she also knew that until she graduated from a Class-Two associate into that golden circle of perfection known as "the Initiated," or "the Ones," her membership and a dollar would buy her a newspaper.

There were five classes of human beings recognized by the association, and none of these classifications were in any way influenced by age, sex, race, or personal beliefs.

Vania was one of the trio of Class-Two security people chosen by Tristan Grandillon to accompany him in the search for Dominic Poduano. Also with them on the flight to Doland, South Dakota, aboard the private Lear jet was one Class-Five security man, James Armstrong. There were only three Class-Five employees and they were considered a necessary evil. The extremely rare Class-Five individual was regarded with a feverishly uncomfortable mixture of disgust, condescension, pity, and, most alarmingly, fear. Vania found her eyes drawn irresistibly to the stocky, balding man throughout the flight.

"Looking at him is like sitting on a spike of ice that extends right up into the base of your brain, huh?" whispered the man sitting next to her. Lloyd Nathan Nesmith was another of the Class-Two security people, and, at six-six and two hundred thirty pounds, he looked capable of tearing telephone books in half; in this case, appearances didn't lie.

Vania wasn't particularly fond of Nesmith, but having to share a flight with both Grandillon—the Ones were intimidating even at their most genial— and Armstrong—Fives called "the Flats" were excessively creepy—she welcomed any sort of reassuring contact.

"He looks so cold," she whispered back, "so completely disconnected with what's going on around him." The fact that this mission was designed to capture and possibly destroy a rogue One didn't alleviate her feelings of unease, either.

"How long have you been at the lake?" Nesmith asked.

"Six months," she answered. In January of that year, she had been brought to the island by her lover, George Hart, who promised to introduce her to a "medical technique" which would restore to her forty-eight-year-old body the appearance and vitality of an eighteen-year-old. That technique had worked perfectly on the five-five, one-hundred-twenty-pound brunette, but, unfortunately, she had not been able to join George at the Class-One level, finding herself stuck, perhaps permanently, among the Twos. Naturally, she and George were no longer lovers.

"You're just a kid, then," Nesmith observed. "This is your first real mission, isn't it?"

She nodded.

"You'll get used to the Flat Fives," he stated, "to an extent." He stared for a moment at the apparently oblivious Armstrong. "You see, they're in a really difficult situation, too. Old Jimmy Armstrong there knows that anybody on this plane—me, the pilot, Mr. Grandillon, even you, a woman—can reduce him to his most basic components with our hands. He could study the martial arts for fifty years and not have the slightest chance in a one-on-one match up with any of us, and he knows that he's going to die after a measly seventy or eighty years. So, he's both scared spitless and as envious as a starving man at a banquet."

"He certainly doesn't look it."

Nesmith grinned. "That's because, in spite of all of his shortcomings, Jimmy's got one advantage that you and I and every other active member of the association gave up at the moment that the Life entered our bloodstreams. He can handle the 'metal' without so much as a twinge."

Vania felt her stomach and throat contract involuntarily. She already knew from painful experience what the mere touch of the metal on her flesh meant in terms of burning, penetrating agony.

Nesmith noted her uncomfortable memories. "Yeah, it hurts, all right. Just think about how it feels to hold small change in your hand, with the diluted amount of metal that coins contain, and then try to imagine what a bullet made of that stuff would do if it drilled into your gut or head."

Vania didn't want to try. "Armstrong's carrying the metal on him?"

"See his sidearm, the .357? Loaded with silver bullets. If he were fast enough, he could disable everyone on this jet. If he found our brains with a shell, he could kill us all."

"Lord." Vania shivered as if a cold wind had blown through her. "But why is he here? I mean, why's he even employed by the association?"

"He knows our secrets. Remember, he was a hopeful young applicant at one time, too. Now, his employment is buying his silence."

Vania's voice rose to almost a too loud pitch, "Then when he was introduced and initiated and found to be a Class Five, why wasn't he—"

Nesmith supplied the word with calm relish, "Killed? The Flats have their uses, Crawford, and since they represent maybe one-hundredth, or one percent of the race, when we come across one it would be pretty wasteful to kill him or her, wouldn't it? Then we wouldn't have our good buddy Armstrong to accompany us in our search for Poduano."

"How on earth can he help us with Poduano?"

Nesmith made a child's pistol of his forefinger and

thumb and went through a cocking-and-firing action. "The silver bullets, babe."

Vania had been unwilling to verbalize her solution to the problem of Flat Fives, a quick and unemotional execution, but she had little difficulty in conceiving of it. When Lloyd intimated that Armstrong would be used to kill a Class-One associate, however, she was so stunned by the idea that even the image of it refused to coalesce in her mind.

"Do you mean that Armstrong might have to *shoot* Mr. Poduano?" she practically gasped.

"Could be." Like everyone else on the flight, Lloyd was dressed in civilian clothing, and as he stretched his long legs into the carpeted aisle which ran between the swivel chairs, he might have been a star basketball player on his way to a speaking engagement. "If Dom is pulling off these crazy murders, it may be that he's just undergoing some transient dementia, in which case we should be able to lure him into the traveling chamber and transfer him back to the lake. But if he's slipped into real mental degeneration or if he's been afflicted by a Class-Four disfunction . . . You've never seen an associate go wildfire Class Four, have you, kid?"

Vania shook her head.

"I have. It's something, take it from me. They lose all integrity of form, of their bodies, and sometimes their mental capacity, as well. They can't exercise any internal control, so they're susceptible to any nearby pattern, sometimes even inanimate objects. Jeez, that's something to see."

"I'll take your word for it." Vania sighed.

Nesmith snorted. "If you come across anyone who's slipped back into Class Four, you're doing him a favor by killing him."

The youthful-appearing woman took her eyes from James Armstrong and gazed through a window at the blue depths of the sky. "I always hoped that my first mission would be an exciting, enjoyable experience."

Nesmith dropped one eyelid in a slow wink. "Give it a chance, darling. You might find that you like it like this."

When they landed at Doland, they secured a serviceable van for their mission.

The hunt did not seem to go well at first, especially since the creature who had killed three young people and seriously injured a fourth had a five-hour head start on them. The unquestioned leader was Grandillon. Naturally the Ones always took the point position in every situation, but he offered no specific plan of action other than to head east on the main road out of Doland. Vania, Lloyd, and Dieter Russmeyer, the third Class-Two operative, made very respectful inquiries concerning the circumstances, but each was summarily dismissed by Grandillon.

James Armstrong said nothing. He merely sat, like a dark-eyed glacier, with one hand on the silver-bearing gun on his hip.

Each member of the mission had a copy of the photograph that Grandillon had made of Poduano's black-and-white convertible. With this in hand, each searcher scanned the portion of the highway to which he had been assigned and prayed that the image would appear in 3-D out there. If Grandillon had to return to the island to face the embarrassment of a failed assignment, his backup team could expect to share in the more unpleasant ramifications, as well.

The morning passed into afternoon and then early evening. Grandillon and the specifically redesigned Class-Two operatives could have carried on the mission for the rest of the day and night without stopping for rest, food, drink, or other relief. But they all realized that a thoroughly perhaps frighteningly unaltered Jimmy Armstrong was suffering the discomforts common to an uninitiated man. Still, he failed to utter a word, and his expression seemed carved into his heavy, round face.

They left South Dakota and entered Minnesota. Minnesota became, in quick succession, northeast Iowa and then southeast Wisconsin. In Illinois, they finally stopped for gas, and Grandillon suggested that they take a few minutes for a meal that none had requested but all appreciated. They ran headlong into nightfall in Indiana, but it wasn't until they crossed the Ohio stateline that the break came.

Fittingly, it was Grandillon who made the sighting. He had driven all day and was continuing to push the van an exact eleven miles over the speed limit when his keen eyes picked out a target ahead of them. There were no triumphant shouts from this coolly-in-charge captain, only a slow and approving smile.

"Gentlemen and Ms. Crawford," he said in an even voice, "please prepare yourselves for action. The moment is at hand."

Dieter Russmeyer, a twenty-four-year-old security officer from Oregon, had been lured by the lateness of the hour and the recent meal into a nearly soporific state. He sat up straight in his seat next to the driver and muttered, "Sorry, sir, what was that?"

Like most other Class Ones, Grandillon seldom chose to repeat himself. He continued to watch the road ahead silently as he guided the van toward the only other vehicle visible on the infrequently traveled highway, leaving Russmeyer to stare in fuzzy-eyed confusion.

"He said that's Mr. Poduano's car ahead, asshole," Lloyd Nesmith replied in a disgusted whisper. He almost stretched one long arm into the front of the van to swat Russmeyer's head but contented himself with checking his own preparations for the upcoming meeting. A rogue Class One was nothing to take lightly.

The car ahead was traveling at a good clip but

Grandillon cruised some ten m.p.h. faster, so the gap between them was closed quickly and allowed the security team to read the New York license plates that had tipped Tristan off to the car's ownership. The van's headlights played upon the rear window of the convertible—its top was up—and the pursuers could see evidence of three people inside the car, two in the front seat and one in the back.

All three appeared to be men, and though none of the shadowed and distorted features seemed to belong to Dominic Poduano, that meant nothing. In a very real sense, there was no single face that belonged to Dominic Poduano.

"What tactic should we employ to handle the situation, sir?" asked Dieter Russmeyer. He was clear-eyed now and eager to erase the memory of his inept performance of a moment earlier.

Hot on the scent, Grandillon was magnanimous. "The direct approach, I should think." The van was quite close to the car now, and when Tristan switched on the emergency flashers, their bright orange pulses could be seen clearly reflected on the glistening white finish. As an added touch, he sounded the horn.

Vania Crawford felt a rush of excitement which produced a sort of fear that was far more pleasureable than she'd ever believed possible.

The results were instantly evident. The convertible weaved in its own lane as the driver turned to peer behind him, but it was clear from the abrupt actions of the second man in the front seat that pulling over to the side of the road was not on the agenda. This second man seemed to be threatening the driver with a weapon.

"I believe Mr. Poduano has picked up a pair of dangerous hitchhikers," Nesmith observed as he squatted between Grandillon and Russmeyer in the front of the van.

"Seems," Grandillon muttered, "we may have to

employ appropriate maneuvers." Abruptly flooring
the gas pedal, he whipped the van to the left, causing it
to rocket into the passing lane and bounce forward so
that the vehicles were pacing each other within seconds. For an instant, they were but inches apart, with
the occupants of each vehicle peering into the eyes of
suspicious-appearing strangers.

Vania stared at the three men, searching for
Poduano. She had never met him, but another of
Grandillon's surveillance photos had shown
Poduano's favored appearance. None of the faces
matched up, however, not even the thin, pasty white
visage of the driver, who seemed to be the captive of
the hairy, ominous-appearing passengers. Still, it was
the right car.

The man sitting in the rear seat of the car produced
a pistol and pointed it directly at Vania.

Grandillon saw and reacted simultaneously. He hit
the brakes and steered into a skid that caused his right
front bumper to hook the left rear fender of the
Chevrolet. The car emitted an agonized wail as it spun
off the road just ahead of the van.

"Be alert," Grandillon ordered as he whipped off
his seat belt. "The two vagabonds are armed." He
stepped from the van without hesitation and was
immediately followed by the security team.

Will I have to kill? Vania asked herself, a question
she never dreamed that she would be forced to
confront. *Can I?*

The sky was dark, with just enough thin cloud cover
to obviate the field of stars above them, so Grandillon
left the awkwardly angled Chevrolet pinned in the
van's headlights as the five of them marched forward.
The trio in the car seemed to be somewhat stunned by
the impact of the collision and subsequent grinding
halt on the roadside. But before Grandillon and
company reached them, the driver roused himself
enough to swing open his door and stumble out to

stare at the damage done to his carefully maintained automobile. He appeared to have totally forgotten the hitchhikers-cum-hijackers.

"I suppose we should exchange insurance information," Tristan said after stopping behind the slender, red-haired driver. "Looks as if that will be at least a thousand dollars."

"Oh, Lord," the little man moaned. "It was so pretty. Oh, my lord. . . ."

"I know a gentleman who owns a classic model the image of this one," Grandillon continued, "a Mr. Dominic Poduano."

That did it. The driver whirled on Grandillon, gazed at his face in the powerful headlights, and broke into a wide smile. "Tristan! What in the name of the Holy Mother are you doing here?" he asked. Then he stood and wrapped the larger man in as much of a bear hug as his thin arms could manage.

Grandillon laughed. "Looking for you, my friend! What else would I be doing in the middle of nowhere?"

The four members of the security team remained grouped behind the two jovial men, their expressions softened by the sight of the reunion of close friends. But one of the four eyed the recovering passengers in the classic car.

"Hey, that's enough of that shit," barked the large man who had been in the front seat with Poduano. He seemed to unfold as he stepped from the car, and his dirty fist clutched a chrome-plated automatic. He wore an obviously weathered sailor's jacket and carried the scent of the ocean with him like an evolutionary defense mechanism.

Grandillon and Poduano ignored him and began to reminisce. There still were no other cars in sight.

"I said hold it!" the hitchhiker roared. He stalked toward the two men, and the other passenger, a slightly shorter version in jeans and T-shirt, left the car holding his gun. "You fags better give a listen or you won't be able to grab ass—"

"Armstrong," Tristan said quietly.

Immediately, two silencer-muffled shots hissed through the night as closely together as handclaps. The sailor went down as the bullet destroyed his brain like a miniature bomb; his shorter cohort was caught in the throat by the second shell, which severed his spinal column and dropped him on his back just beyond the car door.

"Christ," Vania Crawford whispered.

"He's something else, all right," agreed Nesmith. "When you think that he can dispense silver shells with that speed, it makes your butt pucker up, doesn't it?"

"Well put."

Poduano's only response to the activity was to say, "Those guys were getting to be pretty annoying, you know," while he glanced at the bodies. Then he returned his attention to Grandillon. "Why in heaven's name should you be looking for me, Tristan?"

"The reunion, old boy," he answered. "Everyone's asking for you at the island. You know that the gathering won't be the same without you there."

Poduano's borrowed visage expressed shock. "Good God, what day is this? Isn't it Tuesday?"

"That's right, Dom—"

"The twenty-seventh?"

A slip in Grandillon's control allowed the team to recognize the lie that he swiftly composed and then dismissed. Poduano might have been suffering from progressive dementia, but he wasn't stupid. "That's right," Tristan answered, "the twenty-seventh."

"Then there's plenty of time! I hadn't planned to arrive at the lake until the weekend." Poduano patted Tristan's shoulder and strolled by him to where the dead sailor lay in the car's open door. With hardly a flicker of revulsion, he dragged the bleeding man away from the vehicle. "Why don't you and your friends come with me, Tristan? I believe I'll drive on to Cincinnati and have this fender looked after by a genius of an auto refinisher I know there. Then, Lakeland, Florida. They have a sort of commune down there in which the decisions are made by—"

"I think not, Dominic," Grandillon interrupted. He had silently followed Poduano to the open door and indicated that the others should do the same. "There are a number of matters that need your attention right now, so we'd like for you to return with us to Doland. The jet is waiting for us there."

"And leave my car here?" Poduano demanded with an incredulous laugh. "Not on your life, Tristan. You kids run along. I'll be there when I get there."

"Nesmith and Crawford can drive the car to the lake."

"No one drives this beauty but *me*."

Grandillon's voice grew cold and brittle. "No. You must come with us, *Signor* Poduano."

Dom's attitude cooled also. "Don't forget who you're speaking to, sonny boy. I was ahead of this game when Michelangelo took his last breath over the *Pieta*."

Tristan inclined his head in respect. "Of course, *signor*, and I do not take my actions with anything but the greatest respect for you, but many of the other revered elders have requested your presence at the reunion as soon as possible. Surely, the comforts and diversions of the island are more attractive than a long, lonely week on the highway."

"I wasn't lonely when you crashed into me," the older man pointed out, with an eye toward the two dead bodies.

Grandillon sighed a bit. "Just this once, I must insist—"

"Insist away." Poduano stepped over the sailor's body and slid into the front seat of the car.

And, incredibly, Dieter Russmeyer decided to take the matter into his own hands. Without preamble, he grasped the open door, ripped it from its hinges, and then pulled a startled Dominic Poduano from the car. Shock would have been a mild term for the heart-freezing sensation that enveloped Vania, Nesmith, Armstrong, and even Grandillon and left them paralyzed and dumbstruck. Not one of them had ever considered the possibility of a Class Two attacking a Class One without direct orders from another Class One.

Poduano was stunned, too, but not for very long. With a scream that couldn't have come from a purely human throat, he leaped at Russmeyer and as he sailed toward Dieter's neck, his body seemed to become a streak of lightning. The burst of multicolored radiance was so intense that it burned into their eyes and forced them to turn away, crying out in pain.

"Take him!" Grandillon shouted.

Vania and Nesmith ran through the sheet of light which was all that their eyes could detect, while Armstrong bounced back and assumed an offensive posture with the silver-loaded handgun thrust before him. He was blinking furiously to restore his own vision.

Vania sprang upon the writhing forms of Poduano and Russmeyer before her sight returned. She expected to close in on two men, one of whom was rather short and frail, but the thing that her arms wrapped around felt more like a jungle cat than anything human. It was sinewy, covered in short, bristling fur, and as quick as thought. Before she could get a grip on it, something that could have been either a fist or a foot collided with her chin and sent her rolling into the middle of the empty highway.

"Shall I shoot, Mr. Grandillon?" shrieked James Armstrong. His normally ice-cold voice was alive now with fear and eager excitement. "I'm ready, sir! Give the order!"

Grandillon replied from amid the struggling mass of bodies, "No! Hold your fire! This is a capture, not a kill!"

Poduano was now a huge feline, complete with fangs, claws, and a disposition to shame the most savage of tigers. He tore at Russmeyer frenziedly and ripped deep trenches in the young man's chest and abdomen until the three other associates dragged him away, and then he turned his fury on them.

They crashed into the car, only to career away and slam against the front of the van, killing one headlight. Here they seemed to overpower the maddened creature, with Grandillon pinning the forelegs to the thing's deep chest with his own legs while his arms were wrapped about the head and crushing jaws. Riding the elongated back in the fashion of a reversed cowboy, Lloyd Nesmith was able to immobilize one rear leg, and Vania valiantly held onto the other in spite of the way that its claws were flaying her flesh.

Just as they began to experience the initial flush of success, however, Poduano flared in another blast of light and heat. Alarm caused the Class-Two associates to release their holds. They'd never encountered such vivid optical effects in their brief time with the association, and Dominic used the opportunity to flex his powerful and mutating body into a jackknife that slammed Vania into the grillwork of the van and pitched Nesmith some forty feet through the canvas roof of the Chevrolet.

When Vania collected both her senses and sight enough to focus, she found Tristan Grandillon desperately clinging to Poduano, who now seemed to be some sort of mammalian octopus with more thrashing limbs than she could count. She knew that Grandillon was capable of becoming something even larger and more terrible than any form Poduano could assume and thus meet the attack on more than even terms, but he really wished to take the elder associate alive and was holding his natural reactions in check.

"Let me shoot, sir!" Armstrong cried greedily. The killings of the two ordinary humans had not satisfied him, it appeared, and he ached to add a Class-One trophy to his collection.

"Get the hell away from us, Armstrong!" Grandillon commanded. "Security force, now, now!"

Russmeyer lay next to the car, screaming in agony from his severed leg, and Nesmith was nowhere to be seen, but Vania didn't hesitate as she pushed away from the dented grill toward the struggling bodies. She immediately found herself fighting half a dozen long white arms which seemed to have no bones but which did possess the strength of constricting snakes. Losing the bout, she cried out in terror.

"Okay! Get off, get away!" Still trying to hold on to Poduano with his legs, Grandillon twisted about and ripped Vania free of the clutching arms. Then he threw her several feet away and into the brush at the side of the highway. "Stay clear, everybody!" And with that, he began to change.

There was no wild burst of visible light from Tristan, and with just the van's one headlight for illumination, it was difficult to see what was occurring. Tristan retained his leg lock on Poduano's head and neck, but the upper portion of his own body seemed to spring toward the sky even as it flattened and spread like a huge hand fan sliding open. He fell forward, a thin curtain of flesh that had burst through his clothing. As he covered Poduano's numerous struggling limbs, Tristan wrapped his own body around them as if he were made not of flesh but some type of heavy quilting. Vania then understood his intention.

Lloyd Nesmith, stumbling from the other car, did, too.

Somehow, Grandillon retained enough of his vocal apparatus for speech. "Get the cage!"

"Yes, sir!" Nesmith replied as he sprinted to the rear of the van. The "cage" was a hollow box which was six feet long and two feet deep. Though it was constructed of a metallic alloy commonly used as armor plating in tanks, it weighed just a little over twelve hundred pounds. Nesmith swiftly dragged it from the van and hefted it to his shoulder.

"Hurry, damn you!" Grandillon shouted. He had almost completely enveloped Poduano, so that he looked like a gigantic, flesh-colored sac filled with a boiling solution. Only his head remained clearly differentiated.

Nesmith sprinted around the van and stopped before his commander with the box on his shoulder and a stupid look on his face.

"Put it on the ground and open it!" Tristan was being savaged from within, and the pain spilled through his throat like a second voice when he spoke. Poduano's struggles were causing him to roll and slide across the rough pavement almost uncontrollably.

Nesmith slammed the box to the earth. Vania rushed to help him spin the locking wheel and then pull open the end of the cage. It broke the seal with an audible rush of air and swung upward in the fashion of a ship's watertight hatch.

"Help me!" Grandillon ordered.

Nesmith dragged the box closer to the writhing blob of flesh, while Vania tried to help by grasping Grandillon. His skin felt like old leather.

Following some seconds of violent effort, Grandillon was pressed against the open end of the box. Though none of the security team could see it, Tristan then created an opening in the portion of himself which was tented against the hole. Immediately, a stream of dead white flesh shot through the gap as if it were milk being forced through a hose. Before Dominic could realize the deception, Grandillon literally turned himself inside out, vomiting the now-fluid captive into the cage, and, in a twisted image of an almost holy act, he gave birth.

Then he flowed away from the box, yelling, "Close the damned thing!"

Lloyd slammed the lid, and Vania spun the locking mechanism. Less than a second afterward, the captive slammed into the locked door with such force that the box skidded nearly a yard along the road.

Everyone, even Armstrong, collapsed in relief and exhaustion.

Vania laughed almost uncontrollably, in spite of the broken bones she'd suffered and the warm blood that covered the front of her body.

"Can he breathe in there?" she asked when she was finally able to speak again. The cage was still shaking with Poduano's frantic attempts to break out.

Grandillon had re-formed, without a light show, into his familiar persona and now lay supine and naked near the middle of the highway. For more than twenty minutes, no other vehicle had passed on this desolate stretch of back country road. "He doesn't need any more oxygen than the box contains," he replied. "At least, not for several days, by which time we'll be safely back at the island."

Nesmith sat up in a slow, gingerly fashion. "Good work, sir," he said. There was nothing of the sycophant in his tone, just pure admiration. "Damned good work."

Grandillon didn't acknowledge the compliment. Instead, he, too, sat up. "Who's hungry?"

"Starved," Vania answered.

Dieter Russmeyer was still moving weakly, too severely injured for his body to cope alone, but the others ignored him as they gathered at the car. His conduct had earned him a few more minutes of pain.

Only Armstrong failed to join in the repast, returning instead to the van.

"Your choice, sir," Nesmith said from between the bodies of the two hitchhikers.

"The big one, I think," Grandillon replied. He easily lifted the corpse onto the hood of the car, which was the signal to Vania and Lloyd to begin dividing the other body between them.

"Brain?" Nesmith asked gallantly.

"Please," she answered, "unless you'd rather."

He laughed. "I'm a heart man, myself. It's one tough muscle, but it really provides energy."

The three ate quickly, certain that their luck couldn't hold for much longer. They wouldn't have much compunction about killing any nosey passersby, but every murder was another threat to their secrecy.

Grandillon finished first and returned to the van to don an extra suit of clothes that he'd had the foresight to bring along. Nesmith was on hands and knees sucking some fast-congealing blood from the stump of the dead man's neck when Vania heard a strange sound coming from the rear of the car.

Completely recovered from her injuries, Vania nibbled at a forearm, and, taking this with her, she strolled to the car's trunk, where she stood quietly and listened. Yes, there definitely was something moving in there, something alive. She relayed this information to Lloyd.

"So open it," he responded, too busy eating to be bothered.

The keys were in the ignition, but Vania didn't bother with them. Hooking the fingers of her free hand beneath the lid, she applied a little energy to the task, and the trunk sprang open. The shaft of light from the van struck the open lid and bounced down into the well before her. A single blue, living eye stared up at her.

"Oh, Jesus!" Vania cried, dropping the forearm and stepping back. The eye followed her.

"What's wrong?" asked Nesmith. "What is it?"

"I don't . . . God, I'm not sure," she said. She suddenly felt nauseous, but she forced herself to step forward for a closer view. Again, the eye remained locked on her, and the creamy flesh in which it sat seemed to ripple. It was a mound of flesh with only the eye to mar its white smoothness. In fact, with the eye perched at its center like that, it resembled. . . .

"Vania?" Nesmith prompted.

"A breast," she answered. "It looks like a big, human breast. And it's alive!"

Drenched with blood and grinning with a savage mixture of triumph, hunger, and excitement, Lloyd looked as awful as anything Poduano had become during that night of insane images as he joined Vania at the rear of the car and peered into the trunk. "I'll be a son of a bitch," he whispered, "it *is*."

"Well, it's not, really," she said. "It *looks* like one, but it couldn't be."

Nesmith extended a filthy finger and lightly jabbed the shimmering mass. It responded instantly, retreating from his touch, rolling deeper into the trunk and emitting a high, mechanically atonal whine from some hidden orifice. Lloyd was startled by this reaction, and he swiftly jerked his hand out of the trunk with a hissed, "Damn, it's alive!" Coming from a man who had just consumed a raw human heart, it was a rather ludicrous reaction.

This deeply into the game, Vania shouldn't have been surprised or repulsed by anything, but she was.

"Mr. Grandillon," she called, "Would you come here for a moment, please?"

"Will you shut up?" Lloyd demanded tightly. "We don't need to bother him!"

But Tristan didn't seem to be at all bothered by the request. He appeared through the open side door of the van, cleaned, satiated, dressed in new clothing, and smiling broadly. For Tristan Grandillon, there were few sensations more fulfilling than the successful completion of an association mission. He strode quickly across the intervening distance.

"Having difficulties, you two?" he asked with an affectionate condescension.

Nesmith's reply was fast and nervous. "Oh, no, sir, we just—Vania just found something rather interesting in the trunk."

"I'm not sure what it is," the woman said in a whisper.

Grandillon looked at the white, trembling quantity of flesh within the enclosure. "An amorphic," he stated with mild interest and no evident revulsion. "Haven't seen one of these in fifteen or twenty years."

"*That* is human?" Vania asked.

He nodded, prodding the mass with a forefinger as had Lloyd. "Female, I'd say. From the size of it, probably adult."

"What happened to it . . . her?"

Grandillon lifted the creature into the night air and estimated its weight as it squirmed in his hands. "Well, on occasion the physically degenerative processes of a Class-Four victim can lead to a complete amorphism like this, but that's quite rare. This one probably was created."

"Class Four?" Vania repeated, without realizing that she spoke.

"You *do* remember your classifications, don't you, Ms. Crawford?"

Vania, formerly a high-school teacher, was suddenly inundated with all of the long-forgotten horrors to which students are prey.

Nesmith grinned a little meanly. "She's young, sir, inside only half a year." He took a breath and began to recite, "Class One, 'the Initiated,' 'the Ones,' the fully autonomous associates who are in full control of their symbiotic Life forms. Class Two, Security, who host the Life form and are susceptible to metamorphosis but who have little or no control of their physical changes. Class Three, 'the Singles,' who are susceptible to the Life form but who then 'freeze' after at least one change, ridding their systems of the Life and remaining in whatever form they find themselves. Members of Classes One, Two, and Four can regress into Class-Three states. Then there's Class Four, 'wildfire,' who change uncontrollably and at any time. And Class Five, 'the Flats,' who are immune to the symbiotic Life form from the very first."

"Very good, Nesmith," Grandillon said, smiling proudly.

"Mr. Poduano did this to someone?" Vania added.

Tristan shrugged. "Most of us can. But this is no time for further biology lessons, so suffice it to say that this is simply another example of how an innoculating associate can manipulate the quality and effects of the introduced force."

Both Vania and Lloyd looked at the dangling creature and were profoundly thankful that their innoculations had been more conservative in nature.

"Do you think, sir, that Mr. Poduano's advancing difficulties caused this reaction in the subject?" Nesmith asked quietly.

Grandillon shook his head and dropped the mass into the trunk; it landed with a wet plopping noise. "This kind of alteration requires intellectual intent. Dominic is losing his mental stability. The light shows during his changes prove that. But he isn't deteriorating into a Class Four. Visible radiation is a symptom of dementia in ninety percent of the cases."

"What should we do with her?" Vania inquired.

"It's evidence now. It will remain in the car."

"Even while we destroy it?"

"Qualms, Crawford? Look at it. One eye, a nostril hidden somewhere, certainly nothing of intelligence or hope resides in that," he stated. "You'll be doing it a favor." That sounded like Nesmith's view of Class Fours.

Vania stared at the formless thing for a moment before taking a slow breath and closing the trunk.

The three began to return to the skidding and bounding box which contained their captive when Russmeyer called out weakly, "Sir? Would you help me now?" His redesigned body had successfully staunched the river of blood which had emptied at his hip when Poduano wrenched off his leg, but the blood loss and other injuries had left him too depleted to repair himself further.

Tristan gazed at the broken security officer with disgust. Russmeyer's conduct had been abominable and had precipitated a violent conflict that Grandillon could have avoided by judicial conversation— or so he told himself. He *had* brought along the SS thugs, after all. Still, the young associate had believed himself to be assisting in the capture, and he was under Grandillon's supervision.

"Nesmith, Crawford, get the cage back to the van while I take care of this matter," he ordered. The two hurried to comply.

Equipping himself with the appropriate canine teeth, Tristan fastened his mouth to the waiting man's throat and began to work his magic. He concentrated first on the most serious internal damage and progressed next to the skeletal and dermal injuries. In less than half a minute, Dieter Russmeyer was in far better condition than any uninitiated human being in the world aside from the fact that he still had no left leg.

When Russmeyer was entirely himself once more, Grandillon stood, straightened his clothing, and said, "Now come along. We must be on our way before any passersby decide to stop and lend a hand."

Russmeyer sat up with confusion surrounding him like a fog. "But my leg, sir?"

"That you must do for yourself." Tristan's voice was cold, his demeanor authoritarian.

"But, sir, I'm weak. My—my hunger is too much to allow for such sophisticated regeneration." The blond-haired man looked at the remains of the two hitchhikers. "If I might be spared a moment for feeding. . . ."

Grandillon paused for an instant, as if in contemplation. Then he picked up Russmeyer's own bloody, severed leg and thrust it into the man's hands. "Think of it as a form of recycling," he said.

After a few moments of trying to eat, Russmeyer vomited onto the highway and then hopped toward the waiting van.

Vania and Lloyd had wrestled the cage back into the vehicle, though not without a great degree of effort. When they slid it into the rear of the van, the heavy-duty suspension groaned loudly, as it had at the airport. The van had sustained a considerable amount of damage, and to avoid certain uncomfortable questions, they would have to abandon it in the airport parking lot. It would be connected with the private jet, of course, but the lead would go no further than that. The associates and their possessions were very well hidden.

Ever thorough, Grandillon already had plans to kidnap Erika Nancy Robinson, the surviving witness to Poduano's last attack, in case she, too, had been "innoculated."

"Everything ready, sir?" Nesmith asked while he and Vania quickly changed into their extra clothes.

Personal modesty was viewed in a radically different light among the association's members.

Grandillon patted the cage contentedly. "All but one matter. Are you prepared, Armstrong?"

The Class-Five operative stood in the open side door with a set of large tanks strapped to his back. "Ready, sir."

"Proceed." Tristan looked at the box, which shuddered beneath his hand. "I'm awfully sorry, old man."

Outside, Armstrong walked to the Chevrolet. Its left rear fender was crumpled and scarred, its driver's door ripped off, its roof torn open by Nesmith's landing, and its sprung trunk lid half open, but it still was a beautiful piece of work. Armstrong slowly shook his head, thinking, *They sure don't make 'em that way anymore.*

Then he torched it.

The brilliant river of fire flashed from the tanks on his back through the hose in his hands and washed over the car in a sustained wave. The roof went up as if soaked in gasoline and the paint caught so quickly that it looked like plasma, a cloud of glowing gas hugging the body of the automobile. He kept the stream directed at the upper half of the car as he sprayed so that the tires wouldn't explode from the heat.

It took only moments before Armstrong had orchestrated a dazzling and quite well-balanced blaze. Carefully shutting off his equipment, he took a final look at the conflagration and returned to the van, leaving only the bodies of the two men, one frying on the hood and the other a few yards behind the trunk, as witnesses to the event. As he left, he thought that he heard a thin, high, whining sound from somewhere near the rear of the car.

He returned to the van and pulled the side door closed behind him to find Grandillon at the wheel once more.

"I congratulate you every one, my friends," the Class One told them. "It was a difficult mission well accomplished. Now, let's go home."

Marsha had believed that her existence could never have become worse than the black nightmare of the past three days, but when the fire began she honestly thought that she finally had died and been sentenced to eternal hell. She screamed with the voice she had left and rolled away from the heat, as she slowly had learned to do. But there was nowhere to go.

When the trunk lid swung more fully open before the blazing heat, it was pure chance that her eye was in a position to see an avenue of escape. It was ringed by flames, but in its center was a clear spot of marginally cooler air. With her strangely rearranged senses, she could smell the difference in temperatures.

It would mean going through the fire, but to stay in the depths of the trunk would result only in the fire coming to her. She rolled toward the flames.

The metal was so hot that her flesh sizzled when she rippled up and over the lip of the trunk. She could hear it, but, even worse, she felt it. Her screams were as much a mental effort as a physical one. Like paste or raw dough, she oozed most of her mass over the rear of the car and, when overbalanced, dropped to the highway. As she fell, she was on fire.

Pain was as much her reality as the fear that had come to dominate the remainder of her mind. She rolled blindly away in a desperate attempt to escape the inferno, and this instinctive action smothered the flames which were searing her. Still attempting to flee the pain, she continued to roll until she encountered the ravaged body of a man. She climbed atop the chest that had been torn open and she dropped into the cavity, which was awash with blood and pulp.

In all of the ugly moments of her life, and there had been many, she had never tasted human blood other than her own. Now, practically floating in it, she couldn't help but absorb a great amount of it through the porous quality of her flesh and her rudimentary mouths. With almost as much impact as the pain of the fire, an entirely new sensation swept through her, but this was a glorious feeling and she suckled greedily.

Minutes later, she regained enough of her rational mind to take note of what was occurring around her. She was no longer alone. There were people, at least half a dozen, drawn to the spot by the burning car, and none of them had been with the group that had set the blaze. Feeling stronger than at any time since the madness of Poduano's attack, she rolled up and on top of the body into a circle of light cast by the fire. Her burns were healed now, so that she gleamed whitely against the darkness of the night.

She was seen, and someone screamed. It was a deep, hoarse cry, a man's cry, and terror seized her again. There was no help there, only more pain, torture, and eventual death. Panicking, she rolled swiftly off the corpse and into the darkness that lay beyond the shoulder of the road, where she could smell a fast river that had been swollen by a heavy rainfall.

They all shouted and some pursued her, but Marsha Cooper escaped them all and reached the sweet coolness of her new, enveloping home. Without arms or legs, she swam in a skating motion deep into the arms of her first mother, the water.

And as she swam, a world she had never dreamed of awoke before her mind. The blood of the dead man united with the exotic, symbiotic life within her to show her the truth. Silently, she thanked Dominic Poduano for his gift.

CHAPTER ELEVEN

Something of a surprise awaited Chris Wyler on Tuesday. He wasn't fired.

Either Bonzo Buhl was too embarrassed by his ignominious defeat or Neil Merrick, Chris's apparent patron, chose to dismiss the man's charges out of hand. No one came to give Chris the news that his services were no longer needed at Indigo Lake, and those people that he did encounter treated him as before, not as a lame duck who would be a memory by this time tomorrow. Even Buhl, when the two encountered one another on the beach just after lunch, responded to Chris in the manner he had assumed before the boxing match, which meant that he gave the younger man no more notice than he would a spider scrambling frantically to get out of his path.

So Chris decided to celebrate. O'Hanlon's Bar and Grill wasn't very far away and he'd certainly been treated to a good meal the last time he'd been there.

He figured that if he left about nine and got back before lockup time at eleven, no one would miss him at the gym. The sky looked threatening as he walked toward town, but he didn't give it a second thought.

Maurice Willets of the strutting posture and his coterie of hero worshippers were in O'Hanlon's when Wyler strolled through the door. But if Chris was expecting or even hoping for a resumption of their former hostilities, this was quickly negated by the reaction of Willets and company upon seeing him. They all left quickly and quietly. Chris grinned to himself as he found an empty table.

Almost immediately, one of the most awesomely attractive young women he had encountered outside of Caprice Island arrived at his table carrying a menu. She was about five-four, voluptuously figured, and had long, reddish-blond hair and green eyes that sparkled even in the smokey dimness of the bar. Chris was forced to wonder if there were something in the air or water in this part of the country that created such impressive beauty.

Chris had met a lot of beautiful people in his life, and he had been sexually active for years, but he felt like a numbskull around this waitress just as he had when Gabrielle Secretain swept him into her arms. In fact, this girl was like a younger, more approachable version of Gabrielle. He was so rattled that he took the offered menu and mumbled his order without noticing the slip of paper that she tried to give him.

Several of the other patrons of O'Hanlon's showed their good-old-boy senses of humor by chuckling openly until he looked up, confused. Noticing the paper, he clumsily took it and read its printed message:

"Hello. My name is Shannon, and I am unable to hear or speak, but I will do my best to serve you quickly and efficiently. Please indicate your order on the menu and I will relay it to the kitchen for prompt attention. Thank you for your cooperation and consideration."

Chris was embarrassed, true, but he took the ribbing from the guys around him in a good-natured fashion. What did bother him was the fact that a large portion of the general laughter obviously was directed at the handicapped girl, rather than at his own thickheadedness. Still, he was there looking for relaxation, not another argument, so he let it slide.

After the waitress left the table, a couple of Chris's fellow diners gave him a brief rundown on Shannon Kent. She was nineteen, originally from Laconia, New Hampshire, and she had come to the lake to work as a member of the household staff on Caprice Island. For some unknown reason, she either quit or was fired after about eight months and was now working at O'Hanlon's to earn her fare back home. Apparently, she had no family up in Laconia whom she could contact.

This was more information than Chris had asked for; in fact, he hadn't asked anything about the girl. But he realized that Shannon Kent was someone he would like to get to know a lot better, on her terms.

Using her absence from the table, he borrowed a pen from one of the men at the next table and used a pair of napkins to compose his apology and opening line to her. When she returned with the steaming burger and frosty mug, he handed the napkins to her with a smile meant to convey his regret at being so dully insensitive to her hearing impairment and his wish to make up for it.

Shannon read the first missive with a touch of a shy blush that would have charmed Washington right off Rushmore. Laying aside the two napkins, she responded with a brief, elegant motion of her hands, such as Chris had seen used by the staff at the mansion during his short stay there. He took this to mean something like, "Forget it, blockhead," so he nodded and gestured toward the second unread note. She looked at it, and suddenly everything changed.

It was a simple note, at least in Chris's view. In it, he told her that he, too, worked at the resort and had spent some time in the mansion. He ended the note with an apology and a request to take her to dinner on her next night off.

Chris never knew if she got far in the note, because her face darkened and her brow furrowed deeply only moments into reading it. *Something* in that apology touched a raw nerve. She threw down the napkins, made more indecipherable and less elegant motions with her hands, and marched away from the table.

For an instant, Chris forgot the circumstances and called, "Hey, what's wrong? I wasn't trying to hit on you!" Which, of course, was exactly what he had been trying to do.

A few of the others in the dining area got a laugh out of the situation, but Chris wasn't nearly so forgiving this time. A meaningful look cut short the hilarity.

He ate the burger and drank the beer, hardly tasting either. He wasn't upset so much as confused. What in the world had caused her angry reaction? He could move fast at times, but surely that sappy little note hadn't intimated that his only interest in her was a quick coupling followed by a fast fade into the night. Had it?

When he finished, Chris saw the head bartender directing Shannon to return to his table. She obviously didn't want to, but she couldn't afford to offend the boss. Wearing a cool expression like a coat of chain mail, she stopped at Chris's side and handed him another printed message.

It said, "I hope you enjoyed your meal. May I get you anything else?"

"No," he answered, watching her eyes carefully. "Can you read my lips?" He pointed to them.

She understood and shook her head. None of the other staff members at the mansion had mastered this ability, either, which wasn't strange in light of the association's passion for secrecy. He motioned for her to stay and swiftly wrote another note asking what he had done to offend her.

Shannon's response was to tear off his bill from her pad, to slap it on the table before him, and to present her last printed card, which said, "Thank you and please come again."

Chris pointed to his own request.

She held her last message before his face.

"Okay," he said with a sigh, "I understand."

She took his dishes and left.

Shaking his head, he sipped the last of his beer and wondered just what had been so monumentally galling about his simple notes to the young woman.

Naturally, he wasn't supposed to notice a resort guest named Kelly Davis staring at him throughout this little disaster, even though he had. Davis, Chris knew, was a recent arrival at Indigo Lake who passed herself off as a typical vacationer while she actually was a reporter trying to dig up dirt on the folks at Caprice Island. Chris figured she worked for some supermarket rag, and while he saw no disgrace in making an honest buck, even if it were slightly yellow in hue, he wasn't going to be anybody's "inside source."

Shannon hadn't been gone more than a minute before Davis approached him. She was a scruffy-looking little woman, kind of short, kind of overweight, not overly concerned with her appearance, and the type of woman whom Chris, with the thoroughly ingrained and understandable sexism of a seventeen-year-old boy, seldom even noticed. Her short, dull brown hair seemed to sum up her personality in his eyes. But then again, maybe he was allowing his distaste for her profession to affect his assessment of her personality.

What neither Chris nor Kelly noticed was the fact that another woman was watching both of them through cool and perceptive eyes from the rear of the bar.

"Good evening, Mr . . . Lawson, isn't it?" Kelly said as she stopped at his table.

Chris nodded, but he didn't stand. "How's it going?"

"Fine, thanks," she replied. "Mind if I sit down for a minute?"

Would it matter if I did? the boy wondered. "Feel free."

Kelly took the invitation. "My name is Kelly Davis, Mr. Lawson, you may have seen me at the resort. You have? Well, I'm here to offer you a business opportunity."

He smiled wryly. "Really? I've got a job. For now, anyway."

"This is more in the nature of a one-time cooperative effort. You see, I'm a reporter for *Proof!* magazine, and I'd like to ask you a few questions about what you know of this area and the people who live here."

"If my accent hasn't tipped you off already, Miss Davis, I'm a new arrival," he told her. "You'd be better off pumping a local for information."

She took a deep breath. "All right, I'll be more specific. I'm investigating the group of individuals who reside at Caprice Island and I have reason to believe that you know something about them."

"Excuse me, but I have nothing to say."

"Would five hundred dollars buy your cooperation?"

Five hundred bucks was a nice chunk of change to someone in Chris Wyler's position, but he wasn't tempted. If he'd wanted money, he would have slunk back home, tail between his legs, and played perfect little sonny boy. "Sorry. No sale."

Kelly's eyes burned brightly for a moment. When she was on a story her normally repressed personality was transformed. She used whatever she possessed to obtain her goal. Right now, she had some leverage against this cool cucumber across the table from her, and she felt no compunction about using it.

"That's too bad, because I was hoping to keep the authorities out of this. I know that your real name is Christopher Wyler, that you're underaged and a run-away from Georgia, and that if I call the police, you'll be on your way home by midnight." Kelly leaned both elbows on the table and thrust her face toward him. "Do you want to rethink your position now, young man?"

He leaned forward, too, so that they could feel one another's breath. "I don't know what you have to do to keep bread on your table, but I'm not a part of it, lady. You make your calls if you have to. You know where to find me."

Kelly would use anything at her disposal to convince him—anything—so she reached out and placed her hand over his. "We don't have to go for one another's throat this way, Chris. Why don't you come back to my place? We'll have some wine and talk."

He smiled a smile that was bitingly devoid of humor or warmth. "So *that's* what you do to keep bread on your table."

A torch flared in Kelly's chest and engulfed her. Though her rage was focused with laser-beam intensity on the boy in front of her, at least a portion of it originated in the very truth of his statement. Kelly had never slept with anyone in all her thirty-nine years, but through Wyler's eyes, she saw just how far she would go to get her all-important story. As if by reflex, she slapped his face as hard as she could.

Chris took the blow with only a slight widening of his eyes to indicate his surprise, and said nothing.

Kelly struck out at him again, with no conscious thought guiding her hand.

This time Chris used his honed athlete's reflexes to move his face just a fraction of an inch out of harm's way, so that the woman hit nothing but air. "You only get one free shot," he whispered. Chris had never hit a woman in his life, and he wasn't going to hit Kelly now, but he wasn't a masochist, either.

Suddenly shame flooded in to join the fury that filled her. And somewhere in there was fear, as well, not fear of Wyler, but a kind of fear that had been slipping itself around her since the day that she had witnessed Tristan Grandillon's meeting with Blake Corbett. Fear that this time she would be unable to disperse the demons with logic or trickery. Kelly leaped to her feet and ran from the bar.

Chris remained sitting alone with one cheek reddening in the outline of her palm. There were some stares, of course, but they didn't last long. His only comment was, "Stupid jerk," and it was clear that he wasn't directing the remark at Kelly.

It was raining, and Kelly, who had rented a car the day she arrived at Indigo Lake, was staring forlornly into the downpour. Her rented car was sitting snugly back at the resort.

It had seemed reasonable at the time to follow Chris Wyler to this dive on foot and not give herself away too early. Sure, the skies had been a little cloudy and it had been getting dark, but she was on a story and felt certain that things would work themselves out. She had never expected to be part of a sordid little scene.

So now she faced the prospect of slogging through the rain in the dark for a mile or more just because, with typical impetuousness, she had failed to plan ahead. The hell with this. She would simply march back inside and call for a cab, even if it wasn't allowed on her expense account.

"May I offer you a ride?" inquired a smooth, melodic voice from immediately behind her.

Kelly spun around and found herself face to throat with a tall, impeccably dressed woman with classic features, lustrous black hair and dark, glinting eyes that stared at her with almost hypnotic intensity. As Chris Wyler had, Kelly wondered if this part of New York maintained a special farm for growing gorgeous, perfect physical specimens. "Excuse me?" she responded with the only words that came to mind.

The other woman smiled ever so slightly. "I hope that I didn't startle you. I asked if I might offer you a lift? You are staying at the resort, aren't you?"

"Why, yes, I am."

"I thought that I had seen you there."

Well, I sure didn't see you, sister, Kelly thought. "Thanks for your help. A ride certainly appeals to me at this particular moment."

"Fine. My car is just next door, in the lot."

The car turned out to be the latest model, chocolate-colored Mercedes that undoubtably cost as much as the cumulative total of Kelly's earnings for the past five years. The hot juices of envy began to sizzle in her stomach. Surprisingly, the woman had no driver, and when she slid behind the wheel, Kelly sat next to her. Yeah, she could get use to this very easily.

"My name is Adine Pierce," the woman said as she guided the wonderful machine from the sheltered lot into the rain.

"Um, I'm Davis, Kelly Davis."

"It's a pleasure to meet you, Ms. Davis."

"You, too."

"It's really a short drive, Ms. Davis, so I'll get right to business."

Oh, Lord, Kelly thought, *she's going to make a play for me.*

Adine Pierce went on, "I couldn't help but overhear your conversation with Christopher Wyler in the bar. You're interested in the people who are staying at Caprice Island, are you not?"

Kelly relaxed a bit. "You really do go right to the brass tacks, don't you? And you're correct. I *am* interested in finding out a little more about those folks who assemble there every five years. Just to satisfy my own curiosity."

Adine glanced at Kelly briefly. "Neither of us should insist upon continuing our games at this point, Ms. Davis."

Kelly sighed. "Okay. I want to find out about them because I'm a reporter and I think the story would make me a lot of money."

Adine inclined her head slightly, as if thanking her for her honesty. "I can take you there."

"What?" The unexpectedness of the statement was like a fist in Kelly's midsection.

"I can take you to Caprice Island. Tonight."

That damned island. Finally Kelly had to admit to herself that her tentativeness and ineffectual tactics concerning this investigation were due to one thing: her fear of Caprice Island. Something about that place and the people who lived there had affected her in a completely unforeseen way. There was something about the island that was decadent, rotting. Evil.

"Ms. Davis?"

Kelly mentally shook herself. "That's kind of you, but perhaps an interview with you would do just as well. You could probably tell me everything I need to know right now."

Adine directed the Mercedes through the pouring night with a casual sureness. "You would give up the opportunity to witness the story with your own eyes?

Ms. Davis, I don't believe I've ever met a reporter who would agree to that."

A reporter? Kelly asked herself. Or a scared child, a little girl who'd been chasing away the boogeyman for all of her life because, deep in her heart, she knew that he really did exist? But what about this time? He'd always run from her before, but this time he was ready to stand and show himself. Did she have the guts to face him? Or would she run?

The gates to the Indigo Lake Resort flashed damply in the car's headlights.

"Okay," Kelly responded. "Let's go see what's hiding out there."

Adine Pierce smiled very broadly. "You'll never regret this." She drove the sleek car by the guard's hut with barely a glance at the man stationed there and then whipped through the dark, silent resort. Reaching the land bridge, the car continued past the second manned kiosk without slowing and they were on their way to Caprice Island.

"How can you get by the checkposts so easily?" Kelly wondered aloud. "Those guards won't allow anyone else even to think about crossing to the island."

"Simple," Adine replied, and a stray beam of light from somewhere fell upon her sculptured face to make her appear to be a totally different person in Kelly's eyes, a suddenly dangerous person. "I live there."

CHAPTER TWELVE

The van pulled up to the gates and stopped. Though Chester Jefferson, the only man in the guard kiosk, would have let the vehicle pass without identification, he knew that it would be wise to follow procedure with this particularly rules-conscious driver.

"Good morning, sir," the guard said. After last night's prolonged and heavy rains, it was a fine, sunny day. "May I help you?"

The driver's window hummed down soundlessly, and a blond-haired man with piercing blue eyes and an actor's profile leaned slightly through the opening. "Good morning, Chester. Open the gates, please. We've been traveling for almost thirty hours straight and could do with some rest."

"Yes, sir, Mr. Grandillon." Jefferson quickly set the gates in motion. "If I might ask, sir, was your mission successful?"

Grandillon's eyes briefly danced toward the rear of the van. "Eminently," he answered.

"Congratulations, sir. Were there any casualties?"

"Nothing that was beyond repair."

Jefferson's face seemed to light up with relief. "That *is* good news, sir. Please drive through. With your permission, I'll notify the station at the sea road and the estate of your arrival."

"Of course, Chester." Grandillon then guided the finely tuned van through the open gates. As the van passed, Jefferson distinctly heard a muffled bumping sound, as if something heavy had shifted its weight within the rear of it.

Getting Poduano downstairs and securely locked away proved to be almost as difficult as trapping him in the cage had been.

As Grandillon had told Jefferson at the gate, the team had been on the road for thirty hours now, and even with their restructured and marvelously efficient bodies, they were nearing the limits of their endurance. Poduano, on the other hand, seemed to be exploding with energy, even though he had been confined without a source of fresh air throughout the trip.

Vania Crawford and Lloyd Nesmith muscled the three-quarter-ton cage and captive from the interior garage of the mansion, through its hallways, and down several long staircases—the elevators were too small to accommodate the box—to the interconnecting cellars on Tristan's orders. It wouldn't have suited convention for a Class One such as Grandillon to engage in actual manual labor, and Dieter Russmeyer and James Armstrong were of no help, either. The former had not yet been able to reproduce more than half of his severed leg, while the latter, being a Class Five, had no more physical strength than an uninitiated man.

So Vania and Lloyd were left to convey the cage downstairs. Either of them could have handled more than a ton of dead weight, but Poduano's desperate struggles and their exhaustion made it one slow and painful journey.

They smashed against walls, completely broke apart a long section of polished balustrade on one of the staircases, and crushed an antique table and the fine vase that it held when Poduano managed to knock the cage from their shoulders. Naturally, there were a number of other immensely powerful Class-Two employees watching this transfer, and they would have lent their assistance gladly if asked, but that, too, was denied by custom and protocol.

Tristan was properly embarrassed by the difficulty that his people were encountering with this lone captive, but in a way he was gratified by it, as well. This raging resistance proved his assertion that Poduano was dangerously mentally unstable, even as it warned the lower-class staff members that Class-One men and women were profoundly more powerful than they. It was something of a feather in his cap to have found, captured, and returned so imposing a force to the mansion.

Finally, they had passed by the rows of cells filled with screaming prisoners and reached the large and especially constructed room that lay at the very end of the basement. Though neither Grandillon nor any of the other designers of the mansion had ever seen the chamber in which the United States government was holding Rosalie Moorcroft, the two rooms were remarkably similar. The Caprice Island version had certain modifications not dreamed of by the minds at the Institute, however.

Still struggling, Vania and Lloyd dragged the reinforced metal box to the wall which was really the entrance to an "isolation room," where the occasional unfortunate was housed while his fate was debated. Another room much like it lay at the opposite end of the cellar, beyond the showers.

"Affix the mouth into the receptacle," Grandillon ordered briskly.

"Yes, sir," puffed Vania. The stone floor rasped deeply as the weighty box slid across it.

The "receptacle" was an indentation in the metal wall which allowed the traveling cage to be shoved end-on into it. When a button located just above its two-foot-high top was pushed, a steel collar was ejected from above and to either side of the box to form an air-tight seal. A second button caused the single panel of treated steel that separated the mouth of the cage from the room beyond to slide smoothly to the right. The box was positioned perfectly to expel its contents into the cell.

"Very good," Grandillon stated with slight, but real, appreciation. He activated yet another built-in device, and a wide-screen video terminal glowed to life, focusing on the open panel inside the room and the locking wheel at the end of the cage.

"Now what?" asked Vania, who'd never participated in such an operation before.

"Nesmith," Grandillon said quietly.

"Yes, sir." Grinning hugely, Nesmith stooped to the rear of the cage and flipped open a recessed control box that Vania hadn't noticed. Following a few deft motions of his fingers, he stared at the video screen. This system was equipped with an audio relay, too, as Vania discovered when she heard the popping noise that signaled the breaking of the hermetic seal at the other end of the cage; the locking device had been released.

Immediately, the circular door exploded upward. The thing that Dominic Poduano had become hit it like a cannonball and spilled into the other room. Filled with asymetrically distributed claws, fangs, fur, and naked flesh, it was the ugliest thing Vania had ever seen, even more repellent than the breast-like creature that had been in the trunk of his car.

The mass swiftly rolled to the center of the large room, where it stopped and seemed to take stock of its situation with a dozen or more eyes. One eye caught sight of the open panel through which it had been introduced into the chamber, and it launched itself at this possible escape route on six legs driven by massive cords of muscle.

"Close the panel!" Vania screamed as she envisioned the monstrosity slipping through the opening, battering apart the comparatively thin metal collar that pressed against the cage, and then tearing vengefully into the corridor.

Lloyd flashed a somewhat embarrassed smile, and Grandillon calmly touched another button on the control panel.

In the room, a thin strip of flooring flipped open to expose a polished, mirrory surface below it. The creature tried to stop its headlong rush, but even the Class Ones were subject to the laws of physics. One of its feet slipped across the smooth floor onto the band of pure silver.

Poduano screamed as shrilly as a wild jungle bird. White smoke spewed like steam from the point where his metamorphosing flesh touched the embedded silver, and the normal dead-white pallor of the skin flashed a deep red. Still shrieking, he lurched away from the strip and toward the center of the room. With his face boasting a sort of bored satisfaction, Tristan touched the button which closed the inner panels and effectively sealed his captive within the room.

"Wow, was that silver?" Vania asked in an awed tone.

Grandillon fixed her with a cold stare that quietly stated just how ridiculous that question was to him.

The woman swallowed nervously. "Is the entire floor made of silver? Under the covering, I mean?"

"A sufficient portion of it is," he replied. "I congrat-

ulate you all on a job well done, and I suggest we all go
upstairs for a meal and rest."

"Yes, sir," Nesmith said eagerly.

"Should someone stand guard?" Vania asked as she
looked at the still-activated video screen.

Tristan switched it off. *"Signor* Poduano will be
regularly checked by the staff. No one has ever escaped from this chamber."

So Vania followed the men back upstairs toward the
promise of food and sleep, but her mind continued to
replay her last vision of Dominic Poduano in the
center of the restraining chamber. Shrieking mindlessly in pain and fury as he mutated from one terrible
form to another, continuously, like a living fountain.

The miles stayed with them endlessly, in their
kidneys and backs and necks. It was the evening of
June 28th, and they had been on the road for five days
and for more than three thousand miles. During that
time, they had discussed all the pros and cons of using
the satellite dish to transmit their message, as well as
Tristan Grandillon's invitation to Blake to speak at
Grandillon's meeting. They had finally decided that
they no longer wanted to prove anything to the world
or to save mankind from a potentially deadly racial
smugness. All they wanted was rest. And Indigo Lake
was as good a place as any to get that.

Blake was behind the wheel when they drove up the
long drive to the Indigo Lake Resort, as he had been
for most of their cross-country trek. The gates were
closed and the smiling guard in the small kiosk didn't
seem inclined to open them to this less-than-imposing
group in the compact car.

"May I help you, sir?" the guard, an attractive
young woman, asked as the car glided to a stop next to
her.

Blake's eyelids were heavy and his lips thick with

fatigue. "Yes, um, I'd like to see Mr. Tristan Grandillon, please. I believe he's staying here."

The name plucked a responsive chord in the guard's programming. She smiled. "He is in residence at this time. May I ask who wishes to speak with him?"

Though all three occupants of the car realized that they were federal fugitives, Blake had no trepidation at giving the woman their real names rather than the imaginative pseudonyms they'd employed at motels throughout their trip.

The guard consulted the computer screen. "Corbett, Talley, and Grundel," she repeated. "Yes, you've all been included on the preferred guest list. Mr. Douglas Morgan is not with you?"

"No," answered Meg before Blake could respond. "He wasn't able to accompany us."

The guard flipped a switch to open the gates. "Just drive through, please, and follow the road down to the lake. You'll find another guard post at the shore end of the sea road, but I'll phone ahead so that you will have free passage to the island. Once there, an official committee will welcome you to the mansion."

" 'An official committee,' " Nick repeated after they had pulled through the gates and into the resort. "What is it about you that so impressed this Matt Dillon, anyway?"

"Grandillon," Blake corrected him.

"Whoever. Take it from me, A.B., you're not that engaging either as a person or as an author."

"Nick." Meg sighed wearily.

"Forget it, Meg," Blake said. "I don't believe my system could take the shock if he started acting like a human being." To Nick, he replied, "It's not us they're interested in, but what we saw at the Institute. Well, they probably would be very interested in you if they knew what happened to you that night."

From the back seat, Nick grinned his evil, gap-toothed smile which revealed his missing canines.

Both Blake and Meg ignored it. Meg asked, "How do you think that they knew about Nick and me? And Doug? Did Grandillon mention us when he approached you in San Francisco?"

Blake thought for a few seconds as he guided the car through the winding road that cut through the beautiful vacation resort. The lake up ahead looked gorgeous in the bright summer sun.

"No," he finally said, "he never mentioned your names, though I said something about you and Doug being re-incarcerated by the government. You were already underground by that time, and I'd concluded that the Institute had rounded you up again."

"Then why were our names on their preferred guest list?"

"Beats me. Maybe this association has a file on every civilian who was allowed to witness Cummings's transformation last year and survived. That would explain Nick's being on it, too."

"Nothing can explain Nick's being," Meg observed archly.

Blake took a deep and extremely tired breath. "Whatever the reason, I'm too far gone to worry about it. What do you say we just drive across to that glorious island out there and take up thinking again when we're somewhat closer to being capable of human deliberation?"

Without taking a moment to consider her words, Meg laughed and said, "At least, those of us who still fall into the classification of humanity." Like a sudden physical pain, the truth of what she'd said struck her. "Oh, Jesus, I'm sorry, Nickie! I didn't mean . . . It was only a stupid joke."

Grundel leaned his head back on the seat and closed his eyes. "Will you people please stop yammering and let a guy get some sleep?"

*   *   *

The welcome was as lavish as it was unexpected. The guard at the front gate had stated that an official committee would welcome them, and she hadn't overstated the case. Tristan Grandillon and a dozen other chicly dressed men and women were assembled on the expansive front porch of the mansion when the three arrived. They had hardly opened the car doors before uniformed household servants swarmed around the vehicle, removing the meager amount of luggage and guiding the overwhelmed trio into the huge house, where an elaborate dinner awaited them.

The road-weary fugitives were not pressed by the residents of the island to discuss any serious matters, and for this they were quite relieved. Welcomed as if they were long-lost relatives by the invariably impressive members of the association, the three fielded an unending flow of unimportant questions throughout the meal and the afterdinner drinks and tobacco. By the time these proceedings had concluded, night was falling almost as swiftly as their energy levels.

The rooms they were provided with were, like everything else in the mansion, luxurious even as they radiated tasteful understatement. Located three abreast on the fourth floor, each possessed an attached bath, of course, and each traveler was set up for the night. Or so it seemed.

But Meg couldn't get to sleep, no matter what signals of exhaustion her body was sending her. She had to see him and tell him again that she was sorry about the things she'd said and about what had happened to him at the Institute and everything.

Her knock at the bedroom door was answered by his short, gruff, "Yeah?"

"Can I come in, Nick?" she asked softly.

"Meg? Uh, sure." In those few words, his tone modulated from annoyance to surprise to something so hopeful and vulnerable that it seemed totally foreign to Nick's personality.

He was sitting on the spacious, four-poster bed dressed in clean white underwear. He'd showered and shaved a little already, and his smile at seeing her was so warm that Meg felt as if she had walked in on the wrong man.

Though neither had ever admitted it, a strong attraction had begun to develop between them almost a year before, during the earliest stages of their search for a maniacal killer. And while the terrible insanity at the Institute had howled around them, while Gerald Cummings had physically become the embodiment of generations of nightmares, they had taken unthinkable risks to save each other's lives. Nick's sacrifice had resulted in his infection when Nick had tried to escape and Cummings bit him.

"Has anybody ever told you that you're the most magnificent-looking person ever to walk the earth?" Nick asked, stating certainly the sweetest compliment he'd ever uttered.

"Not many have," she admitted.

"Well, those who didn't should have their eyes and hormones examined."

The two young people had never really been alone since Nick's rescue from the Institute van. Blake, without whom they really would have been lost, had been something of a third wheel while they were on the road, though neither had mentioned it to him. The writer had gallantly insisted that they have separate rooms in the motels which he paid for. So it developed that here, summoned by dozens of mysteriously wealthy people in an ostentatious mansion and in hiding from the immense resources of the United States intelligence agencies, Meg and Nick finally began to feel as if they were the only two people who had survived an unimaginable disaster which had engulfed the rest of the world.

They talked for a long time, with only the moon

flowing through an open window for light. Nick was more sensitive and restrained than Meg had ever realized that he could be. It seemed like the most natural thing in the world for the two of them to lie back in the darkness and try to help one another to make sense of what their lives had become. And from there the next level was but a single short step.

Meg had no reason to fear that the bearded young man carried any of the usual diseases, secondary or catastrophic, that were the bane of sexual involvement in the last years of the century, because his system no longer tolerated normal illnesses. Now there was only one condition from which he suffered.

Their desires and needs meshed in that sweetly scented night, and passionate kisses were only part of a prelude to what their souls required to continue the struggle of life. Neither had had the opportunity nor inclination to think of birth control for a long time, but Meg realized that she was at the point of least risk for a short while, so she cooperated with abandon in Nick's overtures.

Still, there was one awfully powerful inhibition remaining in their way: the "disease" that Nick would carry for the rest of his life. It was a form of infection; it had to be. They couldn't surrender their intellects to the tyranny of supernaturalism. But they had no way of knowing if it could be transmitted while the carrier was in his normal state and if no actual biting were involved.

Unwilling to take that chance, Nick withdrew from Meg's embraces.

"No," she whispered, clutching him to her.

"Meg . . . I—I can't." He sighed. "What if I infect you? Christ, I couldn't live with myself if I did that to you."

"I've taken your kisses, Nick Grundel," she reminded him. "I've tasted your tongue and your lips and your neck. I want all of you. Now."

So they shared the night and made gentle love until
dawn, with no thought beyond the moment as they
drifted together. It could be only a brief and limited
escape from the future that they faced, but for these
few hours it was what they needed.

CHAPTER THIRTEEN

Even though the official reunion was not scheduled to begin until Sunday, July second, all known thirty-three members of the North American Association were already in attendance at the island, even though one of these was a prisoner in the depths of the mansion. With a highly atypical number of would-be initiates to introduce to the secrets of their organization, it was decided not to wait for three more days to begin the ceremonies. The opening dinner was set for that night, Thursday, the day after Corbett, Talley, and Grundel's arrival at the lake.

The brief notification of the alteration of the traditional induction routine had caught most of the associates somewhat off guard, but they were nothing if not adaptive. For three days, the Indigo Lake airport had been receiving people of all ages and races, so that, by Thursday evening, twenty-four uninitiated people were among those gathered at the large residence.

Some of these people knew exactly why they were there, while others had some uncertain and nebulous ideas which they'd arrived at by pure guesswork. Nearly half of the group were completely ignorant of the purpose of their visits which had been arranged at the last second because of the association's concern about the shrinking number of associates. These people had been drawn to the resort by the sheer force of the personalities of their individual "sponsors."

Blake Corbett was convinced that he had been invited to attend the gathering only to deliver his firsthand account of the most terrible night of his life. He could hardly have been more wrong.

Chris Wyler felt uncomfortable.

Because he had spent some time in the mansion, this reaction was a little disturbing to him; after all, he knew his way around and was acquainted with a good portion of the big staff. But this time, following Neil's invitation, he clearly felt that he was present for some exceptionally portentous reason, and the deferential manner in which he and the other new arrivals were being treated didn't amuse him as much as it seemed to amuse the others.

He was introduced to a short, nondescript man named Blake Corbett, who seemed to know something about what was going to be addressed at dinner. He'd read several of Corbett's effective horror novels and engaged the author in a rather lengthy conversation regarding his work, but Corbett didn't volunteer any information about the meeting. And Chris didn't bother to ask. He'd been told that it would all be explained during the evening, and that was good enough for him.

Late that afternoon, Chris had made another discovery while browsing through the extensive newspaper file in the library. Georgia was represented only by *The Atlanta Journal*. He was scanning a few fight results from the LA Forum when he glanced over the top of the open newspaper and almost swallowed his tongue.

Shannon Kent had not left for New Hampshire, as he'd been told the night before at O'Hanlon's. She was there, at the mansion.

"Shannon!" he said involuntarily. And, as if she had heard, the beautiful redhead turned away from the associate to whom she had been serving a cocktail to stare at him. But she couldn't have heard him. She was deaf.

"Damn!" spat the seated associate as the gin and tonic spilled over his copy of *La Crónica de Madrid*.

Startled, Shannon turned back to the man and swiftly attempted to mop the alcohol from his trousers with a linen napkin.

Way to go, loud mouth, Chris castigated himself without realizing that his call *couldn't* have caused the girl's surprise. He scrambled out of his armchair to help her placate the red-faced man.

Shannon nervously mopped at the spilled drink while keeping her face turned away from Chris, who was gathering up the damp newspaper that the associate had tossed aside. "It was my fault," he said quickly and apologetically to the man. "I startled her. There's no reason to call Charles about this. It's all my fault." He'd seen how harshly Charles Gladden tended to deal with those under his thumb, and he really didn't want to cause Shannon any grief with that bastard.

Chris could hardly believe that the young woman had returned to the island, a place she obviously hated, but there was no mistaking that clear and dazzling face. Or the body exposed by the old-fashioned French maid's uniform she wore.

"The girl has the grace of a cow," the associate muttered in an unforgiving tone.

As if you couldn't afford another damned pair of

pants, Chris thought angrily.

Neil Merrick, also present in the library, looked up from his magazine and smiled. "It's hardly the bombing of Dresden, is it, Pepe? Think of it as a bold experiment in cologne and let the child bring you another drink."

Pepe grunted shortly.

As matters were set aright, Chris tried to catch Shannon's eye, but she resolutely avoided looking at him. In a few moments, she had completed all of the ministrations possible under the circumstances and gathered up the fallen glass and tray.

Then Charles Gladden strode into the room, and took in the entire scene with a glance. He immediately approached the still-disgruntled associate. "My sincerest apologies, Mr. Alonso," he stated in a tightly controlled voice. "She is a new recruit and very clumsy."

Pepe Alonso didn't ease any of the tension when he replied, "I had been assured that your staff consisted of finely trained individuals, Charles. It seems that my information was faulty, to say the least."

Those words seared through Gladden like the flame of a blowtorch, even though his icy expression remained set as if carved in stone. Chris saw the reaction and stepped closer to the man and Shannon, who was attempting to circle around Gladden and the seated Alonso. Charles caught her by the arm.

"It shall *not* happen again, sir," he said coldly. "You have my word as to that." In punctuation, he squeezed Shannon's arm hard enough to elicit a gasp of pain from her.

"Let her go," Chris said with quiet authority.

Gladden turned to stare at Chris with half-lidded eyes, expressing his resentment of the boy's interference. "This is not your affair, sir," he stated. Then he shoved Shannon roughly toward the door.

Using the violence that had been a part of Chris's entire life, the violence that had been visited upon him from his earliest memories by his own family, the violence that seemed entirely appropriate to him in certain situations, he threw a lightning-fast right hand which collided with Gladden's chin and sounded like billiard balls cracking together. Gladden dropped onto the plush carpeting, and Chris hovered over him like Dempsey above Tunney.

The expression on Charles Gladden's face proclaimed that he was far more shocked to be on his back than he was hurt. "You little son of a bitch," he whispered. "I'll break your spine." He sprang to his feet as if on strings.

Seeing this, Chris smiled.

"Charles, no!" shouted Neil Merrick as he came to his feet.

"But he *struck* me, sir!" Gladden responded plaintively. "And I was only doing my duty—"

"He is a guest," Merrick answered firmly. "I forbid you to assault a guest! Now, go about your business."

"Neil, if he feels that he owes me something, I'm perfectly willing to accommodate him," Chris told them both. "Here or outside."

Merrick dropped a hand on Chris's shoulder. "There's no time for this foolishness, Christopher," he happily pointed out. "Tonight is the most important evening of your life, and as soon as you learn the truth about your future, this will seem as meaningful to you as a playground tussle."

Chris didn't answer. He and Gladden locked eyes and stared at one another for a long, tense moment that seemed as brittle as a paper-thin sheet of glass. Then Gladden looked to Neil and said, "I'll be on my way with your permission, sir." He left without waiting to receive that permission.

"Now, what do you say we redirect some of that

energy into pounding around a racquetball?" Neil carefully steered the still-intense young man toward another exit.

Leaving, Chris glanced at Shannon as she followed the two of them from the room. Her expression contained something of the appreciation that he might have expected due to his intervention, but there was something else there, as well. Something unreadable.

It was almost as if she had seen what had just occurred in that room as being no more real than a half-forgotten dream, even though she had been a part of it. She looked very confused.

Dinner? Banquet would have come closer to describing what took place around those two huge tables in the dining room that evening.

Beginning at seven, the fifty-six men and women—thirty-two associates and twenty-four invited guests—were presented with course after course of sumptuously prepared foods that evaporated any thoughts of abstinence or even moderation. Always the sort of connoisseur for whom grated cheese on a baked potato was exotic, Blake Corbett sampled *hors d'oeuvres* of caviar straight with aquavit, an unnamed soup that seemed to glow more brightly as it settled into his stomach, Chinese gooseberries, mandarin oranges, guavas, papayas, celeriac in remoulade, Turkish sweet coffee, and for the main course. . . .

Because he didn't mind appearing to be the rube that he was in this situation, Corbett asked an associate just what kind of fowl he was being served by the dutiful waitresses.

With an expression that denied any duplicity, the exquisite woman responded, "Swan stuffed with goose, which in turn is stuffed with duck, veal, and larks."

To Blake's left, Nick laughed aloud and said, "You're kidding!"

The woman merely smiled and went back to her meal.

Blake shook his head slowly and marveled at how delicious a course better suited to some mythological king could taste.

In spite of the perfectly chosen and prepared dinner, however, neither he nor his two companions could really enjoy it. They understood that soon, at the conclusion of the meal, they would be enlightened as to who the members of the association really were and just how in the hell they were connected with Gerald Cummings and the soul-withering horror of that night at the Institute.

Blake glanced at the talented string quartet playing sedately in one corner of the room and thought, *Maybe it's all a sham. Maybe* THIS *is where the taxpayers' money goes and we're only being treated to a final evening of luxury before the government swallows us again.*

At the end of the meal, the entire group left the dining room and entered an adjoining den which was so large that it seemed less than half filled when everyone had settled into the overstuffed chairs and sofas. The maids served drinks and tobacco. Everyone was presented with a wide selection of wines and liquors, but Blake chose the house vintage for the evening, Haitian rum served in sugar cane. A very infrequent drinker, he had to struggle with himself to avoid ordering seconds.

"This has got to blow up in our faces soon," he overheard Nick whisper to Meg. "Food, drinks, a palace to sleep in. Man, even the folks on 'Lifestyles of the Rich and Famous' don't live this way. Or look this good."

He's right about that, at least, Blake decided. He'd

never seen so many truly beautiful women assembled in one room, not even at professional beauty pageants, and, damn, as uncomfortable as it made him to admit it, the men were undeniably good-looking, too. Their beauty was so overpowering that the effect became one of suffocation for Blake and the other more average-looking people.

"The New People's Soviet Socialist Revolution has to burst in at any second now and immolate us with Molotov cocktails for violating the natural ban against inordinate pleasure," Nick added.

Blake sipped the last of his rum. "Meanwhile, let's kick back and enjoy the decadence while it lasts."

The end came a few minutes later, and though it had nothing to do with Bolshevik revolutionaries, it still was something of an unpleasant shock to Blake.

Tall, blond, tanned Tristan Grandillon stood at the head of the vast room and, with a wave of his hand, dismissed the servants. The string quartet had not accompanied them into the den. When the room was empty of all but the associates and their guests, he commanded everyone's attention.

"Ladies and gentlemen," he said in that deep, rich, perfect voice, "if there are no objections, we will now begin with the business matters of the evening." There were no objections. "Thank you. At this time, I ask Mr. Allen Blake Corbett to come forward and deliver his report concerning the events which transpired at the Institute of Natural Sciences and Research in California on the night of December 14. Mr. Corbett?"

Blake had spoken to hundreds of audiences, most substantially larger than this one, but it had never been easy for him, and it wasn't now. He felt as if his full stomach were about to drop out of his body. Of course, he had known that the reason he and the others had been invited to this opulent gathering was to deliver this "report," and, as the most publically visible of the three, he was the natural choice as speaker, even though Nick was far more qualified as an expert witness. But he still had dreaded the moment.

"Go get 'em, tiger," Nick prompted in a loud whisper.

To a light and polite round of applause, Blake stood and walked toward Grandillon and the microphone.

As he walked, the doubts continued to assail him like invisible demons circling his head on leathery wings. What did he know about these people, really? Nothing. What proof did he have that this entire setup, even Nick's escape, was anything more than an elaborate program to test his resolve, to see if he would maintain his sworn silence even at these absurd limits? None. How could he be sure. . . .

Come on, A.B., his inner voice interrupted sardonically, *not even an overfed and morally deficient government agency would go to such expense and exertion simply to test the reliability of one man.*

He reached the lectern, and Grandillon smoothly moved aside, pausing only long enough to state into the microphone, "Please understand, Mr. Corbett, that everyone at this gathering is convinced that the 'official' version of the affair, of an 'escaped mutant virus,' is thoroughly bogus. We wish to hear the real truth about Gerald Cummings and we feel certain that you will deliver it."

The real truth, Blake thought. *Okay. Something's got to give, and it might as well be now.*

Only a moment was required for Blake to recall the memories of that night from the shallow, impermanent grave that he had dug for them. Closing his eyes, he gave the assembly the story that they seemed hungry to hear.

"For me, it began almost a year ago. In July.

"I'm a novelist, as I'm sure you know, and I've

always seemed to be most successful writing about horror, so, for the purpose of inspiration, I visited the scenes of recent, violent crimes to soak up the atmosphere and to use it to develop new perspectives in my work. I'll never have to do that again, believe me.

"Anyway, last July, I received a tip from a police informant that an awful double killing had occurred in a small town called Lynnview, just outside of LA, where I lived then. I reached the house before the police could hide the evidence, and I found the dismembered bodies of two people, Stanley and Victoria Gretler. I had seen the aftermath of psychotic attacks before, but I'd never seen anything like that. They were torn to pieces, ripped into chunks of flesh so mutilated that it took the coroner days to determine what belonged to the man and what belonged to the woman.

"For one of the few times since I'd taken up the ugly habit of viewing corpses, I was completely sickened, and when a search team following *human* tracks from the house into the surrounding woods found the woman's leg chewed to the bone, *eaten*, I knew that this was something more than a madman. Even the sickest human being couldn't have been responsible for that.

"The murders had taken place on the night of the full moon.

"A month later, four more people were slaughtered in the same area and in the same manner, also during the time of a full moon. For a supposedly modern man, it was an undeniably ridiculous assumption to make, but I took it. The murderer was a werewolf.

"There was a witness this time, a young woman, Margret Talley. Yes, she is here with us tonight. With her experiences and the help of Nicholas Grundel, also present, and Douglas Morgan, who hasn't been able to join us, we began a loosely organized investigation of this cyclic murderer, whom the press labeled 'the Mangler' and whom we believed to be a living lycanthrope.

"We faced a tidal wave of ridicule, naturally. I don't know that I would feel comfortable living in a society so gullible that the population would freely accept the reality of a supernatural mass killer without solid evidence. So we set out to produce that evidence, in spite of all of the odds against us.

"In a way, what was more unsettling were those people who *did* accept our hypothesis, because almost invariably they brought with them their beliefs in a thousand other blind certainties, everything from ancient astronauts to vampiric mermaids. Hell, after what I've seen, I can't say with any conviction that there *aren't* mermaids.

"Still, we had to have proof to silence the braying critics and our own doubts. But nothing we did seemed to bring us closer to the man or his identity. The only thing that kept our beliefs firm were the murders which came once a month every month, like clockwork. It was a terrible way to be vindicated, but those people would have died even if we'd never begun our search.

"Following a massacre at a cafe in Montana during the October assault, the monster's car was found abandoned, and from its registration he was identified as Gerald Cummings, a college teacher from California. After all of our efforts, after all of the energy that the country's enforcement agencies had applied to stopping him, it was this bit of luck that trapped the man. His photo was shown on TV and in newspapers and magazines across the country—and worldwide— so that he became the number-one topic of discussion in the month leading up to the November full moon.

"Cummings killed again, in Iowa on November 14, and he escaped again. But a couple of weeks later in Kansas City, Missouri, a retired couple who had hired a young transient to do some work on their home recognized the man from his picture which was being displayed like a circus poster throughout the media. They informed the police, and Cummings was taken into custody without a fight a few hours later.

"Gerald Cummings had committed fifteen known and unbelievably savage murders by then, but when he was arrested, he appeared to be as normal and as sane as any person in this room tonight.

"Naturally, speculation ran rampant, not only as to whether he would be ruled incompetent to stand trial for his atrocities, but also if he was really a werewolf, as Meg, Nick, Doug, and I had maintained throughout our five-month search for him. The next full moon would occur on December 14, and the authorities knew that there was no way on earth they could isolate Cummings from the world's press on that particular night. Instead, they placed him in the Institute of Natural Sciences and Research, a high-security government compound in California just south of San Francisco, and invited selected members of the media to attend that evening. There were over two hundred reporters there from just about every place on the globe. Doug Morgan got in due to his newspaper connection, and Meg, Nick, and I were included because of our high profiles during the preceding months. The authorities really thought that this would be the way to discredit and embarrass us for insisting that Cummings was a werewolf.

"You see, they *still* didn't believe.

"Objectively speaking, there was no irrefutable proof that all of the murders had been committed by anyone other than an incredibly vicious maniac. It was hard for the conventionally educated minds of these glorified police officers to entertain the possibility of the supernatural, even though Cummings himself in an article written before he began his spree of slaughter advanced the idea that lycanthropy was *not* a condition beyond the natural, but an infection brought on by an extremely exotic and previously undiscovered viral or bacterial form of life.

"Well, as midnight approached—that was the time of the supposed 'transformation,' rather than the moonrise—we were allowed to interview Cummings. He admitted to the murders, though he appeared to plead not guilty due to a sort of 'physical insanity'; in other words, he claimed that he was, indeed, a werewolf.

"Of course, a few of us believed him or wanted to. The vast majority of the assembly decided that the man either really was crazy or was trying to save his neck by pretending to be and had seized on our assertions as a convenient madhouse routine. What we all knew was that the truth would make itself known in a few hours at midnight.

"Because of this—the difficulty, the *impossibility* of accepting an ancient superstition as a modern reality—the tragedy occurred. It seemed to be foreordained. At midnight, while the assembled reporters waited to see another head case exposed as a victim of drugs or childhood trauma, Cummings was rolled into an observation room strapped to a table. A damned table!

"Meg tried to warn everyone, tell us that this ridiculous attempt at restraint would never hold him, and she knew, because she'd seen him during the height of his madness. And it didn't.

"When midnight arrived, Cummings smashed the table as if it had been made of matchwood. The observation room was packed with medical personnel, and before many of them could escape, he—this *thing* that an apparently normal human being became —slashed and ripped his way through them so maniacally that he must have killed ten people in as many seconds. The rest of us were in an adjoining room with a perfect view of the attack, and it was as if we were frozen. The sight of a literal transformation from one form to something beyond any nightmare from a horror film just overwhelmed us. We watched it. God, we *filmed* it! While that son of a bitch tore the living throats from men and women only a few feet away from us, we responded like recording machines with our cameras and microphones and tape players. I know that none of you can believe this, but you've asked me to tell the truth about that night, and, by God, that is what I'm doing! Gerald Cummings became a living, breathing, murdering creature, with fangs and claws and a coating of hair that covered him like any other furred animal! And we watched it.

"Until he noticed us.

"When he stared through the window into the connecting room and showed us that terrible mouth, with the blood and flesh dripping from it, the spell was shattered. Two hundred people tried to escape into the hallway through two small doors. Nick and Meg made it out somehow, but Doug and I were trapped in the room with most of the others. It was sheer luck that neither of us was killed.

"The building we were in was huge and octagonal with only one designated point of entry and exit, but we were all too terrified to try to reach it. There was the better part of a hundred chambers in that building which operated as combination offices and experimental laboratories. Most of us fled to these and locked the double-chambered doors behind us. We knew that nothing remotely human could smash through those two layers of steel.

"If the head of the Institute, a man named Axton, had reacted in a reasonable manner at that moment, maybe . . . maybe it would have ended that night. I'm sure that some people would have died, anyway, but maybe not so many.

"But I almost believe that Axton was as mad as Cummings. He didn't want to chance having the monster escape into the hills around the Institute—he had to have this fascinating specimen to study and dissect—so that—that crazy bastard had the entire building quarantined. *He sealed us inside with that animal!*

"The Institute staff tried to stop Cummings, of course, with gas, acid solutions, almost anything that could be rigged up quickly with the materials on hand, but it was useless. He was not only incredibly powerful and bloodthirsty, he also seemed to be invulnerable to injury. I swear to God, as I'm standing before you tonight, I saw that man blasted to pieces by high-caliber police weapons, I shot him six times in the *brain*, and none of it affected him for more than a few seconds. He healed with visible speed. None of the cinematic creatures we've ever seen or the nightmares we've imagined were as immune to permanent injury as that thing.

"We had only one opportunity to try to use silver as a weapon against him, at least as far as I know. Nick Grundel had a cross that he used like a knife to stab Cummings, but even though it was effective in driving him away, it didn't kill him.

"Still, all we had to do, according to Axton and his people, was to wait behind locked doors until dawn, when the monster would be returned to human form. Then he killed Axton.

"No matter how many he slaughtered, no matter how much flesh he consumed, it wasn't enough to satiate that thing so long as any of us remained alive in the sealed building. He began to smash his way into the labs, right through the impenetrable steel doors, and whatever he found inside, he killed. Dawn was still hours away, so we no longer could wait him out.

"Nick and Meg had been injured by then, so Doug and I and several other people made a dash through the corridor where Cummings was prowling, in an effort to reach the exit and the chance to persuade the outside guards to open the doors. No one outside the building knew exactly what was going on.

"We were jumped almost immediately by Cummings, and we would have died right there, in his hands and jaws, if it hadn't been for the second most extraordinary thing I've ever witnessed. A boy, a sixteen-year-old boy, who was suffering from some sort of gigantism that had already made him into a seven-foot-tall titan and a mental condition which caused him to believe he was a Middle Ages warrior ripped from his own time . . . Jesus, this wonderfully insane kid came charging out of the lab nearest us and began to fight the monster hand to hand!

"My Lord, what a fight. He actually drove the beast from us and allowed half of our group to make a break for the front exit while Doug, a photographer named Brad Ferguson, and I tried to help him. The two of them must have fought for half an hour. It was the most amazing thing I had ever seen, aside from Cummings's actual transformation into the creature. For a moment, I actually came to believe that the boy would kill Cummings. He had the monster flat on his back and was raining punch after punch into its face, pulping the features, smashing the fangs, beating him right to the very edge. I *wanted* Cummings to die and I tried to help kill him.

"But Walter, the boy, was still a human being, while Cummings had passed beyond that state, so that he didn't tire and every injury healed as soon as it was incurred. Walter took his head and began to pull and twist it, as if he were about to decapitate the thing, but he fell short. Cummings was able to recover and kill him.

"We managed to drive the monster away for a brief time using fire, but Doug and Brad were too injured to continue. I was in no great shape, myself, but I managed to reach one of the front offices, where those who had tried to reach the exit had established outside contact by telephone. The guards had agreed to allow one person from inside the Institute to leave and present eyewitness evidence of what was happening. Somehow, the job fell to me.

"I had a gun given to me by one of the guards, in case Cummings found me before I reached the exit. Which he did, naturally. Christ, you can believe that I emptied every damned shell into that son of a bitch's head, but it hardly slowed him. It was worse than anything I've ever been able to use in my fiction to frighten anyone else. It was a race, and only the fact that the impact of the bullets knocked him from his feet when I shot him allowed me to make it to the doors first.

"When I escaped from the building, though, the situation did not improve. The place was surrounded by an army of troops and local and state police, but they all seemed to be as stunned by the sight of Cummings as we reporters had been in the observation room. So they stood and stared while he chased me halfway across the compound.

"And he ignored them. For some reason, all of his rage and lust was directed solely at me. I knew that I was going to die after so much struggle and being so close to what I believed to be salvation. The memories are blasted white in my mind by the sheer terror that that moment created, so I can't really say how I wound up inside an idling police car, I only know that I did.

"I suppose my only intent was to get away from there, but Cummings wouldn't allow it. He caught my arm through the window and ripped it to the bone. I have a mass of scar tissue from my elbow to my wrist and a certain amount of impaired functioning due to nerve damage. Before he could tear it off as he'd done to so many others that night, I shifted the car into gear and ran over his chest. It freed my arm but didn't stop him. He kept coming for me, roaring and slashing, living only to pull the life from me. I hit him again and again and again! I used that car to run over him at least five times, but he always got up and came at me for more.

"The last time I ran into him, his body was hurled across the compound against a concrete abutment that was designed to prevent washdown from the hill beyond it. I kept my foot on the accelerator so that the front bumper caught him flush in the face while his head was forced back over it, and even Gerald Cummings's body couldn't withstand those pressures. His head was torn from his body.

"For an instant, I didn't think that even that would end it. He actually *lived* for a few seconds more, but finally it was over. More than a hundred people were dead, and I wasn't even certain that *I* hadn't been infected through my arm laid bare to the bones, but it was over.

"Except that it wasn't, of course.

"The government immediately clamped a lid of secrecy over the entire matter and released the escaped-mutant-virus fairy tale, while the survivors were swiftly transported to a security hospital located not very far from the Institute. Our injuries were attended to, and efforts were made to ascertain if we had been infected by contact with Cummings, but there was only one real way of deciding that. The night of the next full moon was January 13 of this year, appropriately, Friday the thirteenth.

"They played a lot of psychological tricks on the survivors, telling us that the date was the thirteenth the day before, or that it was the twelfth on the night itself, and refusing to let us know exactly when midnight arrived. But Nature wouldn't be fooled. At 12 A.M. on that night, technically January 14, a certain number of unlucky men and women went through the same transformation as Gerald Cummings had. A reasonable guess would be that about fifty people proved to be infected.

"Yes, fifty people sentenced to a lifetime of horror, perhaps an unending lifetime.

"I was fortunate, as were Meg and Doug. But Nick . . . We proved to be free of the virus, and when our more ordinary injuries had healed, it was decided to release at least some of those who had passed the test, as long as these people agreed to keep the facts about that night secret as well as everything else concerning the werewolf. I believe that we three were chosen so that we could publicly refute our prior stand about Cummings and add weight to the fable of the mutant virus's escape from one of the labs.

"Once out, I retreated to my home, scared to death of what I had discovered about my so-called 'rational' world. Meg and Doug soon disappeared again, and I like everyone else was convinced that this had something to do with the government and what had happened at the Institute. In fact, they had dropped out of sight voluntarily after being contacted by a rogue employee within the organization itself.

"One week ago, they brought me into their confidence, and we were able to locate and liberate Nick from the Institute's custody while he was being transferred to another installation. Unfortunately, though we've been on the road for the past week, we've been unable to connect again with Doug, who was running interference for us with any government agency in pursuit on the night of the rescue. This leads us to believe that he was captured and we actually exchanged one hostage for another.

"Our goal in undertaking all of this? Simply what Doug implored us to do in his last contact. We have to show the country and the world the truth about that night and prove the reality of what has long been dismissed as mere superstitious absurdity. Gerald

Cummings *was* a werewolf. He left a legacy of dozens of other afflicted people, and being kept ignorant of this fact 'for our own good' by the government serves no purpose other than to leave us totally unprepared to deal with the next Gerald Cummings. You don't restrict the spread of a plague by denying its existence.

"That, ladies and gentlemen, is our story. Perhaps I've simply incriminated the three of us and you will reveal yourselves to be vacationing federal agents, in which case I'm sure I'll be doing any future speech-making from a thoroughly buried jail cell. I have to believe that even our government wouldn't have gone to this much trouble and expense just to catch three fugitives. So I prefer to believe that this gathering will prove to be a collection of sophisticated and generous people who may think that they've just heard the rantings of a writer who engaged in one too many horrific speculations and lost his sanity while attempting to squeeze another dollar out of the reading public.

"But I assure you, for whatever my assurance is worth, every word was true. You can take me into custody, if that's within your power, or you can call the men with the white coats and butterfly nets, but at some time what I've told you is going to erupt into life again. And next time, we won't be able to afford the smugness and ignorance that we displayed in allowing Gerald Cummings to tear the lives from a hundred innocent people.

"Next time, the monster won't be alone."

For a moment, there was no response to Blake's revelations. He stood at the end of that long room and gazed into the perfectly composed faces of these perfect people, lit by artfully subdued soft white lights, and suddenly he knew that *they* knew.

What? How much?

He couldn't be certain, but it was clear that to these assembled listeners—or to most of them, since there were a few startled and unconvinced expressions cloaking the faces of some of the guests—the recitation of the facts of the most terrible night of his life had come as no real surprise. Christ, who were they?

"Thank you, Mr. Corbett," Tristan Grandillon said as he stepped to Blake's side and spoke into the microphone. "It's easy to understand why you are regarded as one of the country's most accomplished authors. Your presentation was eloquent, cleanly structured, and quite powerful."

Confused, Blake muttered, "Um, if there are any questions—"

"I'm certain that there will be," the big man interrupted smoothly, "but they can wait a few moments more. First, it has been delegated to me to explain to you and most of our other invited guests why you all are here tonight and how we members of the association are certain that what you told us of the events of that night at the Institute was the honest truth as you experienced it."

Instinctively, Blake stepped away from the lectern and went back to his seat.

Tristan took the moment to engage in a long, expectant look at his fascinated audience. "Truth has many sides, Mr. Corbett, and while searching for it, one cannot turn a blind eye or a deaf ear to any of its aspects. We associates accept your account of the lycanthropic Gerald Cummings and his atrocities simply because we, too, are werewolves."

CHAPTER FOURTEEN

The reaction was predictably immediate and loud.

One tall, handsome man whom Meg had thought was a member of the association stood and shouted over the general din, "What in the hell kind of joke is this, Lisolette? I don't know what sort of enjoyment you and your rich friends get out of running games like this on ordinary people, but I certainly don't appreciate it!"

The elegantly attractive woman tried to take his hand. "Please, B.D., just listen to the explanation and I promise you'll see—"

"I see that I'm being played for a yokel, that's what I see. There are *no* werewolves, or vampires, or—"

"Don't bet on it, bud," Nick said darkly. Meg, who was gripping his arm in her nervous hands, increased the pressure of her hold.

Half a room away, Chris Wyler whispered through the noisy confusion, "Come on, Neil, is this what you wanted me to hang around the lake to hear? Fables?

This kind of shit went out of style back in the forties with Universal Studios."

Next to him, Neil Merrick smiled faintly. "Give it a chance, son. Every fable has a grain of truth at its origin, and, I give you my word, this truth will far exceed anything a screenwriter ever devised."

"I don't believe in much of anything anymore, Neil."

"You will, my friend, you will."

Altogether, eleven of the twenty-four people invited to the lake by various associate sponsors did not have the slightest idea of the true nature of their hosts, and it was their voices which strove to fill the large room with their shock and disbelief. This group included Meg, Chris, Nick, and Blake.

Grandillon thumped the top of the lectern with the side of his fist, and the microphone magnified the sound. "Please, please, ladies and gentlemen. Please take your seats. I realize that you are all surprised and perhaps alarmed, but we have never before held an induction meeting in such a fashion as this, and I am ready to bear the total responsibility for the resulting apprehension that you feel. Take your seats if you will."

"Just give him a chance," Lisolette Sprouling asked of B.D. Robinson.

The noise level of the room subsided reluctantly. Tristan waited until there was almost complete silence before continuing. "To begin with, we all must accept the veracity of what Mr. Corbett has told us this evening. I'm sure a number of you, familiar with his skillfully crafted short stories and novels, felt that he was invited to give his talk solely for its entertainment value. Sort of a preview of his next book, perhaps.

"But I assure you that werewolves *do* exist and Gerald Cummings was the most homicidal and terrible representative of the species for the past several centuries. Of course, he was an Orphan, inducted into the Life without instruction or support, so we mustn't be too harsh with his memory—"

"Too harsh?" demanded Meg. "He was a *demon*! You didn't see what that monster did!"

Grandillon nodded sympathetically. "I understand your fear and revulsion, Ms. Talley, honestly. The association began a search for Cummings as soon as we had adequate reason to believe that he was one of our number, but this proved to be one of those rare cases when the civilian authorities functioned with a modicum of efficiency."

"But he killed over a hundred people!"

"Entirely against his will, I'm certain. We must view Cummings as a victim, just as much a victim as those who died at his hands. In fact, since he had no help in gaining a perspective on the real nature of his infection, we might even consider him to be no more responsible than a newborn." Tristan's patient tone made it seem as if he looked upon these uninitiated men and women as babies, as well. "For all of the indications in Mr. Corbett's tale, your friend Mr. Grundel was infected by Cummings's attack so that he is one of us now, yet you realize that Mr. Grundel can't be held accountable for any of the murders he commits while under the influence of—"

"I haven't killed anybody!" Nick responded sharply. "And I never will!"

"That's correct, Mr. Grundel. You will never have to worry about becoming a monster like Gerald Cummings simply because we of the association will educate you in self-control which is necessary to take the fullest advantage of your condition."

"Advantage?" Nick asked in a disbelieving tone.

"Exactly. You see—"

"This is a lot of garbage, and I'm not going to let you uppercrust snots make me the butt of it anymore," declared B.D. Robinson as he ignored Lisolette's pleas and stood to leave the room.

A younger woman, Kim Ownsby, joined him while trying to inject a pathetic note of humor in her exit, "Didn't the Doobie Brothers record a song called 'What a Fool Believes'?"

Like a dark cloud passing before the sun, Grandillon's expression took on an entirely new and unsettling aspect. He was a very diplomatic associate and dealt skillfully with the uninitiated human beings he encountered, but everyone has only a limited amount of patience. He said nothing, yet Charles Gladden took his cue from the expression and stepped before the closed doors.

At five-nine, the stocky Gladden was five inches shorter than Robinson, a bulky and quite physical person in his own right, but the look that was reflected in Charles's eyes was powerful enough to stop B.D. and Kim in their tracks.

"I must apologize," Grandillon almost whispered in his smoothly even voice. "I believed that calm conversation would suffice to prepare those uninitiated for the next step, but it is clear now that I was in error. A more literal demonstration is in order to hold your attention. If you all will be so kind as to give me the next few moments of your time." Stepping away from the lectern, he quickly removed his dinner jacket and the expensive silk shirt beneath it.

Grandillon's chest proved to be broad, hairless, and as finely muscled as a competition swimmer's. This exhibition was not aimed at the libidos of any members of his audience, however. "Mr. Robinson, Ms. Ownsby, this is a werewolf."

Reality fled from that room, and perhaps from the world. Before the gaping eyes of eleven people, eight of whom had never in their adult lives entertained the possibility of the supernatural as an actuality, Grandillon's yellow-blond hair spread in a golden foam from his scalp onto his face and neck and then to his shoulders, arms, and chest. They could *see* the hair growing, like fine metal filaments emerging from his flesh and stretching into the cool air of the dimly lit room, then curling into a thick covering like a pelt from some beautiful and exotic animal.

And their staring faces drank in the view of Grandillon's two canine teeth drawing like mechanical prongs up into his gums, only to reappear an instant later as long, gleaming, keen fangs. All without the loss of so much as a drop of blood.

Tristan Grandillon stood before the assembly in the image of the classic movie werewolf, though one of the few of his particular coloring.

Meg, Nick, and Blake had seen this incredible phenomenon once before, six months earlier, on the precipice of the worst nightmare of their lives. To them, Tristan Grandillon could just as well have been Gerald Cummings.

Meg screamed piercingly and tried to spring to her feet, while hands from all sides clutched and held her. Blake staggered back. His stomach seemed to leap into his throat, and he felt as vulnerable as if his very skin had been stripped from his body. The terror had come upon him again, without warning, and he stood helplessly exposed to its irresistible fury once more, just like then, just like on that damned night.

As if awakened by Meg's cry, the voices of the other eight unprepared women and men broke into screams, and they were joined by some of those who had known at least nebulously what to expect.

Grandillon leaned over the microphone. "Stop!" he said forcefully, and it was still his human voice, though somewhat distorted by the fangs and the new, slightly muzzle-like shape of his lower face. "Be quiet, all of you!"

The room fell silent as if a collective breath had been drawn.

Grandillon fixed them with a knifelike gaze. The eyes were still his own. As the audience watched, the

covering of golden fur appeared to be sheared off
below skin level and dropped away from his face and
body in glistening clumps. His face, also, regained its
former contours, though no one could see the replacement of the ugly fangs because his lips were closed
tightly in concentration. Or rage. An instant later,
Tristan stood before them again.

"Convinced?" he asked in a cold tone.

"Oh, Jesus," whimpered someone.

He went on, "But that was no more the extent of our
many lives than the horizon represents the entire
earth. If I may prevail upon those of our number who
have brought candidates to this meeting. . . ."

Among the audience, ten associates took the hands
of their protégés. A woman Meg had never met gently
gripped the awestruck younger woman's hand, even as
another reached up to take Blake's. Shocked, he
turned his face to meet hers.

"If you please," said Grandillon.

The miracle occurred again, ten times over.

Ten people took the genetic patterns from their
uninitiated partners through the contact of flesh with
flesh and casually re-formed their own faces into exact
duplicates of the originals. Ten other people stared at
themselves suddenly reborn. In Blake's case, the woman even used her malleable flesh to create what
appeared to be black-rimmed eyeglasses.

Four of the ten protégés fainted.

It was nearly a quarter of an hour later before the
room returned to something close to normalcy.
Grandillon permitted the servants inside to serve
drinks for those who needed them, and he and several
other associates kept up a calm and reassuring stream
of conversation in an attempt to lower the level of
hysteria. This was a difficult assignment. It was almost
impossible to eradicate the memory of witnessing
another person taking on one's features as easily as an
impressionist switches voices.

Still, once the servants left and heartbeats had slowed somewhat, the meeting continued.

Neil Merrick stood before the lectern now, using his cool, composed personality to carry the exposition in a more soothing fashion than Grandillon's civil bluntness. He no longer looked like Chris Wyler. "We are an old race," he stated in the manner that a historian of a generally recognized ethnic group might have employed. "Our best guess is that the force, the bacterial infection which makes us what we are, is as old as mankind itself. Certain investigators even claim that it is a form of rabies that split from the deadly original pattern some time in the dim mists of prehistory. Certainly, we know that the legends of shape-shifters are to be found in practically every culture's mythology as far back as those tales reach."

"Werewolves," a dazed guest said, and he spoke as if the word itself contained some awe-inspiring power.

Neil smiled benevolently. "We prefer the term shape-shifter, since not all early cultures even knew what a wolf was, and this form of bestial transformation is habituated by the infection only in its earliest stages, in any case."

"You mean you learn to *control* your transformations," a wondering Chris muttered.

"Exactly." Merrick seemed pleased that his guest had stated this obvious fact before anyone else. "The bacterium, which lives symbiotically within each of us, imbues the host with the ability to rearrange his own cell structure at a fantastically accelerated speed. The infection has no intelligence, as such, yet it works in concert with the host's mind so that his physical dimensions become quite literally subjected to his desires." In illustration, the black-haired man raised his right hand and willed it to develop six more perfectly formed fingers.

Despite the dramatic displays they already had witnessed, this second change still drew gasps of disbelief from a number of the audience.

"Following practice, it becomes as easy as writing one's signature," Merrick added.

Blake was seated now and holding Meg's hand. Nick had a firm grip on her other. "Amazing," he whispered. "This is what Gerald Cummings theorized in an article he wrote before his infection."

"He was a perceptive individual," noted Merrick. "It's a shame we weren't able to help him. We could have confined him during his initial psychotic episodes and then educated him in the methods of self-discipline."

"You can use this condition to turn into anything at any time?" Nick asked with a glimmer of previously unforeseen hope.

"And so will you, Mr. Grundel, once you've been properly integrated into our society."

"Anything?" repeated Kim Ownsby.

Neil shrugged. "Practically. Within reason, of course. We have to remain corporeal, of course, no ghostly shades or insubstantial breezes or any such thing. And there is a lower limit to which our forms may be reduced, since our physical minds—the seat of one's being and the home of the soul, if one chooses to subscribe to the belief in a soul—our brains, must remain inviolate while our bodies metamorphose."

"The mind is the constant," Gabrielle Secretain said from among the seated members. "Through all of the centuries, only that remains ours to possess."

"Centuries?"

A number of people voiced this question. It seemed that each second brought with it some unbelieveable, yet undeniable, new facet of reality. Because none of them, not even the angrily suspicious B.D. Robinson, could refute what was being delivered to them in a continuous wave, their only resort was to try to keep their mental balance by moving with it. It was analogous to trying to outrun a tsunami.

"That's right," Merrick replied. "Centuries. When the cells of the body retain their integrity indefinitely, aging is no longer a consideration." He looked directly at Chris. "How old would you say that I am, my friend?"

Too overwhelmed by it all to maintain his usual aura of protective indifference, the boy shrugged and said, "Forty? Forty-five?"

"In six months from today, I will be three hundred and thirty-two years old."

It might have been thought that nothing could have drawn yet another gasp of shock, but this did. Chris sighed. "I know this sounds like the worst cliches from a 'Z' movie, but, man, when you're here, faced with the *proof* . . . it's got to be a dream. This can't be something out of real life."

"I was born on November 29, 1663 in Welshpool, Montgomeryshire, Wales, and I was indoctrinated with the force in the middle of a freezing February night eighteen years later." He glanced at Tristan Grandillon. "And this peach-faced youngster is, if memory serves me, over two hundred and forty, just a year or three older than Pepe. Richard, Richard Comstock, you're closing in on four centuries, aren't you?"

A distinguished-looking, but none-too-aged, associate nodded. "Three-ninety-eight last April third."

"Which brings us to our own *Mademoiselle* Secretain, who may be about . . ." When Gabrielle raised one eyebrow, Neil laughed. "Ah, but a gentleman never broaches the subject of a young lady's age, does he? I believe you see my point, however."

"It makes you immortal . . ." whispered someone.

"That must mean that there are people here who are *thousands* of years old," Blake said in open astonishment. "From ancient Rome, Egypt . . . my God, from the days of the Neanderthals!"

Merrick leaned forward on the lectern and tapped

his fingers together contemplatively. "One might think so, but I'm afraid not. You see, while we're convinced that the force itself is as old as mankind, due to the collateral legends of shape-changers which developed in practically every corner of the world, the Life form itself is as subject to evolution as any other natural organism. It's changed through the ages.

"In the beginning of the symbiotic relationship, all evidence seems to indicate that it merely invoked periodic outbursts of extreme violence in the host, much like the tradition of lycanthropy relates, or as the bacteria dictate in the early stages of every infection. At this point, the force failed to provide any sort of beneficial effects at all. When the caveman saw his companion sprouting fur and fangs, he responded with a stone ax to the foreskull and that was the end of that. Actually, because the fatal blows could be struck without the use of silver, it's rather surprising that the Life form survived through the ages at all."

"Mister, I've seen a werewolf in action, and he wasn't stopped by a few clouts to the head by a stone ax, believe me," Nick stated.

Merrick raised a cautioning hand. "Cummings was a modern-day addition to the number. The force cannot survive for more than seconds outside a host body, and only the human race can accommodate it, so it was passed through the generations from one infected person to the next during the early stages of its existence. Lycanthropes seldom lived long enough to enact more than two or three episodes of transformation, and when a werewolf is in a metamorphic attack, he or she is so efficient a killer that it is unlikely that very many assault victims will survive to develop the condition."

Blake closed his eyes and remembered an afternoon, almost a year before, when he had read practically the same words in a treatise written by Gerald Cummings himself. He was half-convinced that when he opened his eyes again, the entire year would prove to be only a wild nightmare.

Instead, there was Neil Merrick continuing his explanation. "About half a millenium ago, at some point in the sixteenth century, the force mutated. From being a bacterial disease which gave back nothing to its host aside from the periodic outbursts of violence, it changed into an infection that came to work in harmony with the person's mental activities to achieve startling physical transformations. The earliest hosts of this new form had to survive the on-going religiously backed persecution of the time as well as their own desperate feelings of monstrosity inspired by their involuntary attacks upon their neighbors before they realized the true glories of their new states. Then they began to master their own bodies. Ah, how I wish that Giacomo Vilante were here to describe to you those days!"

"But once these—these first victims of the mutated virus realized what the infection *meant* to them, why didn't they go public?" demanded Meg. "Good God, if everything you say is true, it's more like a *blessing* than a curse!"

From the audience, Tristan Grandillon replied, "Now you have it. No associate of my acquaintance would go back to being a normal human being. The 'Larry Talbot Syndrome,' the tortured, suicidal whining over one's situation, seems not to exist once the initiated individual gets beyond the earliest stages and into the area of self-determination."

"Then why isn't it a worldwide condition?" Meg went on. "Living forever, immune to other diseases and injury? Jesus, why have you people kept this knowledge to yourselves?"

"Self-preservation, my dear," answered Neil. "I'm sure you've all heard of the witch hunts of the Middle Ages, but were you aware that a similar religious craze was dedicated to the extermination of lycanthropes just following that dark period? In fact, according to many reputable studies, *more* men and women were put to death for being werewolves than were executed for witchcraft. There was absolutely no question of whether to reveal the condition when the unified might of religious Europe made our so-called 'invulnerability' as effective as a knight's armor following the discovery of guns. It's difficult to maintain your cellular integrity while logs are continually stacked on the blaze."

"Since the Reformation—" Blake began.

"There has been no Reformation as far as most religious thought is concerned. Today, if I were to appear on television and prove to the world as I've proven to you tonight the reality of my condition, you can believe that there would be literally thousands of Bible-quoting 'modern people' who would be eager to tie me to the stake. Perhaps some of the listeners in this room have that same desire."

He paused, and for a few moments, there was complete silence in the hall.

"So, we hid. We covertly sought out others of our kind and used our pooled knowledge to make our lives the most rewarding possible. And, as we expanded into the almost limitless potential of our new lives, a small, intensely secret society began to take shape. The years passed, and then the decades. Finally, the centuries bowed to our vitality.

"Naturally, we had to keep moving from place to place to allay rising suspicions about our continued youth. Some of us adjusted our appearances to give the impression of aging, but generally it was much easier to walk away from one life and into another before any familial ties could grow too strong to break. You see, by this point we had learned to control our regular sessions of physical insanity so well that we could move undisturbed through the light of the brightest full moon, and we men—during those times that we chose to be men—had learned to cleanse our sexual emissions of contagion when lying with women."

At this, Nick and Meg's eyes met and locked. He had no idea how the associates "cleansed" their semen, and now he realized that his tender union with the young woman at his side had infected her, made her what he was. He tried to speak, but she shook her head.

"But our women—when we choose to be women— are unable to do the same with their ova, so that when they become impregnated, the fetus is automatically infected with the force. In a mature host, the force is, as Ms. Talley described it, the greatest blessing. In a developing babe, however, it causes the genetic patterns to shortcircuit wildly, inducing natural abortion or a deformed fetus which should have aborted itself. We cannot procreate in the manner of the uninitiated human, except upon the rarest of occasions."

"And so you developed your own hidden and transient population in the world," Blake observed. "That certainly sounds like a heavy payment for immortality."

Merrick shrugged. "Perhaps. It depends upon your perspective. And not all of us were always so completely hidden."

"Sure, there was the occasional 'Orphan,' like Cummings—"

"I wasn't speaking of the Orphans, Mr. Corbett."

"What do you mean, then?"

"Have you heard, perhaps, of Mysterious Dave Mather, a most deadly Western gunfighter who seemingly came from nowhere and then disappeared following a brief and spectacular career?"

"Well, yes, but—"

Neil gestured to the rear of the room toward one of the male associates. "Please stand for our guests, Joseph." The tall man—weren't all of the men tall?—

rose to his feet as the gathering turned to look at him. "Thank you. I would like to introduce Joseph Sharples Logan, born on March 30, 1814 in New York City, and also known for a time as Mysterious Dave Mather." The man sat next to his coolly appreciative associate companion. "And, Chris, as a student of boxing history, surely you've heard the training camp tales of the unmarked youth who strolled into the Paris gymnasium in December of 1913 where Jack Johnson was training for his fight with Jim Johnson, to defend his title. The story was that the young man stepped into the ring with that greatest of defensive heavyweights on a dare, and knocked the worthy champion unconscious with a single right-hand smash. That 'youth' was actually our own *Mademoiselle* Gabrielle Secretain."

"You're kidding!" Wyler said, grinning and looking at the woman. "I thought that story was just so much hot air!"

Gabrielle normally craved being the center of attention, but she was a bit uncomfortable as the subject of that particular event. "Well, the Negro was making some very inflammatory remarks concerning the athletic prowess of the white race."

"No woman could ever beat Jack Johnson," B.D. Robinson said firmly.

Christ, he's starting to sound like Maurice Willets, thought Chris, even though he knew that now the Willetses and Robinsons of the world were irrelevant and would never again be significant enough to irritate him.

"I was in a somewhat altered form at the time," responded Gabrielle in a dry tone.

"That's sick." B.D. Robinson possessed some very solidly set ideas about the roles and permanency of the sexes.

Merrick was patient. "You must understand the world you are entering, Mr. Robinson. Such formerly

concrete identity labels as sex, race"—he gave
Gabrielle a slight, yet meaningful, glance as an indict-
ment of her comically irrational racism—"size,
health, even biological species have little or no meaning for us. I doubt that any member of the association
in the world has refrained from trying life as the
opposite sex for a time, since this represents an
intriguing mystery even to the most psychically sound
of us. The truth is, however, that practically everyone
settles back into the gender of birth, which adds
credence to the theory that our sexual bearings are
imprinted upon our minds while still in the womb. I
myself have been one of the unfortunately few initiated human beings to successfully give birth—which
was an awesomely significant event in my life, though
hardly as fulfilling or desirable as we males are
regularly led to believe by women—but I have no
doubt concerning my masculinity now. Or my femininity during my other lives."

Robinson settled back into his chair muttering
curses, shaking his head, and resisting the attempted
consolation of his concerned sponsor, Lisolette
Sprouling.

Blake had dealt with shape-shifting, switched identities, and related phenomena for most of his life, but
before it had always been from the perspective of a
disbeliever struggling to persuade others to suspend
their own disbelief. He was a writer, and, as real as his
own stories inevitably were to him as he composed
them, he'd never *really* given the ideas a moment of
gullible, unconditional acceptance. He found himself
sweating, embarrassingly so, from his palm that
cupped Meg's hand to the slick flesh beneath his arms
and the insides of his thighs. But this condition didn't
rise from fear or nervousness or exertion or any of the
emotions to be expected in this situation. He was
surfeited with a sort of wild joy.

"So you're inconstant, physically uncommitted,"

Blake said. "You flow from shape to shape like ice melting and refreezing."

"In a way," Merrick agreed, smiling at his choice of words, "but only at our own pleasure. Once an initiate has mastered the force within himself, there are no further involuntary shifts, no Cummings-style bouts of madness, no undesired blending from Jekyll to Hyde. A number of our group have chosen regularly to find a suitable outward appearance and remain in that form, naturally and without conscious effort, for what amounts to a normal human life span. It's something of a seasonal adventure in the overview of our indefinitely extended existences.

"Nara, dear, do you mind if I make a point, using your nineteenth century venture?"

A stunning woman seated close to Nick responded, "Of course I don't mind, Neil."

So he continued, "On December 31, 1862, a staff officer serving under General W.B. Hazen was killed at the Battle of Stone River. A tragedy, certainly, but hardly a unique one in that most horrible of wars. Nara Beckley, a child of only seventy or so at the time, was passing as a civilian woman, and for various reasons she decided to spend time as an active participant in the conflict, which meant assuming the form of a man. Pre-liberation days, you know.

"The dead officer, his uniform, and his papers were all at her disposal, so it was an eminently simple matter to assume his identity. For more than fifty years, our little Nara faced each sunrise as a man who, through her talents as an author, gained some measure of fame, and it wasn't until 1913 that she tired of the routine and made a renowned 'mysterious' exit."

She couldn't be! Blake gasped silently. *Not him*!

"It's almost impossible for me to equate sunny Nara Beckley with a man who became known as 'Bitter Bierce,' but for a time she was writer Ambrose Bierce."

"I don't believe it," someone whispered.

"Examine the work," Nara suggested. "Nearly all of my output dealt with either war or reincarnation, and one of my stories called 'A Resumed Identity' came as close as I dared to spelling out the entire truth, even to the degree of including the date and location of the real Bierce's death and describing 'his' return to physical existence. Read it."

"I have," Blake said, "and I've never thought of it, but, good Lord, you're absolutely right! You *were* . . . I have so many questions to ask you—"

Neil good-naturedly rapped the lectern with his knuckles to turn aside the mounting dissonant excitement. "There will be plenty of time for personal exchanges following the meeting. If you can endure one more personal anecdote, I believe that I can wipe away any lingering doubts." He stepped away from the lectern and the microphone, which he didn't need, in any case. "Does anyone here find my name familiar?" His slight smile indicated that he was enjoying every moment of the presentation. He prompted them, "Merrick."

"Neil Merrick," Chris repeated.

"Drop the 'Neil' and substitute 'John.'"

"John Merrick," Blake said. Then his eyes lit with realization. "John Merrick! The Elephant Man!" Everyone present had at least heard of the film based on the life of the tragically disfigured Victorian-era Englishman.

"At your service."

"But he was a real person!" Nick said sharply.

"And Mysterious Dave Mather and Bitter Bierce weren't?" asked Neil.

"That's not what I mean, I—"

"I know, I know. You mean to say that you've *heard* of the other two, but you've *seen* the Elephant Man, if only in the cinema. The film's artists did a reasonable job portraying the simulated fibroid tumors that I had decided upon, but, of course, it was only cinematic trickery. If memory serves me, I looked somewhat like this." In seconds and with the casual magic that Grandillon had displayed in showing his werewolf form, a healthy and attractive middle-aged man transformed into a pitiable figure wrapped in spongy masses of fungoid flesh, with a head larger than a basketball and a mass of bone protruding from the mouth so roughly that it inverted the upper lip and forced an almost continuous stream of drool from beneath it. Because he looked so awfully human and vulnerable, to many, this metamorphosis carried more adverse impact than had Tristan's lycanthropic change, and the responses reflected this revulsion.

For some, the reaction was surprisingly related to anger. They had been touched by the descriptions of John Merrick's nightmarish existence of a century before, and to discover that, according to this man who already had revealed so much to them this evening, he had been an *intentional* object of gaping disgust seemed like a betrayal of their compassion. It was a subtle reaction, though, so that no one openly expressed resentment.

Meg came close. "I can't believe that you *chose* to spend years like that. With all of the people who have no option but to live with disabilities day by day, while you can be anything that you happen to fantasize about . . . It's incredible! How could you choose something like that?"

As she had spoken, Merrick had been drifting back to his more normal appearance, sort of like an image regaining clarity through a leisurely focused lens. "Variety," he replied. "Why did Nara decide to become a soldier in the midst of a vicious civil war or Robert Waldron a black man during the nadir of slavery? Dear, when a lifetime is measured in centuries, a few years of moderate discomfort are entirely worth the effort if the payment is a new experience."

"So you became a freak for thirty years—"

"Not so long. Six or seven at most."

Blake felt like the schoolboy who has caught his teacher in a mistake. Quickly, he said, "Neil, I don't mean to be impudent, but we have records of John's life, and he was at least twenty in 1884, when Frederick Treves first met him. He'd been on display for a long time before that." Nara Beckley's appropriation of Ambrose Bierce's identity struck a chord within his memory. "Unless you took over for the real John Merrick."

"I am the 'real' John Merrick," Neil assured him. "The records available to us today are shadowy, contradictory, incomplete, and thoroughly bogus. I was a person of wealth and position in the United Kingdom at that time, so it was simple enough for me to use my power to construct a suitable background. I didn't take up the role until early in '84, but I stayed with it conscientiously until it became annoying and I decided to 'die' in '90."

"That's right, John *died*. He didn't 'fade away' like Bierce or Mather. There are physical remains. I'm sure everyone has heard of the attempts made by Michael Jackson to buy John's skeleton a few years ago."

For the briefest of instants, something like dismay flickered through Merrick's expression, as if he'd moved into an area he had not wanted to explore just yet. But it was gone swiftly. "I provided a corpse. That's another advantage of the initiated. In addition to having control over our own forms, we're able to introduce the force into other bodies, and, if those individuals have not developed the capacity to protect their physical integrity, we actually can change them into whatever shape we decide."

"How, for Christ's sake?" Blake demanded eagerly.

"Those answers will come later. Now, suffice it to say that I left my bed in a secluded portion of the hospital, found another unfortunate patient who actually was passing away at the moment, inoculated him with the force, engineered his transformation into the Elephant Man's identical twin, allowed him to die—as was ordained—in my bed, and, under the cover of his identity, left the hospital. Those remains are quite real, though they are not the original ones."

"You never would have come up with the solution on your own," Gabrielle Secretain observed with a teasing archness.

Deciding to bask in the spotlight for a brief time, she told the assembly of her early brush with death some four hundred years before in France. Actually, this had occurred in July of 1598, and Gabrielle, a very frightened young woman of thirty, stood before the religious front which had been razing Europe in its divinely fanatic search for those who would consort with the devil in order to secure earthly pleasures for themselves. Gabrielle Francoise Secretain already was notorious for her free-spirited and faintly atheistic lifestyle, so when a captured warlock named Jacques Bocquet implicated her in his torture-derived testimony, no one sprang to her defense.

Gabrielle was summarily accused of being both a witch and a werewolf, and the standard round of agonizing inquisition wrung from her a number of confessions to each charge. In reality, one was true: the young woman had already experienced six involuntary transformations into the bestial state following her infection by a fellow libertine three months before. But Gabrielle was as terrified and repulsed by this condition as any of her accusers. Like most of the initiated in those days, she was an Orphan, a lone, isolated, and mortally afraid recipient of the Life form, so she actually viewed her coming execution as something she deserved.

Then, while confined and casually tortured from hour to hour for the entertainment of her "holy" jailers, Gabrielle accomplished a magnificent leap of consciousness. Almost by instinct, she mastered the force within her without instruction.

"I believe perhaps we *do* have an instinct for it," she told the rapt listeners, "or it may be that, somehow, the force does interact with us mentally. All that I can be certain of is that when a young priest came to my cell that day to hear my last confession I had no difficulty at all in taking the man unawares, immobilizing him, infecting him, and then directing the restructuring of his body to match my own while counterfeiting his own for my use. After I switched our clothing, I left the cell a pious soldier of the Lord, and the good father lay in the straw trying to decide just what in the name of that Lord had happened to him." She paused to laugh and fan her face. "My, you should have *heard* the things he screamed while his confederates piled on the faggots!" She burst into more laughter and was joined by many of those about her.

But not everyone felt amused by the image of the fire consuming the transformed priest. Amid the thundering flood of impossibilities that they were being asked, forced, to face in that limited amount of time, it was not easy to submerge and ignore the ugly tangent activities undertaken by the associates. There was the fact that Joseph Logan had used his abilities for his own entertainment by killing other human beings in his gunfighting days, just as Neil Merrick had wallowed in both the disgust and pity of other people after designing his body to incite those responses, again for personal amusement.

Just as disconcerting were the ways in which Neil and Gabrielle had chosen to escape their conditions. Merrick had found an already-dying fellow patient— by a mere stroke of luck?—who just happened to expire on time after being changed to provide the world with a deceased Elephant Man. Gabrielle's situation had been much more desperate and had come down to self-preservation, but there was the delight which she displayed when remembering how the confused, terrified, and possibly completely blameless priest had screamed while being burned to death.

And on top of this, it seemed close to certain that each associate, each *werewolf*, had killed at least one or two innocent people before mastering the infection which made them killers even as it offered them immortality.

It was left up to the youngest person in the room to ask the most incisive question. "Why?"

Merrick looked a bit startled. "Pardon me?"

Chris elaborated, "Why are you telling us this? You said yourself that you've belonged to a secret society for centuries now, and it's clear that most of you don't give a damn about ordinary people, so what's the purpose of this meeting? I can't believe that you just felt like talking to outsiders tonight."

"As always, you cut right to the heart of the matter, young man." Neil rested his elbows upon the lectern. "So I'll give you a direct answer. We are a dying race."

A middle-aged black woman who had said nothing all evening looked betrayed by the admission and blurted out, "But you said that you were immortal! You said that this—this condition cured all other kinds of diseases, even cancer!"

Merrick calmed her with a smile. "That's right, Doreen, it does. No simple germ or virus can survive within the same host as the force. But you're getting ahead of me.

"Lycanthropes have never represented much of a percentage of the world's population, despite our physical advantages. During the insane religious purges of the fourteenth through seventeenth centuries, the vast majority of those slaughtered were innocent men and women and children but they got some of us. Just about wiped us out, in fact. So we went undercover, so to speak, and avoided bringing suspicion upon ourselves, which would have been inevitable had we recruited others. We remained small, secret, and safe.

"It became a habit, one that spread globally. There are members of our group in every nation, but all together the total would probably fall short of five thousand. In the United States, only thirty-two people are fully empowered partners in the association, though, from Mr. Corbett's account, we now have reason to believe that an even greater number are held captive at the Institute."

"With one escapee," Tristan Grandillon observed.

Merrick nodded toward Nick Grundel. "Correct, with one escapee. Welcome to the club, brother." When Nick made no reply, he went on, "For the past hundred and fifty years or so, we associates have held reunions such as this one, so that we can commune with one another, make plans that concern our continued survival and prosperity, propose new members for induction at the next reunion, and welcome a select few number of people into our fold. Immortal or not, we unfortunately lose the occasional associate to some catastrophic accident such as an airline crash or a powerful explosion, so we bring in others who have proven themselves over the preceding five years to fill the void.

"Usually, the number is small, four or five at the highest. The lucky ones this time are Charles Gladden, Audrey Straus, and Leslie Brundage." He motioned to the three beaming faces near the rear of the room.

Chris felt a cold shaft jabbing up his spine. Audrey Straus was the young maid with whom he had become intimate during his stay at the mansion, but he'd had no idea that she was infected, though, naturally, he hadn't even believed in anything like werewolves then.

"The circumstances have changed, however, as they are wont to do," Merrick observed. "You see, we had strong suspicions that Cummings was one of our Orphans, so we planted a spy in the Institute on the night of his scheduled change. Rosalie Moorcroft was an intelligent and competent young woman from whom, unfortunately, we have heard nothing since December. This leads us to believe that either she was killed by Cummings, a very unlikely event due to her own abilities, or she was recognized as a carrier of the force during the quarantine. Should this latter prove to be true, it follows that the world now accepts the reality of our existence. And general disbelief has long been our greatest protection."

"Which means that now that you've told us, we're dead," B.D. Robinson said. One more gasp swept the room.

Merrick rushed to dispel the fear. "Don't be foolish! We've invited you here to *replenish* our number! The days of simply maintaining a population against occasional losses are gone. None of us have any doubts that an intensive government search for more lycanthropes is already under way, and, in the event that some of us will be trapped in that net, we recognize the need to expand our society drastically. At a policy meeting a few days ago, it was decided that everyone who had made contact with a suitable candidate for initiation would bring that person to the lake immediately, rather than going through the usual nominating process. Including Ms. Talley, Mr. Corbett, and Mr. Grundel, who would have to be taken under our wing, in any case, there are twenty-four uninitiated people present tonight, and for a large number of you, this is the first time you've heard of the offer we wish to make."

"You want to turn us into *werewolves*?" someone asked incredulously.

Neil's expression allowed just the briefest flash of discomfort. "We want to share with you immortality. We want you to possess the limitless benefits to be found within our sphere of existence. We want you to be our brothers and sisters."

"And what if we say no?" Chris asked.

"Then you'll be compensated for the time spent here and allowed to return to your former lives, with only an oath of secrecy requested of you." Merrick's reply was swift and, perhaps, convincing. "But don't make that mistake, Christopher. Don't deny yourself this rarest of gifts merely because you have a mistaken concept of some sort of original sin. The past should no longer have a hold on you, and once you realize the complete mastery of your own form, you can make a new beginning anywhere and as whomever you wish."

"To live forever," Blake said in a low breath.

"But we'd have to become *monsters*!" Kim Ownsby argued fearfully. "I don't want to kill anybody!"

"You won't. The indoctrination will take place right here in the mansion, in chambers where you'll be unable to escape and injure anyone else. The five-year apprenticeship that Charles and the others have gone through has been used for some ninety years in order to instruct the new initiate, to show him how to control his abilities and never to fall prey to involuntary seizures. But with drastic new techniques, including hypnosis and drug therapy, we feel that we can slash this time period to months, perhaps even weeks. You'll have to go through your feral episodes a few times upon inoculation and for a full moon or two, but you won't kill anyone and, believe me, the prize is worth the effort."

"That's all?" Chris had learned early to question every "worthwhile" offer. "For all of this power, we just promise to keep the bloodline alive outside of some military complex? There's nothing else we'll have to do?"

For a long moment, Neil didn't answer and the eyes of the associates sought each other. Then Neil responded, "That's all you'll need to know to make your decision. That and a little time."

"How much time?" asked a man who already knew his decision.

"Shall we say twenty-four hours? Following dinner tomorrow night?"

"A night and a day to make a decision that will change our lives forever," Blake observed. "I don't know if I'm up to it."

"At least you've got a choice," Nick pointed out. But in spite of his characteristic acerbity, the young man felt something that had left him with a cold hole in the center of his chest half a year before disappearing. Instead of a future of running, hiding, and praying to no God that he believed in that he wouldn't become a murderer, now he had hope.

Maybe like the old Elephant Man had claimed, it would prove to be worth it all.

The operation took place later that night, and Tristan Grandillon supervised it.

It was association policy that at least one duly empowered Class-One associate take command of any situation which involved another Class One, but no one else bothered to volunteer for the job. They knew that action and violence-loving Grandillon wouldn't be left out of a situation like this one. Naturally, any and all of the Ones could have witnessed the execution had they so desired, but aside from Tristan the other members of the long-lived race avoided even the thought of death whenever they could.

Grandillon brought a recruited squad of Twos and Fives with him to the holding cell, though. It was a good training procedure, he felt.

"Good evening, Mr. Grandillon," said Jackie Kline, the Class-Two man who had been the single guard at the cell since Dom Poduano's arrival. Now he was smiling rather like a retarded child, in Tristan's estimation, but that could have been ascribed to his nervousness. This was a momentous event.

"Kline," Grandillon replied. "Is everything in readiness?"

"Of course, sir. Awaiting your directives."

Grandillon stopped before the video screens, all of which were in operation, and gazed at the figure which was trapped on the other side. Dominic Poduano seemed to have regressed even further than Tristan had anticipated. The man stood no more than inches away from several of the mounted cameras and pounded his bleeding fists into them with an endless ferocity while his mouth was rounded in a wild scream. Grandillon flipped on the sound switch, but rather than the piercing mixture of wailing rage and terror that he had expected to hear, all that came from the cell was a sort of desperate panting, as if Poduano had no voice at all. Odd.

"Mr. Grandillon," said one of the Twos, "why does he look so strange? Like he's—I don't know, like he's unfinished or something?"

"Progressive degeneration," Tristan answered in an off-handed tone. "Probably slipped into a Class-Three phase at the beginning of a transformation and froze his vocal equipment at the same instant. And a Class-Three designation comprises what, Ms. Crawford?" His voice became stern, like a strict teacher's.

Vania Crawford was taken by surprise, but she recovered swiftly. "A Class Three is an initiated person whose body has lost the capacity to host the Life form, therefore they freeze in the last active metamorphosis. Usually permanently."

Tristan smiled slightly. "Very good, Crawford."

A question nagged at her. "As a Class Three, Mr. Poduano is incapable of changing any more, so he's no threat to the association, is he? Should we go through with the execution?"

"Would *you* want to live like that?" Grandillon had asked virtually the same thing of the amorphic blob found in the trunk of Poduano's car. "Well, let's not cause the poor bastard any more anguish than necessary. Kline, would you do the honors?"

The youthful-looking, husky guard nodded. "Thank you, sir." He glanced down at the rows of switches that controlled the fate of the man sealed in the next room. He flipped a pair with confidence.

Inside the cell, jets of a glittering gas spewed from recessed nozzles located in the walls at face level. One stream shot directly into the captive's face and drove him staggering toward the center of the room, with his would-be screams tearing from his throat so violently that each of the witnesses felt sympathetic pain. Where the silvery gas had touched his face, neck, chest, and arms, the man's body responded by producing a blowing gas of its own, but in this case the gas was the result of his cellular structure exploding at the touch of the awful metal.

"What in the hell is that gas made of?" one of the observing Twos asked, forgetting in his awe the standard mode of address when speaking to a superior.

Grinning at the vision of it, Grandillon didn't seem to mind this breach of etiquette. "Basically it's an aerosol propellant, something like freon, but it's impregnated with atomized silver."

Just the thought of contact with that was enough to cause phantom pain in the viewers.

In the cell, the captive lurched to the middle of the room before he stopped and removed his hands from his face. Through the cloud of white smoke that clung to his upper body as his flesh dissolved, the witnesses could see that his eyes had boiled from their sockets and ran like hot grease down his face, joined by the remains of his nose, into his open mouth. That mouth still shrieked its only sound, though it no longer had a tongue or lips. His hands and arms had been eaten to the bone in a number of patches by the gas, as well.

"For Christ's sake, do we have to do it to him that way?" A woman sighed as she looked away.

"How else?" Tristan replied conversationally. "Fire? That would take much longer and be more painful. Crushing? Drowning? Old Dominic is a cunning fox who can spread even the matter of his brain as thin as paste while absorbing oxygen from water more efficiently than any fish."

"But this is like torturing him to death, squirting that damned gas at him when he staggers into range."

"The gas is merely a technique for directing the subject away from one area and into another. Watch. Kline."

The guard selected a switch and threw it into operation.

"Ah, yes," whispered Tristan.

The floor of the cell seemed to split down the middle as the interlocking sections parted and drew back into the walls. Several cameras were trained at the correct angles to reveal the mirrory, concave surface of a huge bowl beneath it. No one asked; they knew that this was another segment of the execution which involved the only known element that was invariably deadly to lycanthropes.

The movement of the floor threw the captive off balance, and he stepped into the widening gap. His naked foot came down on the silver coating and erupted in a new geyser of spewing vapor. Before he could hurl himself blindly back onto the receding floor, a full inch of flesh was seared from the sole upward. He fell, rolling in agony, while the floor carried him ever nearer the nozzles that encircled the room.

"I've got to get out of here," said a woman. She turned to the corridor behind them.

Grandillon didn't break contact with the screens. "Qualen, unless you wish to repeat last year's lesson in extended transmogrification, I suggest you remain at your post."

"Please, Mr. Grandillon—"

"This is an object lesson, children. A display such as this will permanently impress upon your consciousness what you face as members of the initiated. That cursed metal can do this to *any* of us, no matter what class, if we're careless or stupid, and that fact needs to live with us during every second of our existence." It was a harsh, serious lecture, but each student saw the gleam of deep pleasure in his eyes, eyes that remained fixed on the victim's disintegrating body.

Somehow, the dying man found the strength to stagger to the video cameras once more, but Grandillon glanced to Kline, who touched yet another button on the control panel. The nozzle closest to the prisoner expelled its contents directly into his chest this time, and he jerked away so violently that it appeared as if he had been knocked backwards by the blast from a cannon. He landed on his back and slid across the floor until the rear of his head fell into the opening of the silver-lined depression and bounced onto the metal. White vapor spumed upward as the rest of his body jerked wildly.

As he tried to escape the death trap, the bones of his hands and arms, his flesh having dissolved completely now, made loud clicking noises on the floor and began to break away amid the flow of blood from his remaining body. He slipped over the lip into the shiny bowl.

The captive didn't submit to death easily. There

came the fiery radical reaction between his flesh and the silver, of course, and the clouds of smoke that this produced, but what seemed to affect the witnesses in the next room even more was the way his melting muscles spasmed with extraordinary power as they died.

The man was thrown totally clear of the bowl a number of times by this mindless convulsing, so that he resembled, in a remotely lunatic fashion, a dolphin playfully leaping in the ocean. The first several jerks took him as much as six feet above the level of the floor, but each time that he dropped into contact, the silver ate away more tissue, blood, and bone with accompanying frying-meat noises, so that the reactions became weaker. Finally, what was left of the man lay at the bottom of the bowl and dissolved like an ice cube on a hot griddle amid blowing sheets of steam.

Tristan made certain that his people watched it all, even though this display of mortality in a Class-One associate might have served to lessen his stature in their eyes. Naturally, no one said anything to that effect to him. The procedure took almost five minutes, and the impact that it made on them was hardly lessened near the end when nothing remotely human was sizzling down there in the damned recesses of the bowl. Seeing tiny flaps of living flesh writhe and twist torturously was pretty devastating in its own right.

What was left eventually was a room-filling haze that consisted of a mixture of the silver gas and the oxidized remains of Dominic Poduano.

"Done," Grandillon pronounced the result firmly. "I know that it was a difficult matter to view, but there are some things which have to be faced, even though they tear at our emotions." He didn't seem to be in the least upset at the loss of an old friend. "Kline, we'll be leaving you now. Please clear the cell of any remaining noxious gases and then see that the staff gives it a thorough cleaning."

"Certainly, sir," answered Kline.

"A copy of the videotape of this event should be placed in the permanent library for future reference," Tristan added. "An unfortunate situation such as this would make a difference in the way we associates guard our physical and mental integrity if it were required viewing."

"I do agree, sir. It will be taken care of, I assure you."

When Kline was alone in the observation room again, except for the nearly constant cries of the provisions kept in the cells of the adjoining room, he took a moment to look in satisfaction at the misty residue of Dominic Poduano. But that was not Dominic Poduano swirling into eternity in there.

Jackie Kline had been a young man, twenty-eight, and a very inexperienced one, so when he had checked the holding cell earlier in the day to find it empty, he had entered the room, alone. He was afraid that Poduano's escape would be blamed on him, so he had wanted to at least discover the method of the jailbreak before he reported it.

Kline had been struck dumb when the shadow-thin Poduano had dropped from the ceiling to envelop and overpower him. Within seconds, he had been left physically altered and completely mute by the insane, but still quite wily, four hundred-sixty-four-year-old Italian. Naturally, Poduano had left the cell, wearing both Kline's clothing and his form, and now stared at his successful operation.

Poduano hadn't known Kline at all, but he believed that he was a fine enough actor to play the role of a servile Class Two for as long as was needed to enact his own developing scenario. Kline's drawn-out and horrible death had tasted sweet to him, like the fine grains of sugar tasted when biting into a buttery pastry. Not because the victim had been Jackie Kline, but because Kline had been one of *them*, one of the new enemy sworn to destroy Dominic Poduano. They were all enemies now.

Dom switched on the strong fans which rapidly cleared the room of the silver gas and the soul of one Jackie Kline.

PART THREE:
The Payoff

CHAPTER FIFTEEN

Dinner was over, the meeting was concluded. The regal associates, their servants, and thirteen of their invited guests had departed to other sections of the huge house. But in a relatively small and isolated den near the rear of the mansion, eleven people contemplated the decision that would redefine the directions of their lives. For all of the gasping and voiced disbeliefs of a half hour before, this gathering was remarkably subdued. Or stunned.

"I suppose that you might not even want me here," Nick stated while he cradled a glass of Scotch on the rocks in both hands.

"Of course we want you here, Nick," Meg said. "Why shouldn't we?"

"Because I'm not one of 'us.' I'm one of them. My decision's made already. In fact, I never really had a decision. I have to take their offer."

"You're *really* a werewolf," Doreen Shelby said quietly, as if to try to persuade herself of that truth.

"That's right," he answered, nodding. "Since Cummings tore off my left hand six months ago in the Institute." He gazed at its replacement idly. "I grew another during the first change a month later in January."

"You've actually been through it? Changed, I mean?" Of the twenty-four guests invited to the reunion by the associates, thirteen had been fully aware of the society and its designs on them before their arrival at the island. But, like the other ten people in the room, Doreen had been ignorant of the reasons that her fiancé had insisted that she attend this secretive gathering with him. Doreen was sixty-two, a widowed mother of four and grandmother to nine, and a decent, loving woman who never would have dreamed of entering the ranks of the most feared segment of humanity in all of history. But she also was suffering from terminal bone cancer.

Nick responded to her question. "Six times, ma'am, though, thank God, I was safely locked up during each one."

"What's it like?" interrupted Lon Wicker, another protégé who had been unaware of his status before tonight.

"Like nothing you can imagine, brother."

"Do you have any memory of it, the next day?"

Nick sighed. "Nothing at first, but lately, since the fourth or fifth time, I have been able to—"

Doreen turned the conversation back to the element which most interested her. "The changing heals you of everything, right? Any injury or disease?"

"I guess so. I only know I haven't had so much as a cold in the past six months."

"Even cancer?"

"Yeah."

"Well, that makes my decision for me, too. Unless I take advantage of the offer, I won't be alive in three months to accept another one."

Nick placed his hand on Meg's arm. "Yours may be more or less a moot point, as well, babe. I was worried that I might infect you, but, as usual"—his voice choked slightly with emotion—"I thought with my gonads instead of my brain."

"Don't, Nick," she told him quietly but in a forgiving tone. "It was my decision, too."

"You may not be infected at all," Blake pointed out. "These people, with all of their resources, must have a test to determine who is carrying the disease and who isn't."

"I know they use some kind of test at the gate," Chris said. "When Neil and I got here a couple of weeks ago, he had to go inside the guard booth and recite a poem or something while Chester Jefferson compared his voice with an earlier recording."

"More probably his brain waves were checked against those definitely known to belong to Neil Merrick while reciting the same piece of poetry to verify his claimed identity," Blake muttered, extrapolating as he spoke. "When you can change into anyone you wish, thought, voice patterns, photographs, fingerprints, none of these things retain their validity. But that kind of examination wouldn't tell us if Meg has the disease."

"It probably doesn't matter, anyway," she said.

Blake shook his head. "You should have all of the facts, know all of your options, before you make a decision that's clearly the most important of your life, Meg."

"What I mean is that we may not have any real options at all. I doubt that we'll be leaving this island knowing what we know unless we agree to share in the infection."

B.D. Robinson snorted. "Merrick said that we wouldn't be kept here. Hell, he even said we'd be paid for attending!"

"Do you believe everything you hear, man?" asked

Chris darkly. Still, the younger man realized that his decision might have been made for him, and who knew how many of the others had been sexually intimate with their sponsors, even as he and Audrey had?

Lon Wicker didn't seem upset by the prospect of forced recruitment. "So what if they make us take the disease? What would that mean? That we'll live forever? That we can get all of the money we want any time that we need it by turning into a bank president and carrying a load from the vault?" This aspect, too, appeared to hold no ambivalent feelings for him. "Shoot, man, if that's the down side of the situation, tell me what's better?"

"I think I sense a pattern in our choices," Nick whispered to Meg with a dry laugh.

"One more thing," Chris said, as he stood before leaving the room. "They're not telling us everything."

"What do you mean?" Elizabeth Chynnara was another of the group, who was at the point of stepping into an irrevocable direction in her life, but unlike Wicker she wanted to know all of the facts.

Chris rubbed the back of his neck wearily. Emotional abuse can be as wearying as the physical kind. "I don't know, and I probably should have kept my mouth shut. But when Neil was talking to us, I got the idea that there was something—something very important and very bad—that he was intentionally keeping from us. At least until it's too late for us to change our minds." The irony of that phrase struck a twisted nerve connected with his sense of humor, and he grinned secretly.

"Don't be so damned paranoid, boy," Wicker advised. Like the others, he knew nothing of Chris's awesome physical prowess, so he dealt with the younger man with the accepted lack of respect for youth.

Chris was no unpredictable force of nature, though. He simply shrugged and walked toward the door. "I think I'll sleep on it. No reason to make hasty judgments when we've got so much time to reach our own conclusions, right?" He left the room without another word.

"Stupid little bastard," Wicker mumbled. "Stirs up trouble and then struts out on us."

I know what he was talking about, Blake realized. For a moment, he wondered if he'd said that aloud. *I know their secret.*

But the part of him which was so dazzled by the promises that had been made shoved this knowledge deeply into the blackness of his own mind before he could grasp it. Immortality. At the heart of everything wasn't *that* and only that what every writer who'd ever taken up a pen was struggling for? To live beyond life, to touch the consciousness of another person even past the time when death should have come and according to Neil's promises, this immortality could be achieved *without* ever facing death.

In all of his dozens of horror novels, with their hundreds of ravening monsters, A.B. Corbett had identified with the supernatural element only to the extent of establishing his characters. He'd never dreamed of himself as a part of that element.

But the temptations, oh God, the temptations! Could anyone resist them? Certainly not Blake Corbett.

The induction ceremony in another part of the mansion went smoothly enough, though not without disappointment.

Leslis Brundage and Audrey Straus moved easily from the status of five-year apprentices to full membership in the association. Their commitment to the organization had been thoroughly proven during their terms as servants, and their command of the metamorphic properties of their own bodies was easily proven on call before the Ones who were selected to test them. Now they, too, were Ones.

Charles Gladden was not so lucky. His devotion to the association was not questioned. He may have been the best initiate who had ever apprenticed at Caprice Island. But his accomplishment as a shape-changer was not so impressive. In fact, it was discovered that he had become a static Class Two. He didn't slide below that level to where his body mutated uncontrollably or into a state where his body's environment became hostile to the Life form and acted to rid itself of all traces of the disease. He retained his extraordinary strength, stamina, and speed of self-repair.

"But don't worry, Charles," they told him, "your proficiency in handling the household staff will insure that you'll have a position here for as long as you wish."

A "position." A servant's position.

Chris shut off the climate control to his room and opened a window before he slid into bed. He liked the smell of the night air as it came in over the water.

Of course, he knew that he wouldn't be getting any sleep at all tonight. With his head ablaze with the things he'd learned in the past couple of hours, he might just as well have tried to take a midnight stroll on the bottom of the lake out there as fall asleep.

Could he believe it? Monsters *did* exist, he'd seen them himself. They roamed city streets, especially after dark, with blades in their fists and chemical madness surging through their veins and they sat, caged and festering, in the jail cells that he had been tossed into when his own inner monstrousness had spilled out. Sometimes the monsters even rose to rule entire nations.

But Chris could understand those monsters. Hell, he'd lived with them all of his life.

Werewolves?

Could he deny what he had been told? Sure, he had

heard about Gerald Cummings last year, but he had never wasted a moment's time considering that the press's wild speculations about a *real* mythological beast savaging the modern world could be based in truth. A lot of people before Cummings had successfully engaged in mass slaughter without resorting to supernatural assistance, so what reason had there been to suspect that this psycho was special?

Tonight, though, damn. . . .

He knew drugs well enough to be certain that he wasn't high when the associates went into their phantasmagorical series of mutations. That *had* happened. But because they could change their shapes, did it necessarily follow that they were werewolves?

Chris's sudden, explosive laughter seemed to shatter the darkness that enclosed him.

"No, jughead," he said sardonically, "they aren't werewolves, just your garden-variety Greek-fabled shape-shifters."

As if his words had awakened someone else in the house, a brief knock came at his door. Chris was a little startled, since each room had an intercom system and he hardly expected a visit from anyone at that time of night. Switching on the bedlamp, he said, "Yes?"

The knock came again.

Chris propped himself on his elbows. "Yeah? Who is it?"

The only response was the knock once more.

"Come in."

The door opened slowly, and he knew at once from the long, black-stockinged leg that moved into the light that his visitor was one of the household maids. The otherwise elegant and usually understated associates required that their serving girls dress in almost caricatured French maid fashion; Chris had the sneaky suspicion that Grandillon was behind the rule.

Why was the maid here this late? A complimentary

late-evening snack? The last maid who had come to his room at this hour had been Audrey Straus, who, as of tonight was no longer a mere servant.

It was Shannon Kent. The long, reddish-blond hair and sparkling green eyes seemed to glow in the dull yellow radiance of the lamp, and Chris felt himself breaking into a smile at the sight of her.

"Hi, Shannon," he said. "What can I do for you?" Then he recalled her hearing handicap and felt ashamed once more.

But she seemed to understand; maybe she *did* read lips. With an odd expression on her face, a mixture of resolve and regret, though not at all unflattering, she stepped into the room and quietly shut the door. Then she walked to the bed, looked down at him, pointed first to him and then to herself, and placed her hands together, fingers intertwined.

Chris got that message, all right. All right! But, as always, he had second thoughts created by the way she had reacted to him in the bar not so long ago.

Looking up into that lovely, questioning face, it was as difficult as walking through fire for him to reply, "Shannon, if this has anything to do with this afternoon, when I decked Gladden, you don't owe me any kind of repayment." He hoped again that she could read lips, since he certainly didn't know much in the way of legitimate sign language.

In response, she made the coupling motion again.

Chris struggled to keep his head clear. So much of his life had been decided as a result of emotions, his own and others', that he felt the need to maintain a sense of control at all times. Maybe she was so newly receptive to him because she'd discovered that, very soon, he might be a member of the ruling class of this place. He wasn't unaware of the fact that certain "friends" routinely gauged relationships by what they could get out of them.

"Thanks, honey, but I'm not prepared for this right now. Understand? I haven't brought along any protection." He hadn't the slightest idea how he would signal this to her.

She began removing her uniform.

Just how honorable was he supposed to be about this? Then a realization struck him like a golden ray of sunlight breaking through clouds: Shannon didn't know about the lycanthropy! That's why she had been recruited along with other deaf mutes, so that she wouldn't accidentally become aware of her employers' secrets. According to what Neil had said during the gathering in the den, the prospective members of the staff were scrupulously checked to be certain that they weren't proficient in lip-reading. This requirement, of course, was justified under the banner of providing work for those most difficult to employ among the handicapped.

Well, one maid had not been held to those unfortunate standards. He had known from the very first that Audrey Straus was a special case, since she could both hear and speak, and when they had begun a physical relationship he was. . . .

The memory of his nights with Audrey cut short the building sense of triumph, even as Shannon stepped out of her uniform and took away his breath. He knew *now* that Audrey was a lycanthrope-in-training, and their sessions of kissing and sexual involvement may well have made him one, too, without his knowledge or agreement. He couldn't risk doing the same thing to this young woman.

"I can't," he whispered, realizing that she couldn't hear him but hoping that the message came across. He reached out and touched her hand as she began to unfasten the stockings from her garter. He thought that she drew her hand away the least bit from his own. When she looked at him, he shook his head.

Rather than withdrawing, however, she took the initiative by sitting on the bed and stunning him with a tight embrace and an overpowering kiss. Chris knew how he should react; his mind ordered him to turn away and make his reasons perfectly clear to the young woman, but this time the emotions were stronger than the intellect. Maybe he wasn't infectious—or even infected. And if he were, even then, he might be doing her a favor. The disease surely could give her her hearing and a voice.

Naturally, there was no time to put these thoughts into anything like words.

Some time later, as they lay in the darkness together, Chris reached out and found Shannon's shoulder. She was turned away from him and apparently asleep, because she didn't respond to his touch. That didn't matter, though, because he wasn't looking for more sex so much as companionship. Just knowing that there was someone else sharing this particular night with him. His hand remained on her smooth flesh.

"You know," he said, "I think I'll do it. I think I'll take the infection." It was a difficult admission for him to make, steeped as he was in the swamp of his own life. For Chris, the philosophy of, "Live fast, die young, and leave a good-looking corpse," was not so much a personal choice as an unalterable sentence. Until now.

He took a deep breath of the crisp air that seemed so different somehow than at any time in his memory. "I won't be an associate, though. Man, all of this is just as much a cage as the ones the cops toss you into. But starting over somewhere else, not looking like a juvenile delinquent who all of the busybodies on the East Coast are sniffing around for, that would be worth it. And I'm pretty damned sure that Mr. Poor-Me Moaning Jerk, a.k.a. Chris Wyler, will be

able to put those particular new talents to good use
without too much attention." He laughed shortly. All
of this because he'd kicked the legs out from under a
horny, overweight rail bum.

In the dark, he was unable to tell that the young
woman next to him was crying silently into the pillow.

CHAPTER SIXTEEN

"Tonight's the night, then?" Blake asked, displaying a decidedly unoriginal verbal approach to the entirely original situation that he was facing. He, as well as the other ten protégés, had agreed to enter the secret society of lycanthropy.

"The sooner the better," replied Neil Merrick, ready to play the game.

Blake nodded a little nervously. "I just thought that we would wait until the seventeenth, when the next full moon is due."

"That would be appropriate. But with these new chemo-hypnotic techniques which we intend to test on you to educate you to full control over your abilities, it has been decided that immediate inoculation would provide us with those seventeen days of work before your involuntary transformations."

Blake's expression brightened. "Do you mean that we'll never have to go through the change into the most feral basis of our personalities?"

Neil smiled reassuringly at the group. "These new techniques promise to be extraordinarily effective and may reduce the apprenticeship from years to months or perhaps even weeks, but I can't be that optimistic. The seventeenth will still be a period of distress, shall we say. In any case, your initial metamorphosis will also take place tonight."

"Why?" Meg asked quickly. Like Blake and most of the others, she had hoped to bypass the traditional lycanthropic state completely.

"A necessity, I'm afraid." Merrick patted her shoulder the way a father comforts a child. "The first change liberates the Life form throughout the host body. Actually, though it's never been proven or even tested, there exists the remote possibility that an infected person could be cleansed of the force and restored to normalcy if his blood were washed in a kidney-support machine before his first change. Thereafter, it's a lifetime condition."

"Except in the case of a Class Three," added Chris. Merrick had explained the five classes of human beings to them all earlier in the evening.

"Of course."

"How will the infection be administered?" Blake continued.

Merrick had been standing before a discreetly placed bar, and in illustration he picked up a decanter of red wine. "Under ordinary circumstances, something as simple as a sip of infected liquid would suffice, but because we need to induce the first change in each of you, a personal inoculation will be required."

Blake smiled grimly. "Biting, you mean."

"That's an indelicate manner of stating it, but yes. I assure you, it won't be painful. Certainly nothing such as you experienced, Nicholas. This will be rather akin to a sexual experience."

Nick didn't reply directly, but instead stared at Meg

and asked, "Can I volunteer to be one of the 'inoculators'?"

"Sorry, no. You carry the force, naturally, but you don't possess the adroitness. There will have to be some form of intimate contact, Ms. Talley."

"We won't be allowed to hurt anyone else when we—when we change, will we?" she asked. "Any of the staff?"

"Rest assured. Each room will be sufficiently strong to contain you at your most irrational." He set aside the wine and spread his arms before the assembly in a fashion which could have appeared insufferably hammy but which was, in fact, quite comforting. "I realize that all of this must seem frightening to you, but you must trust me when I tell you that very soon it will be remembered as the greatest night of your lives. Take my own case. Attacked and mauled almost to death while walking alone in a remote part of a forest during a very cold February night in 1681, I was so badly hurt that I was unable to crawl from the spot in which I lay for twenty-four hours, until the next nightfall. I suffered all of the unendurable agonies of the near-dead during that time, and I'm convinced that I *would* have died had not the supposed wolf's transformation been voluntary and the next moonrise been a full one. I changed, and therefore I was saved.

"Doesn't sound like much of a beginning to cherish, does it? Yet to this day, I view the episode with a sense of relief. Not just that my life was spared by a thread, but also that the gift of the force was given to me. My one regret is that I never found out who the carrier attacking me that night was in his or her daytime life. I would like to find that person and offer my sincerest gratitude."

"What in the hell are we getting ourselves into?" Meg whispered below her breath to Blake.

"Any other questions?" Merrick asked. No one

responded. "If you will follow me, then, I'll show you to your rooms."

"Just a minute, man," said Lon Wicker. "Don't we get to choose our own partners for this little *tete-a-tete*?"

For the first time since he had met Neil in the stinking freight car, Chris saw genuine rage foaming behind a transparent wall of barely adequate control in Neil's eyes. Merrick took a slow breath, and everyone in the room felt the crackling intensity in the air. "Mr. Wicker," he said evenly, "this service is being performed for you solely due to the graciousness of the members of the association. You are being gifted with the greatest blessing that a human can receive, and it already has been established that each of you prefers heterosexual coupling, so you really have little to say beyond that. When offered eternity, it isn't wise to tweak the nose of the givers, so I hope that you realize that this is not a whorehouse where the employees line up for your convenience." Even after he finished speaking, the atmosphere of the room seemed to ring with his subdued anger.

Wicker coughed. "Uh, okay, sure. Don't get pissed."

Merrick pinned the man in his piercing gaze for a second longer before turning away to lead the procession from the room.

The selected chambers were located in the vast east wing of the mansion, and from the outside they appeared to be no different from any of the bedrooms. What Lon Wicker, in his excitement and arousal, hadn't considered was that most of the initiates would be introduced to the society by the very people who had brought them to the island in the first place, their sponsors. Wicker, Doreen Shelby, Kimberly Ownsby, B.D. Robinson, Elizabeth Chynnarra, Jessie Powers, and Melanie Ryan were met in sequence at the first seven rooms by the women and men whom they'd known as lovers before the previous evening, but never as patrons in this most exclusive of associations.

I guess my "patron" in this thing is Neil, Chris thought as Blake was shown into a room near the end of the corridor, leaving only Meg and himself to be paired with their associates. *This could prove to be a little uncomfortable. What the hell am I thinking? Neil can be anyone he chooses. He had a baby, for Christ's sake. Still . . .*

But the boy's feeling of sexual unease was soothed when Merrick cordially greeted the cool, beautiful woman who already was waiting in the next room. "Christopher, my friend, this is Adine Pierce, who has agreed to be your partner for this evening. She is one of the wisest and most loving individuals our poor race can claim, and you could not be in better hands for the night."

"How do you do, Miss Pierce?" he responded. She was tall, with long, shimmering black hair and equally dark eyes that seemed to reach into his soul and carefully examine what they found there. God, she was beautiful. But, being a Class-One associate, what else would she be?

"Christopher," she said in a low, enchantingly sexy voice. "I have heard quite a lot about you from Neil and Audrey and the others. I'm so glad that you've chosen to join us, and I hope that I can facilitate your passage in some way."

A proper rejoinder failed to leap to his lips, and he could feel himself blushing. To end the discomfort, Adine took his arm in both of her hands, like a woman being escorted in an elaborately old-fashioned style, and drew him into the room with her. Then she shut the door behind them.

Merrick paused for a moment and smiled at the closed door. He was very glad the young man was entering the highly privileged ranks to which he belonged, and though Neil certainly could have performed the rite himself, as Chris had suspected he would, he felt no attraction to the boy aside from strong friendship and empathy. His own youth so long ago had been equally as painful. Besides, with the tremendous realignment in perception that these innocents were facing, Merrick wished to make this initial transition phase as easy as was practically possible.

He knew, of course, about Chris's relationship with Audrey Straus and the boy's belief that he might already be host to the Life form because of that. But Audrey, with five years of training, surely had learned to control her degree of infectiousness in all but the most difficult and intimate of involuntary processes, such as ovulation. Her kisses, and whatever other forms of activity they had engaged in, certainly hadn't offered him any risk.

Neil turned to Meg Talley. Her case was entirely different. "And now our turn has arrived, my dear."

Nick had accompanied them this far, and his bearded face seemed to harden. A true Orphan, Nick possessed all of the potential abilities that Merrick had perfected, yet his very ignorance removed any threat he might have posed to the other man. "Are you sure she has to go through with this?" he grunted.

"Nick, it's all right," Meg said softly, and in none too convincing a tone. Like the others, she was torn between ecstasy and terror. Who had ever prepared herself for going to bed with a werewolf?

"I'm afraid it's entirely necessary, Mr. Grundel," Merrick told them. "To enter the state of salvation requires the opening of the gates." He smiled faintly at his own somewhat bawdy allegory. "But I swear upon my honor that I will be most solicitous and gentle."

"But you said that you—we are infectious even in

our saliva unless we've been trained to control it, and I haven't. Couldn't she already be infected?"

"She almost certainly is." Merrick avoided taking obvious note of Meg's sudden intake of breath. Knowing that something could be true and soon would be true still didn't totally prepare one for the reality of the conclusion.

"Then what's all of this for?" Nick demanded.

"We've been through this," Neil pointed out. "She is going to experience her first change tonight through my direction so that the force can permanently establish itself within her and we may begin her education tomorrow."

"Oh, Lord." Nick sighed.

Meg put her arms around him. In the short time they'd been together something very close to love had grown between them.

"Baby," she whispered to him, "don't worry about me. I know what I'm doing, and when this is finally over, just think of all that we'll have offered to us. Forever. This could be the birth of a whole new species of human beings, and we'll be like the parents. I don't want to go through this without you, but I don't want you to leave me behind, either." She kissed his cheek. "Tell me it's all right."

"You know it is," he answered. "I just wish I could be there to help, so you wouldn't have to go through it alone."

"Some things you just have to face alone, right? And when I change and you don't . . . I couldn't live if I hurt you, Nickie."

He exhaled a laugh that sounded anything but amused. "It's pretty hard to think of myself being in danger from anyone else for once."

Merrick opened the door to the last room. "Shall we go in, Ms. Talley?"

Their hands lingered in one another's for moments

longer, and then she left Nick alone in the hallway and walked into the darkened room which held her future.

Blake Corbett had been alone in his life for a long time. Though he had been married for several years to Beth Dryden, the union had produced no children, so that after their divorce two years ago, he had found himself a solo act once more. He and Beth had remained friends and occasional lovers, however, until the investigation of the Gerald Cummings affair had begun. Their meetings were terminated because Beth didn't enjoy the type of publicity that Blake's werewolf theory had generated. Following the December massacre at the Institute, Blake had been confined to a single room by the government until the next full moon had proven that he had not become a lycanthrope. His imprisonment gave him few opportunities to form a relationship more substantial than those one might imagine with television characters.

After his release, the immensity of the tragedy he had witnessed and the terrible reality of its instigator had caused Blake to withdraw into himself and the small apartment that had become a substitute womb. Then, when he had helped Doug and Meg to rescue Nick from the government, he had been on the run while crossing the country, another circumstance that hadn't invited closeness and companionship.

Meg had been there, of course, but he had come to regard her more as a younger sister or even a daughter and there had been the visible developing connection between Meg and Nick.

For all of those reasons, Blake had become a lonely man, even though he hadn't realized it, and the sight of Gabrielle Secretain reclining on the luxuriously king-sized bed within the room was powerful. She was dressed in an overflowing silken Parisian gown, but its glory faded when compared with the body that it held.

Blake stood in the doorway and stared unabashedly at her elegant breasts and long, stunning legs. She looked like a goddess.

"Come in, please, and close the door," she said.

He obeyed like a robot.

She swung those legs to the carpeted floor and sat up. "Won't you join me?" Without awaiting a reply, she turned to the night table and poured two glasses of wine from a decanter.

Blake crossed the room, feeling as if it were all a dream. Even the lighting contributed to the sensation, as it glowed softly from concealed fixtures near the head of the bed. Gabrielle looked up with a soothing smile glowing in her flawless face, and patted the bed next to her. He sat, and she handed him a glass of wine.

For nearly a minute, they sipped in silence. Her presence next to him was so warm and inviting that even when his nagging conscience tried to thrust to the forefront of his thoughts that this woman was a spiritual sister to Gerald Cummings, he ignored it. And Blake Corbett found it next to impossible to ignore his conscience.

"You know, I've wanted to meet you for some time," Gabrielle said after a while.

"Me?" he asked. The fact that she was both a shape-shifter and the most attractive human being he'd ever seen made Blake's own pretensions to celebrity crumble to dust.

"I find your writing fascinating. Even your werewolf novels are exciting and freshly written." She may have been engaged in subtle game-playing with him, but if so Blake failed to notice. "Your monsters aren't just monsters so much as people swept up by circumstances and trapped by physical laws rather than character flaws. There are times when a person needs to have this reaffirmed, when the memories of less pleasant events surface to cause new wounds." She looked down into her glass.

Blake remembered that she was afflicted with physical and not mental lycanthropy, and that she certainly had been at the heart of a number of awful moments before she had taught herself to control her gift while held in a filthy and primitive prison cell. He wanted to reach out to touch her pale cheek, to reassure her, but he didn't dare. Not yet.

Gabrielle looked at him and beamed with renewed good spirits. "But we have all of the time in the world to talk once you've partaken of the force. Would you like to begin?"

His lips felt as dry as his palms were damp. "Now? Make love, you mean?"

She winked playfully. "Only if that's the manner which you choose. There are other ways, of course."

Blake didn't mean to say anything. He meant to leap up, tear off his clothes, and fall into the sensual joy of her arms, but he heard his voice asking, "What ways?"

She took his glass and sat both of them aside. "Oh, there's the standard way, the way that your friend Grundel experienced. I could bite you." In spite of the mention of Nick's ordeal and the invocation of pain that it carried, her suggestion only increased Blake's arousal. His clothes were beginning to feel very tight. "But that's terribly primitive. Or I could be the efficient practical nurse and use a syringe to inject you with a bit of my activated blood. Do you like medical fantasies?"

For an instant, Blake couldn't answer. "Uh, well, not really."

Gabrielle knew exactly what she was doing to him, and it gave her as much pleasure as he received. "Then there is the really disgusting one. I could spit into your wine and have you drink it."

That was going a little too far, however. "No, I don't think so."

"Good." She laughed. "You have to carry out those last two very quickly, anyway, since the force can't survive outside the body for more than a few seconds. Even in the best of wines."

Again Blake spoke without meaning to. "That's not true in every case, you understand. Cummings, before he changed that last night, told us that he was infected by a powdery substance that he was forced to drink down in Santa Rosalia. It contained the crystallized saliva of a werewolf who had been killed twelve years before."

"Interesting," she said in a tone that contradicted the statement. "You should tell this to Neil or Tristan."

"I will. It's amazing that we've discovered something that your association hasn't been able to for hundreds of years—"

"Who cares?" Gabrielle whispered. She touched the bulge in Blake's trousers and neither of them said anything else.

She was more beautiful naked than he had believed possible. Her passion gave him no chance to have second thoughts or doubts. He didn't dwell on the morality of what he was doing, or the physical condition into which he was entering, or the people that Gabrielle had killed when she had transformed into a beast before discovering how to control her talent, or the stupefied priest who had died at the stake in her place. He didn't even think about immortality.

They rolled on the soft bed, experiencing every facet of each other. Blake tasted her lips, her breasts, her thighs and wonderous seat of femininity, and she did things to him that he had never even read in the few pornographic books he'd seen. Time meant nothing now. The moment was all, and the world in which death and responsibility resided no longer even existed.

For the very first instant since that night when he had watched Cummings metamorphose into something other than human, Blake burst through the gathered blackness into freedom.

He came three times within the span of a couple of hours. It wasn't a competition, naturally, and he wasn't keeping count, but Gabrielle's aggressiveness meshed perfectly with his own drives and needs, to lift him to a level that he had never suspected. All of his fear and desperation became sexual energy that she accepted from him with a love that left him drained, exhausted, and entirely content. As he lay on his back, he didn't even feel that he had cheated on Beth, for a change.

"You're wonderful," he said quietly in the aftermath. "That was the most amazing time . . . I've never been with anyone like you before." Nor had he ever experienced such sexual satisfaction either. His male ego whispered that *she* should be telling *him* these things, but he just told his ego to shut up.

Her hands began to caress his neck. "Is that all for tonight, darling?" she asked.

Blake was torn by conflicting emotions. In one way he was pretty darned sure that it was all for tonight, or at least for some hours; in another way, he felt like praying that Gabrielle would arouse him to more glorious activity. He said, "I don't know, baby. What do you think?"

"There will be plenty of other nights for us, Blake, all the nights in the world." She seemed to enjoy that phrase.

Grinning, Blake allowed himself the small conceit. "If you're tired . . ."

She rolled atop him, still massaging his neck. "Let's finish it, then."

Confused, he said nothing until he felt her warm

breath washing over the right side of his neck. "Hey, wait a minute. Let me get over a bit—"

"Just lie still, my darling," she told him. "I'll take care of this."

"Take care of what?"

"The second part of the session. Your change."

Panic sparkled deep in Blake's soul. The sheer somatic bliss that had pervaded him during their lovemaking receded like the tide, and the void was filled by his old friends, fear and dread. "I thought I was infected already by the kisses and—"

"You are, dear, the force is racing through your system like sunshine driving away the night."

As if in response, his entire body reacted with a tiny, but perceptible, shiver.

Gabrielle laughed softly. "Don't worry. Soon enough that knowledge will warm the core of you better than any lover could. Now—"

"You're going to change me?" he asked.

"I'll incite it. You'll change. It's not like the changes that are made in most other cases, where one initiated body takes control over a second and causes it to mimic the metamorphosis of the first. The Life force within you now is capable of creating this basic change at any time if something in your subconscious triggers it, something like the rising of the full moon. The moon has no physical effect on us at all. It's what you *think* about the moon that activates the inner person. In the old days, the phases of the moon meant nothing to us."

"But you have to bite me?"

"Only this much." She kissed his neck quickly and he gasped. "See how the thought of it raises your emotional awareness. For some people, that would be enough to begin the transformation just by itself. A slight nip, with no real pain, will start the proper emotional reactions."

"I don't want to hurt you, Gabrielle."

"Don't worry, love. I'll be well away before you lose total control."

"Oh, my God, I don't know if I can . . ."

What else could he say? It was too late for words now, anyway, the infection was already breeding inside him. He closed his eyes and rolled back his head to expose his throat to her. As a writer and a horror buff for most of his life, he was immediately reminded of the thousands of spotless maidens who had given their necks to vampire lovers, but this was distinctly different. Of course, he was neither a maiden nor spotless, and this was no fictional vampire drawing off his life in exchange for a moribund nocturnal existence.

No, Gabrielle was giving, not taking.

The three lay in remarkably similar poses, waiting. In sound-proofed rooms, they rested on soft beds as thirteen of their fellows had reclined the night before, knowing to an extent what to expect.

Neil Merrick had been kind with Meg, as he had promised, but she knew that the lovemaking hadn't really been necessary. He could have inoculated her with his teeth, which he had to use to incite the first change in her, anyway. Also, there was the fact that in all probability she had picked up the infection from Nick.

She felt frightened and excited, as did Chris and Blake, but she also recognized a faint sensation of victimization. Had she been raped? No, she couldn't trivialize that awful crime against women by equating it with what she had just done, because she had offered her body to Merrick in exchange for what he would bestow upon her. If anything, it was more prostitution than rape.

Chris held on to the remnants of the best sex he'd

ever experienced and alternated this terrific feeling with anticipatory joy at what was promised him and cold fear. What if he proved to be a Class Five, unable to host the disease? Then he'd be no worse off than he was now. What if he were a Two? In that case, he'd hit the road again as soon as possible, because he sure as hell wasn't going to spend even a week as a mop-pushing flunkie of the association. What if—what if he'd made the wrong choice altogether?

They thought of long life, health, power, and a thousand selfish and selfless things, but not one of them dreamed of becoming a real life flesh-rending animal. And for all of their considerable imaginative power, none had an inkling of what the next six hours would actually feel like.

Gerald Cummings had shown him that it would come at midnight, but Blake had forgotten. The full moon, accelerated healing, elimination of aging, and a dozen other characteristics of the modern werewolf owed as much to the novelists and the screenwriters of the last century as to real lycanthropy, because the mind had complete control over the infection, at least according to Gerald Cummings's own article.

Meeting actual representatives of the society had proven that some of the points in that paper were spurious, however. Workable invulnerability and the cessation of aging had been accomplished without cooperation from the hosts' minds centuries before the first film was made. But one thing that Cummings's subsequent savage attacks had imparted to the newest members of the club was that the involuntary transformation took place not at night-fall, but at midnight. Even Blake, who was a novelist, a would-be screenwriter, and perhaps the most knowl-edgeable tracker of Cummings while the madman was free, had forgotten the twelve o'clock rule. Such was

Gerald Cummings's contribution to the mythos.

Even when the wall clock in the dark room began chiming the hour softly, Blake paid no attention to it. He was as tight as a wound spring wondering when and what would happen, as well as why he suddenly was itching—all over! From head to foot! It was like being on fire and it was *hot*! What . . .

He sat up swiftly, clawing at the whole surface of his nude body. "Wait!" he called to no one as he was alone in the room. "I don't know what I'm supposed to do! Gabrielle! Merrick!" Then the cry that was boiling up his throat like molten lava altered before reaching his vocal cords into a lusting, savage growl.

Still himself mentally and not recognizing the sound, Blake started violently and fell from the bed onto the floor.

"*Jesus*!" he screamed, and the imploring of a higher being for help echoed in nine other rooms, spoken by believers and agnostics alike. "What's happening to me?"

Then he knew. And it was . . . wonderful. He sprang to his feet while the hair welled from his flesh and his upper canine teeth dropped from his wide mouth onto the carpet and were replaced by needle-sharp fangs. He didn't know where he was, who he was, or why this had happened to him, but he did realize that his single intent in life was to find meat and blood and rip open its living envelope so that it could flow down his wailing throat to feed the new creature within him. It was glorious, understanding the sole reason for one's existence, but it also brought with it unbearable frustration when he could find no victim to satiate this mad hunger.

The room was empty, and he established this by tearing apart most of its furnishings in his search. He attacked the walls and door with the full measure of his raging power in an effort to escape and visit his insanity on someone—anyone—who might feed his hunger.

There were no Class Fives in that group, so all ten rooms barely resisted the cyclonic efforts of their transformed captives to escape and satisfy a rampaging lust for flesh in an unsuspecting world. A world which was now their hunting ground.

CHAPTER SEVENTEEN

The sound of his own name being repeated gently but continuously drifted through the layers of viscous fluid that swamped his mind and nudged him toward the world again.

"Mr. Corbett, would you like to have breakfast now? Mr. Corbett?"

He coughed thickly, and the sound was hoarse and full of breaking congestion deep in his throat. He opened his eyes.

Why was he lying on the floor? The carpet was thick and soft, almost caressive as it fluffed about his neck and back, but if this were a bedroom, it had to have a bed, didn't it? He turned his head to look at his surroundings.

For a moment, he had to wonder how he had survived the explosion. The room seemed to have been devastated by a bomb. The large and heavy bed had been reduced to twisted springs, a shredded mattress, and kindling composed of what once had been polished hardwood. The curtains that he believed had hung over the room's single window had been ripped down and left in strips to reveal a blank wall rather than a window; and the walls themselves showed extensive damage done by something—apparently steel prongs—raking over them in chaotic patterns. Even the carpet lay in ruins at various points about the floor. He gazed at the wreckage in quiet awe.

"Mr. Corbett?" asked that insistent, if polite, voice again. "Are you ready for breakfast, sir?"

Blake's eyes found the source of the sounds high on the wall above the closed door. It was a speaker for an intercom system, and even though it was some nine feet up, its metal grill had been slightly mutilated by the force that had ravaged the rest of the room.

"Mr. Corbett?"

Blake sat up and found he was naked and partially covered in patches of long brown hair. He'd never had a particularly hirsute body, so this discovery was every bit as shocking as the condition of the room. When he touched these patches with shaky fingers, the hair broke off at skin level with a dry readiness and drifted from him to the carpet in big clumps.

"I'll be damned," he whispered, and even this brought with it a new discovery. His voice sounded different, more sibilant, and his tongue pressed against new spaces where his eyeteeth had been only the night before. He slapped his right hand over his mouth. He'd never had a tooth pulled in his life!

"Mr. Corbett? Are you awake?"

Once more he stared at the speaker, as if to discern the face of the woman behind that voice, and the next shock in a seemingly unending string slammed into his consciousness with enough velocity to almost rob him of his tenuous grip on reality. He could *see* the grill quite clearly, even though . . . even though he had been considerably myopic since birth and he wasn't wearing his glasses.

"Oh, my God," he said, several times, in fact.

"Mr. Corbett, please don't be alarmed," the voice said in a soothing tone. "We realize that you are experiencing a profound period of disorientation, but if you wish to—"

"What's happened to me?" Blake screamed.

"Please, you are fine now, please remain calm. Would you like for someone to come into the room and assist you? One of the staff or an associate, perhaps?"

Through it all, the deeply ingrained emotion of shame asserted itself. Blake glanced at his nakedness. Practically all of the body hair had fallen away at his abrupt movements, leaving him a strangely youthful-looking, mannequin-like copy of himself, and he blushed. "Uh, no," he muttered. "I don't . . . I don't have any clothes."

Obviously, the intercom worked as a condenser microphone because the woman replied, "If you would like to shower in the adjoining bath, a number of dressing gowns are available so that you may return to your room before taking your meal."

"Yeah, that's fine," he said. "What bath?"

Her response was to activate a sliding panel in the wall to the right side of the door, which revealed to him a moderately large and very well supplied bathroom. This place had everything.

"Thank you," he said, standing. "I'll, uh, contact you from my room about breakfast."

"Very good, sir."

Dizziness and weakness assaulted Blake as he took his first step, but these symptoms were actually attributable to his mental confusion rather than any physical source. It was as if his subconscious were purposely keeping him muddled about where he was and what had happened until he was better able to accept it, because, really, he felt fine. He felt great. All of the minor twinges that take up residence in even the most fit of bodies after the age of thirty had vanished. His muscles seemed comfortably primed, and his sinuses were clear. (He never had sinus difficulties except in the first half hour or so after awakening).

But the most amazing thing was his sight. He'd never experienced such acuity with glasses. The images were sharper and the colors brighter than he had ever known and this alone snatched away any lingering feelings of unease about the state of the room he was leaving or the hair that had dropped from his skin as he moved. It was nearly as if he'd awakened in the wrong body.

That struck the note that awakened all of his memories. His firm stride developed into a stagger in mid-step, and he clutched the sides of the bathroom sink as he reached it for support. He found himself staring with those newly keen eyes at his own stunned face in the mirror.

I am a WEREWOLF, he thought. *She did it to me, she made me one of them.*

It was perhaps ten minutes later before he entered the shower. The hot water failed to shock him out of his stupor, and he watched with detached disinterest as the claws, thick, glossy chestnut in color and wickedly sharp, like the claws of a cat broke off his fingers under the pressure of the hard shower and clinked to the tile floor. He felt no pain at this or when the water washed over the raw pink flesh left uncovered by the nails, and in a few seconds even the minimal bleeding had stopped.

He finished the shower, slowly recovering. The sight of the remainder of his inches-long "fur" swirling down the drain worked against his continual denial, so that by the time he'd toweled off and pulled on a long robe, he accepted the fact that he was a permanent member of a select group of people.

Returning to the bedroom, he found what was left of his clothing in shreds and patches of material. His glasses were smashed to powder and their tough frames had been ripped apart. But he had more clothes in his room. He left for that destination in the opposite wing of the mansion without a second thought to the sense of offended modesty that he had felt earlier.

He encountered a few members of the staff in the hallways, but Blake ignored them, being too preoccupied with his circumstances to remember the amenities that he had once dispensed to associate and servant alike. Once dressed, he knew that he should take a long time, maybe even all day, to sit and contemplate what had happened to him and how it would affect the rest of his life, as well as to take notes for the book that would come out of all of this. ("Always the writer first, aren't you, A.B.?" Nick's ghostly voice inquired.)

But this wasn't the time for meditation. For one thing, his former shock was rapidly being fanned into barely controllable excitement; he suddenly wanted to shout, run, leap to catch the sun in his hands, and talk with Meg or Nick or *anyone* about what he'd just gone through. For another, he realized that he was ravenously hungry. Apparently, transformation took a toll on the energy reserves.

Using the intercom callbox found in every guest room, though not in the room he'd spent the night, Blake discovered that he could have a complete breakfast delivered to him or he could join several other associates who were dining on the south terrace. There was no need to debate his choice. He practically jogged through the house to reach the terrace with its brilliant July sunshine and the companionship of his brothers and sisters in this marvelous event.

"Would you look who's deigned to join us in crullers and apple cider?" said a grinning Nick as Blake approached the table on the far side of the

terrace where he and Meg sat. Nick stood and extended his hand. "Looking pretty chipper this morning, you weakeyed, humpbacked scrivener."

Blake took Nick's hand and shook it heartily.
Actually, he felt like grasping Nick and squeezing the
life from him in an exuberant bear hug, but for all of
his changes in the past day, he hadn't changed *that*
much. Instead, he stooped and transferred the impulse to Meg's shoulders.

"Well, I don't suppose we have to ask if *you* had a
successful night." Nick laughed as the two men seated
themselves.

"Nick, Meg, I . . . I did it!" *Don't gush*, Blake
cautioned himself, *try to maintain some degree of
mature sophistication.* "After all that we'd seen, with
Neil and Grandillon and the others transforming right
before our eyes, I can't say that I really, viscerally
believed in it. After all, this is not something that a
person can just blithely incorporate into a private
frame of reference, right? But once it *happens* to you,
man, it's—"

"Tell me about it," Nick interrupted. "You remember, of course, that I was introduced to the club
several months ago"—he flicked a glance toward
Meg, who had not as yet parted her smiling, tightly
pressed lips—"and I didn't even have a sweet lover to
guide me on my way."

Blake missed the thinly veiled jealous comment,
but a sudden fear did strike him. "Um, you were
successful in the transformation, weren't you, Meg?"

She laughed shortly with much of the bubbling
joyousness that was possessing Blake. "I'd call it a
resounding success." Her eyeteeth were missing.

"Me, too!" Like a child, Blake opened his mouth
and darted his tongue into the gaps left by his canines.

"What a qualification to join a club," observed
Nick, whose own teeth had been missing—except for
five regular periods of a few hours apiece—since late

January. "I think the first thing I want Merrick to show me how to do is grow replacements for these. You seem to be missing some facial adornment, as well, Mr. Hemingway." He touched the bridge of his nose in illustration.

Blake's eyes grew even wider. "Ask me to read something, anything! See that newspaper that guy is reading way over there, at the table next to the entrance? I can make out the text of it without so much as a squint! I even put on a spare set of glasses in my room, and it was like looking through an ice sculpture or something!"

"That's nice—" Nick began.

"'Nice'?" Blake repeated incredulously. "Your birthday is 'nice,' attending a Broadway play is 'nice,' but this is damned *great*! You've never been called four-eyes, have you? You've never had to fake your way through a class because you were seated in the rear of the room and couldn't read the blackboard. You haven't wondered just what all of the hilarity was about when everyone around you read the joke on a banner trailing from an airplane while it looked like so much Chinese to you, right?"

"Okay, okay, I surrender." Nick chuckled. "It's great."

"And what about the rest of it? I haven't been able to throw a decent baseball since I wrecked my shoulder during a high-school basketball game—"

"Basketball?"

"Basketball. But look at this!" Blake whipped his right arm about in a fast windmilling arc and watched it with apparent awe. "Not a twinge of pain!"

"Congratulations," said Meg happily. No one else seemed self-conscious about missing teeth, so she was beginning to loosen up a bit, as well.

"Settle back to earth for a while, A.B.," Nick advised. "I know all of this is fantastic to you. How do you think I felt when I found myself with a left hand again? And it's great to find out that, after training, we won't be forced to undergo the change every few weeks against our wills, and the rest of it is . . . son of a gun, the rest of it is almost too much even to think about. But there is something that we need to consider, you know."

"Like what, Nickie?" Meg asked.

"Like, what are we, for instance?"

Blake, only now recalling that he was extremely hungry, signaled to catch the attention of one of the deaf staff members and responded, "We're werewolves, man. It may be difficult to admit to ourselves, but I think I've made some real strides in that direction already."

"No, Blake, I mean what kind of werewolves are we? What class?"

That did intrude upon their euphoria with a harsh power. For a short time, they were quiet. A kitchen maid approached the table with the printed menus for the morning, and in deference to her disability, each of the three pointed to certain selections. Then they resumed the topic of conversation.

Meg spoke first. "Didn't the fact that we changed prove that we're Class Ones?"

"No. Nick's right," Blake answered. "That just proved that we aren't Class Five, the people who are immune to the disease. But we could be any of the other four."

"Or either of the first two, really," Nick corrected him. "The people in Three and Four start out as Class Ones or Twos, and anybody can degenerate from that into the wildfire Fours who change without control or into the Threes, where they host the disease for a while before freezing and developing an immunity to it. But both of those are pretty rare cases, anyway, so we've got to figure that we're either Ones with all of the abilities and privileges, or Twos and—"

"We'll spend the rest of our lives as servants," Meg

finished glumly. Her assessment of that state was easy to read in her tone.

"Still, it's not a bad trade off for an extended lifetime," Blake noted, none too enthusiastically, as their juice and coffee arrived.

"Extended servitude for extended life," the young woman replied. That simple statement summed up the matter with admirable succinctness.

"Maybe we'll all be royal," Blake said.

"Calling on the great god of luck again, A.B.?" Nick asked.

"Let's say I'm not ruling him out."

Nick swallowed nearly half of his steaming coffee in a smooth gulp. "Well, while you two were busy last night, I had a lot of time on my hands. It wasn't my number, you'll recall. My—*our* next spotlight focuses on the seventeenth of this month." Meg and Blake each took deep breaths. "Anyhow, I talked with a lot of the locals, Ones and Twos, and I found out that even they aren't able to tell what category we'll fall into until we start our intensive education and show an ability to master our disease—or fail to."

"But Twos don't change at the full moon, do they? If we do on the seventeenth, that'll prove what we are," Meg said.

Nick shook his head. "Twos don't change only after they learn to sublimate the involuntary impulse. Even our old Buddy Cummings might have been one of them."

How in the world can anyone ever sublimate what I felt last night? Blake wondered.

"So, when do we begin our lessons?" Meg asked. "Soon, I hope."

Nick shrugged.

They started that same morning.

And the lessons came four times a day.

They took place in a chemo-hypnotic state brought

on by injections composed of a derivative of thiopental sodium, other exotic drugs which had seemed promising to Neil Merrick, and one completely new ingredient, an ingredient which had been used in only one case, the blood of Gabrielle Secretain.

The Life force was the same in all of the initiates, it was agreed. It certainly wasn't like the common cold, a crazy quilt collection of viruses and bacteria masquerading as a single complaint. It was a specific infection that someday would be isolated by proper scientific investigation. But the intuitive mind of Neil Merrick developed the theory that, due to variance in the *hosts*, each symbiotic union between the disease and human being could well offer a correspondingly different genetic "look."

He picked Gabrielle's blood to test his theory because she was one of perhaps fifteen associates worldwide who claimed to have developed control over her mind/Life form connection entirely without aid or instruction and within a very limited period of time. Gabrielle had conquered the mysteries of transformation, duplication, and linked-mind domination in the space of three days while being tortured for supposed religious crimes and actual ones, since she *was* a werewolf, and her accomplishment was made all the more impressive when taken in the context of her horrible situation.

It was Merrick's opinion that Gabrielle and the other early conquerors of their infections had either contracted a more pure, governable strain of the force or their own human stock had been somewhat different (hardier?) than that of the initiates who followed them. He also felt that including this "pure" strain would increase the effectiveness of his chemically reinforced hypnotic sessions with the newest initiates.

Neil had planned to conduct the experiments quite scientifically, by utilizing the blood properties of two of the original associates, with Dom Poduano being the second donor. But then Dom had become danger-ously erratic, a condition Merrick was not willing to induce in half of his test group, and Poduano's dementia had progressed to the point where it had become necessary and humane to destroy him.

Merrick's first trial using his concoction of drugs, blood, and suggestion had come on the morning of June 28, and had involved a recruit from the resort. The results had been less than encouraging. The young woman had been duly infected, but she had shown absolutely no response to the three treatments he had given her. Rather than admitting to anyone, especially himself, that the entire effort had been a failure, Neil had proclaimed that the woman was a Class Two, who wouldn't have benefited from the injections anyway, and prepared for his next group of subjects, the reunion inductees.

His very first session with these twenty-four people, including the already-infected Nick Grundel, was vitally important to Merrick. With the men and women almost filling a quiet and isolated room in the west wing of the mansion, he brought the assembly into a light hypnotic state with the use of vocal techniques which he had been refining for more than two centuries. Then he and three Class-Two assistants filled syringes with the drugs and blood to take the subjects even deeper, down to the level at which Neil felt certain that he could mold their subcon-sciousnesses into mature and powerful entities capa-ble of total control of their own forms.

Since the Life form couldn't survive for very long outside a host body—Merrick hadn't yet been in-formed about the crystallized powder that had in-fected Gerald Cummings a year before—and Gabrielle Secretain was not interested in playing the part of a mobile tissue culture every time Neil felt the urge to perform his mad-scientist chores, she had graciously consented to creating a separate living portion of herself. She extruded a kidney-shaped lump of flesh from her body in the form of a self-sustaining, blood-manufacturing tumor. Mixing his drug formula with serum from this organ, he began the first of the intensive sessions.

Whether it was the properties of the blood or his own impressive hypnotic performance, the results this time rated as an unqualified success. In twenty-three of the twenty-four cases, he achieved rudimentary physical regeneration by restoring their canine teeth which they'd lost during their feral states the night before. It was a small victory, certainly, but still, it was unheard of to bring about even this minor, self-motivated and controlled alteration so soon after infection. Merrick was so excited that he found it difficult to keep his voice modulated and calming as he walked among the couches, implanting the new knowledge within his subjects.

Naturally, his findings indicated that one unfortunate, Roland Myhrbridge, fell into the Class-Two category (and further sessions confirmed this), but the addition of twenty-three Class Ones to a standing population of just over thirty was quite an achievement for twelve hours' work.

Of course, even with the hypno-sessions, their graduation into full-fledged and fully responsible associates would take weeks; the question of their morality and character would not be answered for years. But in cutting this period to an infinitesimal fraction of its former time, Neil Merrick felt as if he had just taken the biggest step for the members of his particular sub-species since some long-forgotten ancestor first gave in to the irresistible impulse to fall upon all fours and slip, hungering, into the cool night.

Through the four-a-day lessons and through their own hard work and powerful desires, the once ordinary men and women moved slowly into the realm of the superhuman. To their senses, it was a slow and laborious process, and even though they could recall little, if any, of what their psyches were absorbing while they lay on the couches, they knew that they were making progress.

For Chris Wyler, the past few days had proven to be among the best of his life, and the solitary, suspicious, and quite hopeless blanket that enshrouded him had begun to slip aside in a tentative manner that revealed the awakening boy beneath it.

His transformation on Friday night had created just as much of a personality crisis in Chris as it had in his companions, but all in all it had proven to be a beneficial episode for his underdeveloped self-image. Like many abused children, at some deeply subconscious level, Chris remained convinced that he was responsible for the physical beatings and psychological injury he had suffered from his earliest memories at his parents' hands. Being an only child of quite wealthy parents hadn't served to spare him any of the resulting pain of the first seventeen years of his life. But now, facing the almost certain potential that a Class-One status bestowed upon him, he knew that he could get that fresh start that he had always dreamed of.

Just running away from home and what it represented and changing his name never would have exorcised the demons that plagued him. If for no other reason than he was heir to a substantial family fortune, someone would always be looking for Christopher Andrew Wyler. But if he could change his very features, add or lose inches and pounds, redesign what he considered to be a thoroughly ordinary face, *that* was his definition of a fresh start.

So he faced the daily sessions eagerly. Whatever it took to become the master of oneself in body as well as in mind was small payment for true independence in the young man's eyes.

Tuesday, July Fourth, brought with it a real feeling of celebration. Shannon Kent had come to Chris's bed again on Saturday night following his initiation by Adine Pierce, apparently anticipating the reluctant objections that he might raise. The girl had brought with her a letter from Adine explaining that Shannon was more than just a house servant. Actually, she had been a candidate for inclusion in the association, with the desperate hope that the Life force would provide an answer to her profound hearing impairment, but, unfortunately, she had proven to be among the two percent of all human beings to fall into the Class-Five category, the one which represented those who are fully and permanently immune to the force.

If there were a brighter side to Shannon's condition, the letter explained, it was that she already knew of the evolution Chris was experiencing and was safe from the infection. So Adine and the other associates had no reservations if the lovestruck Shannon and Chris expressed their feelings for one another in healthy and athletic ways, so long as Chris himself had no objections. Chris held none whatsoever.

He knew it wasn't love on the girl's part. She was using him in a sexual way just as blatantly as he'd ever used any woman, but that was okay, too. They had spent every night together since Saturday, and tonight, on the Fourth, they were picnicking along with a number of resort guests on the shore side of the lake, with expectations of enjoying yet another uninhibited and mutually pleasureable evening.

The association sponsored the yearly fireworks display, and, naturally, they did nothing halfway. It was the most elaborate exhibition that Chris had ever witnessed, and in addition to the residents of the island and the resort, the crowd of about eight thousand people watching the event from the shore of the lake beyond the resort boundaries included just about every resident of the town as well as a large number who had driven in from surrounding cities. It was the biggest gathering that little Indigo Lake would see for the entire year.

Chris and Shannon watched from the picnic area for a few minutes before he noticed that she really wasn't having that much fun. He figured that the rolling blasts that stung his eardrums weren't bothering her, but the invisible billowings of energy created by the explosions caused almost as much discomfort to her as they slammed into her face and chest as the sounds had on him. Not to mention the dazzling bursts of multicolored light that accompanied the blasts.

He saw her wince and felt her hand shiver in his as the celebration continued to delight most of the gathering. There was nothing phony in these reactions, and Chris took no pleasure in them. When a particularly brilliant red flare lit up the now well-darkened sky, he caught her attention with a tap on the shoulder and pointed to the glow.

Shannon understood, and, with a short shrug, she shook her head.

Chris then pointed toward the island, and she nodded.

"I suppose that America can have a nice enough birthday party even if we step out early," he muttered, smiling as he stood and helped his beautiful young companion to her feet.

To return to the island, the two had to walk across the sea road, though they had no difficulty in passing by the guards' station, since both were well known by sight by the security people. The fireworks display continued with rising enthusiasm above and behind them, and while Shannon strolled slightly ahead of him, Chris cast an eye to the ongoing performance. He liked fireworks.

Because he was looking back, he happened to notice three furtive shadows as they crept with barely controlled eagerness along the thin ribbon of shore that lay some six feet below the top of the sea road, as if they belonged to some ninja assault force making a rush at the mysterious island. He laughed to himself, recognizing resort regulars, Danny Orlando, K.T. Kellerman, and Shane Magill, as the creeping trio.

Going to use the rockets' red glare to sneak onto the island and see what we're really up to, huh, kids? he thought. *You can try but I'll bet money that you'll never get by the guards.*

Before the amused guards in the kiosk could shout down to the three children that they were trespassing on private property, the leader of the group, Danny Orlando, stood up, drew back his arm, and tossed something small and sparkling up and onto the sea road no more than a few feet behind Chris and Shannon.

Chris saw it was a firecracker even before it struck the road, and he instinctively raised one arm in front of his face. The miniature bomb exploded with only a minimum amount of flash and a maximum amount of noise. It almost deafened him.

In quick succession, Shannon gasped, the guards cursed from their station, and Danny chortled, "We got you, Wyler! You're dead, man! We got you!" before leaping into the lake and swimming for the shore with K.T. and Shane in close pursuit.

"Are you all right, Mr. Wyler?" one of the guards called solicitously, his tone projecting the concern due a Class One by a Class Two.

His voice was thin and weak in Chris's numbed ears. "Yeah, I'm fine."

"I know those three, sir, and if you wish I will have their parents informed of this—"

"No, no," Chris said quickly. "They're okay. They were just goofing around."

"Very dangerous tomfoolery, sir, if I may say so!"

"They're good kids. Just forget it."

"As you wish."

Chris turned to Shannon, who had stopped a few feet ahead and was staring at him through the randomly shattered darkness of the night. Her eyes were wide, her face quite pale, and her chest rose and fell swiftly in an attempt to recapture her breath. Well, why shouldn't she be startled? Chris's own heart was thudding pretty damned hard, after hearing something so loud and so close. Then the truth hit him as if a curtain had been drawn back.

She had heard the firecracker.

She had been walking away from the explosion, looking toward the island, and the muted white flash surely would have been eclipsed by the blazing bursts from the skyrockets. There had been a little bit of a sonic wave in the air from the detonation, naturally, but it was nothing compared to the waves which were continually bombarding them from overhead. She wouldn't have noticed it amid the rest of the rumbling and shrieking, yet she had gasped at the very moment the firecracker had gone off and turned back toward him. How could she have known what had happened, unless. . . .

"You *heard* it," he whispered.

Her eyes flickered to his lips, giving further testimony to the fact in the midst of all of the other sounds.

"You heard me!" he stated more loudly. "Shannon, this is great! You're able to *hear*! This is terrific!" He reached out to take her hands in his.

Shannon avoided his touch and turned to run toward the island. There was nothing playful or the least happy in her actions, and Chris was stunned. He called to her, convinced now that she heard his voice, but she continued to race to the mansion. As confused by this as he had been by anything in the last several days, he chased her.

When he caught up with her, some of Chris's bewilderment had changed to mild anger, because he felt sure that he'd been made the butt of some elaborate joke. Catching her by the shoulder, he dragged the girl to a stop and forced her to face him.

"What's going on?" he demanded. "What the hell kind of trick are you pulling?" Since they had shared a bed several times already, he used the term in more than one sense.

Shannon struggled weakly and refused to meet his eyes.

"Answer me!" he shouted. "I know you can hear me!"

Instead, she lashed at his face with her hand.

Chris was taken by surprise, but his defensive abilities allowed him to blunt the impact of the blow high on his cheek easily enough. To his relief, his own hands did not whip back with dangerous counterblows; maybe he wasn't an animal after all.

"Stop it!" he told her. "I'm not going to hurt you. I only want to find out why you've been pretending to . . ." Then his eyes met hers, and a connection that Chris hadn't suspected between them was completed again. The eyes were green and beautiful, Shannon's eyes, but the shining intelligence—though muted or restrained by something he couldn't understand—behind them belonged to someone other than Shannon Kent. That girl was gone, probably riding a bus back to Laconia, New Hampshire. The person who stood before him was someone else.

"Oh, my God," he whispered. "Who are you?"

In his imagination, the green eyes darkened to brown, the face became that of the last woman to strike him. And he knew.

"Kelly?" he asked in a lower whisper.

She nodded hesitantly, not at all like the aggressively confident reporter Kelly Davis, but he couldn't deny what he had recognized in her.

"This is . . . you've changed yourself, and you're one of them—us?"

She shook her head and pointed to the mansion.

"They did it to you? Why? I mean, I don't understand what the disguise is for." "Disguise," that sounded totally inadequate and ridiculous in this situation. But, wrapped in a foamy blanket of shock and disbelief, he didn't bother with such inanities.

She began to make tentative motions with her hands.

"Stop that crap!" he yelled abruptly. "*Talk* to me!"

She touched her throat and shook her head.

Chris took a long, deep breath. The prospects of his own metamorphic future were like money in the bank to him, but, for reasons he couldn't fathom, having Kelly Davis before him in another woman's body was both frightening and a little repulsive. "They did this to you?" he asked, indicating the people in the mansion.

She nodded.

He clutched her wrist and loped toward the mansion. Somebody had a lot of explaining to do.

The first person Chris and Kelly encountered was, fittingly, Neil Merrick, whom the boy had been searching for, anyway. He was descending one of the long, polished staircases when they entered the front door, and his smile was a genuine welcome.

"Ah, Christopher and his young paramour. Back so soon from the festivities?" he asked happily.

"The noise was too much for *both* of us," Chris darkly replied. When Neil seemed not to have picked up that clue, he continued, "What in the hell is going on in this place, Neil?"

Merrick looked as startled and confused as his urbane associate status allowed. "You have me at a loss, Christopher. Is there a problem?"

Wyler's voice almost slipped his control. "*She's* wrong! This is Kelly Davis, not Shannon Kent! What's with the masquerade? Who is the joke on, Neil? Did you and your effete buddies get a real good time out of doing this to her and then forcing her to sleep with me? Is that the only way you can get your rocks off, by watching?"

The rage in Chris's voice seemed almost to push Merrick back up a step, and in the fraction of a second following this reaction, Neil recovered his usually conciliatory attitude. He stepped to the floor and led the two young people into the connecting room, a well-furnished parlor.

"Sit down, won't you, Chris, and we'll talk," he said.

But Chris remained standing and holding Kelly's wrist as if she were exhibit one in his case against the association. "I want some answers, Neil, and I'd like to think that you have enough respect for me to provide them. What's going on?"

Merrick did take a chair. "I respect you, Chris, and in that respect is the knowledge that you'll take a moment to step back, get a grip on your emotions, and wait for the explanation." Chris said nothing, so Merrick took this as a small success. "Now then, first, yes, I am well aware that the lady at your side possesses the psychological orientation of Kelly Davis, but you'll have to get used to such surprises, son. In this life things are hardly ever what they appear to be."

That's a comforting thought, Chris told himself sardonically. "Stop blowing smoke, Neil. I know that Kelly would never volunteer to be changed into—into someone else. She was pretty damned sure of who she was and how she wanted to live her life." In spite of the fact that the woman was standing next to him, listening to his nervous speech, he couldn't help but refer to her in the third person, as if she had died in some way when her body had been altered. Another uncomfortable reality of his strange new existence.

"Don't assume so much, my friend," Merrick stated with a smile. "When you've been around as long as I have, you come to realize that what lives in the secret heart of any person is seldom remotely similar to the outward persona. Still, to answer you, Ms. Davis came to us a week ago, last Tuesday night, following the unfortunate incident between the two of you at the bar."

At the reminder of the confrontation, Chris glanced at Shannon, who was really Kelly, and he immediately released her wrist, as if to assure her that she should feel no threat from him. For her part, Kelly stepped away from him with an expression that combined both horror of the memory and a kind of innocent confusion Chris had never recognized in her other face, her real face.

"She understood that a change in her rather humdrum little existence and from her vulgar job was necessary," Neil went on. "When she discovered the truth of our organization, she knew that we could provide her with a new life. And, of course, her implied threat to expose us was all the incentive we needed to comply with her wish."

"And she chose to start another life as a household maid?" he asked disbelievingly.

"Certainly not. Adine Pierce introduced the Life form into Kelly's system, but, unfortunately, she proved to be a Class-Two individual."

Though Chris had known about shape-shifters and their classes for only a few days, and had been a member of the group for even less time, already the words "Class Two" had taken on a meaning that was usually designated to terms like "retarded" or "deformed." Chris was disgusted with his own reaction.

"How do you know she's a Class Two?" he demanded. "We were told just the other day that no one can be certain about classifications until the first full moon, and that won't be for another couple of weeks."

"We've been through this, Chris," Merrick said, exposing Wyler's own tactics of denial for what they were. "My new chemo-hypnotic treatment using Gabrielle's blood as a base ingredient allows me to incite voluntary metamorphic control in even the newest recruit. Kelly displayed no such control. She was my first subject, and I thought that my treatment might be insufficient for the task—"

"That's right, you might not be able to make an accurate decision."

"Until I achieved such success with your group. There was one Class Two among you, as well, Roland Myhrbridge, so I'm afraid that my diagnosis of Ms. Davis's condition was correct."

Chris decided to sit now. "That still isn't an answer. Why did you change her like this and take away her voice?"

"Adine decided that, actually. With the departure of the 'real' Shannon Kent, so to speak, we had an opening for another staff member, and rather than have her depend upon self-discipline to maintain the image of the deaf mute, it was much simpler to take away her vocal equipment, though it was decided to retain her hearing—"

"Why change her at all, for God's sake? Why didn't you just let her go back to her life?"

"This is her life," Merrick responded coolly. "She is a member of the association now just as much as you or I. Once the decision is made to accept the gift, it is irrevocable. There's no retirement plan."

"It should have been up to her, anyway." Chris sighed. "Who says she has to live her life in somebody else's body?"

"Adine."

"And I suppose Kelly jumped at the chance to become a babydoll plaything of the Class Ones, right?"

"No, as a matter of fact. She was rather obstinate in the beginning, so it was necessary for Adine to adjust her mental alignment properly a bit to—"

"What?" Chris sprang to his feet, his eyes bright with shock. "She messed with her *brain*?"

"A minor harmonizing to eliminate her most intrusive characteristics and moderate the awful fears of other human beings that were instilled in her during her early years—"

"But our *minds* are all we can hold on to through the years!" Chris said. "It was explained to us, every time we change we get a little further away from our original physical make-up, and finally we'll be re-creating only *memories* of our first bodies, right?"

"Astutely put, Christopher, but—"

"Which means that the only real part of ourselves that we can keep is our minds. That is what *we* are, our identities! And the first thing that bitch did was change Kelly's brain!"

Neil Merrick was a long-suffering individual, especially so for a powerful member of the association, but there were certain, definite limits to his good nature. "Watch your tongue, young man!" he said as sharply as he had ever spoken to Chris. "You're speaking of a brilliant woman who has more than two centuries of experience."

"I don't give a damn how old she is!" Chris practically shouted. The object of this rapidly escalating scene, the young woman who was no longer completely Kelly Davis in either a physical or mental sense, covered her ears with both hands and turned her face away from the men as if unable to bear the knowledge that it was her life they were discussing.

"Control yourself, Chris," Merrick advised.

"Or what?" he asked. "Are you going to change *me* into something, too? Another broom jockey or a trained monkey or something? You're not gods, Neil! Just because you have the ability to do things like this to other people doesn't give you the *right*! You can't go around screwing up other people's minds!"

Merrick shook his head wearily. "Your concerns are

admirable, son, really, but they're also incredibly shortsighted. When you've lived as one of us for a few decades and come to realize just what your place is among the miserable short-timers that make up the vast majority of the race, then you'll see that the concerns you have for one mere Class-Two representative are insignificant."

"Shut up!" the boy exploded. "If living with people like you makes me believe that nine out of every ten people in the world are 'insignificant,' then I'm walking!"

"You don't realize what you're saying, Chris."

"Just tell me where she is."

"Who?"

"Adine!" Chris took Kelly's arm, ready to leave the room. "She's going to change Kelly back into herself, and then we're getting our asses away from you people! Where is she?"

"My boy, you're in no way prepared to face your new life alone! When the seventeenth arrives, you'll become an uncontrollable monster and destroy the lives of other innocent men, women and children. Is that what you want?"

"Let me worry about that, okay?"

Merrick decided to try another route. "And you certainly don't want anyone inciting further changes in Ms. Davis's brain. We hardly knew her to begin with, so any physical change would remove her even more from her original personality."

"Damn," Chris spat.

"And as for her somatic appearance, well, the same is true. Adine—or any one of us—would simply be molding a copy from a basically untrustworthy memory. Besides, pardon me for being so blunt, dear, in this form you've dropped roughly half your former age and you are clearly more pleasing to the eye then before."

"Don't you understand it, man? It's not your decision to make! It's Kelly's mind and body!"

"Then why don't you ask the lady what she would prefer to do with her life?"

"She can't tell me anything, thanks to you and your kind!"

"*Our* kind," Neil reminded him. Standing, he placed a hand on Chris's shoulder. "You're tired, both of you. Give it a night, and in the morning we can discuss things coolly and logically—"

"Don't touch me, man! None of you are ever going to lay a hand on me again, I guarantee that!" Chris's face was filled with a burning revulsion that was made all the more powerful by the fact that part of it was directed at what he had allowed himself to become.

For all of the fondness that Neil Merrick felt for Chris Wyler, for his understanding of Chris's distrustful and dangerous attitude, and for the hope that he had of delivering another of his "children" into the paradise of the shape-shifters' life, Merrick knew where his ultimate allegiance lay. Using this knowledge, he reached an extremely difficult decision in that instant. Again reaching for the boy's shoulder, he began to form the difficult words of that decision.

But before Neil could speak, all hell broke loose beneath their feet.

CHAPTER EIGHTEEN

Blake, Meg, and Melanie Ryan were ashore watching the fireworks display when another resident of the island made a brief, deadly bid for freedom. They were sitting at the picnic tables somewhat south of the sea road and therefore out of the path of the ensuing madness, but they did hear the screaming and see the sudden charge away from that area when it began.

"What in the world is going on over there?" Melanie asked. She was another new inductee into the association, having received the Life force on the same night as Meg and Blake. She was a short, blonde-haired woman of twenty-three—at least, that was who she was now. Who could say what the future held for her?

Blake chuckled briefly. "In this place, even the world might not cover the range of possibilities."

Meg shielded her eyes from the overhead blasts of color. "I don't know, Blake. It doesn't look like they're having fun over there. It looks like—like a panic. I don't like it."

Blake stood and peered through the darkness toward the developing drama. Once, very recently, he would have squinted to make out what others saw without difficulty, but now his vision was as razor-keen as his eyes had always been in his dreams. What he saw on this occasion wasn't reassuring, though.

"You know, something *is* wrong," he muttered. "Stay here for a minute." He began walking in the direction of the confusion.

"'Wait here'?" Meg repeated. "Who are you, John Wayne or somebody?" She began following him.

"Ask me that in six months, and you may be surprised," he answered.

Not wanting to be left out, Melanie joined the pair.

They were halfway to the sea road when Maxwell Buhl made his abortive attempt to stop the runaway's rampage, and the noise of six gunshots made them all jump.

"Good God!" Blake whispered, as he quickened his stride in the direction of the sounds.

"Blake, no!" cried Meg, catching his arm. "You don't know what's happening there, and you could be hurt!"

He grinned with ugly ferocity, and it was an expression that Meg had not seen from him since that night at the Institute. The experience of violence carried with it a kind of addictive quality, the young woman knew. "I'm just going to check it out, Meg. Don't worry."

"And what about the police? With shooting going on, you know that they'll be here soon. Do we just give them our names and addresses?"

That brought him up short. "Damn. You're right. We'd better get back to the island."

With that matter settled, the three hurried through

the chaos of the frightened crowd and onto the sea road. Reaching the guard's station, they found one of the two men painfully pulling himself ashore from the lake and the other lying dead just outside the little building. He looked as if he had been butchered by an inexperienced apprentice meat-cutter.

Melanie, who had never seen a dead body, almost gave in to hysteria, but with Meg and Blake taking her arms, she found herself rushing across the road and onto the grounds of the mansion. Here, they were nearly bowled over by a group of uniformed men and one woman heading toward the sea road. The guards, displaying none of the usual respect for their Class-One superiors, ignored all of the questions tossed at them and disappeared into the darkness.

During their run to the mansion, the fireworks had stopped and a new celestial sight-and-sound show began in accompaniment to the wailing of police sirens arriving at the resort's gates. High in the sky, the throbbing engines of heavy helicopters rumbled, and the stabbing beams of their searchlights created darting circles and ovals on the lawn and the sides of the house.

"Helicopters?" Meg wondered aloud. "What kind of invasion is this?"

Blake urged both young women along. "Let's get inside, and then we'll ask our questions."

Inside the mansion seemed no less confused than had the shore. Associates were running in every direction without regard to the calm sense of protocol which had held sway at the estate during the preceding days, and none of them paid any attention to the new arrivals until Neil Merrick sprinted up the staircase which led to the vast basement below the building. Spying them, he called the three to one side, out of the swift flow of the traffic.

"Would any of you have an idea where Jessie

Powers, Elizabeth Chynnarra, or Lon Wicker happen to be?" he asked before they could begin with their own questions.

"We saw Elizabeth and Jessie in the picnic area on shore just before the fireworks began, but I don't know if Lon was over there or not," Blake responded. "But what's going on here, Neil?"

The man attempted to wave aside their concern with his standard aplomb. "Don't allow it to worry you. It's a minor difficulty that will be cleared up in a matter of minutes, I assure you."

"Minor, hell! Did you know that there are helicopters landing outside?"

"Helicopters?" Neil repeated with real alarm. "They're landing on the island?"

"That's what it sounded like to us."

Merrick's demeanor changed dramatically. Though he was hardly as brusque or overpowering as Tristan Grandillon as he steered the three toward the stairs he had just ascended, there was no mistaking the urgency of his actions. "This certainly is serious, Blake, and I hope that you'll forgive me, but I have to ask that you and the ladies follow my instructions without question. Please go downstairs and join those who are assembling near the eastern foundation. Charles and a number of other staff members will be there to assist you."

"But who's in the helicopters?" Blake demanded. "What do they want?"

Merrick stopped for a moment to answer. "I'll have to be blunt. Considering the swift reaction time, I must conclude that those vehicles are operated by the United States government and are filled with trained agents who have been led to us by you and your companions."

"The government? Damn! I always thought that Nick's escape was too pat! They must have set it up so that they could follow us and locate any other witnesses to the Institute massacre who were planning to expose the truth!''

Merrick began nudging them toward the stairs again. "It seems most likely, but right now you have to help me by following instructions."

Blake continued to shake his head and curse himself, so that Meg had to take his arm and pull him to the staircase.

Like the ground floor, the basement was swarming with activity. Blake's report of the landing aircraft had prompted Neil to switch on an alarm that echoed throughout the huge house and appeared to double the speed of the general activity. Under the military-style direction of the staff, Blake, Meg, and Melanie were ushered immediately to the left upon reaching the basement, along with dozens of other confused residents.

Since none of them had been down there before, they had no way of knowing that a section of the wall forming the foundation had been mechanically drawn aside to expose the long, tile-floored tunnel which they found themselves entering. The tunnel, illuminated by cool white fluorescent strip lights, seemed to run on forever at a slight downward slope.

Nick abruptly appeared next to Meg and Blake from the low-level tumult. "Do these people think of everything or what?"

"Oh, Nick, what's going on?" asked Meg.

"It's pretty obvious, isn't it? We're in a situation calling for evacuation, and this is an evacuation tunnel," he answered.

"But why? Who are we running from?"

"The fuzz, the feds, Brother Larry Self-Righteous and his Inquisition Ragtime Band. Take your pick."

The collection of mystified people had come to a stop just inside the tunnel, and Blake stared back into the long cellar behind them, wondering just what those barred rooms set into the wall were designed to accommodate. "Okay, Nick, but what started everything? Who was shot on the shore?"

"Somebody went apeshit," the young man replied. "I saw him. I don't know who it was, but he was in full-blown psychotic metamorphosis, just like Old Man Cummings. The guards blasted him, but he got away and hightailed it across the sea road."

Blake nodded. "The police were alerted to the presence of a 'monster' and their radio calls tipped off the government squad that is landing outside right now."

Nick's eyes grew wide. "The government is in on this?"

"I'm afraid so. They must have tracked us all across the country. The entire 'escape' from the transfer van was just a setup so that they could find out if we were part of an underground exposé movement or . . . Hell, they've got Cummings's body and probably a living shape-shifter in Rosalie Moorcroft. Maybe they suspected the existence of the association."

"So why in the hell are we standing here jabbering like magpies while they prepare to batten down the doors and put us to the torch?" he asked.

Blake glanced down the long corridor ahead. "Waiting for directions."

"Ladies and gentlemen!" came the exasperated voice of one of the Class-Two guards behind them. "Please move into the tunnel! This is most urgent! Everyone must move quickly into the tunnel!"

Like obedient school children, the people began to shuffle deeper into the opening when they all were startled by a series of loud and desperate cries from behind them. From those strange, recessed cells.

"For God's sake, you can't leave us!" a man screamed. "Let us out! We'll go with you! We won't be a threat to anyone!" There were at least a dozen other similar pleas from the other cells, as well as a few equally passionate calls from faceless prisoners for the first group to shut up. Apparently, this latter group wanted to be left behind for the authorities to discover. Everyone in the tunnel froze.

Blake was near one of those cells, one of the largest ones, and his eyes were drawn to its barred window as if magnetized. What he saw almost stopped his heart in his chest.

There were people in there, men and women, who weren't really people but more like . . . caricatures, twisted, mutated, possessed of sizes and forms so foreign to Blake's mind that he was unable to accept what his eyes revealed. His mouth went as dry as dust.

Charles Gladden was suddenly among the staring people, and all pretense to civility vanished as he used his extraordinary physical strength to plow through them like an ice breaker. He actually grasped one of the newly initiated Class Ones, Laura Qualen, by the arm and dragged her several feet along the corridor. As the others followed, they turned along a slight bend and faced a long string of tram cars, not unlike those used at large amusement parks to convey visitors from their cars to the front gates.

"Now get your butts in gear and get on this thing!" Gladden ordered. He climbed into the lead car. "I'm leaving in fifteen seconds and anybody left behind can either walk or trust themselves to the kindness of those idiots breaking in upstairs." This contained just the right balance of alarm and intimidation to spur the listeners into action.

Within seconds, the first tram departed at a surprisingly swift rate for its unstated destination, and moments later its twin revved its electric motor and sped after it, loaded with the clearly upset associates who *knew* where they were going and why.

The tunnel ran beneath the lake and came up on the shore opposite the resort in the basement of a

moderate-sized transportation company which was
owned by the association, though this was not public
knowledge. The quite legal "burying" of the company's ownership proved to be effective for the area
had not been staked out by the government operatives
who were arriving on the island and resort via helicopters like a swarm of insects.

While the majority of the transportation company's
vehicles were standard trucks, there were also a pair of
large, double-decked passenger buses in the warehouse, and the employees loaded everyone onto these
with the swiftness of practiced drill sergeants. There
had been no actual evacuation plans made by any of
the Class-One associates or their staffs, but everyone
understood the necessity of putting Indigo Lake as far
behind them as possible. Because it seemed certain
that the federal boys would have staked out the
airport, the buses were the best hope of escape. In
tandem, the two vehicles pulled out of the warehouse
and headed west.

In the midst of the escape, even the most compel-
ling of issues were reduced to secondary status. Even
though Chris now knew that Shannon Kent was in
fact a woman who had been stripped of her true
identity and changed against her will into the image of
someone else, for the hours that were occupied by the
flight from Indigo Lake, his naggingly persistent conscience was shut down. Though he and Blake and Meg
and Nick and all of the other new converts to the
association had witnessed in the runaway and in the
people in the cells the unexpected birth of their own
potential ugliness at a time when they felt completely
in control of their bodies, between the full moons, no
one broached this subject to the experienced associates during the first night and day of the trip west.

And perhaps most surprisingly, no voice raised the
question that weighed on everyone like the top quar-

ter of a mountain: Who *were* those people in the basement cells?

The buses drove west for eighteen hours, interrupting the unplanned journey only for fuel and food stops. The vehicles contained their own bathrooms, so this cut back on the unavoidable breaks in the trip even more. Considering the nature of their take-out meals, most of the members of the group didn't set foot off the buses in the long stretch of driving that followed their escape from Indigo Lake.

It was Wednesday, late afternoon, before the routine changed. They had crossed the Illinois state line and were nearing Champaign when the brain trust of the company decided that they could chance leaving the highway long enough to decide exactly what their next move should be. No evidence of pursuit had been detected, but, of course, the supposedly supersensitive intelligence network at the island had failed to alert them to the impending government assault to begin with.

A summer resort not unlike that at Indigo Lake seemed a suitable site to spend a day or two planning. An entire section of duplex cabins was rented, and the associates moved in—minus any luggage—after paying in cash. They knew that credit checks or confirmations would provide screaming signals to any interested eyes, so all financial transactions would heretofore involve only hard cash, of which the associates had an abundant supply.

After a needed night's rest, a general conference was called for early the next morning.

As head of security at Caprice Island, Tristan Grandillon tried to take full responsibility for what had occurred. He even offered a plan.

"I suggest that I be allowed to surrender to our pursuers and provide them with a manufactured tale which will be convincing enough to confuse them and allow the other members of the association the time to determine their future actions," he told the assembly.

DeLaurence Long, a two-hundred-thirty-six-year-old associate who had been born in the area which would be admitted to the Union as Arkansas more than three-quarters of a century later, acted as *ad hoc* moderator for the meeting. He spoke for the entire group when he replied, "That will hardly be necessary. I'm sure that no one holds you accountable for the debacle at the lake, Tristan. No one could have known that the government would mount such a massive offensive, or that they would have a clue as to our existence, much less our location."

"You couldn't have known that someone else, some outsider, would lead the enemy to our doorstep," observed Pepe Alonso archly.

Blake coughed shortly and stared at his shoes.

The conversation continued for the better part of an hour, with Lisolette Sprouling, the associate who had brought her lover, B.D. Robinson, to the island, introducing the summation of the gathering with a single sentence, "I believe that we should leave the States."

DeLaurence Long regarded the observation for a moment. "We are rather close to the Canadian border, and if we obtain automobiles and cross in smaller groups—"

"I don't mean to Canada or Mexico," Lisolette interrupted, surprising in any conversation involving two or more Class Ones. Even in the middle of this mess, the Class Ones were unfailingly courteous to one another. Maybe it came from their extended lifetimes of training, knowing that an individual as powerful as a self-determinate lycanthrope/shapeshifter should always be treated courteously.

Lisolette continued, "The entire North American continent is too firmly under the thumb of the U.S. intelligence community. No matter how we rearranged our appearances or blanketed our sources of income, there would always be someone whose suspicions about us would be aroused and someone else who would know where to report those suspicions. I don't want to live that way. The government believes in us now, but perhaps other governments don't. We have to camouflage ourselves in foreign countries until the average fearful and violent uninitiated mind can evolve into the realization that *we* are not nightmares from the past but the heralds of their own future."

"You're suggesting, then, that we leave the Western hemisphere for Europe or Asia," Neil Merrick pointed out.

"Not necessarily. To some, South America would seem to be safe for decades. I would stay away from England or Australia, though."

"I don't like running away," Merrick said. "We knew that someday medical science would progress enough to recognize the reality of our existence, and now that the day has come we can only think of abandoning our nation—"

"Neil, you're Welsh," Lisolette reminded him.

"I've lived in the United States for longer than any uninitiated man or woman in its history. For myself, I say that we should meet with representatives of the government."

That statement triggered an immediate response. The decorum of the meeting dropped away like a desiccated husk, and some of the associates even raised their voices very nearly into shouts.

"Breeding will tell," Nick whispered with sarcasm to Meg and Blake.

Neil's powerful words quieted the room swiftly. "I'm not suggesting that we surrender! What I am interested in is arranging a conference on *our* terms between selected representatives of both sides. I hereby volunteer to be one of the emissaries."

Pepe Alonso, now a tall and powerfully built man with graying black hair and fiercely black eyes, stood as if he were a lawyer objecting to a particularly repugnant line of questioning. "Neil, you're one of the oldest and best friends that I have, but what you're proposing amounts to racial suicide! You know that there are legal considerations to deal with. Our lawyers have informed us of that, and you must be aware that the authorities will have those we left behind in custody by now. I don't intend to spend the rest of my lifetime confined to a laboratory or a silver-lined prison cell."

Merrick sighed expressively. "Pepe, believe me, I respect your anxieties, but I don't think that our past indiscretions—or what the uninitiated world will perceive as our indiscretions—will be held against us once they realize that we are offering them immortality."

In a cool voice that was almost too quiet to be heard, Adine Pierce said, "I'm not sure that I wish to live in a world where everyone possesses the Life form."

Calmer debate followed, and it eventually was decided that each member would decide whether to emigrate to other portions of the world—primarily Europe, which maintained a healthy population of shape-shifters of its own—or to remain behind with Neil to confront the aroused legal and scientific communities of the United States. Merrick gave his word that he would do nothing to expose his brothers and sisters to any danger. The vote became something of a landslide.

"Neil, my good friend, I wish there were something I could say to convince you of the wisdom of our decision." Long sighed when the voting ended. "This country is too dangerous for people like us, and I would hate to think of you spending the next several decades locked away in some steel box of a room, an experimental subject to be poked and probed by your conscienceless jailors."

"I appreciate your concern, DeLaurence," Merrick replied, "but I feel that the only future any of us can hope to claim will come after we've realigned ourselves with the whole human race. That's what I intend to work toward. You know that I'll wait until all of you are securely out of the country and I'll never breathe a hint of your location, or even your existence."

"But this is such a monumental job," Leslie Harlan said. "You're trying to do too much alone."

"I'll have Tristan," he reminded her. "As well as Ms. Talley, Mr. Corbett, Mr. Grundel, Mr. Gladden, Ms. Ryan, Ms. Davis, and Mr. Wicker." As he recited the names of the only people who had agreed not to leave the country, Merrick stood and walked among them, touching some on the shoulder and shaking Tristan Grandillon's hand firmly. "But I don't wish to presume too much. I'll not ask anyone to join me in this endeavor. I'll continue the new chemo-hypnotic therapy with our newest fellow associates until they are fully prepared to control their own destinies, and then I'll allow them that control."

Grandillon held on to the other man's hand. "I'm with you all the way, Neil." Had they been superhuman enough to read his mind, the others would have seen that Grandillon saw this as the most exciting challenge of his lengthy existence.

"Thank you, Tristan," Neil responded. He surveyed the assembly. "And thank you all, for the greatest support and best friendship that any man ever experienced. Thank you for the confidence you've shown me today, and thank you for providing this opportunity to take the next giant step in our evolution as a species. Soon, perhaps no further into the future than next year, we may be able to walk among our uninitiated siblings without disguise or fear.

"Indeed, in one short year, we may be regarded as the saviors of a world which sometimes seems so blindly lurching toward the precipice of self-destruction."

What followed was a painful separation, but a swift one.

By the next afternoon, a clear and promising day, the majority of the members of the American association took the two buses and left for Baton Rouge, Louisiana, where another "safe house," a compound not unlike the one at Indigo Lake, awaited them. There they could rest and prepare for the exodus from the country which had been home for them for so long. This compound would also provide them with substantial amounts of secreted cash, all of the clothing they would need, and the forged passports necessary to leave the country and to establish new identities elsewhere.

Merrick and his group numbered nine people. They were going on the road again, too, to yet another association-maintained residence, located in California, only an hour's drive from the Institute of Natural Sciences and Research.

Certainly, a return to that awful place was the last plan that Blake, Meg, and Nick would have voted for, at least from an emotional standpoint. The Institute was lodged in their memories like a cold lump of fear, seething in its own juices and launching nightmares that destroyed their sleep even now, even after they had learned the truth about Gerald Cummings's affliction, even after they had become like him.

But Merrick had explained to them that his plan to establish a bridge of understanding between the "normal" world and that of the shape-shifters dictated that he be able to appear personally at the Institute in just over a week. The three realized that if they were ever again to have lives of their own, they would have to rely on Merrick's wisdom, at least for now.

They looked west once more, to the future, but none could forget the full moon that was hurtling toward them in less than two weeks' time.

CHAPTER NINETEEN

"Got a big Friday night planned?" Blake asked happily as he and the other six newest associates left the shaded den in which another of their chemo-hypnotic sessions had been held by Neil.

It was Friday afternoon, July 14, and they had been in residence at the ranch since early Monday morning.

Meg smiled brightly in response. "Oh, sure, a real model of Western decadence. I plan to settle into an easy chair at eight and watch a colorized broadcast of *The Wizard of Oz* on television."

"But that's already in color."

"Ah, but now the opening and closing sequences have been provided with dazzling computer-directed shades and hues and to balance out the additions, the central part has been stripped to black and white." Meg laughed at her own joke. "You know, all of that dull stuff that takes place over the rainbow."

Blake joined in the mirth. "Well, I hope that your system can stand the strain."

"I'll just have to risk it."

The spirits of the two were so high in spite of their continuing exile from general society because they had just again proven to themselves that they were on the verge of mastering their own cellular codings. Along with a substantial amount of untraceable cash, the most important item that Merrick had managed to bring from the island during the evacuation was the blood-producing organ that had been produced from the living body of Gabrielle Secretain. Using this and his own chemical compounds, Neil had continued the regular indoctrination classes since arriving at the ranch.

These classes now were showing some encouraging results, the most obvious of which could be seen in Meg, Blake, and Nick, the three people who had been cosmetically altered by Merrick before the trip west. They now were reverting to their original appearances. Meg's eyes had already returned to a bright green, and her recently darkened hair had lightened to reddish-blonde near her scalp, giving a new meaning to the old colored-roots condition. Her olive complexion was visibly brighter, as well.

Like Meg, Blake had something of a two-tone hairstyle now, as his normal dark brown shade was just beginning to show below the disguising red that Merrick had given him six days before. His eye color was halfway between blue and green, and there was a returning roundness to his face that caused him to breathe a sigh of relief when he glanced into a reflective surface. At this rate, he would be completely normal before the month ended.

"Want to join me in scanning the skies for exciting television events tonight, Nickie?" Meg asked him while the two of them strolled down the hallway to their rooms.

"I didn't enjoy watching Judy Garland serenade two thousand midgets before the mad colorizers got their greedy hands on the original film," he answered with a gruffness that was more typical of the old five-foot-five-inch Grundel. He wasn't as pleased with his slow reversion to the original model as were Meg and Blake. He'd already lost two borrowed inches in height.

"Oh, I was just joking about *Oz*. Not even the most mercenary television exec would tamper with a classic like that."

"Right, and there's redeeming social and artistic value in professional wrestling, too."

Meg conceded with a shrug. "Well, what do you say? Want to watch TV in my room?"

Finally, Nick surrendered to the smile that had been struggling to escape throughout the conversation. "It sure beats sitting in the prison wing, doesn't it?"

"Wow, when you use sweet talk like that, how can any girl resist you?" Meg said with more than a touch of sarcasm.

Behind them, also leaving the den, were two other young people engaged in a rather awkward conversation. The reasons behind this uncomfortable exchange were entirely different, however.

"Kelly, wait a second," Chris Wyler said while breaking into a short trot to catch up to the slim, attractive young woman. "I want to talk to you."

Though Merrick hadn't realized it at the time of their departure from the mansion, Chris would never have run out on the association the way he finally had been forced to leave his abusive homelife. With some justification, he felt responsible for what had happened to Kelly Davis, and his innate sense of duty kept him focused on what he could do to correct this wrong. He knew now that she had been physically restructured and sent to his bed after proving to be a Class Two. Adine Pierce, having witnessed his failed attempt to pick up the real Shannon Kent in

O'Hanlon's Bar and Grill, changed Kelly physically to look like Shannon so she would appeal to Chris. He also knew that he couldn't offer Kelly any help if he turned tail for Europe or faded away into the American underbrush.

"What do you want?" she asked in a hoarse whisper. The first thing that Chris had done after their arrival at the ranch was to convince Neil to give Kelly back her ability to speak. Because he had little recollection of how the real woman had sounded before her transformation by Adine, Neil had been forced to improvise the vocal qualities, and the result had proven to be a husky, breathy, not-unalluring tone that Kelly still found embarrassing. Throughout the week, she had remained largely silent, and when she did speak, it was in that near-whisper that seemed to attest to her embarrassment.

Or maybe Chris was just jumping to conclusions and Kelly's supposed embarrassment was actually due somehow to her physical and mental confusion. God knew, she had reason enough to be confused.

Chris took her arm and led her aside in the corridor, out of the path of the other people, who were departing the room. His face was slightly reddened, and his own voice was nervous when he replied, "I just think that we should, you know, talk about this."

"What?" The question seemed genuine.

"Well, what's happened to you. I kind of feel, you know, kind of responsible."

"Why? It's not your fault that I'm a Class Two."

He sighed heavily. "Sure. That's not what I mean. I thought that . . . uh, if it hadn't been for that scene we had, in that bar, you probably never would have gone to the island and Adine wouldn't have infected you just for the hell of it and. . . ."

Her wide green eyes, so unlike the brown and suspicious ones that Chris had come to know first, seemed to mist with confusion. "The bar? I don't . . .

oh. Oh. Yes, that night, when it was raining. You said something to make me . . . You hurt me that night, didn't you?"

"I'm sorry, God, I'm sorry," he told her desperately. "But I promise that I'll get Neil to fix you. Or if he can't because he didn't know you well enough, *I* can. When I've learned how to do those things, how to control the structures of others—"

"I'm not a doll!" Kelly stated with sudden passion, more loudly than he'd heard her say anything since the night of the incident. "I—I'm all mixed up, like my mind is twisted and tied in knots, but that doesn't give you the right to treat me this way! I'm not something for you to play with or experiment on! I'm still a person!"

"Kelly, Jesus, I'm sorry!" he responded quickly. "Believe me, I won't do anything to you if you don't want it. I only meant that I would do my best to return you to who you were."

"And get into my brain again? And squeeze out what you don't like and make me forget all that other . . . everything?"

"I didn't do that to you, Kelly! It was Adine, not me!"

"You, Adine, Neil . . . How do I know who any of you are? Or who you'll be tomorrow? How can you be sure that you're who you think you are and not some great joke being played by one of them? Chris, I can't . . ." Suddenly she was crying, softly and without self-pity. "I don't even know who *I* am. It's like I was born two weeks ago with a head full of nonsensical dreams instead of memories. Oh, Lord, *I can't even remember my last name!*"

Chris said nothing; there was nothing to say. The yoke of personal accountability tightened like a rope around his neck. She *wasn't* Kelly Davis anymore, not really, because a woman who had had two hundred years to forget what it meant to be human had blithely

reached into the seat of Kelly Davis's soul and rearranged what she found there to her own specifications.
This woman before him was a new creature, as well as
a confused and frightened one.

Eventually, Chris managed to say, "Adine had no
right to do that to you." But the words sounded
pathetically inadequate even to himself.

As quickly as the tears had come to Kelly's eyes,
they vanished. She wiped her face with her fingers and
said, "I'm sorry. I have to go to the kitchen now."
Since in Neil and Tristan's estimation the mundane
household duties such as cooking and cleaning fell to
a level far below that appropriate to a Class-One
individual, the only Class Twos available, Kelly and
Charles Gladden, naturally inherited the responsibilities.

"Yeah? Well, maybe I could give you a hand?" Chris
couldn't cook toast, but he also couldn't leave matters
the way they were.

She shook her head. "I don't think so. Charles
doesn't like you very much."

"Charles is a conceited asshole."

She actually smiled at that. "You know what they
say about cooking, um, about too many cooks and
the . . ." Her face clouded as the remainder of the
ancient line eluded her. "Never mind." She turned to
leave.

Chris caught her arm again.

Kelly snatched it from his grasp with startling
energy. "Don't touch me!" she hissed. "Don't ever
. . . Just leave me alone, okay?"

He said nothing as she hurried down the hall to the
kitchen.

Blake watched Meg and Nick's hesitant courtship
with amusement and a certain amount of pride. When
all of this had begun, only a year ago, he wouldn't have
bet five dollars that the two young people would ever

be attracted to one another. Now, they were almost inseparable.

Love among the lycanthropes, he thought with a silent chuckle.

"Oh, Blake, would you mind coming into my office for a moment?" Neil asked, drawing the author from his reverie.

"Of course, Neil," he answered.

As befitted their leader, the office was large and combined the expensive elegance of Victorian leather-covered furnishings with the super-sophisticated communications equipment that covered one entire wall. Neil seated himself behind a huge mahogany desk and waved Corbett to a heavily stuffed armchair. "I've asked you here to congratulate you, Blake."

"Really?" With that, Blake began to lose the sensation that he had just stepped into the principal's office.

"You and your companions. Today's session in the den was nothing short of miraculous. You're all progressing at a rate practically unheard of in our community since the days of Giacomo Vilante."

Blake felt like cheering aloud, but he controlled himself. "So you think that we'll graduate to a self-determinate plateau soon?"

"Soon? How about by August?"

Corbett whistled. "By then? Neil, I talked to the others, at the lake, and most of them said I faced a long, uphill struggle. One, Carrie Ann Pellaton, told me that she was subject to the full-moon changes for almost five years."

Merrick nodded slowly. "True enough, but Carrie Ann was a long-time Orphan. She was born back in 1722 in Manitoba, Canada, when the word 'wilderness' meant far more than being outside of driving range to a shopping mall. She lost her family in the attack that infected her at age six and lived a feral existence not unlike that of Kamala and Amala of so-called 'wolf girl' fame in the early part of this century. She was totally without instruction from any other associate during that time and created quite a wealth of folklore among the surrounding Amerindians, believe me."

"An atypical case," Blake admitted. "But just as recently as Gerald Cummings, the infected man transformed ten times between March and December of last year, and Nick's gone through it six times already."

"The average length of time to reach self-determination is about eleven months, even with instruction and mind-control techniques," Merrick said with a touch of a sly smile.

"But you believe that we might be able to achieve it in less than one?"

"Until now, the instructions have never included hypno therapy and injections of the original bloodstock."

"Which means that *you* are responsible for the new success rate."

Merrick chuckled. "Not to sound immodest—"

"Why the hell not?" Now laughing openly, Blake stood and reached across the desk to shake his patron's hand. "Man, you're a genius! I don't mind telling you, even though I have no real memory of going through that spell in the bedroom the other night, I really dreaded reverting to a spitting monster once a month for the next four or five years. And to think that I may have to endure it only once more—"

"Perhaps not even once."

"What do you mean?" Blake asked. "The moon's full on Monday night!"

"True enough, but you six—you, especially, Blake —are so advanced at this point that I have confidence that it's possible you will be able to maintain self-control on Monday.

"Today, while you were at the deepest point of the trance, I'm certain that at my suggestion you would have gone into a full feral metamorphosis without the direct impetus of another associate's contact or the psychological trigger of a full moon at midnight. And that, my friend, is a very big step on the road to complete self-government."

Blake stood and leaned onto the desk. "Why didn't you give us the suggestion then?"

Merrick shook his head. "It's considerably easier to direct a young associate into the change than it is to bring him out once he's become so psychologically unstable, and six enraged werewolves would be something of a handful even for Tristan, Charles, and me." He leaned back in his swivel chair. "But Monday night, with your permission, I intend to try an experiment."

With my permission, Corbett repeated to himself. *He's really coming to consider me a Class One, if not quite an equal.*

Neil continued, "You know, of course, that we've planned to confine each of you to one of the cells in the west wing. What I haven't told you is that I have intended to place you all in chemical trances at the appropriate time and strongly present the command that you resist the psychosomatic impulse to change into your violent status—"

"That's terrific!" Blake interrupted. "If it works, we can do this every time until it isn't necessary anymore!"

Merrick silenced him with a motion. "Blake, I'm going to do that to your companions, but I'd like to leave you and Chris untreated." He didn't allow Blake's startled expression to sidetrack him. "You two are the most advanced, and I honestly believe that through your own powers of concentration you can overcome the impulse. If this proves true, if you can remain in control of your senses and bodies, the rest of your evolution is pure sweetbread. It's like undamming a river of knowledge. Get through Monday night's trial, and by the end of this month you'll be capable of any physical activity that I or any other veteran associate has achieved."

It was almost overwhelming to Blake. "You really think I can do it?"

Merrick nodded. "Completely."

"But you'll still lock me in a cell, right?"

He grinned. "I may have complete confidence in my beliefs, but I'm not foolhardy. You and Wyler may prove to be the most naturally talented shape-shifters since Gabrielle Secretain herself." Neil's expression clouded slightly with memories. "You know that she died at the mansion as a result of treason, of course," he added practically to himself.

Blake had heard of Gabrielle's death, though he'd never been told the cause and hadn't thought it prudent to ask. He said nothing now.

Merrick continued. "We found her in the cellar during the evacuation. Virtually unrecognizable, as if she had been attacked with a silver weapon. And then, somehow, Theodore Jarvis, without doubt the most dangerous and uncontrolled permanent feral in our number was released to make that disasterous assault on the civilian portion of the resort. Quite a coincidence, hmm? Almost too much of one."

As one of the very newest recruits to the association, Blake understood that any suspicions of treachery would fall on him, and he could only hope that Merrick's confidence in him extended deeply enough to cover this.

Apparently, it did. "My guess is that the military authorities had a spy planted in our midst, a member of the mansion's uninitiated staff, since it's obvious that no member of the association would have dreamed of such actions. At least, no associate more sane than the late Dominic Poduano."

Corbett breathed a silent sight of relief.

At that moment, the mood of quiet contemplation

was broken by a sudden, brisk ringing of a bell from the communications panel behind Merrick. Blake was a bit startled, but Neil responded with cool elan. "This should be interesting. No one knows this private shortwave frequency aside from our friends who've chosen to emigrate. I didn't expect them to be ready to depart, yet, but it seems they've decided not to waste any time." He reached for a call button on the desk before him.

"I'll talk to you later, then," Blake said.

"No, stay, please. You're a full-fledged member of the association now, so you shouldn't feel uncomfortable about hearing association business."

Again, feeling flattered and lucky, Blake settled back into the chair.

Merrick touched the button. "This is LMW-335-11 responding. Please identify yourself."

From a speaker on the desk, a surprisingly strong and clear voice replied, "Roger, LMW-335-11, this is LMW-337-26. Repeat, LMW-337-26. Do you copy?"

"Roger, LMW-337-26," Merrick answered. He glanced at a dial on the wall panel. "Encoding signal rating is plus seven. Please continue."

The man's voice at the other end of the transmission instantly became more relaxed and personal. "Neil, old man, you made it home, did you?"

Merrick's response was equally warm. "Without a hitch, Sergei, though at the expense of a few numbed posteriors. We drove all the way. How did your party fare?"

"The same. We made Baton Rouge late Saturday, rested and handled business matters through Wednesday, and then moved to New Orleans, our last port of call, so to speak."

Blake noticed a flicker of sadness in Neil's expression as he asked, "The plans are still in effect, then? You're going?"

"Tonight, Neil. We'll be flying out at 11 P.M. locally,

landing in Lisbon, and departing for various points immediately thereafter. We thought it best to contact you through the scrambler with the details rather than trust the postal service."

"Good thinking. You've made the appropriate financial arrangements, I hope?"

A short laugh came through the speaker. "As many as time and security permitted. About seventy percent of our capital has been transferred to European accounts, all legally. It will raise a lot of eyebrows, but we haven't given the government any free shots at impounding it."

"Any *legal* free shots," Merrick interrupted. "Let's not take fair play for granted at this point."

"Exactly. Anyway, the remaining thirty percent has been switched to the backup association accounts in this country, hoping that they haven't been ferreted out and shut down. Naturally, you and Tristan have full authority to withdraw the capital or transfer it to other holdings, but I advise extreme caution if you do so. The federal boys could be perched atop the accounts like starving lions waiting for a lamb."

"I'll go through the accepted intermediaries if I decide to tap into it," Neil assured him. "But Tristan and I should be well fixed for the next decade or so without it, and, with any luck, the necessity for such secrecy will be long over by then."

"You're going ahead with your contact plans, then?"

"Roger. But not for several months. I'll give you plenty of time to establish yourselves over there."

"Thanks. Well, Neil, it's not a good idea to linger too long on the air, even with the scrambling, so what can I say other than good-bye, old friend, and all the luck in the world to you. We all admire your courage."

"I appreciate that, Sergei. And I admire your foresight and judgment. If all goes well, we'll be reunited before the year's out, though you have my word that I won't do anything to endanger your position."

"That goes without saying, Neil. Our flight number will be—"

"Is it wise to reveal that over the air?"

"After admitting that we're leaving from New Orleans for Lisbon at eleven tonight, does it matter?"

"Still, I'd feel better if you didn't."

"Whatever you wish. Good-bye, old man, but only for now."

"Good-bye, Sergei."

"LMW-337-26, out."

Merrick switched off the speaker phone and stared off into the farthest corner of the dimly lit room for a moment. Blake still felt that it was not the time for him to bring up the mundane hopes and fears of a virgin associate. He realized that Neil had just said farewell to a group of people who had been his friends possibly since the time of the Industrial Revolution. They were, in fact, his family.

And so it was Merrick who broke the silence. "I believe I know what you're thinking."

I wouldn't be surprised if you could read my mind, Blake observed. "What?"

"That, in spite of your excellent imagination, which you've demonstrated in dozens of fine novels, you never dreamed of anything as outrageous as this."

"Neil, I'm not certain that I haven't been carted off to my neighborhood mental institution, where I'm babbling placidly in my straitjacket right now."

David Anthony Knox was a twenty-two-year-old airport employee, who had just gone on a fifteen-minute break. It was going to be a long night, he knew, with an unnaturally heavy passenger load. Man, there were more than seventy people on the 147 to Portugal alone. So he figured that a man with his responsibilities deserved a couple of cups of coffee and a doughnut to maintain his edge during the coming wet night.

He didn't quite make it to the snack bar.

"Hey, boy, excuse me," someone called from a hallway as David passed.

The word stung like fire, even though David knew that he was cursed with "boyish" looks and probably would be until he hit fifty. But the uniform, jerk, didn't the uniform make him more than a "boy"? With a sigh, he stopped and looked at the man. "Yes, sir?" He was a big son of a gun, over six feet and about two hundred pounds. He was well dressed, but there was still something kind of seedy about him.

"Yeah, I wonder if you can help me here," the man said.

David sighed. There went at least one cup of coffee. "What seems to be the problem, sir?"

"It's this damned knee of mine. Gives out on me when the weather's bad like tonight."

David suddenly noticed that the man was leaning heavily against the corridor wall. "Do you need a wheelchair, sir? I can get you one in a minute—"

"No, it's not that bad," the man said. "It's just out of joint, you know, from football, and if you'll give me a hand, I think I can pop it back and get on the plane. It hasn't left, yet, has it? The 147 to Lisbon?"

The young man reached him and tentatively took his arm. "No, sir, not yet, but you've only got about ten minutes."

"Time enough," the man said, and with the speed of a rattlesnake, he stood away from the wall, grasped Knox's entire face in his hand, and twisted his head sharply. David heard the sound of his neck snapping before he died.

The man remained in motion, dragging the limp body of the young man into a restroom which was located only a couple of yards down the narrow hallway. This room was empty, as he'd previously ascertained, and he carried the corpse—and his small black bag—into one of the stalls and locked the door.

After carefully placing the bag on the rear of the toilet, the big man stripped away his clothing, which he then rolled into a rough ball with the shoes at the center. When he was nude, he almost gently took the face of the late David Knox in both of his hands and stared into the dead eyes.

This was the fast and efficient way of duplicating the physical form of another, by direct cell-upon-cell contact, allowing his mutable body to connect with the genetic pattern of the body to be copied. He could change his shape in practically any way imaginable, re-create the appearance of creatures which were only remotely related to known species, simply by the active imposition of his will on his body. But to produce an exact duplicate in this fashion took a small if definite amount of time longer than the touch mimicking, and the man didn't have much time.

Within seconds, there were two David Knoxes in the restroom, one dead and the second standing over him. The man removed the clothing of the other and donned it, so that, following a little arrangement of the hair in mirrors mounted above the sinks, he was the identical twin of the dead man on the outside as well as to the last cell of his intestines. Only their brains remained different.

His disguise complete now, he stepped on the closed lid of the toilet bowl, carefully pushed up a section of the overhead ceiling tile from its network of hanging rods, and slid aside one section onto the back of another next to it. Feeling in the darkness with his hand, the clone found the top of the block wall which formed the rear of the restroom and to which were attached the hanging rods. Then, with no evident strain, he picked up the dead body and balanced it on this narrow ridge and out of sight.

After placing the ball formed of his own clothing on the chest of the corpse, the man eased the ceiling back into place, thus effectively concealing the murder. He didn't fear the authorities and being discovered—Christ, this was hardly his first murder—but he didn't want to have to deal with any interference now.

Then the "new" David Knox carried the small black bag past all of the usually efficient safeguards and to the luggage compartment of Celestial Airlines Flight 147.

CHAPTER TWENTY

The residents at the ranch were not very concerned
with news broadcasts. Immediately following the incident at Indigo Lake, they had scanned newspapers
and diligently kept up with television and radio
coverage, only to find that the government disinforma-
tion officers had successfully thrown up a smoke
screen again. Something about how a military veteran
of the Middle-East conflict had "flashed back" during
the July Fourth fireworks and sent more than a third
of the resort's guests to private, government hospitals.
But after that they hadn't given the story much
thought. The more optimistic were sure that even the
federal boys couldn't maintain a charade that impris-
oned firsthand witnesses like Patricia Leffert, Garri-
son Whitechapel, and the first cousin of the President
of the United States of America for very long.

Generally speaking, their attention was occupied by

what would happen in only three days July 17, when the full moon would rise.

For this reason, no one at the ranch became aware of the fate of Celestial Airlines Flight 147 until mid-afternoon on that Saturday.

They were leaving another of the increasingly successful hypnotic sessions with high spirits. Kelly Davis heard the ominous announcement first. Though she definitely was a Class Two, a nonvoluntary shapeshifter, and Merrick was practically convinced that she wouldn't undergo the change to feral form at the impetus of the full moon, she was included in these gatherings at Neil's insistence. He was giving her a solid psychological foundation for self-control should she ever progress into the abilities and advantages of a Class One, which was known to happen from time to time.

She was passing one of the inset wall radio speakers which had been playing easy-listening tunes throughout the estate when one of the short newsbreaks interrupted the music. The first story had to do with Flight 147.

"Mr. Merrick," she said with a rare urgency, "what airline did the others use when they left last night?"

Neil, who had been discussing something with Lon Wicker, turned to the young woman. "I don't know, Kelly. Why do you ask?"

"I just heard on the radio, there was a big crash last night over the Atlantic, and I think they said the plane was heading to Portugal."

Neil Merrick, ever cordial and calm, went dead-white and whispered, "Dear God."

Wicker didn't understand what any of this had to do with him, never having given any attention to the plans of those who had chosen to "run like whipped dogs" from their own country. He turned to Kelly and, with the quickly acquired self-importance of the typical Class One, said, "Davis, you'd be better off if you didn't interrupt your superiors when they're—"

"Wicker, will you please shut up!" Merrick snapped. Then he pushed by the startled man and pressed his ear close to the wall speaker.

The others were shocked into silence by this uncharacteristic outburst, too, and cut off their own conversations to listen.

It was too late, though. The velvet-voiced announcer had moved on to another topic by then, something having to do with the IRA and another senseless bombing. Merrick clutched Kelly's arm fiercely. "What did he say?" he demanded of her. "What was the exact report?"

Rattled and in pain from the pressure of his grip, she took a moment to compose her thoughts for a response. "Um, it wasn't much, just that the Navy has a ship in the area of the Atlantic where a passenger jet bound for Portugal is thought to have crashed sometime last night. They don't know for sure, though, because they haven't found any wreckage or anything."

"Did he say from where the plane departed?"

"No. I mean, I don't think so."

"The airline? The flight number?"

"Celestial, yes, Celestial Airlines, but that's all."

With a flicker of movement, Merrick released her and darted ahead of the staring people into the media room, where he quickly switched on a wide-screen television and tuned it to an all-news satellite station. It was two-fifty-five, and he knew that the headlines would be repeated at the top of the hour.

"Blake, you don't think that the plane was the one that the others were on, do you?" Meg asked him tensely. She didn't know those people very well and had been put off by some of the ones whom she had met, but more and more she was coming to think of them as *her* people, almost her relatives.

"I don't know, Meg," Blake answered, though to himself he added, *how many flights from the U.S. to Portugal could there have been last night?* With the others, he hurried into the media room.

The newscast affirmed their worst fears. It had been Celestial Airlines Flight 147 which had left New Orleans for Lisbon the evening before only to disappear approximately halfway through its journey. So far, there was absolutely no clue as to what had happened to it, no last second communications from the aircraft itself, no oil slick, no bright orange liferafts signaling survivors. There hadn't been, as yet, even a claim of responsibility for the disappearance of the jet by any of the usual political extremists.

"That's it, then," Lon Wicker stated slowly, but with only feigned emotion, "they're all dead."

"We won't jump to conclusions without all of the facts." The sentence was again in the Merrick range of easy authority, but the unspoken order to keep his opinions to himself was not lost on Wicker.

"I wish that we could find out *something*." Meg sighed. "I mean, not knowing for sure if it was their flight is almost as bad as being certain that it was."

Neil rose from the sofa before the television with a clear set to his features. "We can," he said. "I'm going to my study and I don't want to be disturbed." He began to leave the room.

"Neil, maybe it would be better if you had someone with you—" Blake called after him.

"I said I didn't want to be disturbed, Mr. Corbett!"

Blake whistled silently. Oh, well, from equal participant in the adventure to disciplined schoolboy in one short step.

Merrick knowingly made three extremely dangerous calls on his possibly tapped telephone. Even if the government assault team didn't know that this secluded residence was another association hideout, it seemed quite possible that they were on to his sources in and around New Orleans—wasn't the crash evidence of that strong probability?—and could trace the calls back to him. What other mysterious, wealthy caller would be using illegal methods to find out the names on the passenger list of Flight 147 before this information was released to the public?

At that moment, however, he didn't give a damn about the risks.

He knew who would have been on that jet; the calls only put the words into the mouths of others. For a long time, he sat behind his large desk and rested his face in his hands.

The meeting was called for six that evening, when normally they would have been sitting down to dinner. It was a silent and downcast gathering. For all they knew, they were the last members of their race on the North American continent.

"I'm not going to waste your time with speeches," Merrick told them. "We know that Adine and Pepe and Lisolette and all of the others are dead."

"But we can't be sure," Melanie Ryan interrupted. Unlike Lon Wicker, her pain was real. "Maybe they survived and they'll be picked up. Sometimes people live for weeks on rafts."

Somehow, Merrick summoned a warm smile for her. "Yes, I suppose it's possible," he said a bit hoarsely, "but we can't go on that assumption. They must have died when the plane was shot out of the sky."

"Shot down?" Nick repeated. "Who would have done that? They were in the middle of the goddamned ocean, not near any borders or war zones or . . ." Realization spread across his face painfully.

Merrick nodded. "I knew that out of all of us you would understand the soonest, Nicholas, after what they already have done to you."

"Who?" asked Meg. "What are you talking about?"

"Our friends in the government," Merrick replied.

"No." Meg looked from Neil to Nick, shaking her head at each of them. "No, you're wrong, they wouldn't do that. They wouldn't shoot down a planeload of people—a planeload of mostly *ordinary* people just to stop a few of us from escaping the country!"

"Babe," Grundel began slowly, "I . . . Who else?"

"That's crazy! *You're* crazy, both of you! They wouldn't do that!"

"Meg, while I was inside, they . . . Well, there were rumors in the general pop that the scientists who were studying us had culled a few subjects for surgical study. While they were still alive. I guess it's called vivisection. They find us very intriguing."

Meg closed her eyes tightly.

"Maybe it's time we retaliate," said a rather surprising voice. Every eye in the room was instantly drawn to Tristan Grandillon. They respected the sheer power that radiated from the man who had been the association's equivalent of a military leader, and, if the truth were known, they were each afraid of him, as well. "If these cowardly pigs have decided to declare war on us, the best response is to show them that we're ready to fight back, to kick some ass ourselves."

"Yeah," Lon Wicker agreed in a low breath.

"We've hidden like rats in our holes for long enough," Grandillon continued, "and it's time to let it be known that we are *here*, we're established, viable, and damned certainly ready and able to fight for our place. Neil, I'm not going to stand by while they act like superstitious savages and eliminate us from the face of the earth."

Charles Gladden seemed inspired by those words. "I think he's right, Mr. Merrick! If we don't make a stand now, we'll lose whatever chance we have of convincing them that we have a right to exist." A number of other voices joined in that sentiment.

Merrick raised his hand, and the room fell silent. They may have respected Grandillon for his threatening presence, but they knew that Neil commanded the same consideration for his mind. "No blind, futile gestures, please," he said calmly. "As Ms. Talley has pointed out, we don't have any solid evidence that the jet was shot down. It may have been mechanical failure—"

"The one time that it was carrying forty-three members of the association?" Gladden demanded angrily. "Goddamn it, Neil, I don't believe in coincidences!"

Merrick moved nothing other than his eyes, but these fixed on the Class-Two housekeeper and drained every atom of rage and indignation from Gladden's soul. He mumbled an apology that barely made it past his lips and sank back into his chair.

Merrick went on, "Accident or act of war, we can't change the past. But I do have a plan in mind. I've just learned from my own sources that a very important meeting—a demonstration, if you will—is scheduled for Monday night. Yes, Nick, I have my own network of information gatherers, though there is no one actually inside the government itself, or I would have known that your escape was a planned exercise to locate the rest of us.

"Monday's meeting will take place in San Francisco rather than at the Institute, and it is designed to be a highly secretive demonstration of just what happened in December of last year."

"They're going to tell the world about us?" asked Nick. "That's what *we* were trying to do while we were running from the idiots! Why in the hell did they have to pull that ridiculous attack back at the island?"

"I didn't say that they were going to tell the world about us, Nick, only selected segments of it."

Chris caught the meaning of that instantly. "Selected government segments."

"That's right. My inside man tells me that there will be several U.S. senators there, as well as invited guests of similar federal standing from a number of other countries: Canada, Great Britain, France, Germany, perhaps ten or fifteen others. You see, the purpose of the event will be to present all of the known facts about us to the representatives and then to rip away all shreds of disbelief by showing some of those who were infected by Cummings during and after total transformation at midnight."

"Those sons of bitches!" Nick spat.

"A secret meeting," Merrick went on, almost to himself. "Secret in planning, production, and post-production. What those people from other lands will do is set up task forces in their own countries to locate and 'neutralize' their home-grown lycanthropes before all of this becomes public knowledge. The secrecy is to avoid—"

"Public panic," Nick finished sardonically.

"Exactly." Merrick lightly massaged his temple with his hand. "Before . . . before what occurred last night and before I learned of this upcoming meeting, I had planned to bring all of you along into full awareness and control of your new abilities. Then, with your permission, I was going to take you to the Institute during the night of a full moon in, say, October or November, and show the terrified bastards how you were able to conquer the most unfortunate aspects of infection in a relatively short period of time. But this demonstration changes everything. We can't allow them to spread their attitudes of fear and anger to other countries. There are nations whose policies in this regard will make our own look compassionate."

"But what can we do about it?" Melanie asked.

"We could kill them," Grandillon stated.

"All that would do would be to give them real grounds for their fears," Merrick disagreed. "Someone has to go there, to be there when the other unfortunates are metamorphosing and convincing a collection of modern men and women that ancient horrors do exist. Then that someone will have to show the representatives that the primal regressions can be overcome and the initiated person can lead a life rich beyond their fantasies."

"Let me go with you, Neil," Corbett said.

"No. Thank you for volunteering, Blake, but it can't be risked. You may be at the point where you can resist the compulsion to change that way, all of you may, but you understand that one failure would destroy the effort entirely, and none of us would leave the building alive. No, this job is solely for experienced and fully realized Class-One individuals. Since last night, only Tristan and I fill that description."

"I'm with you, Neil," Grandillon said.

"I know you are, Tristan. Just remember why we're doing this."

"But to expose yourselves to them . . . It seems so dangerous, almost like suicide," Meg whispered.

Merrick smiled. "Don't worry about us, my dear. We've been in rough spots before, and we've always come through. Actually, I'm rather looking forward to it."

"So am I," echoed Grandillon, but his voice contained an entirely different emotion.

When the bus made a fifteen-minute stop in San Antonio, Texas, the man got off to buy a morning newspaper. He purposely didn't look at the headlines as he removed it from the box and placed it, folded, under his arm. In fact he saved it, like a child saving the last bit of dessert, until he could stand the temptation no longer while on the bus that left the city limits and rolled smoothly along the westbound highway. It was then that he opened the paper and gazed at the headlines that screamed about the loss of an American passenger jet somewhere over the deep Atlantic.

He laughed to himself. *We made the big time, baby.*

Naturally, there were other travel options open to the man, including a few that would have brought him to his destination in northern California that same evening. But he didn't want to arrive too early and allow the pitiful remnants of the association the chance to recognize and prepare themselves against him.

He wished to make his appearance for this final act right on cue, which would be Monday night.

Charles Gladdon gazed at his prisoners and thought, *This is right, this is the way that it should be.*

The Class-Two associate was in charge now, perhaps for the last time in his life. Merrick and Grandillon were gone, heading north into San Francisco to crash the top-secret government party and the others were safely locked in their cells in the west wing, where they would undergo their most basic transformation because they were as yet unable to resist the purely psychological dictates of the full moon that was beaming brightly outside.

It was Monday, 9 P.M., three hours away from the most critical minutes of the entire history of the association in North America.

Gladdon enjoyed looking at his charges at this moment, as they sat either morosely or nervously on

the simple cots behind the bars that made the entire
wing resemble the set of a thirties penitentiary melo-
drama. The cells were so sparsely furnished because
there was no reason to provide anything more when
they were used only a few hours every month and the
detainees passed those hours in homicidal manic
states.

I could kill them, thought Gladden. He could take
the gun and the shells from the safe upstairs, come
down here, and blast their brains to jelly. It might take
awhile, maybe he would have to reload a few times,
but he could manage that. Then he could kill Neil and
Tristan in the morning, and no one would be left to
remind him that he was only a Class Two, who could
be twisted into any sort of clown that they decided. He
could do it.

The eyes of the seven confined people stared back at
him as if they were aware of what sort of fantasies
were spinning within his head. They may not have
known the exact words of his scenario, but they had
no trouble in reading the hatred that inspired his
thoughts.

"Are you going to stand there and gawk at us for the
whole damned night?" Lon Wicker demanded nervously.

Rage flooded through Charles, rage and violent
disappointment. By a sheer accident of luck, this
petty, frightened little man, who never should have
expected to evolve beyond being the owner of a
negligible Lewiston bistro, stood at the threshold to a
life of godlike proportions while he, Charles Gladden,
who had devoted his entire existence to attaining such
a state, was condemned to an eternity of servitude.

I could kill him with my hands, Gladden decided. *I
wouldn't even need the gun.* Until Wicker learned to
control the limitless power that lived within him, he
was no more dangerous than an uninfected man. *I*

could pull his brain from his skull like the fruit of a melon or squeeze his heart until it ran through my fingers.

But he did neither.

"I'm sorry, Mr. Wicker, but I have my instructions," Gladden, the perpetual second-class human being, answered. "Mr. Merrick has outlined my duties for tonight, and one of them is to maintain constant attention should you need assistance."

"Yeah, like *you* could do anything for us," Wicker grunted. "Hell, you're like a damned eunuch, you can't even change the color of your hair."

Charles's eyes went hard, like sharp chips of blue ice, but with a titanic effort of will, he said nothing.

"Quit staring at me," Lon muttered.

Gladden slowly turned his gaze from the man. After all, with seven individuals locked in as many cells, he had plenty of other subjects to scrutinize.

Silence fell on the long room as the group of people watched a soundless wall clock which was slowly dragging them toward their private fractions of hell. In fact, it was almost a quarter of an hour before Melanie Ryan, the twenty-three-year-old secretary from Des Moines, who seemed entirely lost in the events that had flooded over her in the past weeks, spoke, "God, I hope that Neil convinces them to stop the killing."

"Don't worry about Neil. He's very persuasive," Blake noted. "I just wish that we were advanced enough to have helped him in the effort. Charles, while we have a moment, I wonder if you'd answer a few questions for us."

Gladden was seated in a straight-backed chair next to the entrance to the room, and he nodded briefly. "Anything I can, Mr. Corbett."

"Well, this is something that has been bothering me since the Fourth. I didn't want to trouble Neil with it, since he's had so much on his mind and all—"

"That's our good friend and professional author, ladies and gentlemen," Nick said from his cell across the room. "As enlightening and succinct as a Gregorian chant."

Gladden forced a short smile. "Please don't feel embarrassed about asking me anything, Mr. Corbett."

Blake took a deep breath. "Okay. Being locked up this way tonight reminded me. Who were those people in the cellar at the mansion?"

To Charles, the question was like the blindside tackle that knocks a quarterback from the game. He knew who the prisoners had been, of course. He'd put a few of them down there himself, but Neil Merrick had made it clear in terms as strong as he had ever employed with Charles that this subject was never to be discussed with the new associates. Maybe the older man had planned to keep them ignorant of the reason for imprisoning those people in the hopes that the new members might not develop a taste for the matter, or maybe Neil had just wanted to explain the situation to them himself. For whatever reason, Gladden understood that if he so much as hinted to this audience the truth about that collection of rebellious Class Twos, fading Class Threes, dangerous Class Fours and Fives, or the uninitiated men and women with them, he himself would be in deep shit.

"Charles?" Blake prompted.

His first response was a form of denial. "I'm afraid I don't know who you're talking about."

"The hell you don't!" said Wicker. "We all saw them while we were running through the tunnel under the lake. They were screaming and crying like kids. Don't tell us you've never seen them before! Answer me, hotshot!" he demanded. "Did you forget that you're only a Class Two and I'm a Class One? I'm *ordering* you to answer!"

"Lon, take it easy!" Blake said quickly. "Man, I didn't mean to start an argument or anything. If Charles says that he doesn't know who they were, I'm willing to take him at his word. It wasn't that important, anyway."

But Wicker wouldn't let it go. "I gave this asshole a direct order, Corbett, and I'd appreciate it if you wouldn't undercut my authority."

"All right!" At Gladden's shout the room fell silent. His face told them all that he had finally crossed the line over into insanity, the seething resentment that had been boiling inside him like a pool of lava since he discovered that he had slipped out of the sacred Class-One status exploded over the rim, and there would be no banking of the fires now. He stood and walked down the center of the room without looking to either side at the faces that were fixed upon him. But they each felt his hatred.

"All right, you want to know the truth?" he asked. "Then I'll tell you. Merrick will flip out over it, but he's probably going to get his butt fried by the Army tonight, anyway. Hell, we all may be dead by daybreak."

He reached the end of the room and stopped, pausing an instant before turning on them like a prosecutor in a bad courtroom drama. "Who were they? Some were Class Twos, Threes, and Fives, people who had been inducted into the organization and either lost their ability to control the Life force or proved they were immune to it from the beginning. Do you know what it's like to be admitted to the most glorious circle of people that your mind can imagine and then have it snatched away from you?" he snapped at a wide-eyed Melanie Ryan. When she didn't answer, he went on, "It's like—no, it's worse than losing your arms or your legs or your sight! My God, it's like being allowed a vision of a heaven and then having the door slammed in your face."

"All of the non-self-determinate associates are locked away like that?" Blake asked with a trace of repulsion in his voice.

Gladden sneered at the inanity of the question. "Of course not. I'm here, right? All any of them would have had to do was agree to become a scraping bootlicker like me and they would have been as free as the air. Or as free as the Ones will permit.

"The guys in the cells were the Twos, Threes, and Fives who decided that they deserved as much of a say in the affairs of the association as the revered Ones, and if they didn't have it, they would reveal our existence to the world."

"What's the big secret, then?" Wicker said. "It sounds perfectly reasonable to me. Damn, man, every organization has to have some kind of internal policing agency."

All the way, Charles told himself, *don't hold back*. If Merrick and Grandillon didn't get shot to pieces tonight, he could still get the hell out of there before they came back. What was he waiting for? He grinned at them. "Because those people you saw weren't just being held in custody, jerk, they were being saved for food."

There were no cries of outrage or disbelief, but the collective intake of breath contained as much passion as any words. Gladden laughed aloud.

"What the hell did you think, you imbeciles?" he shouted. "We're werewolves! Those little bastards swimming around in our bloodstreams *crave* flesh! Human flesh! Did you think that all of the legends were garbage? Why were Peter Stump and Giles Garnier burned to death? You have to be crazy or retarded not to know!"

"You're lying, you son of a bitch!" Nick screamed. "We're not like that!"

"Who infected you, brother? Cummings, wasn't it? Didn't you see what he was doing to those other pathetic clowns at the Institute?"

Nick staggered back from the bars in his cell and sat heavily on the cot. He felt as if some invisible force had engulfed his stomach and ripped it from his body, leaving behind a freezing emptiness. Doubling over with both arms wrapped about his midsection, he began whispering, "No, no, no, no . . ."

"Nickie!" cried Meg, who could see him from her cell.

Gladden continued to press in the knife. "Oh, you'll change your tune soon enough. Once you've gotten your first taste of it, you'll wonder how in God's name you were ever able to eat anything else. It's the best, like honey in your mouth, and the blood tastes like wine—"

"Shut up!" Chris shouted, gripping the bars as if holding the edge of a cliff.

"Or what, J.D.?" Charles asked baitingly.

"Or I'll bust your head open and wipe your face in what spills out." Chris's voice was low but heavy with threat.

With one hand, Gladden caught the back of the heavy chair in which he had been sitting and smashed it into splinters against the wall. "Not likely, tough guy. I'm not some drunken martial-arts dropout. I'd snap your spine with no more effort than that. You may be a Class One, you little shit, and I'll never be, but to me, right now, you're nothing more than strutting Southern trash."

"Open this damned door and we'll see what I am," Chris whispered.

Gladden fingered the keyring at his belt. "Boy, I'm going to ignore that and save your life." He looked about the room. "Think about it, folks, stew in it. You may believe you're some kind of blessed new race, but I know . . . Jesus, I've *seen* your insides! Yeah, right,

Saint Neil Merrick has promised that he can guide you around the muck and make this some kind of spiritual transition, but you'll find out. One smell of fresh blood and you'll find out what kind of addiction you're facing. A year from now you'll be scratching the dirt off graves just for a taste."

Melanie turned away from him, crying.

"You asked me who they were, didn't you?" he observed archly.

"Neil is going to put you in your place when he finds out about this, you sadistic creep," Wicker told him.

"The hell with Merrick! The hell with all of you!" As if suddenly struck by inspiration, and feeling power welling inside him, Gladden ripped the keyring from his belt and stalked to the cell holding Kelly Davis. She tried to evade his grasp after he had opened the door and stepped inside, but he caught her wrist and dragged her into the room after him. She cursed and fought him, but with his superhuman muscle, he hardly seemed to notice.

"Gladden, stop it!" Blake shouted, trying to make his words sound harsh and commanding, a difficult effort in the circumstances. "What do you think you're doing?"

Gladden's reply was devastating in its tone, if not its content. "Babydoll and I are going to do the dishes."

"Let her go!" Chris shrieked. He hit the bars of his cell so heavily with his forearm that they seemed to vibrate. "You lousy jackass, I'll kill you!"

Charles stopped at the doorway long enough to respond, "You've never killed anybody, little boy, but I have." Then he pulled Kelly from the room and slammed the door.

Meg sat limply on her cot. "Oh, my God, is this what we're becoming? Cannibals, murderers? *Grave robbers?*"

Chris pressed his face into the bars with fierce energy and squeezed his eyes shut.

Perhaps five minutes later, the door opened again and Neil Merrick strolled through as if on his way to his study for an afterdinner drink. "Good evening, everyone," he said.

"Neil!" Meg cried. "Thank God! You've got to stop him!"

Merrick seemed mildly intrigued by her urgency. "Stop whom, my dear?"

"Gladden!" Chris yelled as he leaped to the bars again. "He took Kelly upstairs somewhere! Hurry, man! We've got to do something!"

Merrick made calming motions with his hands. "Please, don't upset yourself. Everything's fine."

"You stopped the animal? Kelly's okay?"

"Of course I did. Just take it easy, son, because I've taken care of everything." Merrick shook his head in good-natured exasperation at their worry.

But everything wasn't fine. At the same instant both Chris and Blake were struck by the *wrongness* of this suddenly appearing man. The features . . . Well, they were perfect, they *were* Neil Merrick's features, and the voice was the same. But there was something in the phrasing and the timbre. . . .

Chris struggled to present what he hoped was a relieved expression. "That's great, Neil. How about letting me out of here?"

"Oh, let's not go through all of that rigmarole of unlocking and then relocking your cell as the hour approaches. Just relax, perhaps you can doze a bit. I just came down to check on everyone and ask a few questions."

"Open the door, Neil," Chris said with more emphasis.

Merrick ignored him. "Has anyone seen Tristan

lately? Within the last hour or so?"

That surprised the group, but it also alarmed Blake. Before he could comment, however, Lon Wicker asked, "What are you talking about, man? He left with you just forty-five minutes ago for San Francisco."

"Oh? What location?"

"Lon, be quiet!" Blake ordered. "Neil, who am I?"

Merrick turned to face him. "Memory problems, old boy? If you're experiencing mental difficulty, perhaps we should move you upstairs for a closer examination." He walked to Corbett's cell.

Blake backed away. "Tell me my name, Neil! Name anyone in this room!"

Wicker sighed in disgust. "Jeez, Corbett, be real, will you? We've got more important things to think about than your stupid little games."

Merrick smiled. "Yes, Corbett, let's not waste time with this foolishness."

"You keep your mouth shut, Wicker! Identify some-one else, Neil, anyone!" He stared at this person who was representing himself as his friend and searched his face for any sign of recognition; there was none. "Who in the hell are you?"

Wicker snorted a derisive laugh. "Damn, Corbett, you really are mental, aren't you? Who does he look like? Michael Jackson?"

"Merrick" joined the big man's laughter as he sidled to Wicker's cell. Then, with breathtaking abruptness, his hand snaked between two bars, gripped Wicker's shirtfront, and jerked the startled captive up against the bars. "All right, my friend, let's be very cooperative. Where did Grandillon go?"

"Lon, don't say anything!" Blake warned.

But Wicker's fear was more powerful than anything Blake could offer to counter it. "He went with you, man, to 'Frisco! What's going on?"

"Where in San Francisco? And why?" The man

tensed his arm and raised Wicker several inches off the floor.

"It's not Merrick!" Chris shouted. "He's somebody else, Lon, don't say anything!"

The man shook Wicker, banging his head against the bars. "Where?"

"Charles!" screamed Melanie. "Help us, Charles!"

The pain flashed through Wicker and burned away any resolve he might have possessed. "The, uh, the Berlinger Building, I don't know where it's located, I swear!"

"Why?"

"The meeting—some kind of government meeting with a bunch of foreign representatives and some werewolves to prove that we're real!"

The man nodded slowly and then thrust Wicker away from him as easily as he might have tossed aside an empty suit of clothes. "Midnight, then. Just about enough time." He began to walk toward the door through which he'd entered only a few minutes before.

"Wait a minute! What's going on? Who are you?" Blake called after the man. Intellectually, he'd been aware that life among voluntary shape-shifters would mean that no one could ever know for sure who another person was, but until this moment the full emotional impact of that reality had not struck him. When it did, the effect was overwhelming.

The man looked back at them. With a swift, strobe-like flash of white light, the Neil Merrick face wrinkled and remolded itself into a visage that none of them recognized. When he spoke, the voice was different, as well. "When Charles asks you who upset his lord and master's careful plans to make us respectable, tell him that Dom Poduano sends his regards." Then he left.

* * *

They shouted for attention and banged the bars and walls of their cells, but if Gladden heard them, he chose not to respond. The clock on the wall was inching toward ten.

After he had temporarily exhausted his fury in useless effort Chris slumped onto his cot. Yeah, in a couple of hours he would be a raging nightmare full of power and deadly, inexhaustable strength, but right now he was just ordinary Chris Wyler. Kelly was being brutalized, Neil and Tristan would be betrayed and probably killed by something that called itself Dom Poduano, and there wasn't a damned thing he could do to stop either event. He had to find an answer, something that would put an end to this craziness.

Blake's cell was next to his, and though Chris couldn't see him well due to the fact that a solid block wall separated them, the two could speak easily. "Blake," he said while the others shouted or cursed about them, "at that dinner, when you explained to us about what happened to you at the Institute when Cummings changed, you said there was this guy who actually fought him, hand to hand, right?"

Blake's voice was tired and resigned. "You mean Walter. Walter Taylor. Yes, that was really a sight to see."

"He did pretty good for a normal person, didn't he?" The plan was forming rapidly in Chris's mind now, and though he wouldn't admit it, it was scaring the spit from his mouth.

Blake responded with a weary laugh. "Oh, man, he was great. He had a mental problem, a type of autism that made him see the world as if he were some kind of barbarian warrior, a real Conan, and he was gigantic, over seven feet tall and strong as a bull. He wrenched a leg from a metal table for a club and nearly beat Cummings to death. If he'd been fighting anyone but a werewolf—"

"And this Walter was only, what, sixteen?"

"I believe so. What are you thinking, Chris?"

"Nothing. Just passing the time."

Blake's voice swung a bit toward alarm. "I know that you think you have to do something, son, we all do, but you can't fight Charles! My Lord, he has five times your strength!"

Jeff Banky, in the box car, had been two or three times as strong as him. "Muscle doesn't always make the difference in the end." Of course, Banky had been fifty pounds overweight with a bad leg, too.

That didn't convince Blake. "We'll reason with him when he comes back—*if* he ever comes back. I know that he doesn't sound as if he cares about Neil or Tristan anymore, but he has to feel some sense of loyalty to them. When we tell him about Poduano—"

"Damn, man, you know what he's doing to Kelly! He doesn't give a damn about Neil. No, he *hates* him, just like he hates all of us, because we're Ones and he's stuck as a Two. He's going to split out of here just as soon as he's finished with Kelly. I only hope that he brings her back to lock her up before he leaves so that I can bait him into a match. If he hasn't killed her already."

Blake punched the bars before him with the side of his clenched fist. "Walter's *dead*, Chris! Cummings ripped out his throat! Yeah, he put up one hell of a fight, and his intervention saved a lot of lives, including mine, but when it came down to it, his normal human strength couldn't withstand Cummings's teeth and claws!"

Talk me out of it, man, Chris thought with a private grin. "There are differences, Blake. Gladden's no werewolf, not really. I know he's strong, but he's not particularly fast, and I decked him with one shot just a few days ago."

"You did?" Blake responded in surprise. "Well, he

still has the ability to recover from any injury at an accelerated rate. I think that's what finally killed Walter, the fact that whatever amount of damage he inflicted on Cummings was instantly repaired."

"I didn't see him, but I did see that man at the island torn open by bullets and jump to his feet and run away. I don't think that Class Twos heal that fast. If I can put him out for just a while, only a ten count maybe, then I can let everybody else out and we can try to get to San Francisco before Poduano ruins everything. Or before we change tonight."

"Chris, this is admirable of you, really, but I don't believe it will be necessary." Blake sighed, but it was as much a hopeful sound as weariness. "I think that I'm near the point where I can control my own transformations."

"You're kidding! This soon?"

"I really think so. It's due to the new chemo-hypnosis sessions. You're probably as advanced as I am, and I know that as midnight gets closer the strange sensation is getting stronger."

Chris thought about this. He *did* feel weird. Psychological or not, that damned full moon was powerful!

"You don't have to let him kill you, Chris," Blake said. "Just wait until he leaves us alone again, and then at least one of us should be able to conquer our impulses enough to hold on to our minds and get out of this place. Whoever's successful can take the van to San Francisco and warn Neil before the change comes."

Chris had never lost a fight in his life—at least, not one that could have been considered to have been remotely fair—but he'd never gone against anyone with the sheer muscle of Charles Gladden, either. He wanted to warn Neil of the disguised danger that was racing north toward him and he ached to repay Gladden for what must be happening to Kelly at that moment, but he didn't want to die. Blake's strategy told him that he wouldn't have to. He settled back onto his cot to wait.

It was ten-fifteen when Gladden returned. He pulled Kelly after him, and from the blood and bruises on her face and the stunned, vacant look in her eyes, Chris knew that his worst fears had been on target. Charles was grinning like a monkey.

"You dirty son of a bitch," Chris whispered.

"Chris, please!" Blake said. "Just let him know who was here, and if that doesn't work, don't do anything to cause him to hang around."

"Yeah." The boy stared at Kelly's swollen features. "Yeah."

Blake raised his voice. "Charles, someone else is in the house."

Gladden's face registered an instant of shock and a little fear. "Who? Wait, how would *you* know?"

"He came down here to speak to us. He looked like Neil."

The flash of fear was definite this time. Gladden had hoped to be long gone and lost in the anonymity of the population of California before Merrick had a hint of his intentions. "Where is he? Why did he come back from San Francisco before the meeting?"

"He *looked* like Neil, but it wasn't him," Lon Wicker said quickly. "He fooled me, all of us, and he tricked us into telling him where Merrick really was."

Blake hadn't wanted to release all of that information to the dangerously angry Gladden yet, but it was too late.

Charles relaxed visibly. "Quit trying to jerk me around, Wicker. You don't expect me to believe a load of garbage like that, do you?"

"It's true, man, I swear to God! I thought he was going to kill me!"

"Damn. You mean to say that another Class One

who knew the codes to get him through both the gates and the front door sneaked in here as Neil and pumped you for information?" Gladden asked contemptuously.

"That's the only answer," Blake replied. "We saw his face change when he was leaving."

"In case you forgot, dumbass, there are no other Class Ones on this continent! Uncle Sam blasted them all to hell, remember?" He tugged Kelly toward the empty cell from which he had taken her. "I don't know what you idiots think that you can accomplish by this, but I'm not going to waste my time playing games with you." He started to shove her inside.

Desperate now, Blake said, "He told us his name. Dom Poduano."

That froze Gladden in his tracks. "Dom? What do you know about Dom?"

"Just that he was the man who came in here. He tried to pretend that he was Neil, but we saw through him, so he forced the information out of Lon and then left. But before he went, he said to tell you that Dom Poduano was going to upset the plans that Neil and Tristan had made. Charles, you've got to warn them. If he changes his appearance again, they wouldn't have a prayer of recognizing him before he does something to sabotage the demonstration!"

Gladden shook his head. "Poduano's dead, Corbett. I saw the films myself. He went loco, and Tristan tracked him and caught him and locked him in the containment unit on the island. Then they used the gas and the bowl to burn him into about a half pound of smoking sludge."

"Well, that's who the guy claimed to be, and he certainly sounded crazy to me."

Gladden considered this a moment longer. "You're the crazy ones if you think I'm going to fall for that crap. Nobody could get into this place without my knowing it, though, I have to admit, my girlfriend and

I were a little busy at the time." He laughed coldly.

"Eunuch!" Kelly spat. Her bloodied lips twisted into a harsh smile, too. "You talk big, but you couldn't deliver on the promise, could you?"

Gladden slapped her face.

Chris threw himself against the bars. "Stop hitting her, you shithead! If you don't leave her alone, I'll beat you to death, I promise you that!"

Still holding on to Kelly's arm, Gladden seemed ready to answer the threat, but a sudden thought stopped him. He grinned. Instead of locking the young woman in her own cell, he forced her across the room to Chris's door, where he placed one large hand about her throat.

"Get back or I'll break her neck," he ordered.

Chris was confused by the demand, but he stepped to the rear of the cell as Charles took the keyring from his belt and unlocked the door. He had no chance to move when Gladden opened the door just wide enough to permit Kelly to squeeze through and pushed her roughly toward Chris.

"Now you lovebirds can be together at the big moment," he said, closing the door.

Chris caught Kelly as she stumbled forward, but she pulled away from him fiercely. "Don't touch me!" she cried, throwing herself onto the cot and refusing to look at him. He stood helplessly, his questioning face turning from her to Gladden and back again.

"Have fun," Charles whispered. "I believe I'd like to watch this." He strolled to the wall opposite the cell and leaned against it, a stocky, muscular, and thoroughly intimidating presence, who looked bigger and meaner than Sonny Liston in Chris's eyes. "I can spare an hour and a half."

The truth of the situation hammered into the boy's mind. "Charles, wait! For Christ's sake, you can't leave her in here with *me*! What about midnight?

When I change? *I'll kill her!"*

"Brain damage really slows down the memory, huh, Wyler?" Gladden answered.

Meg understood, too. "Charles, please, just put her in another cell!"

Gladden's smile was swept aside by anger. "Don't tell me what to do, bitch! You're not in charge here! None of you are! So just sit down and shut up!"

"But I won't be able to stop myself!" shouted Chris. His fear and rage at Gladden and at what he'd already done couldn't sustain itself against the horror he felt at what *he*, Chris Wyler, might be compelled to do. Kelly was staring at him now with eyes as big as windows. "Charles, I know—I know that you hate us, but don't do this. If you won't get in touch with Neil, at least don't force me into this. I don't want to hurt her!"

"Thirty seconds ago, you said you'd kill me," Gladden observed. "Rather selective in our sympathies, aren't we?" And following that, he said nothing more, completely ignoring any further questions, pleas, or demands.

The minutes seemed to race by. He had to think of something, come up with some way to get Kelly out of harm's way, but Chris's mind remained as blank as a fresh field of snow.

He couldn't rely on Blake's imaginary "self-control."

He couldn't kill Kelly.

He had to do something. Now.

"If I lose it and become a Two, will it happen to me, too, Gladden?" he asked in a low voice that carried through the silent room with raw power.

Charles roused himself from his reverie and stood away from the wall. There was no furniture outside the cells other than the chair that he already had smashed, which meant that he would have to stand or sit on the floor until midnight, but that was no problem for a man of his restructured body. "What are you talking about?"

Chris kept his tone level and passionless. "You know, if I slip down a class, will I lose my manhood the way you did?"

"You shut your filthy mouth, you little bastard!" Gladden's voice had risen to almost a shriek.

Chris painted his face with the innocent expression that covered his youthful features so easily. "But you couldn't do it to Kelly, could you? I just figured that it was a result of, you know, losing your ability to—"

"She kicked me, the little animal hurt me!"

Kelly tore her eyes away from Chris and spat in Gladden's direction.

Chris nodded. "Oh. I can understand that. But is that why you only fight girls now? Because you're a Class Two, I mean?"

Gladden seemed to have regained a bit more self-control. "Just sit down and shut up or I'll show you who I'm going to fight next."

"I'd beat you." Chris added acid to the words by ending them with a sly grin.

"Sure, kid, sure. I'd smash your skull like a marshmallow."

Chris laughed. "Like Kelly said, big talk. Especially from that side of the bars. I already put you on your ass once."

Chris knew that this would be his last fight as an ordinary human being. He would pit his ordinary bone and muscle against a man who had five times his strength. It might really *be* his last fight.

"Don't get too brave off of a cheap shot, bozo," Gladden advised him. "I don't give second chances."

"I won't ask for one. Open the door. We'll go one on one, and if I win, you'll let us drive to San Francisco to warn Neil about Poduano."

Gladden was walking about the room now,

loosening his shoulders and cutting sidelong glances at the awesomely conceited boy. "If you lose?"

Chris shrugged. "That's up to you, isn't it?"

"You bet it is, chappie." The man took the keyring from his belt and tossed it with a jangle into the doorway at the far end of the long room. "There's your reward. Get past me and you can unlock any door you want, but I'm going to give you fair warning. I'm going to snap your spine, rip off your head, and piss down your neck. It won't make a tinker's damn to you what happens at midnight."

"You got it, man."

"Chris, no!" Meg cried.

"He's not going to let you kill him, Gladden!" Blake shouted. "*We're* not going to let you! Now, be an adult, for God's sake, and let me try to get to Merrick before it's too late."

"We've reached our deal," Charles told them all. "There's one way out of those cells. If he's as tough as he claims to be, good enough. If not, you'd better pray that Neil or Tristan live long enough to get back here, or you'll starve right where you are."

Kelly looked up at the boy and seemed to understand, really, for the first time what he was willing to do for her. "Don't do it, Chris. He's so damned strong. He'll kill you."

Chris looked at her and closed his eyes for a moment. Then he walked to the cell door. Smiling, Charles retrieved the keys.

When Gladden unlocked the door and Chris stepped out, Kelly tried to thrust herself through the opening as well, apparently to help him against this human bulldozer. Gladden caught her face in one hand, shoved her back to the cot, and slammed the door.

With hysterical strength, Chris hit Gladden at the base of his neck with a double-fisted blow that drove the man staggering to his left. Nick and Wicker screamed in triumph, and with Charles hurt, however momentarily, Chris forced his advantage by hooking his right leg before both of Gladden's and clubbing him again to the side of the head. Gladden went to the floor hard, and the others nearly exploded in a united paroxysm of joy.

Chris leaped for the keys that Charles had dropped upon being hit the first time. In a way, he was counting on Gladden's sense of sport—hadn't he said that all Chris had to do was get the keys?—but he also knew that he could use all the help that he could get. His fingers failed to close about the metal ring at the end of his dive, because Gladden managed to catch his ankle, but he hit the ring hard enough to send the keys skittering through the bars into Wicker's cell. Lon immediately snatched them up.

"That's it!" Chris yelled happily. "We've got the keys! It's over! Let everybody out, Lon!"

Gladden rolled into a sitting position while still holding Chris's ankle in a viselike grip. "You open that door and I'll kill you, Wicker!" he bellowed. "I mean it!"

Wicker stared at the keys in his hands and then at Gladden's terrifying face.

Chris rolled to his back, twisting his leg half a turn. "You said that all I had to do was get them. I got them, man! That's the end of it!"

"Do you believe everything you're told, kid?" sneered Gladden. "This thing is between you and me, not them. When it's over, one of us will be dead and the other will be the winner. Want to guess who the betting favorite is?"

"I don't bet." With this, the boy lashed out with his free foot and smashed Gladden's face.

It was a solid kick, one that would have left most men either unconscious or easy prey for more blows, but it did no more than break Gladden's nose; he didn't even lose his grip on Chris's ankle. Crying out in pain, he threw Chris away from him and clutched his face with both hands.

Chris flew across the stone floor as if he had been shot from a cannon. Where his bare flesh touched the rock, he was immediately burned by the friction. His short cry of anguish was choked off when he collided with the wall next to the only exit from the room. His head bounced off it and shattered his consciousness into a million glistening shards, so that he dropped limply to the floor.

When he came around after only a few seconds, the first thing he saw was Charles climbing unsteadily to his feet across the room, blood gushing from his nose and an almost palpable hatred radiating from his eyes. Though everyone in the cellar seemed to be calling his name, Chris distinctly heard Gladden hiss, "I'm going to tear out your heart and eat it."

"Lon, open the door and get us out of here!" Blake roared. "Move, you idiot! We've got to help him!"

This drew Gladden's attention for a vital moment. "I told you I'd kill you," he said shortly. Wicker's eyes widened with fear.

"Then throw them to me!" Blake ordered from across the room. "I'll do it! Don't just stand there! Lon!"

Wicker continued to look at the keys in his hands until his fingers opened as if drained of life and the ring jangled to the floor.

Chris had desperately needed this moment to compose himself and painfully work himself to his feet. His leg hurt, but it didn't seem to be seriously injured. When Gladden turned that baleful stare on him, everything snapped back into focus. This was real. This was win or die.

"You don't stay down, do you, boy?" Gladden said through the flowing blood. As Chris had suspected, the rate of recovery of the average Class Two was not as accelerated as a Class One's. This, added to Gladden's thoroughly normal reflex speed were the only pluses on Chris's side.

The breeze from the open door behind Chris whispered across his back like breath from a grave. Kelly noticed the exit, too, and cried out, "Run, Chris! Get outside and he'll never catch you!"

Blake's face broke into delight. "Get to a phone and call the Berlinger Building! Tell them there's a bomb, and they'll never go through with the demonstration!"

God, it made sense to Chris. His leg ached, but it was still functional, and he knew that Gladden couldn't catch him in a sprint, even if the bastard's strength and stamina might win out over the long run. Chris might find a weapon by that time. . . .

Gladden read the thoughts in his eyes. "Run out on me now, pissant, and I'll kill every person in this room, starting with your girlfriend."

That didn't frighten Kelly. "Get out of here, you stupid jerk!"

But Chris had read Charles's eyes, too. He wiped his sweating hands on his thighs and raised his fists up to his chest.

Charles grinned. "All right. Let's rock and roll."

Chris had to stay away from that power. Technique meant zero when the punches were backed by that much strength. Chris knew of Gladden's extensive martial-arts training, but he wasn't overly concerned with this threat, having seen karate and kung-fu bully boys beaten senseless by street toughs. But that raw muscle. . . .

Gladden threw a sucker right hand, and Chris established himself immediately. Ducking the ridge punch, he landed four shots to the man's stomach in the space of a heartbeat. Gladden grunted and folded at the waist from the impact, allowing Chris to score with a clean right uppercut. Gladden staggered back, and the boy followed, throwing and landing blows with the power and speed of a demon. Charles slammed against the wall and, for a moment, was pinned there by the ferocity of the punishment that Chris was delivering.

He threw everything, not about to let this golden opportunity slip away. Elbows, head butts, knees, and shoulder blocks exploded into the man's face, throat, and groin. Gladden's body crashed again and again into the block wall, as his head made drum sounds while bouncing against it.

Led by Nick's profanity-laced cries, the captives cheered on this boy who shouldn't have stood a chance in hell against the human powerhouse he faced.

Jesus, I'm going to kill him! Chris thought in horror. Though every instinct that he had ever developed in his brutal life screamed for him to continue, he dropped his burning arms and stepped back, giving Gladden room to fall. No one could have taken all of that and remained conscious.

Charles's face was a bloody mask, but the extraordinary strength with which he had endowed himself before he had receded to Class-Two status somehow kept him on his feet. He wasn't unnaturally fast, true, but Chris's surprise when he remained up allowed the man to lash back with a single punch that seemed to detonate in the boy's face.

It seemed that the entire world had crashed into Chris's head. His left cheek shattered as if it had been an eggshell hit by a hammer, and his feet flew from beneath him. He didn't hear the cries of the others, just as he didn't feel the steel bars of Kelly's cell when he hit them and slid limply to the floor. His mind dived deeply into the blackness of death even as Gladden began to recover enough to understand what his blind punch had accomplished.

Blake snapped his face away from the sight. For a fleeting moment, he had believed that a truly exceptional athlete could match his skills against a superhuman being, and damn if Chris Wyler hadn't made that fantasy look like reality—until that single, awful punch. Blake had seen Walter Taylor die; he couldn't watch it happen to another boy.

Chris slumped against the cell bars with his face blazing like an out-of-control gas fire, and Kelly aggravated the condition by trying to rouse him. "Get the keys, baby," she whispered urgently. "Let me out of here, and I'll help you, I'll kill him for you, but you've got to get the *keys!*" She shook him roughly.

Thirty feet away, Charles balanced uncertainly on his weak legs and shook the bells out of his head. Chris had done some serious damage of his own already.

Chris groaned, coming around.

Gladden pushed off from the wall and lurched across the room to the cell. His powerful hands caught Kelly's and ripped them from the boy's shoulders. Kelly shrieked in pain as she was thrust back across the cell, and this sound more than the searing pain from his face cut through the deadening haze that had enveloped Chris's mind. He looked up, found Gladden standing astride him, and kicked the man as hard as he could in the groin.

The blow actually lifted Charles from the floor. He fell back, screaming shrilly, and began to roll away from Chris without the breath to prolong that first anguished cry.

"Hot damn! Get him, Chris, stomp him!" yelled Nick.

Kelly ran to the bars again and wrapped her bleeding fingers about them. "Get the keys! Wicker, throw them over here!"

Lon was startled that the fight had lasted this long,

and at the sound of his name, he seemed to realize
that he still held the power to release everyone in the
room and provide the kid with help to subdue Gladden. He stood from his cot and drew back his arm to
toss the keyring to Kelly, when Charles reached
another cell and levered himself to his feet with the
tremendous strength of one arm. At that, Wicker sank
back into a sitting position.

"I'll kill you!" Gladden wailed at Chris. He staggered forward, half-dead from the waist down. "I'll
tear out your lungs and eat your eyes!"

Chris may not have been superhuman, yet, but
through a series of lucky accidents involving heredity,
environment, and personality, he was as close to that
state as a normal human could be, at least so far as
fighting was concerned. This was what Chris did to
affirm his own worth, so, in a very real way, this was
who he was. He climbed to his feet to meet Gladden's
charge.

He knew the bones in the left side of his face were
shattered, and his eye already had swollen to a slit on
that side to reduce his vision by half, but he didn't
run. Gladden lurched in with another wild punch, and
Chris slipped it, ghostlike, and countered with a
terrible right cross that landed flush on the man's
chin. Charles wavered, but he didn't go down.

The pattern was fixed at that. Gladden's unnatural
strength allowed him to rush time and again after the
wraith whose fists and feet lashed him with pain.
Chris's incredible natural gifts worked to steer him
inches away from quick death even as he fired back
with devastating blows aimed to beat the consciousness from the man. He knew that, given just a few
moments, Gladden could restore his injured body to
optimum performance, which would insure Chris's
own death, so he held nothing back this time.

Of course, Charles did manage to connect with

some blows of his own, since even ghosts aren't perfect. One punch to the stomach felt as if it were tearing Chris in half. But as the seconds passed, the boy stood up to the most incredible challenge that anyone had ever faced and did more than battle on even terms. He became the victor.

After seven minutes of outrageously brutal and awe-inspiring unarmed warfare, the principals found themselves in a position identical to the one in which Chris had first tried to end the conflict. Gladden was backed to the block wall in a sharp corner this time and Chris was belaboring him with an unending flow of punches to the head and body. Chris would have like to have leaped to Wicker's cell and grabbed the keys which would bring him all the help he needed, but each time that he eased up on the punishment that he was delivering, the unbelievable strength lodged in Gladden's machinelike body drove him to attack again. If he ever got those crushing hands around the boy's neck, nothing that Chris could do would save his life.

Finally, after a series of blows that blurred in the sight of the onlookers, Gladden sank to his knees. Chris almost launched a kick to his face but was stopped short when he saw the man struggling to his feet one more time.

He stepped back. "For God's sake, that's enough, Charles!" he gasped, blood spraying in pink clouds through his lips. "Don't make me kill you!"

Gladden's face was a horrible ruin, but he knew that he could recover from this damage; nothing this savage bastard could mete out would be enough to stop him. "Eat your heart," he mumbled again. "Tear it out . . . make you watch . . ." He fell forward, reaching for the boy's neck.

This was the first opponent Chris had ever faced who was completely impossible to knock out. If only he could put the man out for a few seconds, just long enough to get those goddamned keys but Charles kept coming after him, trying to squeeze his head from his body.

Chris knew what he would have to do.

When Gladden lunged within range, Chris hit him with a left hook that spun him to one side. Falling back into his martial-arts training, Charles threw a roundhouse kick that would have broken the boy's neck had it landed, but with heartbreaking predictability, Chris ducked under it. This time was different, though, because Chris bounced up to smash his shoulder into Charles's thigh, wrapped his arms about his body, and lifted him off the floor.

"I'll kill you, you little son of a bitch!" Gladden's hands gripped Chris's hair and tore out bloody chunks of it.

Screaming in agony and rage, Chris ran into the wall with Gladden's body thrust forward like a battering ram. The man's head crashed into the blocks with the impact of a pair of colliding trains. They dropped together to the floor with Charles's body covering Chris.

He lost consciousness from total exhaustion for a few seconds while lying beneath Gladden. While the sound of his name being called repeatedly by a variety of voices slowly roused him, it was the wrenching pain that caused Chris to roll the motionless baggage from atop him. Without thought, he was still trying to escape the hurting, as he had been trying to do most of his life.

About a minute following the collision with the wall, he struggled back to awareness to find himself staring at what remained of Charles Gladden's face. He almost vomited. His fists and feet had done awful damage to the man's formerly sharp features, but it had been the last act, the impact of Gladden's head with the block wall, that had caused the worst, that had stopped him.

Gladden had been a Class Two, with no longer any voluntary control over his physical makeup. He had extraordinary strength and the powerfully reinforced skeleton to anchor and command it, but his brain had been totally unprotected. As a result, his skull eventually had split under the terrible punishment that Chris had administered, and his brain had spilled onto the floor—and the boy's body—like his partially solidified soul. Charles Vincent Gladden was dead.

Chris choked back his stomach's spasms and crawled away from the corpse.

"All right, man, I knew you could do it!" Nick shouted triumphantly. "Good God, you're something! I never saw anybody like you in my life!"

Chris ignored him. He didn't feel too incredible at the moment.

Though he was alive with hot pain from a dozen sources, enough of the veneer of desensitized madness remained from the fight to allow him to shunt aside the worst of his injuries and climb to his feet to wobble to Lon Wicker's cell. The older man crawled onto his cot and pressed his face against the cold wall.

"Don't hurt me," he whined, "please, kid, I wanted to help you, honest, I did, but the bastard said he would kill me, please—"

"Give me the keys," Chris whispered through his smashed cheek and torn lips.

Wicker continued to mumble his excuses. "I thought that you could do better alone, you know? I knew—I knew you could beat him without me so I thought I'd stay out of the—"

With a monumental effort fueled by rage, Chris grasped the bars of the cell and rattled them. "Give me the goddamned keys!"

Wicker tossed them toward him without having the courage to face the boy.

It was the hardest thing he'd ever done, but Chris stooped to the floor, clutched the keyring, then staggered to the cell in which Kelly stood nervously. After a couple of fumbling attempts, the young woman took the keys from his broken hands and unlocked the door herself. Then she carefully helped him to the cot and eased him onto it.

"Oh, Christ, your face, your beautiful face," she said in an aching voice, and there were tears in her eyes. "What's he done to you, Chris? I told you to run away!"

Somehow, through it all, he found a smile. "I wish you'd told me a lot harder." He rested his head against the wall. "Let the others out, okay?"

"That can wait! I've got to help you!"

"Kelly, please!" Blake called frantically. "We've got to warn Neil about Poduano! Let me out!"

Chris patted her shoulder weakly. "I'm okay, babe. Nothing can hurt me. Let them out."

Reluctantly, she left him on the cot and rushed to the next cell. When Blake was free, he sprinted instantly into the main body of the house, which forced Kelly to release Meg, before she could give up the keys and return to Chris. Kelly's life and mind had been torn apart, brutally handled, and crushed back into a totally altered basis of reality since she had first overheard Blake and Grandillon's exchange in that parking lot. So knowing that she could never return to the person she once was, either physically or mentally, and because of the never-ending disorientation, she thought that she could never trust or care for anyone else ever again. But this wounded boy, who could have run away to save his own life, somehow seeped through her enveloping pain to find and squeeze her heart back into life. She didn't know if she loved Chris

Wyler, but she was sure that if she had been offered a chance to change places with him and endure the suffering he'd taken to save them all, she would have leaped to accept.

Meg released the others, except for the weeping embarrassment that was Lon Wicker, and they all crowded into Chris's cell.

"Jeez, you look grotesque," Nick stated.

Meg clipped his shoulder with her fist. "Will you shut up? When did you receive a medical degree, anyway?"

"A simple observation doesn't require an M.D."

"He'll be okay," Kelly whispered practically to herself, like a prayer. "We'll get him to a hospital, and everything will be okay."

Chris's eyes had been sinking shut, but he forced them open and sighed. "You folks are starting to convince me that this is serious."

Kelly touched his lips with her fingers. "Shhh, rest, rest. We'll take care of you now."

At that moment, Blake came bounding back into the room. "Damn it, that jerk has cut off the phones! They're as dead as—" He glanced at Gladden's still body and cut himself off. "Uh, Kelly, do you know anything about the telephone system in the house?"

"No," she answered.

"Well, I guess I'll have to take the van to the nearest gas station and find another phone."

"We've got to get Chris to a doctor!" Kelly said fiercely.

Blake looked startled. "Of course. Nick, give me a hand." He entered the cell and gently guided Meg and Melanie to one side.

As the two men took his arms, Chris shook his head. "Don't," he said weakly. "Don't pull at me." He tried to stand alone.

Chris steadied his legs and draped his arms about

the men's shoulders, but as he took the first step, he looked up, toward the cool fluorescent lighting overhead, and smiled. A sort of beatific expression crossed his injured face. "Look," he said, his voice barely detectable.

Then he fell back onto the cot and died.

CHAPTER TWENTY-ONE

"It's a beautiful night," Dr. Eugenia Daugherty said as she gazed at the dazzling full moon from the balcony of the Berlinger Building.

Dr. Isador Redmond, married for the last thirty of his fifty-one years, had never looked at his colleague in a sexual way but tonight she appeared to be almost lovely. Tonight was her night. Eugenia was about to take center stage in a demonstration that might rival the impact of the explosion of the first atomic bomb.

"It's gorgeous," Redmond replied, referring to the night and much more. Redmond was not a seeker of the limelight, and he didn't mind playing sidekick to Eugenia's night of triumph. She was the primary force behind the investigation into this stunningly fascinating subject of shape-changers, as well as probably the most brilliant member of the investigative team. Let her enjoy the moment.

"I am rather uncomfortable with General Hall, though," he added as an afterthought. "He seems awfully set on the Final Solution-type of conviction."

Eugenia dismissed the head of the United States military "advisors" with a brief toss of her head. "Hall is the living cliche of a soldier who wouldn't understand the simplest mechanics of physical metamorphosis if he were provided with an intra-cranial computer terminal."

"Exactly my point," Redmond said. "He makes no secret of the fact that his solution to the entire matter of lycanthropy is to begin mass extermination."

This, too, failed to upset Daugherty. "The White House will never allow him to take away all of our subjects. We'll have as many as we need until we crack the code."

"But, Eugenia, they are *people*, you know, infected or not."

"They *were* people. Now they're an entirely separate species, and until we can master their physical control to the extent that we can provide the human race with the same advantages and protections, they'll remain bestial and dangerous. You've seen them in full transformation often enough. Do you think that any of them would suffer pangs of conscience over ripping out your throat? Or mine?"

"Of course not, but we can't hold them responsible for their actions while in the throes of that . . . well, lunacy. Between the seizures, they're as rational as you and I or—"

"And what about Moorcroft?" she demanded. There was a sparkle of triumph in her eyes that didn't come only from the brilliant moon above them. "It changes when and how it chooses—when we allow it enough energy—and I don't fancy my chances with that thing in an unsupervised environment any more than with one of the primal changers."

"She hasn't actually been given reason to trust or like us," he pointed out.

"She is what all of our subjects will become if we

keep them alive long enough. I'm not sure that at this
point I don't agree with Hall's general sterilization
theory. This could be the most dangerous infection
ever to take hold in the human animal, more virulent
and contageous than AIDS or the plagues, *the* most
dangerous."

"Or it could be our salvation, once we've harnassed
it the way that Moorcroft and those people at Indigo
Lake seemed to have."

Eugenia smiled. "That we can learn from a few
selected guinea pigs after we've convinced our government and the others of the world to deal with the
trouble of the at-large carriers of the disease."

Redmond shook his head slowly. He well knew her
dedication and immense intelligence, but he'd never
really witnessed the off-handed cruelty that she possessed. His only response was a reprise of his first
objection. "But you're talking about slaughtering people, maybe hundreds or thousands of them worldwide. All of the people at the Institute, all of those
men and women except Moorcroft, were completely
normal and healthy before Cummings infected them
last year!"

"Our people, yes," she corrected him, "but their
brothers and sisters must have been preying on the
innocents of the world for centuries, and that, Isador,
amounts to thousands and tens of thousands of victims." The woman glanced back into the heart of the
building, where ten elaborately designed cages held
the proof of the greatest discovery of her life, and then
she looked down at a side street forty stories below.
"Anyway, the decision isn't up to us. General Bernard
Roy Hall will decide whether we ask our allies to help
us study the lycanthropes or kill them."

Forty stories below, Dom Poduano sat in that dark
alley and sucked down the shredded membranes that
once had been the brain of a human being. This

particular human being just recently had been a tremendously large white separatist "skinhead" who had made the mistake of selecting the fat, bald man as his latest mugging victim. Dom lapped his buttery-tasting blood from his own face with a tongue long enough to reach his chest.

The stupid patsy who had given him a ride into San Francisco had been quite filling, but Dom hated to pass up sustenance which was begging to be sampled.

Scooping a palmful of fresh brain from the mugger's skull as dessert, Poduano stood and continued his jaunty walk through the alley on his way to his destiny in the Berlinger Building.

"Oh, my God, he's not dead, he's not dead!"

Kelly shoved Blake aside and pressed her ear to Chris's chest. Taken off balance, Blake fell backwards until he dropped onto his butt, where he sat, shaking his head.

"I'm sorry," he whispered. "He must have been injured inside. I didn't know. He was so . . . so damned good with his fists, and when he beat that monster, I didn't dream that he might have been hurt."

Incapable of speech and with her voice shivering in rhythm with her breath, Kelly began pounding on the boy's chest desperately. Her clouded memory was obscuring the details of CPR, but she knew that she had to do something.

Meg winced and closed her eyes. "Kelly, Kelly, listen," she said, "that can't help him now. It's too late, honey."

"He's not dead. We've got to help him!" In spite of her passion, she allowed Meg and Melanie to ease her away from the body.

"Damn, if we could have helped him." Nick ground his teeth as if he were trying to chew stones. His eyes seemed to be searching for something, and then they fell on Lon Wicker, still locked in his cell. Nick's face reddened. "If that son of a bitch had let us out, we could have helped him!" He ran across the room and kicked the cell door fiercely with the heel of his foot. Wicker cried out.

"Forget it, Nick." Blake sighed as he climbed to his feet. "That won't help."

"The hell it won't! Give me the keys!"

"What?"

"Give me the goddamned keys! I'm going to knock that bastard's teeth out!"

Blake instinctively clutched the keyring in his pocket. "We don't have time for that now! We've got to decide what we're going to do about the demonstration. I still think that calling in a bomb threat is the best idea, and then, when Neil and Tristan return, we can tell them about Poduano."

"Wait a minute," Nick said, his voice hoarse with a dawning sense of possibility. A horror film kept playing itself before his mind's eye while he stared down at Chris, and this created a feeling of unease, as if he were spitting on the boy's grave. But horror films had brought him to this point. Without a lifelong and intense relationship with them, he never would have guessed the truth about Gerald Cummings and joined in the effort to track down the killer and become infected. "*Frankenstein Meets the Wolfman*, near the beginning," he muttered.

"What is it, Nick?" Meg asked, more attuned than the others to his moods.

"How do we know that Chris is really dead?"

She sighed. "He's not breathing. There's no heartbeat."

"We've forgotten what we are! We're werewolves, damn it! We can't die that easy! What did you have to do to Cummings, Corbett?"

Blake's eyes widened. "I had to rip off his head with the patrol car! My God, do you think—"

Nick looked at the wall clock. "It's just over an hour 'til midnight, but if the disease is still in him, still living, the brain is still intact physically!"

"I shot Cummings six times in the head, point blank, and he kept recovering!" Blake added. "Lord, if the disease can somehow live within him until it's time for the change!"

"Neil will know what to do!" Meg said quickly. "Even if midnight doesn't inspire anything in him, Neil can help, I know he can!"

Kelly had been crouched in a corner of the cell, slowly rocking herself like an autistic child, but her numbness was blown away by these words. "He's alive?" she asked. "Help him! Make him breathe again!"

"We've got to get him to Neil," Blake said. "As soon as possible! If he doesn't change at twelve, we can't afford to wait until tomorrow. Give me a hand!" He began pulling Chris into a sitting position.

"No—aw, hell!" Nick almost spat the words. "That means we'll have to drive him there, and we'll be on the road at midnight! Jesus, I haven't killed anybody yet, and I won't start now, Blake! I have to be locked up when the time comes!"

Blake looked frantically about the room, as if searching for a way out of the trap that circumstances had sprung on them again. "One of us will have to do it."

"Blake, we can't," Meg argued. "We can't control ourselves, you know that!" she pointed out painfully. "Maybe Kelly?"

Kelly tried to pull the boy's body to her chest and to stand, but her redesigned form wasn't equal to the effort. "I'll carry him, just give me a hand!" she gasped.

She might not change, Blake thought. Neil said he didn't think that she'd ever be susceptible to the Life form again. "Can you drive, Kelly?" He was acutely aware of the cloudiness Adine Pierce's tampering had caused in her mind but he had seen her master the mechanics of the vacuum cleaner since arriving at the ranch.

"Drive what? What do you mean?"

His spirits dropped by a mile. "The van. It's a straight shift. Can you drive it?"

"Show me how," she whispered, and there was an intense determination etched in her face. "I'll do it if you show me how."

But there was no time for driver's ed. classes. Even if she somehow caught the gist of handling the big vehicle, there was no chance that she could find San Francisco or the Berlinger Building. Or Neil Merrick. "I'll go. Let's get him in the van," Blake said.

"Aren't you listening, Corbett?" Nick shouted. "We're going to change in a little more than an hour, you, me, Meg, Melanie, even that slimeball Wicker! You've only been through it once, so you probably can't even remember what it's like to be caught up in that madness, but *I* can! There's no way on God's green earth that you're going to be able to maintain enough of your personality to understand that you're still a human being, much less drive a damned van!"

"Will you just shut up for a minute, Nick!" Blake exploded. "I know how you've been through it six times already and how that scares the life out of you, but I think I can overcome it! Merrick's new techniques have—"

"Merrick's new techniques are bullshit!" Nick's words were being forced from him by an unstoppable wave of horror, horror of self. "He's a cheerleader trying to convince us that we can control ourselves. It's nothing but a mind game."

"It caused us to be able to replace our missing teeth, didn't it?"

"Yeah? You were stoned while that happened, remember? How do you know that Merrick himself didn't slide his fangs into us and stimulate the new teeth?" Nick was normally argumentative and aggressive, but this went beyond any sort of twisted reflex. Something very painful was forcing this response from him. He paused and took a deep breath. "Blake, I should have told you, I know, but when I was in the Institute, back in April I escaped from my cell. During the change. They recaptured me before morning, but I know that I got out. I remember that much. No one would tell me if I managed to kill . . ."

"Oh, God," whispered Meg.

"I can't take that chance again. I've got to be locked up at midnight."

Blake's reply was low and understanding, but he, too, realized what had to be done. "You don't want us to take away Chris's only chance, Nick. I know you don't want to let Poduano ruin everything that Neil's trying to do for us. You see how it is, don't you? We've got to try."

"Not all of us," he answered.

"No. You're right. Just me. Now help me get Chris out to the van."

"Sure, man."

"I'm going, too," Kelly told them quietly.

"Kelly, if I fail, if I do change, it would be terribly dangerous for you to be close by," Blake said.

Some of Nick's characteristic fire returned to his voice. "Chris killed Gladden so that he wouldn't be locked in the cell with you when he changed, girl. Don't be so stupid now."

"I'm going," was her simple reply.

Nick started to speak, but Blake shook his head. "Maybe she can make it the rest of the way if I can't, but we've got to get going now."

When the van carrying Blake, Kelly, and a body which might yet encase the soul of Chris Wyler had left at breakneck speed on its way north, the remaining members of the group retreated again into the safety of the prison wing of the ranch. They locked themselves into the cells, and Meg kept the keys, hiding them from her other self beneath the strapped down mattress of her cot.

All of their hopes and good wishes went with the people racing to San Francisco, but they still wanted to be aole to leave their prison when dawn came.

"Nickie, tell me something," Meg said softly as she sat on the floor.

He sighed audibly from the cell next to her. "No, I can't really describe what it'll feel like, other than to say that it will combine the worst sensations imaginable with the best. Lord, in its own way, it's almost an addictive feeling."

"That's not what I meant."

"Okay. What?"

"How on earth did *Frankenstein Meets the Wolfman* make you realize that Chris might still be alive?"

He laughed. Despite the weary resignation in the sound, Meg could detect some real affection and trust that his speculations were right. "You remember it, don't you? Naturally you do. I've never met anybody besides you who even approaches me in the number of fantasy films they've seen. Well, then you have to recall how Larry Talbot is brought back from the dead."

"Sure, a couple of grave robbers break into his burial vault during a night of the full moon, and when it shines on Chaney's face, he—" The young woman's voice broke off abruptly, as she visualized the moment when the Wolfman sprang, raging back across the gulf between life and death to mutilate the pair who had accidentally summoned him.

Nick picked up on her awed memories. "Yeah, an impressive scene, right? Scared the pants off me when I saw it as a kid. And Talbot had been beaten to death with a silver-headed cane and shut up in that coffin for a long time."

"But that was just a movie," Meg felt obligated to remind him.

"So? We already know that the disease maintains an intimate relationship with the host's mind, and this includes the host's preconceptions that he's picked up from the movies about lycanthropy. That's why we change at the full moon. Old-time werewolves didn't. Maybe Chris was indoctrinated well enough so that his soul, I'd guess you'd say, will hang around in his body for a while, at least until midnight."

"Let's hope that he saw the film."

"Good point. If you don't know what you're supposed to do, rising from the grave can be hell."

She had to smile at that. "God, how I envy you your way with words."

They reached the Berlinger Building at twelve minutes until midnight. Kelly drove at nightmare speeds, sometimes hitting one hundred miles an hour.

"Here we are!" she practically screamed as the van skidded into a parking space across the street from the forty-three-story building. The street was well lit and seemed strangely empty for a business area in a city like San Francisco. But, then, it was the middle of the night on a Monday.

Blake had been sitting in the back of the van with Chris, and his eyes practically glowed with excitement when he looked at Kelly. He spoke as if addressing a small child, "I'm going inside the building to find Neil, and I want you to stay here and stand watch for me."

Kelly eyed Chris and got out and scrambled into the back of the van.

"Now, look under the back seat, please, and get the tire iron. If anyone bothers you, do what you have to to stop them. Don't kill, but you understand how important this is to you and me, Chris, and everyone in the whole world, don't you?"

She nodded. "I understand."

Blake stepped out the side door. "I'll try to be back before twelve. If I'm not, then take off. Find somewhere safe, okay?"

Kelly nodded again and he closed the door and walked across the street.

How am I going to do this? Blake asked himself. *What if I can't even get into the building?*

He could still telephone the police with the bomb story, and there was a long row of pay phones at the side of the entrance. That would stop the demonstration, but what if it meant that Neil or Tristan were caught up in the legal reaction? Instead, he walked directly to the nearest door and grasped its handle. It was locked.

He pressed his face to the glass and peered into the lobby beyond. Halfway across the huge room was a security desk, and behind it sat a single man in a blue-and-gray uniform. He seemed to be intently studying the screen of a computer terminal. Blake rapped on the door.

The reaction was immediate. The man glanced up with a severe expression and then sprang to his feet. He practically ran across the room while working the keyring from his belt.

He was a big son of a gun, with a sidearm that looked even bigger to Blake, who still had no idea what he was to say or do. *If I try to shove past him, he'll either hammer me to the floor or put a bullet into my spine*, he thought. *I suppose it's time to find out just how extraordinary my new powers really are.*

The guard unlocked the door with a twist of motion and jerked the door inward, which threw Blake off balance and sent him staggering inside. *Now, run like a thief,* Blake told himself, *run before he can pull that damned gun*!

"Blake Corbett, what in God's name are you doing here so close to midnight?" the guard asked.

That question froze Blake even before he started his sprint. "How do you know me? Who are you?"

The man smiled, and Blake recognized the still-cool eyes, even if the remainder of the face continued to elude his memory. "Tristan?" he ventured. "Tristan Grandillon?"

"You're getting rather good at the game, Mr. Corbett," Grandillon admitted as he shut the door again and locked it. "But as I asked, what are you doing outside of your cell at this hour?"

"Christ, Tristan, this entire night's gone insane! Charles is dead and—"

"Dead?"

"Yes, Chris beat him to death but he had to. The idiot wasn't going to let us out to warn you! And now I think Chris is dead, too, and you've got to get Neil!"

"The demonstration's underway up on the fortieth floor," Grandillon answered. "The government people already have explained the situation to the foreign representatives, and they're waiting for the transformations to substantiate the story. Neil and I appropriated these official uniforms and the physical images from a couple of the federal security men, and now he's upstairs to deliver *our* message once the demonstration has taken place. There's no way that I could interrupt that—"

"For God's sake, Dom Poduano's here somewhere!"

Grandillon's face stiffened with shock. "That's not possible."

"It damned sure is! I didn't know you, so how could you know him? Listen to me, he came to the ranch, while we were locked up and Charles was out of the room. He was disguised as Neil and he forced Lon to tell him where you were, but as he left, he told us who he really was, and he said he was going to do something to ruin this whole gathering!" The words were tumbling out of Blake now, and he felt the seconds slipping away from him like rain through his fingers. "Charles wouldn't believe us. I think he suffered some kind of mental breakdown. He tried to rape Kelly and then he threatened to leave us all locked up to starve if you and Neil were captured or killed. Anyway, Chris agreed to fight him, and, I'll be damned, he beat him. God, he was sensational! But we think he died, too, and you and Neil have to help him before it's too late!"

"All right, keep your head, Blake," Tristan said soothingly. "I can contact Neil by short wave from the desk. He'll be down quickly to go with you, but I'll have to stay here to try and find Dominic before he can do any irrevocable damage to our movement—"

"Then get him!" Blake snapped. "Chris is in the van across the street!"

Grandillon ran to the desk, tossing over his shoulder, "Good, smart thinking! Wait right there!"

Where would I be going now? Blake asked himself. He looked at his watch and the fist of ice around his heart closed a little tighter.

Dominic Poduano felt the breeze as it caressed his flat, kite-like body and tried to nudge him away from the side of the Berlinger Building. He dug his claws into the stone siding and anchored himself more firmly in place.

The man clung to the wall some forty stories above the ground, but his shape was so flattened and camouflaged that he would have been invisible to anyone peering out of a window on that floor.

He opened his mouth and tasted the wind with a tongue unlike that ever employed by a human being.

Almost time, almost midnight. He would allow them to witness this most majestic of moments and give Merrick a chance to present his futile presentation designed to unite the two species of humankind in brotherhood. Then he would show them what it really meant to attempt to assassinate Dominic Poduano.

He licked the wind once more and laughed to himself.

The audience was aware of the credentials of the committee presenting this extraordinary story, and they had heard many remarkable reports at similar meetings in the past. All of those prior sessions had centered about incredible medical advances which were yet available only to the inner coterie of government officials in their respective nations. From limb and brain transplants to youth-prolonging radiation treatments, all of these discoveries had proven to be genuine blessings to the very few people privileged to know of them, but this . . . *werewolves?*

The two dozen men and women were seated in chairs arranged about the center of the large room, so that each individual had a clear view of the ten clear acrylic boxes positioned there. In nine of the boxes, five men and four women sat on the floor, naked, frightened, and thoroughly pathetic in appearance. These were the "werewolves."

The tenth cage had been empty since the start of the meeting, but as the minute hand crept toward midnight, two of the uniformed federal guardsmen appeared from somewhere, carrying a black metal box between them. It was a relatively small box, like a coffin for a ventriloquist's dummy. The men carried it to the empty glass cage and, after opening the panel that served as both the door and one wall, sat it inside and pulled back the top. With none too careful hands, they removed a body that resembled a tiny, hairless monkey.

The monkey lay motionless on the floor of the cage, hunched and gnarled-looking, making one think of a clenched fist. It also appeared to be dead.

"Time to wake up, Rosalie baby," whispered one of the men, though no one outside the cage heard this. He took a prepared syringe from his jacket and flipped off the needle cap before jabbing it into the creature's abdomen and emptying the clear fluid into its body. The reaction was immediate.

"Oh, man, let's haul ass!" one guard said nervously. "She's coming around!"

The second didn't argue. Pulling the transfer box with them, they exited the glass booth and swiftly locked the door. The monkey was still lying on the bare floor, but it was trembling now, violently.

Rosalie Moorcroft had been unconscious for more than one week, trapped in her depleted condition by her captors so that she wouldn't have the internal energy to initiate the apparently unlimited range of metamorphoses that she had displayed at the Institute. The disease which provided her with the power to control her own form needed sustenance, however, and while it was a benevolent symbiotic partner under most circumstances, its own survival took natural precedence. It had been ingesting the woman's own tissues throughout the famine.

The Life form had no intelligence, as such, but it was no less involved in the struggle to survive than any other bacterium.

What was left of Rosalie's mind slowly recovered as the high nutrient solution from the syringe began to circulate through her body. She rolled over, gasping, and slowly shook her head, like a woozy prizefighter. She opened her eyes and gazed at the assembly who was staring so passionately at her recovery, before opening her toothless mouth in a keening plea for food. She was so hungry that it felt as if every cell of her being were screaming in that plea.

The pink gums abruptly split along their ridges to produce fifty gleaming white teeth.

"I still don't know how you got him here so quickly, but you did exactly the right thing," Neil said as he and Blake hurried across the street to the van. Grandillon had abandoned his post in the lobby to begin an unobtrusive search for Poduano in the floors above. "Unless his brain was completely destroyed, as you say Charles's was, there is a brief grace period during which the Life form maintains the body without cellular degeneration."

"Thank God for that," Blake puffed.

They reached the van, and Merrick pulled open the side door and scrambled inside.

"Who are you? What do you want?" cried Kelly frantically as she tried to drag Chris's body away from him.

"Please relax, Kelly. I'm Neil Merrick," he answered. "Tristan and I merely took the forms of a pair of security guards who were assigned to the lobby of the building so that we could move freely about during the demonstration."

"It's okay, Kelly," Blake said, climbing into the vehicle behind Merrick. "We've got to help Chris before it's too late." He stole a glance at his wristwatch, and alarm flooded through him. "Oh, Jesus, it's two minutes until midnight! Neil, what are we going to do?" Blake asked. "I don't want to hurt anybody!"

But Merrick was far too busy to respond. Gently easing Kelly away from the body, he bent over the boy's exposed neck as if he were a vampire hovering above a victim. But when his teeth slipped through the skin, his purpose was to establish a contact between the two colonies of the disease that resided in

their forms, rather than to steal any type of sustenance. He ignored the two distraught people near him
while this took place.

Less than half a minute passed before he sat up and
cleared his head. "The Life form is still viable within
him," Neil told them. "There is no respiration or
circulation, but it's possible that the body's functions
can be incited into activity again. Certainly there's
been no deterioration of his cells yet."

"Then *do* something!" Kelly begged him. "Bring
him back!"

"I've done all that I can, child. I've reinvigorated
his portion of the Life form and heightened the
survival qualities. We can only wait and hope now."

"Wait for what?"

"Midnight. If Chris's impressions of the power of
that moment were strong enough to imprint a permanent coding into his Life form, that will bring him
back to us. If not—"

With a wild shriek, Kelly threw herself at Neil.

Instinctively, Blake pulled her off Neil and dragged
her, struggling, to the floor. With a tremendous effort,
he wrestled her into the rear of the vehicle next to
Chris's still form, but when he looked up at Merrick,
the pleading in his eyes had nothing to do with Kelly's
momentary insanity. "You've got to help me, Neil! I
don't think I can control myself when it happens, and
I don't want to hurt them!"

"Too late, Blake," the man replied, rearranging his
clothes which Kelly had grabbed. "Only you can help
yourself now. Be strong and take your mind back into
our sessions."

Blake suddenly felt a rush of icy-cold adrenalin
cascading through his body. "*I don't remember*!"

"Do it, Blake! Become your own master and stride
into our world with your mind clear and powerful!"

"Help me!" he shouted.

* * *

Forty stories above them, all of the sophisticated ennui of twenty-four international representatives evaporated before the sight of five men and four women transforming into wailing embodiments of a racially recalled nightmare.

From the balcony, an unseen Dominic Poduano laughed quietly.

"Zero! Here we go, ladies and gentlemen!" Nick called as the clock on the wall registered midnight. He fell back onto his cot, his eyes pressed closed and his forehead down on his raised knees. He knew this moment. Lord, he knew it so well. It was a total disintegration of the self, sort of a sheer explosion in which his personality split the boundaries of its containment and soared to the depths of the universe while an evil which must have existed before the primal birth of time and space screamed into his body to fill the void that was left there. It was the most terrible sensation that a human mind could conceive, and, in a way, it became more seductive each time that he experienced it.

The insistent itching swept through his body, externally and internally, and Nick spread his lips to join in the feral screaming that already was taking place in the cells holding Melanie Ryan and Lon Wicker.

Then he heard the sound of metal scraping metal. It should have been lost in the high-pitched cacophony that filled the room, not to mention in his own madness, but somehow Nick's ears picked out that faint noise from amid all the rest. It sounded like it was coming from very close to him, maybe as closely as Meg's cell, just to his left. Then he heard the short wail of the cell door as it opened.

The demand to change was overwhelming, but Nick fought it down for the instant. He stumbled to feet which already were producing hard and sharp claws from the bare toes and staggered to his own door. He clutched the bars, resisting the compulsion to tear them out of their settings, and looked out to see Meg leaving her cell.

Melanie and Wicker had already fully transformed into nightmare creatures, but Meg was still . . . Meg. She was gasping with effort and coated with a gleaming sheen of perspiration, but she was still human and so beautiful that Nick realized that he had to be dreaming. Holding the keyring in her hand and grasping the bars of the cell for support with her other hand, she tottered out, turned to face him, and began to move in his direction.

"Nick," she whispered, a sigh of triumph through her struggle, "we have to help each other."

His reply was something close to a shriek. "What in the world are you doing, Meg?" He almost choked when the Life form ejected his eyeteeth in a welter of blood to supply his mutating jaws with ripping fangs, but he spat this aside. "You can't do that. Don't open my door!"

"Fight it," she responded, inserting the key into the lock. "We can do it if we fight." Her face seemed to become fuzzy and unfocused, but it wasn't Nick's vision at fault. Her flesh was desperately trying to conform to the demands of the disease that was raging within her. Yet, she still held on. "Remember what Neil told us, during the sessions." She opened the door.

He leaped away. The fire was practically consuming him now, as he knew that it must be flaring within Meg, but he wasn't afraid of her. He was afraid *for* her. "Please, Meg, for God's sake, don't come in here! I don't want to kill you! I can't!" He backed into a corner, slipped to the floor, and wrapped his arms about his head as he literally shook with the effort to control his impulse to spring forward, tearing, biting, eating.

"The curse of the werewolf is to kill the ones he

loves the best," the old gypsy had told Lawrence Talbot, and Nick shook from the memory of that line.

"Get out, get out," he whispered. His voice was getting fainter.

Then her small, white, and beautiful foot stepped before him, and he saw that she, in fact, had won her battle. She stooped to his side and took his half-transformed body in her arms. "You see, don't you, Nickie? We *can*! We can do it! We just have to fight it together!"

Nick, who had been reduced to the worst essence of the darkest side of his soul on six previous occasions, knew at that moment what he had to do. Opening his arms, he raised his face to look into her perfect features. Their eyes met, so that their minds connected with a unity achieved by very few and each knew the most hidden secrets of the other. Then their lips met, as well.

Laughing in exultation, Meg Talley and Nick Grundel shared the first real moments of their new lives.

CHAPTER TWENTY-TWO

He won!

It was trying to rip away all of the insulating control that separated his actions from his emotions and change him into something that would slaughter Kelly and steal from him forever his privilege of walking free among other human beings. And it was strong, God, it was so strong. More than any hunger or need or desire, more than any sexual compulsion or dark fantasy than he had ever felt, almost more than he could resist.

But he would not be defined by the carnal urges or the commands of the unique type of life that dwelt inside his body. While Kelly stared at him emptily, and Neil chanted encouragement like a high-school cheerleader, Blake Corbett made the discovery that saved his sanity.

There was no disease. Until that very instant, he had considered himself to be infected with an external organism that was not too different from a common cold, aside from the fact that it offered him perfect health and possibly eternal life. But as he fought to maintain a level of determination over his existence, he realized that this was *not* a symbiotic relationship, no matter how often Merrick and the others had chosen to use that terminology. He was *not* Blake Corbett with the disease, any more than he was Blake Corbett with platelets in his bloodstream or fingernails on his hands. He *absorbed* the disease and became a new Blake Corbett.

"New," perhaps, but still free, in charge, and not a slave to any outside impulses. He fought the Life form and defeated it. Now he knew he could control this aspect of his existence so well that he could even regulate his contagion or eliminate it entirely. He could give blood without passing on the condition; he could even father a completely uninfected child.

He had won.

Blake looked at the two faces which were gazing so intently at him inside the van, and he grinned. "I'm all right."

Neil was elated. He grasped Blake's shoulders in powerful hands and almost crushed him in a bear hug.

"Welcome, my friend," the man said happily. "Now you truly are one of the elite."

Blake wasn't sure if Merrick was so cheerful because of any sense of friendship they shared or because his own extraordinary new educational techniques had been validated, but he did know that the emotions were genuine. Blake himself felt as if half of the world had been lifted from his shoulders.

"What about Chris?" Kelly asked in a small voice.

The men turned their attention to the boy in her lap. His battered face rested there, his eyes closed, the left swollen shut and purple, as if asleep and his chest unmoving. The urgent joy of the instant fled before the confirmation of death. It now was well past a minute after midnight.

"Kelly," Neil said softly, and this emotion was as honest as what he had expressed at Blake's success, "I'm sorry. He must have been beaten too badly, suffered too much to recover before he came to control his own ability to heal."

"No, don't say that." Her voice was barely audible to them. Blake could hardly believe that this was the same woman he had seen battle with vicious futility against Charles Gladden as he dragged her into another room to molest her.

Like a little girl, Kelly cradled Chris's head to her bosom and began rocking back and forth, whispering an old song that Blake hadn't heard in twenty years about what a strange world it was.

A fog of crushing defeat filled the van, so crushing that the almost imperturbable Neil Merrick wouldn't accept it. While Blake took his initial tentative steps into immortality, there was no justice in the death of this child who had suffered so much in his short life and had given all that he possibly could give to save the rest of them.

Merrick took the body from Kelly, ignoring her tears, and held the face very close to his own. "Christopher!" he shouted. "Christopher, wake up! I mean it, son, if you don't come back to us right now, we're all going to die, Kelly and Blake and Meg and all of us! Do you hear me?"

"He can't hear us anymore, Neil," Blake said. "There's no reason to go on with it, is there?"

Merrick wiped away a trickle of sweat from his transformed face. "Sometimes, in the few cases that I've encountered, the Life force seems to concentrate in the physical brain at death, and it maintains the cellular integrity for a time." He shook his head. "I thought that if somehow I could penetrate that space between life and death, spark a flame of recognition with this side . . . but the gulf is too wide now, I suppose."

Blake knew that now was the moment to try anything, no matter how ridiculous or unlikely. As a boxing fan for over twenty years, he knew the (possibly apocryphal) story of how an old fan, standing over Stanley Ketchel's coffin after the twenty-four-year-old middleweight champion had been shot in the back of the head by a jealous employee, had whispered, "Start counting over him, and he'll get up."

Why not?

Leaning next to the boy's ear, Blake began, "One . . . two . . . don't let them count you out . . . three . . . four . . . five . . . six—"

A tremor passed through Chris's body, like a flicker of light, and Blake fell back, gasping.

"Count, count!" cried Kelly.

Blake's voice rose in pitch. "Seven! The count's at seven, Chris, get up! Eight!"

Chris gulped an explosive breath. Merrick slammed the inside of the van so fiercely in his jubilation that he left a dent in the metal as large as his head.

Blake leaned over Chris's body and screamed directly into his face now, "Get off your ass, man! Nine! Only one more and you're out! Get up, get up!"

Chris's eyes crept open and he sighed. "I'm up, man," Then he spoke the litany repeated by every prizefighter in history, no matter how desperately injured, no matter how close to death, "I'm okay. I'm okay!"

"That leaves us with the problem of Dominic," Merrick stated, virtually to himself, as the others struggled to accept the miracle that was Chris's return to life. "Perhaps Tristan has found him by now, but that isn't always possible when dealing with a person who can become anything he wishes."

Blake slapped his forehead. "My God, I forgot all

about him!" He glanced to the huge building that thrust its way to the stars across the street from them. It seemed to be quiet and solid, even though nearly five minutes had passed since the change should have overtaken those poor captives who had been brought from the Institute for the demonstration.

"Apparently, he wants to take some sort of vengeance against us all, since we tried to destroy him and put an end to his suffering." Neil chuckled shortly and without mirth. "I thought that we had. I wonder who we killed?" He opened the door and stepped into the night. "If Tristan or I haven't returned within the hour, head back to the ranch and take what you will need to escape the authorities. Money and clothing, whatever you feel might be of use."

"Let me go with you, Neil," Blake said. "I'm fully a member of the association now."

"No, Blake, you still have a lot of learning ahead of you." He looked to Chris, who had been drawn back into this world by their calls and then strengthened against involuntary transformation by their instruction and support. "You and Chris have to show the others the way, and if whatever occurs here tonight incites a global oppression of our kind once again, you may have to re-establish our race."

Nervous and embarrassed, Blake coughed shortly. "I'm not worried about any of that, Neil. You'll do whatever needs to be done in there." He extended his hand to the man. "Good luck."

They shook. "You, too, my friend." Then Merrick was gone, as swiftly as the breeze and as soundlessly as a shadow.

Life can be designed, step by step, if one has the foresight and the courage to master the intricacies.

Dr. Eugenia Jacqueline Daugherty was forty-four years old, and she had believed that precept all of her life and it had thoroughly shaped the woman she was. Brilliant, she didn't rely on that alone to bring her to the pinnacle of existence, as she defined it; instead, Eugenia was always the hardest worker, the first to begin her studies and the last to finish them. From the fifth grade, it was quite rare for her to encounter a teacher who really could offer her any insights into the educational material once the semester was a few weeks old. Only after reaching college did she meet with minds on her level or occasionally more advanced, and even then none of them could match her passion for work.

This single-minded pursuit of excellence produced a genius. That couldn't be contested, but it cost Eugenia in other areas of her life. The childlike side of her failed to develop in this sterile atmosphere of pure knowledge. As a result, Eugenia never understood the concept of love or caring when it had nothing to do with her mental exercises. As a teenager, she had coolly performed extraordinarily cruel "tests" upon the young children whom she baby-sat for minimum wage. Even though this eventually became public, she felt no remorse for the damage that she had done to their tender psyches or for the shame and sorrow she had brought to her own family.

In fact, her younger brother had secretly been one of her "subjects" since the cradle, and he would never climb to his own pinnacle of life due to the psychological and physical tampering that he had endured.

In the discovery of living lycanthropes, Eugenia had discovered the work of her life, the challenge that was equal to her talents, and in General Hall, she had met a matching soul.

The sounds were a mixture of feeding time at the zoo and the populace of Tokyo fleeing the approach of Godzilla.

"Do you think they're convinced?" Isador Redmond shouted happily over the din. In the center of the vast room, the foreign representatives receded in a circular wave away from the ten glass cages in which a group of men and women who had seemed to be only naked, pathetic prisoners a minute earlier had metamorphosed into raging demons. The alarmed cries of the guests left no doubt as to their total belief in what they were witnessing.

"There's no cinematic tomfoolery that can equal that, and every one of them knows it," Eugenia Daugherty replied. Her joy at their terror practically radiated in her face. "Now we finally can get underway with our real business. Tracking down and confining the carriers of this condition worldwide."

The booming voice of General Bernard Roy Hall cut through the near-hysteria that was swelling within the room. "Please remain calm, ladies and gentlemen, there is no reason for panic! The subjects cannot escape the restraining receptacles!" The public-address system magnified his already powerful voice and effectively quelled the startled reactions of the gathering. The invited dignitaries broke off their terrified cries and turned to stare at the incredible demonstration that already had achieved its designed effect.

Hall continued, "These acrylic cages have been especially constructed and rigorously tested. They will contain the creatures without difficulty, but imagine, if you will, how those monsters would tear through this gathering if they were *not* caged. Savage, invulnerable to our weapons, insatiable, their only desire is to rip open human flesh and devour it!"

At fifty-four, Hall was among the youngest generals in the U.S. armed forces, but his mostly gray hair and heavy mustache added considerable weight to his image, and his rigid character reinforced that. "And now, ladies and gentlemen, think about the certainty that there are thousands of these supposedly mythological beasts living secret lives throughout the world, in your own countries."

A layer of shock blanketed the room. The heavy glass cabinets muffled the screams of the transformed lycanthropes almost completely, and the only sounds from the observers were soft moans of fear.

"This is great!" Eugenia whispered to Redmond.

Hall held the gathering in the palm of his hand, and he knew it. "What can we do about this most severe threat to our safety, to our very way of life? Are we to remain the unsuspecting prey of this race of shape-changing devils who have survived on the bodies of our ancestors for literally centuries? Let me introduce you now to someone who knows more about this problem than anyone else in the world, perhaps the most brilliant scientist that the world has to offer, Dr. Eugenia Daugherty."

The lights went out. All of them. Those focused on Hall at the speaker's podium, the others which were illuminating the majority of the room with a diffused glow, even the battery of floodlights which were trained on the ten cages and their contents. Without a flicker of warning, the entire building was plunged into total darkness.

There were some screams from the audience, of course, especially from those who hadn't turned their eyes from the awesome spectacle of the werewolves when Hall began his speech. A number of the soldiers on the security team for the assembly cursed, but, surprisingly, no one moved. What had been blood-chilling in the light became absolutely unendurable under the cover of darkness and froze everyone in place.

After a moment in the silent blackness, the senses became attuned so that the faint glow of the full moon seeped through the curtains that covered the windows and the muted roars of the creatures caused hearts to seize or to race with fear.

"Please remain calm!" Hall called out to them, and though he was without the service of the public-address system now, his voice was still strong enough to fill the room. "The situation is under control, so please stay where you are."

Eugenia reached through the darkness, found Redmond's arm, and gripped it fiercely. "What's wrong, Isador?" she demanded, as if the circumstances were his fault.

"Power failure," he replied, going for the obvious explanation. "The lights are probably out all over the city."

But they weren't, as was proven when a man standing near the windows eased back a curtain and scanned the skyline. It appeared that only the Berlinger Building had gone dark.

As the seconds stretched into a minute and another after that, not even General Hall's assurances could keep the assembly calm. Some people were convinced that the federal supervisors of the demonstration had cut the light purposely, either to heighten the dramatic presentation's impact or to disguise sloppy bogus Hollywood special effects. A small current of conversation was born beneath Hall's ongoing declarations that the problem soon would be remedied by the men he had sent to the basement generator room, and it grew substantially louder in a short amount of time.

As the level of incipient panic grew, Hall became more concerned with the situation. Grasping an aide roughly by the shoulder, he drew the man close to his side and hissed, "Damn it, Perkins, what's holding up the lights?"

"I don't know, sir," the other answered, "but you have to remember that since the power is off, the elevators aren't running, and our people really haven't had the time to get down to the basement and back up here by the stairs."

"I'm not interested in excuses, mister. Get some kind of illumination in this room right now. Flashlights, gas lanterns, whatever we have on hand."

Perkins said, "There are some portable spots in the transports on the roof that would light up this place like high noon."

In the darkness, Hall rolled his eyes at the exquisite incompetence of every noncommissioned and junior officer he had ever encountered. "Then have some men bring them down here before I bust your ass to civilian, all right?"

"Yes, sir!"

Before Perkins could pull free of his grip, Hall added, "And make sure that the containment men are ready to deploy around the room."

Perkins stopped short. "Do you think there's some danger of escape?"

"Shut your mouth and carry out your instructions, Perkins." Hall's tone was low and even, but the authority in his words sent Perkins rushing through the gloom to comply.

It wasn't surprising that, with the encompassing darkness and the fears it inspired, no one noticed when a strange, liquid form of life, the exact color of the outside of the building, flowed up the exterior wall, over the balcony parapet, and across to the slightly open sliding doors which led into the room. Once inside, this life took on a uniform blackness so that it seemed to mix its very molecules with the darkness that filled the building.

It moved across the carpet, fluid yet animate, avoiding the feet of the blind and fearful people, until it reached the center of the room. Where the cages sat. It extended a pseudo-limb up the clear door to one of the cages and into the sophisticated-locking mechanism which supposedly was beyond the ability of the most accomplished safecracker. Only seconds passed before the hermetic seal of the cage was breached with a tiny hiss that was lost in the conversation in the room.

The amorphic thing moved on to the next cage.

The first person to notice the change in the tone of the mad cries from within the glass boxes was Javier Suerna, a representative of the government of Costa Rica. He had been struggling to present a cool and *varonil* image to reassure his security-cleared companion for the evening that everything was under control. To this end, he had refused to move away from the cage which he had been inspecting when the lights went off, though he had turned his back to it. When the door opened less than a foot away from him, he clearly noted the sudden increase in urgency in the lusting growl of the captive.

"*Quien vive?*" Those were the only words Suerna managed to speak as he turned in the blackness to face the creature that was discovering its own freedom.

The door exploded open, and a mass of fury sprang upon Suerna as all the tales of medieval hell coalesced into hungering reality. The man's companion screamed, and then all of the doors burst open.

Blake was standing at the open side door of the van when the lights of the Berlinger Building went out. He noticed but he didn't notice, since there hadn't been that much illumination in it to begin with (the government demonstration was the only activity taking place at that hour) and the grounds lamps and streetlights surrounding it remained burning. Blake was watching Kelly as she tried to explain to a still-befuddled Chris what had happened to him. He remembered nothing beyond collapsing in the cell following the fight. He knew nothing of how he'd been dragged back to life—if indeed he'd really been dead—and why he hadn't changed into his uncontrolled feral form at midnight. So Blake unconsciously dismissed the loss of power across the street as a trick of his vision.

Only minutes later, however, he clearly heard the eruption of choral screams from so high above and with instinctive accuracy snapped his gaze to the fortieth floor and connected the power outage with the cries.

"Oh, my God," he whispered.

The theologians of the Middle Ages churches could never have created an enclosed globe of terror to equal what took place in that room in the moments following the release of the captives.

Nine insane engines of death rushed into the darkness, their preternatural senses showing them their targets even as those men and women ran blindly from them, into one another, and into the mouths of the very nightmares they were so desperately trying to escape. Fangs which had replaced human teeth closed on naked throats and then twisted to rip open the flesh and expose the blood and pulsing organs beneath. Blood sprayed like fountains and was sucked down nine shrieking gullets in futile attempts to satiate the awful hungers that drove the hosts; and the thickest bones snapped with gunfire-like reports in clawed hands that could not have bruised the layers of muscle around them only minutes before.

And near the floor, one tiny being who resembled a shaven monkey was too weak yet to transform into the nighttime horrors as represented by her larger fellows, so she had to content herself with the juices and meat that dropped down to her level. Each swallow brought her a huge step closer to full strength.

A real animal, upon making a kill, will stay with the

body and eat until its physical needs are met, but these monsters were both more and less than real animals. The best taste, the one which came closest to matching the craving that inhabits the host stronger than drugs control the junkie, comes at the very moment of attack, when the flesh is quivering with the pure wine of vitality. The Life form knew this, and through it the hosts knew, as well, so they barely lingered over one victim before casting out in madness to bring down another. Sometimes the first target wasn't even dead and would survive for the month essential to delivering another member into the brotherhood of living demons.

There was no electrical power to dispel the darkness, but the fear could not have been greater had they been capable of seeing.

Those people who had maintained enough of their sense of direction from the moments just before the failure of the lights ran over furniture and other people to reach the five exits into the hallway, but even here they found no hope. General Hall's security men had been stationed at each door with instructions that no one was to leave without his direct order or the order of his second-in-command while the demonstration was in progress. Certainly, Hall hadn't intended that the display last all night or develop into circumstances such as these, but those were their orders and the men were committed to carrying them out. When civilians stumbled into them, frantic to shove by into the relative safety of the corridors beyond, these soldiers physically blocked the way and threw men and women alike back into the maelstrom. Their weapons were drawn and ready, but they refrained from using them.

Dominic Poduano, on the ceiling of the room, watched the terrible events that he had inspired with vision that almost brought the scene into noontime brightness. He laughed, without bothering to muffle or disguise the sound in the screaming, roaring gale that snatched it from his lips. This was the finest moment that he had experienced in the four-hundred-and-sixty-four years of his life.

Poduano had never before been an associate who threatened his own kind. He had preyed upon uninfected humans for centuries, of course, and his acting games, such as those employed with Harry Mitchellson and Marsha Cooper, were a bit *outre* for the average member of the association, but he explained that he used them to remain sane. Dom was an eccentric uncle, perhaps, who always had been able to mesmerize an audience with his tales of the very earliest days of the association's formation following the miraculous mutation of the lycanthropic condition. He'd never been a source of fear among his initiated brothers and sisters.

You thought that you could wipe me from the earth as easily as you crush a bug, didn't you? he demanded of Neil Merrick and Tristan Grandillon, whom he felt certain were being engulfed in the struggle down there.

Once this farce was concluded, Dom would kill those helpless idiots at the ranch and stand as the only self-determinate metamorphic being on the North American continent.

Ready to seek out and destroy Merrick and Grandillon, Poduano flowed across the ceiling by gripping its tiny imperfections with thousands of nearly microscopic fingers until he reached an empty corner. Then he slowly dropped to the floor with the viscous reluctance of thick cake batter dripping from a spoon. Each ounce of himself that stretched in a stream onto the carpeting re-formed into the overall image of a solid, awesomely powerful man.

"Where are you, boys?" he whispered to himself. "The boogeyman is coming to get you."

"Well, he won't have to search far," responded a familiar voice from immediately behind him. "I'm right here, you damned son of a whore!" Then Tristan Grandillon fell on him with slashing claws and teeth.

If a person can witness her entire world ripped apart at its most basic level, Eugenia Daugherty did.

The loss of life all about her was of little immediate concern; in fact, wouldn't the display serve to emphasize the necessity of capturing or destroying every lycanthrope throughout the globe? But the totally uncontrolled savagery of it made it clear to her that any number of unacceptable results could take place within the next few seconds, even before she could fight her way through the maniacal crowd of victims and monstrosities into the hallway.

First, Hall could order the total destruction of every living thing in the room. The general was little more than a bomb who had exploded several times in Vietnam and other battlefields. Only sheer luck and swift reaction by military intelligence had kept his atrocities from becoming public.

Eugenia had provided the man with the most effective manner for destroying lycanthropes: sustained exposure to high temperature streams of fire. A primitive method which might prove useless against advanced practitioners of the shape-shifting art, but surely thorough enough for the neophytes assembled there.

If Hall ordered this sterilization by fire, she knew that he wouldn't stop with the obvious targets. In his own way, as mad as the lycanthropes, the general would take "preventive measures" and fry every last individual who was not a member of his own military unit. Eugenia worked for the government, but she was not in the armed forces, and she was not ready to die.

A second, all-too-possible eventuality was that the monsters would find Eugenia in the dark and eat her alive as if she were no more important than any of the shrieking foreigners in their clutches right now. In that case, the most advanced mind in the ranks of humankind would be nothing more than succulent flesh.

The third option was less likely than the first two and, in its own way, even more terrifying. Eugenia might be assaulted by one of the creatures and survive, alive but infected. In other words, she would *be* a lycanthrope. She wanted the Life form, and she would inoculate herself with it someday, but *only* after she had recognized and conquered all of its countless mysteries. She would never allow herself to be subjected to the wild and ungovernable passions that seized these beings on a regular basis, and she could never be locked away at the Institute in the same cells which held the subjects upon whom she had performed conscienceless research for the last six months!

She could not become the object of the game!

Fighting with all of the fury of the afflicted people from the cages, Eugenia slapped and kicked her way to one of the five doors. "Let me through!" she screamed at the huge soldier who stood there, blocking the way. "I'm Dr. Eugenia Daugherty, and I *order* you to let me out of this room!"

The man grasped the front of her dress with a hand the size of a baseball mitt and threw her back into the awful storm.

Eugenia landed on her back on the floor. Feet stabbed at her and bruised her ribs and thighs, bloodied her face, and caused kaleidoscopic explosions of light within her brain. Somehow, she held on to her consciousness.

She had managed to sit up and clasp the legs of an overturned chair when Isador found her. He didn't know that it was she he was grasping by the arms and dragging to her feet, nor did she realize that those were his hands. But when they were both on their feet and bumping against one another, the natural extrasensory perception of long association revealed the truth to both.

"Eugenia, are you all right?" he called over the cacophony. "We were separated—"

"Get me out of here, Isador!" she screamed. "Now, before they can catch me!"

"This way," Redmond grunted. Tall, but not very heavily built, he nevertheless plowed through the swarm of people at a surprising rate of speed. Within moments, they had almost reached the same door from which Eugenia had been barred only minutes before. This time, quiet, scholarly, and previously totally unimpressive Isador Redmond didn't bother to ask the big soldier to move. He shoved the man staggering out of the way.

"Stay close!" he called, letting go of her to use both hands in forcing open the heavy door.

Before he could catch the so-called panic bar handle of the exit and push it, it swung outward and into the hallway and a great wave of searing white light flooded into the room. It was a stunningly brilliant battery-powered lantern which had been brought down from the helicopters which sat on the roof landing pad. Redmond, catching the full impact of the light in his wide open pupils, cried piercingly and stumbled back, with both hands covering his face. Eugenia's vision was slammed, as well, but her head had been turned just enough to save her from the full power of it.

In fact, she was able to see Redmond fall backward into the center of the room and the waiting arms of Jacob Bronck. Bronck had been a short, overweight

Danish reporter assigned to cover the trial of mass
murderer Gerald Cummings when he entered the
Institute in December of the previous year. Now he
was a screaming madman with the jaws of a huge
carnivorous animal. As the arms wrapped about
Redmond's upper body, those jaws opened wide to
receive his throat.

Two security men used their sidearms, now that
they had the light by which to aim, but their bullets
were of standard military issue and had next to no
effect when they hit Bronck. Isador fought wildly, but
he couldn't escape the beast that was devouring him.
Then the second soldier stepped through the doorway
with the equipment he had retrieved from a helicopter
on the roof.

The sound of the stream of flame as it leaped across
space was so loud that it washed aside the fountain of
screams that had filled the room since the moment of
the first attack. The flame that burst over Bronck and
Isador Redmond was something close to beautiful in
contrast to the blackness that had preceded it. For an
instant, it seemed to magnify the two forms that it
engulfed with a radiance like some religious apotheo-
sis, but only for that instant. In this night of transformations, yet one more turned the men from glorified
ciphers into a pair of flaring suns which wheeled in
their indescribable agony into opposite sides of the
room.

The trapped crowd somehow forgot what had been
terrifying them seconds before and parted in unison
as the burning men ran amid them. Eugenia backed
into a wall and dropped to her knees. The soldier with
the flame thrower strapped to his back continued to
train it on the pair, alternating his bursts, until they
fell and writhed in lessening energy near the windows
at the far side of the room. It lasted only seconds, but
even the remaining werewolves were fascinated into

stillness by the power of the fires.

The other doors to the room flew open before Redmond or Bronck died, and four more teams of soldiers with lanterns and flame throwers ran inside. There were eight figures caught in these new beams of light, who were obviously transformed lycanthropes, and these were the immediate targets. Assaulted by the powerful jets of fire, the werewolves overcame even their permeating hunger in desperate attempts to escape, but there was no escape. The flames leaped upon them, wrapped them, and stripped away layer after layer of flesh faster than the disease within them could restore them.

Hall's men weren't discriminating in their assault, however, and the brutalized audience very quickly understood that they weren't being spared death, only offered a different, perhaps more terrible form of it. The furnishings of the room ignited one after another, and the water which suddenly spewed down from the sprinkler system had no effect upon the growing conflagration. Burning bodies crashed through the tempered windows to plunge cometlike into the streets below, desperately seeking a quicker end to their anguish.

The fire, the screaming, the demons in human form and the humans in demon form combined to turn that isolated fraction of space into an overwhelming hell.

Eugenia Daugherty crouched on the floor. Her mind had never been incapable of protecting her from life before, but a fear beyond anything she had ever imagined seemed to be drowning her. She saw the devastation for which she was largely responsible, but it didn't register with her as thought. Even when she saw two violently struggling bodies tearing at one another with strength much greater than human at the far side of the room only to fall through the heavy curtains onto the balcony beyond, the intelligent

Eugenia should have realized that these two were advanced lycanthropes who hadn't been figured into the equation.

She probably would have crouched there in her mentally empty shell until Hall's assassins got around to charring the life from her had not one more hand extended out of the whirlpool to grasp her shoulder. Her eyes shot to the hand, illuminated redly in the fires, and her upper lip curled back from her teeth.

It was a soldier. "Dr. Daugherty!" he shouted. "Come with me! Quickly!"

"Don't touch me!" she screamed. "Jesus, help me, please, Jesus!"

The soldier's hand closed tighter and his voice dropped to a dangerous register. "If you want to live, come with me right now! I'm going to get you out of this!"

Eugenia gasped at this intimation of hope and scrambled to her feet. "Yes! Oh, please, get me out of here!"

Without thought to the horrendous death that was claiming Isador Redmond or the way in which dozens of other people were going to die, Eugenia followed the soldier out of hell and into the corridor which was infinitely darker yet as inviting as a mother's womb. She only wanted to run, to get away from the edge of this nightmare, no matter who she left behind. She clutched the man's hand so fiercely that her nails cut through his skin and drew blood.

The soldier, who had to be as blind as she, seemed to know his way about the building very well, because he literally ran through the hall for at least fifteen yards before abruptly stopping and opening a door which Eugenia still couldn't see. "This is the stairwell!" he told her. "We have to hurry!"

She punched his back hard with the heel of her free hand. "Just go, damn you!"

The man plunged ahead and dragged her with him. Down.

"Wait, wait!" she cried. "The helicopters are on the roof!"

"We have to get to the street!" he replied. "Hall's ordered that you be killed on sight, but if we reach the Institute first, we can get in touch with the senator—"

"I understand! Keep going!"

They had descended twenty floors through the inky blackness when the lights came back on.

"Don't follow me!" Blake shouted at the two people who were leaving the van behind him. He had struggled to follow Neil's instructions, but when the smoke began pouring out of the fortieth floor windows along with the awful screams, he knew that he had to find out what was going on up there and stop it if he could.

Naturally, Kelly and Chris felt they were ready to accompany him.

"Get back in there. I'll take care of this!"

"If you don't shut up, you won't have the breath left to climb those stairs," Chris responded as he stepped rather gingerly into the street. His face and body retained no evidence of the savage beating he had taken at Charles Gladden's hands, but he wasn't one hundred percent back from wherever he'd been yet.

Kelly was holding his arm as he climbed from the vehicle. "Something's got to happen now, Blake. We've got to stop this before the whole world falls in on us."

Neither of the men understood exactly what she was trying to tell them, but they knew that they would have to leave her behind.

"Damn!" Blake sighed. "You have to stay with the van, Kelly. We'll need it to get away. You do understand, don't you?"

Kelly looked at both men then smiled wistfully.

"Okay, but if you guys are not back soon, I'm coming in after you. Deal?"

"Deal," Blake answered, and turning to Chris said, "come on."

Blake and Chris had no plan, but they were driven forward by a primal desire to do *something* that would end those screams which were ripping apart the night above them. The lobby of the building was quite dark, lit as it was only by street illumination through the windows and doors, but when they opened one door to a stairwell and stepped inside, it seemed as if their very eyes had been snatched from them.

Blake began to climb the stairs with Chris trailing him. They reached the eighteenth floor by mental count when the lights flickered on. Even the emergency signs which were designed to lead trapped people out of the building during blackouts had failed; the tampering with the computer-controlled services had been very ingenious.

"The elevators. Good," Chris said while they blinked in the sudden brightness.

Corbett caught his arm. The image of the black smoke boiling from the windows above mixed with the faint odor that he detected even down here. "Stay away from the elevators!" he told him.

"Why?"

"The fire. It might short out the circuits and we wouldn't know what we'd find when the doors opened."

Chris shook his head. "Back to shoe leather."

Only three minutes later, they almost collided with a soldier and a woman rushing down the stairs. Neither of these people emitted so much as a grunt of surprise as they passed and vanished in the depths below. In the confusion, Blake failed to recognize the woman as one of the many, many probing minds who had examined him during his own internment at the

Institute, and Eugenia's eyes were still too full of what she had witnessed on the fortieth floor even to notice him.

Finally, they reached the floor. Gasping a little less than his companion, Chris waved Blake away from the door while he felt along its edges and knob.

"Feels cool," he said. "Unless this thing is really thick, I don't believe that there's any fire near it on the other side."

"Give it a try," Blake advised.

Carefully, Chris twisted the knob and eased the door into the stairwell.

Smoke quickly rolled through the widening gap, but there was neither flame nor ominous reflections of it in concert with the sooty, awful-smelling fumes. Chris held his breath and peered into the corridor to find the source of the smoke as a room some fifty feet away, where a partially open door was emitting foul waves of it.

"Man, that stinks," he said as he pulled back into the stairwell. "It smells like bad cooking, meat frying—"

The terrible truth of the smoke's origin hit the two men at once, and without another word Chris darted through the opening, followed closely by Blake. They had practically come to ignore the continuous screams from this floor up until that point, but in the hallway the urgent, yet hopeless, quality of them crashed into the men like breakers from the ocean. When they reached the second door, they plunged through without breaking stride, but the unbelieveable vision that met them stopped them in their tracks.

It was worse than any butchery that they could have imagined. Nine human-shaped bodies lay strewn about the interior of the room, each charred and/or burning hideously, and though the two couldn't know it, only five of those bodies represented lycanthropes.

The other four had belonged to members of the audience unlucky enough to have come between the soldiers and their primary targets. But that wasn't the worst of it.

Four metamorphosed werewolves had managed to reason to some minute extent even in the throes of their lunar madness. They realized that their fantastic recuperative abilities couldn't match the unceasing sprays of fire, so they had retreated into the small spaces which seemed to offer them some form of protection, the glass cages. All that the soldiers had to do was slam the doors and lock the creatures inside, but other minds had veered into insanity. Eight soldiers, two to a cage, were inundating them with continuous rivers of stunningly bright flame while their partners held the remaining audience members cowering in one corner of the room.

"*No!*" screamed Chris. "You idiots! You don't have to *kill* them! Just lock the doors!" Fully recovered from his battle with Gladden and as explosively physical as ever, the boy ran into the room, intending to grab the nearest of the soldiers, but he was tackled by three more of the guards and wrestled to the floor. Even then, he began to fight madly with the men and seemed about to wriggle free, when a soldier leaped into the melee and a forty-five caliber handgun was shoved into Chris's neck.

"Don't shoot him!" Blake yelled. "Stop! Stop!" His eyes were torn between the two terrors, the possible execution of Chris and the ongoing incineration of the trapped lycanthropes in the cages. "They couldn't help it! They didn't know what they were doing!" He might have been speaking of either group.

A soldier whose uniform marked him as a major appeared in the doorway behind Corbett. "Listen up! We're pulling out, now! Institute cleanup procedure, everyone ambulatory goes up top in the choppers! Move your asses!"

Chris slapped the gun away from his neck and spun around, but it was too late. There was nothing alive in the cages anymore. Nine men and women who hadn't considered the possibility of lycanthropy less than a year before had had their altered lives seared from their bodies in less than ten minutes. And five of their victims, who may or may not have been infected by them, were lying dead, also, their flesh blackened to crusty ash.

Rough hands gripped Chris and Blake by their arms and clothing and guns were thrust into their sides and backs. *He can't kill me*, Chris thought wildly. *Even if he pulls the trigger and puts one through my neck, my body can heal itself now! I came back from what Gladden did, didn't I? I can take him and get Blake out of here.*

They had almost made it into the hall when the weirdest noise cracked through the night air from somewhere beyond the windows. There were plenty of sounds coming up from the streets, predominantly the wailing of fire-truck sirens in response to the smoke of burning flesh that had escaped the windows. But this clearly was coming from some point much closer to the fortieth floor, though still outside the building.

The sprinkler system, which had been shut off manually by the soldiers, had left small pools of water on the floor. The last soldiers in the room, those holding Blake and Chris, virtually dragged their captives through these pools onto the balcony to investigate the strange sounds. When they all looked over the side toward the street so far below, they saw in half silhouette a scene unlike any they had ever seen.

A rolling, seething, erupting mass of white flesh was stuck to the exterior of the building by some undiscernable manner six floors below them. It appeared to be trying to tear itself apart. Molding temporarily solid features and limbs from its own doughy body, the thing transformed itself at incredible speeds. Heads with long, wide, and wickedly fanged mouths rose out of the blob as if they were dinosaurs thrusting up out of white pools of tar. Then, gleaming in the lights which played on them from the building and the streetlights below and dripping pieces of themselves, these heads slashed down, apparently back into the original liquidy source to rip itself with terrible cries. Hands and arms shot from the central mass only to turn into more mouths as the attack continued.

"Neil," Blake whispered. "And Poduano?"

The soldiers knew of the possibility of advanced transformations once the lycanthrope had developed beyond its initial stages, and some of them had seen tapes of Rosalie Moorcroft going through remarkable changes, but none of them had ever seen anything at all like this. One decided to act without awaiting orders. His heavy machine gun roared to life and spat fifty shells into the writhing lump of flesh with enough impact to blast it away from the wall and into the empty night air.

Kelly witnessed the fall of the thing from the side of the Berlinger Building along with a couple of dozen other awestruck women and men in the street below. As she had stood on the sidewalk, the fire trucks and rubberneckers had begun to arrive. But she had stayed to find out what would happen to Blake, Merrick, Chris and Grandillon.

That's why she saw the huge wad of flesh that was stuck to the building like a rotting mushroom.

Of course, the thing had something to do with the lycanthropes. It *had* to have. She didn't know what or who the creature was, but she watched its self-mutilation with rapt attention. She couldn't make out the details of the battle as well as those looking down from the floors above it—after all, the thing was still more than thirty stories from the ground—yet she did see the claws and the teeth which were shredding the main part of the body so viciously, just as she heard the cries.

The flash of the soldier's gun startled Kelly, so that she almost choked on the spittle that had collected near the back of her mouth. But she still couldn't pull her eyes away from the sight as the blob was knocked from the building and drifted, quite slowly it seemed, out over a narrow strip of lawn before it began a sharp plunge to the earth.

It appeared that about halfway down the thing tried to change its shape again, to spread out one side of its fluid mass into a wing or perhaps a parachutic form. But then the schizophrenic nature of the creature reasserted itself so that its second half twisted and hung over the wing, creating once more the fast-falling contour.

"Jesus Christ, look out!" shouted one of the firemen as he leaped from the rear of the truck.

His warning was just in time, and the last man had just dived into the street when the mass hit the vehicle and splashed. Liquid the color and texture of thick pus was thrown outward in a rough circle from the point of impact. Where it landed, it seemed to continue to tremble and slither with a self-contained life, in some spots wriggling into the cracks in the sidewalks and melting away into the porous ground. Kelly, who knew that it had to be one of the transformed lycanthropes, still couldn't believe what she was seeing.

Then, while the shouts of the uncomprehending witnesses filled the night, a pair of relatively larger lumps of the material fell out of the body of the fire truck and began moving over the street in the full glare of the streetlights and the assorted headlights of the vehicles surrounding the spot. One remained amorphous, sickly white, and sluglike as it snaked in a weaving pattern over the pavement. The second, however, went through yet another change after dropping behind the first.

Since much of the mass of the thing had been dissipated by the splashing effect of the fall, this second portion of flesh had little matter to draw upon as it changed, but it still became something recognizably human. A three-foot, naked, featureless homunculus stood behind the first mass and took only an instant to collect itself before running after the slug-thing as if it were a child chasing a pet.

The comparison evaporated when the childlike creature caught the depleted and weakened slug. Bounding upon it, the child's blank face changed once more, even as it whipped downward toward the struggling prize. It seemed to clench itself. All of its structures—eyes, mouth, rudimentary ears—rushed to the center where the nose should have developed and then fused into a long tubal arrangement that resembled the bottom of a funnel or the mouth of an anteater. It proved to be much more rigid than either of those, however.

As the homunculus had metamorphosed, so had the captive. Its slack and soft surface had hardened in the first creature's hands so that it had crusted into something like horn or even bone. When the human-like being's pointed face slammed against this tough exoskeleton, it bounced back with a sound reminiscent of billiard balls striking one another fiercely.

A considerable crowd of people had gathered about the two by this time, with Kelly at their head, and their shock at the supposedly impossible nature of the creatures and their transformations kept them planted where they stood, like carved statues. All except for three men who fainted.

The homunculus wouldn't give up. With its neck muscles swelling to produce power, it drove its facial spike into the slug a second time, and that was enough to create a tiny crack in the smaller thing's petrified surface. It was a small advantage but enough for the little human.

From the tip of its spike shot tens of glistening threads of flesh, like tendrils of some horribly mutated insect, and they frenziedly wiped across the shell, found the minute crack, and jabbed together into the meat that lay below. The slug jerked so explosively that it broke open its only protection even more, so that the child's funnel-mouth was able to thrust into it all of the way up to what remained of its own face.

It's done for now, Kelly somehow managed to conclude, in spite of the way that her consciousness was wavering on the edge of a bottomless canyon. *It'll never escape now.*

Her instincts were perfect. In the following seconds the slug-thing transformed into more shapes than had Proteus himself in his efforts to escape from his various pursuers, and the speed with which these changes took place was stunning. But the child-thing maintained its hold and continued to suck with tremendous force through that artfully designed tube, so that the soft insides of the slug were drawn into its own body. After a minute, the insanely frantic struggles abruptly ended, as the last bits of the defeated creature slipped among the spiral rows of razor-keen teeth and then into child-thing's gut. The first monster was dead or, at the very least, assimilated.

The child-thing rose up to its knees and gazed at the assembled crowd through re-formed but filmed eyes. It was totally exhausted by its tremendous effort to overcome the first creature, and after only a few seconds of silent stillness, it collapsed first onto its behind, and then to its back. A strangely familiar face began to evolve underneath the eyes.

"I'll be damned!" gasped a fireman, the first words spoken in more than a minute.

The drained being raised one hand from the street

in a calming motion. "There's nothing to be afraid of now," it told them weakly. "He's dead. Poduano's dead for certain this time, and I . . . won't hurt any of you. You have my word."

As if speech from this creature were more terrifying than all of the transformations that they had witnessed, the ring of observers backed away, cursing and crying, some actually hissing in primitive response to the unknown and unacceptable. And Kelly recognized the face of the thing.

She was about to call his name when suddenly there were soldiers everywhere. They poured out of the Berlinger Building as if in the middle of an assault on an enemy stronghold. They pushed their way through the assembly to surround the exhausted shape-shifter and pointed the barrels of guns and flame throwers at his limp figure.

"Prepare to fire!" screamed one of the soldiers. The others who had composed the upper half of the circle moved out of the line of fire.

Panic flared in the little creature's face. "I surrender!" it said quickly. "I won't resist you. I don't want to fight! Just allow me to marshall a bit of strength, and I'll go with you willingly!"

"Fire!" the leader cried.

Shells and flames engulfed the creature. It came to its feet amid the terrible shower, shrieking in agony.

"For Christ's sake, he was giving himself up!" Kelly shouted. "Stop it, you bastards, stop!" She clutched the arm of one of the men with the flame throwers. A fraction of a second later, the butt of a rifle smashed into her skull and sent her, half-conscious, to her knees.

They bathed the creature in a continuous stream of fire until, with an incredible effort of will, it summoned the strength from somewhere to break away from their aim and run screaming into the empty streets ahead. Several soldiers began to chase him.

"No!" barked the leader. "It's finished! Let it die in some ditch. We have to get out of here! To the transports!" He jabbed a finger at the still-dazed Kelly. "She comes with us! Move it, move it!"

Two sets of bruising hands grasped Kelly and dragged her to her feet and into the awful intestines of the Berlinger Building.

CHAPTER TWENTY-THREE

The roof of the building seemed to be three-quarters of the way to heaven and burning with the lights of hell to Kelly's throbbing mind. The wind tore at her, and her legs seemed to want to move independently of the signals that her brain was sending to them, but the rough hands at her arms and shoulders kept her moving in the direction they chose. She felt as if she were going to vomit.

"Soldier! She goes in here!" shouted a grating voice from their left as they passed the first of four revving military helicopters.

Kelly was shoved into the interior of the chopper.

"Negative, soldier. You go with your unit!" the same commanding voice ordered loudly.

"Sir, will you need assistance in guarding the prisoners?" asked the man who had shoved Kelly into the vehicle.

"These are our guests, soldier, and the pilot and I can handle them on our own." The man laughed and there was more than a touch of madness in the sound. "I'm carrying silver bullets, son, just like the Lone Ranger, so these people won't give me any problems. Now, haul your ass into your chopper!"

"Yes, sir!"

Groaning, Kelly rolled over onto her back and stared up into the tense faces of Chris and Blake. "What are you two doing here?" she whispered.

The car raced along the deserted country road, but still Dr. Eugenia Daugherty felt as if a giant, invisible hand were reaching out from the Berlinger Building and closing about her throat to drag her back there, into that mind-shattering scene of terror.

"Can't you go any faster?" she demanded of the soldier in the front seat.

"This is as fast as conditions allow, Dr. Daugherty," he answered with commendable calm. "Faster, actually."

"Well, what are we doing driving these cattle paths, anyway? I don't remember ever going to the Institute by getting off the main highways."

"This is a shortcut that will knock off at least twenty miles, ma'am," he assured her. "Don't worry. We'll beat old Hardass Hall back home."

Her stomach contracted violently at the mention of the man's name. "Hardass Hall is going home in a goddamned helicopter, if you've forgotten, you incredible cretin, and if he gets there before I do, I'm as dead as last week's newspapers."

"I know that, ma'am," the soldier said quietly.

Eugenia leaned back in the rear seat of the stolen civilian car and inhaled slowly. How had it happened? How had it all gotten away from her? Not by accident, that was for damned sure. The lights *accidentally* went out at the same time that the locks on the cages *accidentally* failed and released the subjects into the helpless crowd? Not *too* likely.

Maybe it had been Redmond's fault. Yes, that glory-hungry bastard had always been searching for a way to claim Eugenia's triumphs as his own, so he could have rigged the demonstration to become a total disaster. Or Hall. The general was terrified of the disease and was convinced that mankind's only hope was to wipe it out down to the last carrier before a plague swept the globe, even though it already was centuries-old and had claimed only a microscopic number of victims.

Hall could be responsible. He certainly hadn't been shy in using the flame throwers on lycanthrope and diplomat alike.

"Dr. Daugherty?"

The soldier's question startled her from her angry reverie. "Yes? What is it?"

"Do you have a family?"

That took her off guard. "A family? Well, my parents are dead some twenty years, but I do have a younger brother somewhere back east." She smiled fleetingly in the darkness of the car. "I suppose you could still call him my brother."

"Everyone should have a family," the man said in a quietly contemplative voice, "even if it's not really your own. Do you know what I mean?"

Already, Eugenia was bored with the conversation. "Not at all," she replied.

"I'm sorry, it's hard to really express what I mean." He didn't look back at her but kept his gaze fixed on the empty road ahead as it cut a channel through the deep forest that rose on either side of them. "But you should have some group of people to, you know, anchor yourself to as the years pass. You don't have any children or a husband?"

Eugenia almost laughed at the thought. Marriage and childbirth, in any order, had never appealed to the youthful Eugenia, so she had undergone sterilization as soon as she was legally old enough to request it, though, as a scientific aside, she had arranged for a certain number of her ova to be cryogenically preserved. "No, I don't have a husband or children. What exactly is all of this leading to, private?"

For almost a minute, he said nothing. Then he abruptly pulled the car to the side of the road and slammed it into park. "Families are the most important things in the world, Dr. Daugherty," he told her, and there was a new, disquieting harshness in his tone.

"What do you think you're doing?" she demanded. "Get back on the road! This is no time for foolishness!"

The soldier turned to face her now, and the same note of harshness was present in his face. "There's no worse crime known to humanity than to kill someone's family, like you've killed mine."

"Are you crazy?" She fumbled frantically in the darkness to clutch the door handle. This was going as wrong as the demonstration had. "I've never killed anyone in my life!"

"What about those nine innocents you brought to play in your freak show tonight? The ones that mad son of a bitch Hall burned to death?" His voice rose in power and loss of control. "What about the helpless fools you are killing an inch at a time at the Institute, not to mention the ones you've already vivisected? They're my family, Daugherty, my brothers and sisters!"

Eugenia found the handle, popped it open, and tried to leap out of the car. With animallike speed and strength, the man caught her wrist and held her inside.

"Not yet," he stated, grinning. "You've got bills to pay first."

Eugenia had never formally studied self-defense, but she knew how to handle herself. In that confined spot, she instantly went for the man's most vulnerable area with her free hand: his leering eyes. She missed the left eye altogether, her long nails digging two deep trenches into his forehead, but her small and ring fingers jabbed with cruel accuracy into the other. The eyeball burst with a wet pop, and blood and vitreous fluid gushed over her hand.

But he didn't let go!

The man's viselike hand remained closed about her wrist, and he didn't even scream as his eye washed in a great, red surge down his cheek.

"Nice move," he said with casual appreciation. Then he opened the front door of the car with his free hand and, carefully maintaining his grip while changing hands, he pulled her from the back seat into the deserted road.

"Don't hurt me!" Eugenia heard herself begging. Even while her father had beaten her for what she had done to her brother and the other children, she had forced herself to remain rebelliously silent, but now she begged. "Please don't, Jesus, I'm sorry! I'm sorry!"

The man pulled her away from the car. "You still haven't caught on, have you? This is dues collection time, Eugenia."

She beat at him with her hand even as she apologized and pleaded for mercy. He seemed not to notice. When she refused to move a step farther, he jerked her so roughly that she tumbled into the road. He squatted next to her in the dazzling glow of the headlights.

"Don't kill me, please, I didn't mean to hurt you or anybody!" she wept. "I don't even know who you are! I swear!"

This seemed to surprise him a little. "Oh. Well, we can't let you go to your reward in ignorance, can we?" He smiled in the high beams of light and changed.

Eugenia gasped. She'd witnessed this metamorphosis often enough from her one self-determinate experimental subject at the Institute, but until that very moment, she hadn't been aware that the soldier was one of *them*—or that, Lord God in heaven, this was Rosalie Moorcroft!

"I thought you were dead," she whispered to the woman who now held her arm in her still-terrible grip.

It was Moorcroft, in body as well as in uninjured face, and the soldier's fatigues that she had been wearing actually had been only a sophisticated camouflage tactic that she had designed out of her own skin. Now she was naked and as pure and unmarked as she had been during her first days at the Institute, before the denial of sustenance had demanded that she use her available flesh to maintain her life.

"It was for science, Rosalie," Eugenia explained. "You can see that, can't you? Everything I did to you was to find out more about the disease that you have!"

"Why didn't you ask me?" Rosalie responded in her old voice. "Eugenia, I'm one hundred eighteen years old, and in that time I've learned one hell of a lot about who I am and *what* I am." Her two eyes flashed with anger in the headlights. "Why is it always attack and kill and burn? Why should we have to live in secret like animals? It's always been this way, because you people are so incredibly fearful—"

"Because you *are* animals!" Eugenia was startled by her own vehemence; she wasn't begging now. "You kill *us*, or have you forgotten? Normal human beings are your choice of food, you self-righteous bitch! How are we supposed to react?"

"I haven't killed anyone in seventy years," Rosalie answered, suddenly on the defensive. "We can educate ourselves away from the craving for human flesh, it's not an irresistible compulsion for most of us."

"Like Gerald Cummings?"

"He was different, he was an Orphan. He never had a chance to understand what had happened to him, what he had been given." With a tiny but quite real shake of her head, Rosalie re-established the hierarchy of the moment. "And I've never hurt anyone connected with *you*! Those people you've treated like lab rats for the past six months have never even had the opportunity to hurt anybody else! But tonight, ah, tonight I tasted human flesh again after so long, because it was the only food offered to me, and I had to have something to keep me from death." A small red tongue slipped across her lips. "It tasted wonderful, Eugenia."

Eugenia's rage and resistance blew away as if it had been a mist before a high wind. "Oh, God, please! Don't eat me, please!"

Rosalie smiled again, and this time her small white teeth had been replaced by dripping fangs. She opened her mouth impossibly wide and leaned over the struggling woman.

"You goddamned animal!" Eugenia screamed. "Help me, somebody!"

And Rosalie's lusting mouth laughed. "Animal, Eugenia? Perhaps, but I'm still better than you are." She stood up, leaving her supposed victim lying at her feet. "I'm not going to eat you, no matter how succulent you might taste, because I'm beyond that now. I wonder if you could say the same were our situations reversed?" She began to walk back to the car.

Eugenia sat up tentatively. "You—you're not going to hurt me?"

Rosalie stopped at the open driver's door. "Did I say that? Oh, I'm beyond cannibalism, but not revenge, that most human of emotions. I'm going to get you, honey, if not right now. Someday, somewhere, I'm going to get you. And you'll never know who I'll be when it happens." In illustration, the woman's face swiftly and smoothly ran through a series of ten transformations which encompassed all ages, races, and shades. "I'll be seeing you, Eugenia. Count on it."

The doctor watched in stunned paralysis as Rosalie cranked the car and drove away, leaving her alone miles from nowhere beneath a full moon which she knew could incite some people to become monsters. Eugenia slowly climbed to her feet and peered into the darkness. Fear and relief raced through her body; overall, she counted herself lucky to be out of that mad bitch's control.

But what if the next person she encountered were Rosalie in disguise? Or the one following that? Or her fellow workers at the Institute, or—or crazyass General Roy Hall? Even without Rosalie, there was always that homicidal idiot to worry about.

As she stood there, now truly isolated Eugenia Daugherty saw the cloud of paranoia drifting out of the recesses of her mind to envelop her as clearly as she saw the moon overhead, and she knew that there was not one damned thing her vaunted "superior" intelligence could do to stop it. Jesus, not for the rest of her life!

"Rosalie, please!" she screamed into the night. "I'm sorry!"

Then she fell to her knees in the middle of the road, crying, and no one heard her other than the creatures that inhabited the forest after the sun died. Or might it have been something other than an animal. . . .

There were five people in the helicopter, and the emotions of each were drawn as tightly as a bowstring against the blade of a knife.

"What are you going to do with us?" Kelly asked through dry lips.

General Roy Hall stared at the woman with eyes as powerful as lasers. He was sitting near the front of the large helicopter, just behind the pilot, and the other three people were seated together near the rear. Hall was pointing a pair of pearl-handled .45s at them, and each gun, as he quickly had informed them, contained shells loaded with silver. A chopper was no place to employ a flame thrower, but if any of these bastards was a werewolf—a so-called "self-determinate lycan-thrope" like Moorcroft—it wasn't likely that they would chance eating four or five silver bullets.

"I'd like to know," Kelly said quietly. Maybe silver held no terrors for her, but she sure wasn't bullet-proof.

"That's my decision to make, isn't it?" Hall's voice was low and breathy, so that it was almost lost amid the sounds of the helicopter.

"What's the mystery?" Kelly asked archly. "We saw at the building what you do to 'monsters.' You roast them alive."

"Kelly!" Blake whispered sharply.

Hall chuckled to himself. "Don't worry, man, I was already pretty damned sure that at least one of you was a werewolf. Yeah, we know that once you get past a certain stage you can change any way that you want. All of you are diseased."

Hall laid one pistol on the seat next to him long enough to slip a cigar from his jacket and light it. "Now sit back and relax. You're not in any danger so long as you don't threaten me or my flyboy." He nudged the back of the pilot's seat, but the man didn't acknowledge it. "When we get back to the Institute . . . Well, we'll see."

" 'The Final Solution,' " Blake said. "It didn't work for Hitler, so why should you presume to have any better luck?"

The general puffed his cigar. "Better organization, fewer opponents. The way I see it, this is a matter of national security, and when it comes to that, I've been given complete control over the lycanthropic prob-lem. Even those foreign representatives, with all of their diplomatic immunity, are securely under my thumb. If they don't subscribe to the true events of tonight's fiasco, that you and your kind created the whole mess and killed some of those diplomats, I guarantee you that no matter what kinds of fits their governments pitch, they'll never see daylight again."

"You can sentence them to life imprisonment?" Blake asked incredulously.

"National emergency." He pointed the cigar at them like a weapon. "An emergency caused by one of *your* people, not mine."

The three people exchanged silent looks. This was something they couldn't deny, because they'd heard enough to know that some totally insane individual had released the subjects into the room—which he previously had blacked out by shutting down the building's generators—in the midst of their transformational madness. Not even a conscienceless sack of hatred such as Hall would have done that, and the only totally insane person who came to mind was Dominic Poduano.

Blake sighed. "Because one guy out of thirty thousand goes crazy, you're ready to exterminate the entire race."

"Maybe I should wait until fifty of you attack a grade school and make meals out of the student body."

Fire leaped into Blake's chest. "That wouldn't happen!"

"You can guarantee me that?"

"Well, yes, by God, I can! Did you believe in werewolves before you saw the tapes of Gerald Cummings?"

Hall exhaled a blue breath. "That has nothing to do with this."

"You're damned right it does. Our kind has existed for thousands of years, and we've controlled ourselves so completely that the rest of the world hasn't even believed in our existence."

"They will now." The military man remained maddeningly calm. "I'll make sure that everybody sees our photographic evidence of the presence of a hidden, cannibalistic sect in our ranks and just how dangerous you really are."

"We're not dangerous, damn you!" Kelly suddenly spat.

"You eat people. I think that qualifies."

Blake snorted derisively. "For a few weeks until we learn to master our impulses. We"—he gestured to himself, Kelly, and Chris—"have never killed anybody, not even tonight, and it's a full moon out there, in case you haven't looked!"

"I told you, we're aware that after a time you learn to keep from changing against your will—" Hall began.

"We were infected *three weeks ago!*"

Finally, something seemed to have penetrated the protective aura and really shocked Roy Hall. "That all?"

"Yes! And we're in charge of ourselves. We'll never have to become like that again."

He nodded slightly. "That's impressive, all right. How'd you manage it?"

Maybe this is the chink I need to get through to this asshole, Blake thought. "It's a brand-new technique devised by Neil Merrick, who you probably killed back there in that hellhole. It involves drug therapy and hypnosis." He didn't think it wise to bring up Gabrielle's blood at this point. "With this way of educating new members of the group and all that we have to offer the human race, perfect health, eternal youth, the means to become whatever you—"

"There's your problem. Your mind set. It must come with the infection, because all of you want to spread your sickness to the entire world, and that means that it's not safe for any of you to live among decent people. Not here, and, hell, not even in Russia."

"You're crazy!" Blake exploded. "I just told you

that we've been a self-maintaining minority throughout history!"

"Then I'll just help to keep you that way." Hall
raised the gun suggestively, though it didn't seem that
he was really ready to use it just then.

"You don't have the right," Chris said tersely.

"This gun and these bars give me all the rights I
need, jerkoff," Hall responded. "The government gave
you to me."

"I wasn't talking about us. You don't have the right
to deny our condition to the rest of the world. How
many people do you think would turn it down, man?"

"Everyone who saw what kind of monsters you
really are—"

"Nobody who's ever grown old or gotten sick or
suffered an injury that won't heal." Surprisingly,
Chris laughed this time. "Hell, we're not angels, and
Poduano's certainly not the only one of us to go nuts.
One look inside the basement back at Caprice Island
would convince anybody of that. And I know you
were leading that raid, weren't you?

"We've got our headcases just like the rest of the
world, and we've killed and eaten more than a few
innocent people down through the centuries. But how
many men, women, and children have been raped and
slaughtered by the military, General? Millions? I'm
not talking about the victims of wars, just those folks
who've been stomped down by some half-assed little
impotent bastard who had the Army on his side. Talk
about your glass houses, man, you military idiots
don't even have glass. More like spun sugar, I'd say.
Does that mean we get rid of all of the armies?"

"Don't be ridiculous, punk. You'd come begging
when the first tinhorn dictator decided he liked your
neighborhood better than his own," sneered Hall.

"Probably, just like you'll beg when you find out
that you have inoperable cancer or diabetes. Men have
mistreated women since the beginning of time, Hall,

and you'd better believe it's gone the other way, too, but I sure as hell won't vote to do away with either sex. What right do you have to deny the world all of my advantages?"

Blake spoke with honest awe in his voice. "Chris, you should have been a writer."

The boy grinned in the gloom of the helicopter's interior. "No thanks, man, it makes my brain hurt too much. I'll stick to boxing."

Hall wasn't impressed. "It's all academic, isn't it? Because I'm not going to give any of you the chance to make your pitch on national TV."

"You're still going to kill us?" Kelly asked. Something truly chilling seemed to glow behind her eyes. "All werewolves?"

Hall's reply was almost compassionate. Almost. "I can't let you spread your disease any further, honey. We have to leave the past where it belongs and look to the future. Maybe killing you all won't be necessary, maybe you can live at the Institute or some other place like it, forever. But, really, wouldn't you prefer a nice, quick death instead of eternal imprisonment? I know I would."

"Then you'll get your chance, son of a bitch!" Before any of the others could react, Kelly leaped to her feet, tore open the inside of her own wrist with her teeth, and threw herself across the center of the craft and onto Hall. He was shocked, but the gun still went off. Its silver shell missed her side by no more than the width of a hand and whined off the roof. Meanwhile, Kelly had descended on the man like one of the mythological Furies and smeared her bleeding wrist into his face. It wasn't a terribly severe wound, but there was plenty of blood.

"Goddamn you, I'll kill you!" Hall screamed. He shoved the girl away and took aim with the gun.

A second body hit him with the impact of a bolt of lightning, and he abruptly found himself fighting a

monster that hadn't bothered to change from its
human form. Hall was larger and stronger than Chris,
as well as expert in a number of hand-to-hand fighting
disciplines, but he really had no chance. The pistol
was knocked from his fist within the first second of the
battle, and the second one, the one he had left in the
seat next to him, was sent skittering across the floor a
moment later. Blake dashed in to help Chris.

Hall was driven back into the foremost part of the
vessel, where he collided with the uniformed pilot and
caused the craft to bank dangerously. "Help me!" he
shouted.

"Sir, I have to fly! I can't release the controls!" the
pilot cried as he fought to right the chopper.

There was no time for further exchange, because
Chris grasped the general's feet and dragged him back
into the belly of the craft, where two vicious head
punches left him semiconscious.

"Now what are you going to do?" Kelly demanded
in nearly hysterical triumph. "Are you going to commit suicide? Cut your own throat?"

Hall rolled away from Chris, groaning.

The boy was busy with other matters by then.
Locating one of the two pistols, he swept it up in one
hand and then hissed in pain as the mere proximity of
the silver blistered his palm.

"Throw it out!" Blake told him. He turned the
handle of the sliding side door and pulled it open just
a little, allowing the roaring night to squeeze inside.
"We don't need it! We can take care of the bastard
ourselves! Toss it!"

Not inclined to argue, Chris hurriedly pitched the
weapon into the darkness. He scanned the floor.
"Where's the other one? He had a pair of them."

"I don't see it!" Blake responded.

Kelly was crouched next to the dazed Hall. "How
does it feel, jackass? You're one of us now, you're
contaminated, and once you're a member of the

group, there's no way to resign. All of those tiny creatures are wriggling in your bloodstream now, reproducing, making you into one of us. All that it takes is one drop of tainted blood."

Hall touched his bleeding mouth and looked at his fingers, as if he expected to be able to distinguish between his blood and hers. "No," he said, so low as to be barely audible, "it's not true."

"It *is* true, you pompous ass! You're a werewolf!" The girl laughed.

He scrambled frantically toward the front of the helicopter. "Soldier, soldier, radio the Institute for help! Tell them what's happened and to have a blood-filtering machine ready!"

Blake joined in Kelly's laughter. "It won't help," he said, even though Neil had told him that early dialysis indeed might cleanse infected blood just after exposure and Kelly probably wasn't contagious, in any case. He wanted to see the animal sweat and maybe change his outlook on the situation. "How objective are you now, man?"

Hall climbed to his feet with the aid of a chair. If Kelly's expression before her attack had been unsettling, the look in his eyes was enough to freeze their spines. "I won't d–do it," he stated. He sounded as if he were speaking in a dream. "I won't become like you."

"What choice do you have?" Kelly sneered. "I can't wait until the next full moon. I hope we get the same cell block so I can watch you grow hair all over your body and start spitting and scratching and trying to tear your way out—"

"Don't say that!" Hall wailed. "No!"

"Or maybe tonight! The moon's still up! All you have to do is convince yourself that you're going to change!"

"No, no, no, no, no!" The tall man stared desperately about the craft, as if searching for some magic icon with which to clean himself of the polluted blood. To Chris, it appeared that he might even throw himself out of the helicopter, so the boy stepped in front of the still-open side door. "I won't be this!"

"Then die," Kelly whispered.

In a single smooth motion, Hall dropped to his knees and shoved both hands into a large military bag next to the pilot's seat.

"Watch out for a gun!" Blake shouted.

But when the man turned back to them, he held in each fist a hand grenade. "You can't make me become one of you, and you can't do this to anybody else!" With his thumbs, he flipped the pins.

"You're not infected!" cried Blake. "Kelly's not contagious!"

"Too late for lies." Hall threw the two live grenades into the back of the craft and grabbed and armed two more.

Kelly seemed turned to stone. Both Blake and Chris realized that it was far too late for action, yet both sprang toward the general. Death raced through the seconds toward them.

The pilot leaped from behind the controls of the helicopter. He shouldered past the now completely insane Hall and moved with more than human speed into the belly of the vessel. As he moved, he changed. His arms spread wide and grew dramatically, like opening mandibles, and his body lengthened and flattened. Not even Chris, with his trained athlete's reflexes, could snap out of his path before one of those gigantic arms slammed across his chest and drove him toward the open door. The other two were swept back with Chris so that they were knocked head over heels through the door and Hall was left alone on the craft, like a startled sacrifice to a god he didn't know.

The night clawed at the trio and shrieked in their ears. Their own cries were too insignificant to register over the howling wind. The full moon, which in a way was responsible for all of this, shown brilliantly beneath their feet. Then it was gone and they were staring at the silver-and-black earth so far away. They rotated a little more so that they had a clear view of the helicopter which roared on through the sky and exploded into a devastatingly bright red sun to make the moon fade into insignificance. If they hadn't been falling, they would have been incinerated by its eruption.

But they were falling.

EPILOGUE

They changed.

As the wildness of nature whipped by them and tried to flay the flesh from their bodies, while they screamed a single, one-pitch and unending scream that they knew signaled the last action of their lives, while they plunged toward the earth that always won its eternal battles with the pitiful beings who struggled through finite existences to escape its grasp, Blake and Chris changed.

Their bodies were throbbing with a second form of life that was desperate to do something to preserve the hosts, but the two men themselves had neither the experience nor instinct to rearrange their physical structures in order to stop or slow their fall. The pilot took care of this.

He was already well altered when he threw the three people through the helicopter door before him, and the shape that would save him from death was, of course, birdlike, with a forty-foot wingspread and a torso that was both wider and thinner than any of the dinosaurs that had soared the younger skies of earth. He caught the single immutable body that fell before him, that of Kelly Davis, with feet that had become grasping hands the size of suitcases. Perhaps he could have saved Chris and Blake in a similar fashion, after forming pseudo-hands out of other shoots of flesh, but the weight of three human bodies would have put a terrible strain on the strength of even this gigantic creature.

Instead, the pilot used those probing tentacles of mass to reach through the darkness and touch the two free-falling men. Then, employing arcane knowledge that he had won from hard experience over the centuries, the bird-pilot injected teeth into their necks, established sufficient contact between the Life form within him and the brother colonies that coursed through their systems, and incited his own metamorphosis into the two of them. Their bodies were liberated by what their minds had yet to understand.

They became birds. Their arms grew into tremendous wings without feathers, as every other portion of them changed in concert so that they were truly, wonderfully airborne. It was perhaps the oldest desire in the racial memory of the human soul, the answer to uncountable falling dreams, and the discovery of a sensation that surpassed any they had ever imagined possible.

They flew.

They were clumsy and hardly aesthetic, but, by God, they *were* capable of independent flight. They played in the radiance of the moon like newborn children. They dipped and climbed and banked and soared. For a few minutes they were free of every care and binding that becomes attached to the least worldly of us, and though they knew that it couldn't last much longer, they gave themselves to the joy of the instant with an unreserved totality found in very rare moments.

Then their strength began to fade so that they were forced to follow the pilot down to the earth. This was accomplished by a long, shallow glide that was almost as enjoyable as the actual flying. The instincts that the pilot had instilled in them during the brief contact allowed them to make relatively painless landings next to him and his stunned companion, who could not connect with the feelings which had flowed through Chris and Blake during those minutes when they used their own muscle and sinew to propel themselves to the edge of heaven itself.

Once on the ground, the two regained their familiar forms by intuitive impulse and collapsed to the ground. But for a time, for a short, glorious time. . . .

The pilot naturally was none other than Neil Merrick. He explained what happened as the other three lay on their backs in the moderately comfortable fallow field approximately halfway between San Francisco and the Institute.

"I was in the basement trying to get the generators back on line when most of the action was taking place," he said. "I realized that we would have no chance at all of locating and stopping Poduano in the dark, but by the time I reached the fortieth floor, he and Tristan already were plunging into the street. I started to rush down to help, but then I saw you two being taken captive, and I thought that my first allegiance was to you, since it was I who brought you into this in the beginning. I made my way to the roof, subdued the pilot, and took his place. Then I suggested to Hall that he isolate you two and you, Kelly, when you were captured, on board the craft to find out just what you 'outsiders' knew about the matter. I'm not even sure what happened to Dom and Tristan."

"He killed him," Kelly responded. Of the group,

she was the quietest and most reserved. "They survived the fall, and then Tristan became like a human again, like a kid, and he ate the other guy."

Revulsion rose in them all. "That's one way to handle it, I guess," Blake commented.

"In those circumstances, probably the only way," Neil agreed. "What of Tristan?"

"I'm not sure," she replied. "Some soldiers came out of the building and surrounded him. He tried to give up, but they turned the flame throwers on him anyway. The last I saw, he was running down the street on fire. He might have survived. They didn't chase him."

Merrick closed his eyes. "Perhaps they *will* destroy us all."

Kelly's expression hardened. "Maybe Dom was right, maybe the only way to treat them is like food."

"No," Chris said firmly. "This isn't 'us' against 'them.' I meant what I said in that helicopter. We owe something to the rest of the world. Some of us will have to go on and show them what the disease can offer. No threats or coercion, just an invitation."

Blake looked to Merrick. "He's right, Neil, and you're the only one with that kind of experience. We'll help you any way that we can."

"I was planning to spirit you and the others out of the country," the older man pointed out.

"Forget about that, man. I'm staying for the duration," Chris said.

"Me, too," added Kelly.

"You've got to let us grow up sometime, Neil," Blake stated. "You've given us a lot, but now we can control our own destinies. Damn, we've already undergone transformations that are light years beyond the feral. We'll be okay at the ranch, while we experiment and learn even more."

Merrick looked at the group and then to the skies, where at least one military helicopter had returned to search for them. It was getting closer. "I did have something in mind. I thought that if I could go deeply undercover, really down there, into the very heart of the normal world's resistance to us, perhaps I could enact some subtle attitude changes which would make us more acceptable to them. I'm considering disguising myself as Hall."

"Hall?" Kelly repeated in disbelief.

"Why not? The Army can't know that he's dead, yet, and they'll never be able to identify whatever's left of him in the wreckage of the helicopter. I got a reading on his genetic pattern when I touched him, so there will be no problem there."

"But his voice, his mannerisms, damn, his memories," Chris said without confidence. "You won't even know the people he worked with. Don't you think that will tip off the other members of the investigation team? They know that we can duplicate any form that we want."

Neil smiled at his perceptiveness. "Nice extrapolating, my friend, but you know that I've picked up a trick here and there over my three hundred thirty-one years. You've seen how an associate can influence the very physical structure of another person's brain." He resisted the temptation to add, "The way Adine Pierce meddled with Kelly's mind." "What you didn't know was that the circuit can be switched into reverse. Only a few of us ever try it, since our minds are all that are constant within our lives, but I've managed to acquire the ability to use that vast fallow portion of my brain that we all retain to duplicate the mental structure of another person. Actually, I now have what you might term a 'sub-mind' interacting with my own. I don't know *everything* that Hall ever saw or felt, but I have enough to get by. Such as the fact that your friend Douglas Morgan is alive and well at the Institute, though quite angry at his incarceration."

"That's incredible," Blake said.

"Just so long as it doesn't threaten my own identity, which it doesn't. I'll work slowly and carefully, nothing to make anyone suspicious. I'll gradually call off the general state of alarm and persecution and eventually redirect the official military and governmental positions into more conciliatory ones accepting of the lycanthropic state. We'll save the world, yet, you and I."

Kelly pointed up the road to a number of bright headlights which were rounding a corner. "Someone's coming."

Merrick cranked up his night vision to its highest level. "Army vehicles. They've dispatched troops for a ground search." Even as he spoke he was creating in his body various burns and injuries which might have been incurred when he was thrown from an exploding helicopter. He had lost the upper portion of his uniform upon changing into the flying creature, as Blake and Chris had ripped their shorts, and his pants gave no clue as to his identity. When he looked back to the small group, he was the image of a hurt, barefoot, and thoroughly convincing General Bernard Roy Hall.

When he spoke, even his voice was Hall's. "I suppose my toughest problem will be explaining to the diplomats and their nations how the demonstration went to hell tonight and convincing these gentlemen who are driving up the road that I did indeed survive a fall of several thousand feet into that lake over there."

"Good luck," Chris said with a grin.

The good-byes took a moment, but not long enough for them to be seen by the approaching soldiers. A lot of emotions were exchanged during those few seconds, and they all, even wise old Neil Merrick, were silently struck by the ways in which their lives had been forever changed in only a matter of weeks. If there were a tomorrow, what could it offer to match these days just passed?

Blake, Kelly, and Chris slipped away into the shadows cast by the strong moonlight and waited for the military vehicles to arrive and collect the man the soldiers believed to be Roy Hall. After that, the three began the long walk that would take them to a place where they could call the ranch for transportation.

"Why don't we take one of those?" Kelly asked hesitantly as they passed a quiet farmhouse with a serviceable-looking car in its drive. "I can . . . I think I can remember how to fix it so that it'll run without a key."

Chris laughed quietly and hugged her in real affection. She didn't resist. "Not now, babe," he said. "We don't need to get the law down on us now."

Blake was watching the big, white, silent moon ahead of them. It was all going to work out. They were alive, maybe forever, and they had the greatest gift that ever could have been offered to the world. He had no knowledge of the problems that awaited them—an embittered associate named Rosalie Moorcroft, who now hated normal humans passionately; a newly infected psychopathic killer named Marsha Cooper, who was just coming into control over her awesome abilities; Tristan Grandillon, perhaps the most powerful creature on the face of the planet and one who had been viciously attacked by the very race that Blake and his group sought to help; and even more. But Blake knew that they could overcome anything. The future was there to be taken.

"Chris is right," he said. "If this plan is to be successful, we have to hope that no lycanthrope anywhere gives the uninfected people reason to fear us or to be suspicious of our motives. Let's keep walking."

The moon seemed to reach down to embrace them.

WILLIAM SCHOELL

TERRIFYING TALES YOU WON'T BE ABLE TO PUT DOWN!

SHIVERS. Deep beneath the city streets it lurked — a creature so hideous and powerful that it could destroy a victim by thought alone. Humans trembled with horror as it moved in for the kill, and there was seemingly no escape from the torture.

____2607-4 $3.95US/$4.95CAN

BRIDE OF SATAN. It was unconquerable in its quest for evil and blood. It turned its victims' hands into gnarled, four-fingered claws; it was so elusive that only two people guessed at its existence — and had to find it before it found them.

____2423-3 $3.95US/$4.95CAN

CLASSIC HORROR
by DRAKE DOUGLAS

OBELISK
AN ANCIENT TERROR TO CHILL THE MARROW OF YOUR BONES
by Ehren M. Ehly

Trapped in the hot, fetid darkness of an ancient Egyptian tomb, Steve Harrison was suddenly assaulted by bizarre and horrific images of a past he had never known. Even when he returned to New York, he found himself driven by strange cravings and erotic desires he couldn't explain; his girl friend suddenly feared for her life and that of her unborn child. Steve Harrison only had one chance to restore his deteriorating body and cleanse his diseased mind—a final confrontation with incredible forces of evil, this time in Central Park, this time in the shadow of the forbidding...

OBELISK

____2612-0 $3.95US/$4.95CAN

SPEND YOUR LEISURE MOMENTS WITH US.

Hundreds of exciting titles to choose from—something for everyone's taste in fine books: breathtaking historical romance, chilling horror, spine-tingling suspense, taut medical thrillers, involving mysteries, action-packed men's adventure and wild Westerns.

SEND FOR A FREE CATALOGUE TODAY!

Leisure Books
Attn: Customer Service Department
276 5th Avenue, New York, NY 10001